*To Fran's
inner child*

# SECOND CHILDHOOD

## Donna McMahon

**Drowned City Press**

Gibson's Landing, British Columbia
www.drownedcitypress.ca

This is a work of fiction. All the characters and events portrayed in this novel are either fictitious or are used fictitiously.

Library and Archives Canada Cataloguing in Publication

McMahon, Donna
      Second childhood / Donna McMahon.

ISBN 978-0-9865484-1-3

      I. Title.

PS8575.M244S43 2010     C813'.6     C2010-901245-3

Published by
Drowned City Press
Gibsons Landing, BC, Canada
**www.drownedcitypress.ca**

Cover Design by Brenna Johnson (www.brennajo.com)
Photo by Novak Rogic (supernovak.com)
Chinese Text translation by Patsy Leung

*It's never too late to have a happy childhood.*

- Tom Robbins

the RMS *Empress of Japan*, c.1894
(public domain photo from Wikipedia Commons)

Read more about *The Empress* at www.drownedcitypress.ca.

## ACKNOWLEDGEMENTS

Writing science fiction involves a great deal of research into extremely disparate topics, ranging from living on Cortes Island to the science of neural-computer interface to how to set up a 22nd century woodworking shop. I'd like to thank some of the people who helped me with this novel by answering my peculiar questions (sometimes so long ago they've probably forgotten):

Howard Davidson, Eugene James,
Susan Mayse, Pat Rich, David Rousseau,
Frank Shaw, Robin Somes, Peter Watts

And apologies to anybody I have omitted.

# 1

March, 2109
Cortes Island

Wind thrummed across the sunlit wharf, a deep organ chord that drowned the sounds of death. Blade gripped thin old ankles and heaved Choi's frail body into the air, then he smashed down, cracking Choi's skull against the concrete deck. Again! Again! Crimson splatters flew. Blood drenched thin white hair. Blade's heart soared with exultant rage. Die! Die again!

A hand touched his shoulder. Blade whirled, dropping Choi's limp weight, and turning his motion into a blow. Boosted muscles spun his hundred kilo frame through a blur of scenery and he slammed into the person behind him, then caught a glimpse of a young woman's face framed by unruly auburn hair, mouth half open, eyes pleading at him. Klale! NO!

Too late. Simon felt ribs shatter under Blade's arm, saw her body fly back, whipping her neck forward. Her body crumpled wetly onto concrete. Hazel eyes stared up at him, empty.

Simon tried to flee, but he was trapped inside Blade's brutal flesh. Abruptly the music stopped. In the sudden silence wind hissed in his ears, carrying moans and terrified sobs. He stared around. Bodies lay strewn everywhere—faces battered and vacant. He knew all the faces. Mary. Alberta. Rill. Dr. Lau. Klale.

One small body lay face down. Choi. But Choi had white wisps of old man hair, not springy black curls. Simon reached down and flopped the corpse over with Blade's blood-sticky hands. Toni's face stared up at him.

No! Not Toni! NOOO!!!

Terror welled up. Then he heard Choi's icy, sarcastic voice, so familiar that it resonated in his bones.

"Did you think I would die so easily?"

Panic exploded inside Simon. Every instinct screamed to run, but he sank automatically to his knees, throwing himself prostrate. He lay motionless as he had so many times before, willing himself to immobility and silence, and straining not to hear the old man's inexorable footsteps circling slowly round him. Waiting for agony....

A hand gripped his shoulder, shaking it. Simon tried to flinch, but his muscles wouldn't respond. His body lay inert and heavy, and he couldn't breathe. His face was buried in soft fabric. His stomach clenched with old terror, and warm, acrid vomit flooded his mouth.

Hands raised his head, pulling the covers away, and soft light fell on him. A towel was placed under his chin as Simon heaved up warm juice, smelling of stomach acid. Heartbeats pounded in his ears and his lungs labored, then the spasms eased. A soft cloth brushed his mouth.

"It's all right, Simon. You're safe. That was just a dream. It can't hurt you."

Toni's voice. Simon felt a glow of impossible hope. He couldn't turn his head to look, but he felt warm smooth fingers against his cheek, then caught a glimpse of graying black curls, hazy in his peripheral vision. Toni, alive! He savored the feel of her hands as they stroked his shoulder, and the sound of her words, recited with patient weariness as if she'd said them too many times.

"It's OK, Simon. Relax as much as you can. The neural restraint will release you when your adrenaline level drops. I can't roll you over, you're too heavy, so I'll prop up your head. Just lie easy."

Simon tried to relax, but he had no control over Blade's body. It lay separate from him, fear-twisted into a gross, shuddering heap, with sheets wound tight and clinging to damp skin. Terror still sucked at him, so Simon concentrated on dancing up, away from it.

He ran up the tongue and groove cedar wall onto the slanted ceiling, then looked back down. Blade lay sprawled on a futon. Toni sat beside him on the worn wooden floor wearing a night robe over jeans—a small Afroid woman, her hands tiny against Blade's bulk. At the back of her head, a bald circle etched in her short, curly hair revealed a scarlet rose and skull that bled two luminescent red drops down the back of her neck. Simon didn't like blood, so he studied the bright patchwork quilt on the bed and the amber curtains that swayed gently with gusts of cool night air. The island air

2

felt wonderful—rich with scents of forest rain and low tide, and ghosts of the cedar trees felled to build the cabin walls. Simon ached to flee Blade's body and dance in the tree-ringed clearing outside the cabin, whirling and soaring under the sky.

"OK, Simon, try to move."

Reluctantly, Simon sank back inside the ugly hulk, and this time his limbs responded. He turned over, muscles aching where he'd lain clenched on his right side. His eyes were blurred with tears, his nose dripped mucus, and he was shivering.

Toni looked down at him with weary concern and handed him a damp washcloth. There were shadows under her eyes.

"That was your third nightmare tonight. We can take a break and then try natural sleep again, or we can plug you into the sleep-ware. It's your choice, Simon."

Instinctively Simon cringed and brushed a hand across his smooth skull to feel for the small plastic Davidson cups that uplinked data to surgically implanted chips in his brain. They weren't there, but it would only take a few seconds to attach them. Then Toni could activate a sleep cycle. Or pain....

"Easy, Simon! I won't hurt you. Never." She put her hand on his shoulder and used a commanding tone. "Emancipation. Relax."

Simon automatically closed his eyes at the keyword and inhaled slowly. Toni's hand on his shoulder grew immensely heavy.

"You're sinking under hypnosis, down... down... down...."

Calm closed over Simon, like a warm sea. He drifted in it. A long distance away he heard Toni sigh.

"OK, we'll take a break. I'm going down to the kitchen. While I'm gone, I want you to count slowly backwards from one hundred. When you get to zero, you'll wake up feeling relaxed and calm."

Simon blew a Chinese hundred out of his mouth, and the soap bubble character drifted up to bump against the cross beam of the slanted ceiling. He puffed out ninety-nine, distantly aware of Toni getting up, tossing a towel into the laundry hamper and then treading down the creaky stairs. As ninety twirled lazily in the air, she turned on a tap in the kitchen and water pipes groaned.

Numbers accumulated up at the ceiling and Simon had to concentrate harder. When the one stroke finally arrived, he floated gently upward with it and broke surface. He opened his eyes.

Abruptly he noticed the aroma of chocolate. Toni was holding a mug out to him, so he sat up and reached out with his left hand, then noticed it was bandaged and switched to his right. Toni pulled over a cushion chair and sat, cradling a glass of whisky in her hands. The sweet chocolate steam at Simon's nose made him feel ravenous but he drank slowly, cupping the warmth in his hands and swirling rich, sweet flavor around his mouth. When he finally put the mug down, Toni took his right hand and Simon savored the soft shock of her skin against his palm.

"Simon, stay here in your body and talk to me, OK? I want you to tell me about your dream. Where were you just now?"

He swallowed, feeling the edges of old fear. "Vancouver. Pier B-C."

"What happened?"

"Blade went berserk. He killed people."

"Simon, you are Blade. You're one person."

Simon stared away, trying to strip Toni's words of meaning and lose them in the air like numbers. Words without meaning held no terror.

"Simon!" Toni's voice was sharp. "Listen to me. Tell me what happened at the pier last October."

Toni's bloody skull had felt wet and grotesquely broken in his hands. Simon stifled a stab of panic. Don't feel anything. Be wood. Be stone.

"Blade killed Klale," he told her flatly.

"No, Simon." Toni's voice took on an edge of frustration. "We've been through this before. You killed Captain Dhillon after she pulled a gun on me. Dhillon was wearing Klale's sweater. You killed four people, but you didn't hurt Klale." She was trying to trap his eyes. "Klale's here, remember?"

Sometimes in the mornings she pressed warm lips to his cheek and put her arms around him.

"It's a dream," he whispered.

"No, Klale is real."

Simon's stomach hurt. He pulled his knees tighter against his chest and wrapped his arms around them. Toni's hand retreated. He huddled, longing to float away, but Toni's orders pinned him to the bed.

4

The curtains on the window hung partly open and he caught sight of Toni's reflection. She was rubbing her temples with both hands, then she reached forward and picked up her whisky. For a long second she looked into the tumbler, then she stood abruptly, carried it down the hall, and Simon heard a splash in the bathroom sink. She came back and leaned in the doorway looking down at him wearily.

"Simon, I'm far too tired for this. We just go over the same ground again and again, and nothing I say seems to stick. I'm running out of ideas. Look..." she ran a hand through her close-cropped, woolly hair and snared him with intense brown eyes, "please, please tell me why you won't help me."

Her eyes sucked a whisper out of him.

"I'm afraid."

"I know that, Simon. I understand." Toni kept his eyes pinned to hers. "Can you tell me what you're afraid of?"

"Him." He couldn't say the name, but even so every muscle clenched with the old terror

"Choi is dead."

"No! He's waiting for me!"

Abruptly Toni kneeled in front of him and grabbed his hands, her fingernails digging into his palm. "Choi is dead, Simon. You belong to me now. You gave yourself to me. Choi only exists in your dreams. But I will always be here to wake you up. I will always protect you. You must believe me!"

Simon closed his eyes. His stomach hurt again and his throat ached, and he could feel the first faint hum of Blade's rage rising inside him, like a giant wave that would build and build and then break, smashing everything in its path.

Sometimes he glimpsed the real monster lurking beneath Blade's rage, waiting with icy, implacable patience. Choi had seared himself onto Simon's forehead with a branding iron, and twisted himself into Simon's mind with nanocircuits and poison.

Choi was not dead. Choi lived inside Simon. And Choi would destroy Toni.

# 2

Saturday, May 18, 2109
Vancouver

It felt strange to walk through familiar streets with a new face. Less than a year ago the grizzled Afroid vendor at the spuddy cart on the corner had known "Dr. Smith" by sight, but now her eyes scanned past Yasmin without recognition. Just another tourist. She didn't even bother to call "Get it hot! Get it now!" Guild tourists didn't eat at Downtown greaseries. Yasmin smiled with delight.

The vendor's eyes went past Tor, too, then flicked back, and Yasmin saw a faint frown before the old American turned her gaze further down the street. Damn! That was exactly what Yasmin had feared. Tor's blond Nordic features were new, but his height was the same and, worst of all, so was his stance. She'd tried to teach him to walk differently, but he had no skill at it, and she didn't have the time or equipment to do subtle physiosurgery. The wedge-heeled aggro boots she'd bought him didn't make enough difference. She'd brought Tor to Vancouver for protection, but if anyone recognized him as a former Viet Ching gang member he'd be a disastrous liability instead.

Well, too late to worry now. She pushed back her thick, glossy new hair, straightened her crisp shirt and took Tor's arm, giving him a smile that he echoed back with delight. It felt wonderful to be free, strolling in spring sunshine on the road that had been tantalizingly out of her reach for so long. A dense crowd flowed slowly along Robson Street, squeezing around vendors' stalls and pushcarts that filled the space between the derelict office towers. Even the sky looked crowded. The ancient concrete towers were festooned with the detritus of squatter family living—laundry, chicken cages, kitchen gardens, wind rotors, bird netting—and the air reeked of steaming cabbage, human sweat, and chicken dung.

Yasmin had hated that odor when it wafted through the windows of her laboratory prison, but now that she was free, she found it no longer annoyed her.

Just ahead, a Guild family on a Saturday slumming trip walked three abreast, jabbering and blocking the narrow street. Almost half a block ahead of them she glimpsed Doc's balding head bobbing purposefully forward. During the hours they'd tailed the old sot he'd dawdled, talking to people, collecting payments and dispensing malpractice, but now that the streets were packed he'd decided to hurry. Of course he might already have unloaded the packet he was carrying, but Yasmin had a hunch that he hadn't.

She moved her glance away from him and stared around, mimicking other tourists. The multilingual hubbub sounded the same as always, and everywhere hands gestured in Slang—the local patois sign language—but she noticed changes, too. Bands of City Watch officers in green hats and armbands patrolled the streets, and so far Yasmin hadn't seen a single gang member. But there were plenty of dirty, malnourished beggars entreating passersby—more than she remembered. Homeless, probably. Since the City had reoccupied Downtown in October, they'd torn down dozens of derelict buildings. Near the harbor, whole blocks had been leveled, and construction hoarding enclosed a huge excavation at the site of the new mag-lev railway terminal.

Staying in character, she dug a coin out of her pocket and tossed it to a big-eyed beggar child, then the family ahead of her stopped abruptly and she nearly collided with a beefy Citizen in a smartweave-shirt that flashed soccer slogans. He was gawping at a dentist's stall, with a giant, weather-worn plastiche tooth hanging in front of it and a groaning flot seated in a folding chair, mouth full of antique steel cutlery. Genetically optimized Citizens with Guild-funded medical care rarely suffered from dental disease. They stared at the stall with horrified fascination and the kids pointed their phones, vidding their friends back in Shaughnessy. Yasmin elbowed past them and looked ahead again, but this time she couldn't pick out Doc.

"Tor!"

Tor craned. He stood taller than most of the crowd.

"He's turning left. I think... He's going into the KlonDyke."

"Wait here two minutes, then follow me and take a table by yourself," she told him, and strolled toward a tall, narrow tower topped by the wreckage of a rotary restaurant—an oddly naked spire of concrete amid jungled buildings. At street level, red carpeted stairs led up to double doors covered by a white awning with a crimson biolume "K". A bouncer stood beside it, arms crossed. Yasmin tossed another coin to a dirty red-haired beggar crouching at the bottom of the steps, then walked up and through the doors, past the bouncer's incurious glance.

After the sunshine, it felt like walking into a cave, and Yasmin paused, waiting for her eyes to adjust. During her captivity, the implanted Viet Ching surveillance chip hadn't allowed her to stray further than a hundred meters from the lab so she'd never seen the KlonDyke. Her first reaction to Downtown's most famous bar was that it was both bigger than she expected, and tattier. A jumble of mismatched chairs, tables and desks salvaged from old office towers were arranged on three levels circling an empty stage. Shafts of daylight from a couple of skylights illuminated dingy stage curtains and stains on the floor. It looked like a junk sale, and smelled like stale beer, fried apples and Fireweed.

The only elegant touch was a polished wood bar stretching along one wall. Doc leaned against it, looking like a derelict with disheveled gray hair and beard, and a beer gut straining against his rumpled shirt. Yasmin wondered again why the city hadn't run him out of Downtown yet. Were they hoping that his trade would dry up as flots and squats gained access to licensed medics?

A bartender in a feathered wig and luminescent gold body paint poured Doc a pint. Tourists stood gawking nearby, and Yasmin strolled up behind them, just in time to catch an excited voice mention "assassins." Of course. Her eyes dropped past the bartender's nipple rings to a spray of splintered bullet holes in the front of the bar. This was where Mary Tungsten Smarch, manager of the KlonDyke, had almost been killed by a death squad last October—the incident which sparked an all-out tong war and finally forced the City of Vancouver to re-occupy Downtown, fifty years after abandoning the quake-devastated island to vagrants and refugees. The tong war and resulting riots had also, inadvertently, been Yasmin's deliverance.

Tourists goggled, no doubt eager to view the scene before this dilapidated building was demolished, too.

As if on cue, the kitchen door swung open and Mary Smarch stepped out, a plump Native woman in a flowing cobalt salwar kameez. She'd let her hair turn gray and her face age naturally into deep seams. A clever move, decided Yasmin. It gave her tremendous presence among all those look-alike Citizens with their face sculpts and juvving treatments. The tourists nudged each other and stared. Doc put down his beer stein, already half empty, and his deep voice boomed over the background din.

"Mary, my dear! Your beauty and your beer are a delight, as always."

As Smarch went over to greet him, Yasmin's attention sharpened. Doc was reaching into a grimy trouser pocket. Yasmin pretended to study the liquor bottles lining the mirrored shelves behind the bar while Doc drained his glass, then slapped his hand onto the bar, as if offering payment. Smarch took his glass, and, just as casually, put her brown hand over a small package and slid it underneath the bar.

Intriguing, thought Yasmin. Mary Smarch, famous do-gooding crusader of Downtown, was taking delivery of elicit software used for mind twisting. Did she know what it was?

The tourists moved off and Yasmin looked for a table close to the bar. As she sat down, she glanced around the room with apparent casualness. She recognized no one except Tor, just seating himself at a table on the middle level.

Pulling out her phone, she unrolled the display and fingerpad. Her up-link didn't flash on—the KlonDyke must be jammed—but she had what she needed in memory and scanned quickly for information about the KlonDyke. She'd bought the data from a stolen tong data cache and it was six months out of date, but it should suffice. Mary Smarch's profile was irreproachable—respected Tlingit citizen, and co-founder of SisOpp, the licit venture that ran the KlonDyke—but many of the KlonDyke's staffers were former smuts or addicts, with tong connections. And Mary's head bartender, Toni, was rumored to have trained slaves for the blackmailer, Choi Shung Wai!

Choi. Yasmin found herself scowling and smoothed her face

with effort. That vicious old bastard had hunted her down and sold her to the Viet Ching, a captivity that lasted eight interminable years.

Official reports listed Choi as a casualty of the tong war, but Yasmin doubted the wily old bastard was dead. An explosion that buried all evidence below a collapsed office tower seemed much too convenient. And Choi's enforcer had been seen alive afterward. Yasmin was willing to bet that Doc's supplies were destined for Toni, who was either retraining Choi's old enforcer, or making a new one.

Toni would lead her to Choi. And to retribution.

Yasmin smiled as she put her phone away, then ordered a pot of green Darjeeling chai and sat back to watch. Hours ticked by. Doc drank two more beers and departed. Mary Smarch disappeared in the back for long periods, returning periodically to help at the bar and chat with customers. At five, a jazz group took the stage. As more customers arrived Yasmin's new face and flaming red hair attracted interest and she had to discourage both men and women from sitting at her table. She ordered food. Around seven-thirty, as her patience was wearing thin, a husky young woman with a tangled mane of auburn hair strode up to the bar, shrugging a heavy duffel bag off her shoulder. The insignia on the girl's Cowichan sweater, plus the hempen pants and heavy boots marked her as Working Guild. But she seemed very much at ease in the bar, greeting servers by name and calling out to Smarch.

Yasmin took a surreptitious scan with her phone and ran a visual recognition query. She got an immediate match: Klale (pronounced clay-lee) Renhardt, a Fisher Guild runaway who worked at the KlonDyke. Rumored to be Toni's lover.

Yasmin looked up again, just in time to see Smarch pass an envelope to Renhardt, who shoved it in her pocket, picked up her bag and headed for the main door.

The envelope looked new, but all Yasmin's instincts shouted that it contained Doc's packet. She stood, stretched, and reached for her coat. A few tables away, Tor rose also. Too obvious, thought Yasmin, suppressing a flash of annoyance. Tor had no talent for surveillance, but he was the only one from the lab she'd been able to save. The rest of her trusted staff had died in the fire, or at the hands of the mob waiting outside.

Tor trailed behind her for a block, then caught up when she beckoned. It was dusk, and they had to hurry to keep up with Renhardt, shouldering her way purposefully up the still crowded thoroughfare. At Bute Street, the girl turned north toward the harbor, and they followed, dropping a bit further behind. Renhardt didn't look back, though. She hurried between makeshift shacks and vendor stalls, then out onto one of the piers that had been built hastily over top of older wharves during the last century's sea level rise. Dilapidated loading equipment littered the open expanse of stained concrete and the whole area reeked of seawater, marine lube, rust and rot. Yasmin stopped in the shadows of a warehouse, not wanting to follow too closely. There were few people around here.

In the relative quiet Renhardt's steps clumped past the looming bulk of a tramp carrier tied up at wharf, then she stopped beside another rusting ship and called up. A crewer stepped to the railing above and waved, then disappeared inside, leaving the girl shifting impatiently from foot to foot. Long moments later the crewer reappeared, carrying a blue foil cube about the size of a loaf of bread. Yasmin watched carefully through a pair of full spectrum zooms as Renhardt zapped a phone payment to him, then caught the cube as it was tossed down, and stuffed it into her duffel bag. She hoisted the bag back on her shoulder, turned and started retracing her path at a jog. Yasmin and Tor backed up and ducked around the corner of the warehouse.

"Lookin' for somebody?"

Yasmin jumped. A uniformed security guard leaned against the building. His pose affected casualness, but his right hand hung free, near his belt. Worse, she recognized him. He had been a member of the Tigers, the Viet Ching's gang. And he was staring at Tor.

She stepped in front of Tor and smiled.

"I'm afraid we're lost," she said. "We're looking for the ferry."

"That way." The hench pointed west, still frowning at Tor. Damn.

"Thanks," she said, and took Tor's hand. "I told you it was this way, honey!"

They almost bumped into Renhardt as she came trotting past. They followed in her wake, walking until they got out of sight of the security guard, then breaking into a run.

Renhardt was already out of sight, but when they reached the next corner Yasmin looked right and spotted the girl's distinctive black and gray sweater bobbing through a crowd at the passenger ferry terminal—that same brightly lit oasis of modernity that Yasmin had arrived at from Seattle the previous day. She seemed to be heading for a boat at Berth Four. A lumed billboard at the entrance to the pier announced: "4: M.V. Salish Pride departing for Vancouver Island: Nanaimo, Qualicum Beach, Fanny Bay, Comox, Campbell River, Sayward, Port McNeill, Port Hardy. Connections to Northern Gulf Islands. 6 minutes to departure."

Yasmin followed the girl onto the pier, then glanced over her shoulder and felt her whole body tense. The security guard who'd stopped them had just rounded the corner. And he'd acquired two friends. Damn! She could catch this ferry, but if the henches followed, she'd be cornered. Badly as she wanted to follow Renhardt, Yasmin couldn't risk recapture by the Viet Ching, and she didn't want to lead the tong to Choi. She needed another way out, and fast.

Two pedicabs stood idle nearby, drivers leaning against them. Not fast enough. And they'd have to go right past the approaching henches. I need a real taxi, Yasmin thought with irritation, wishing there were more motorized vehicles Downtown. She pulled out her phone, feigning tourist confusion, and linked to the ferry terminal. Announcements flashed and blared. She searched for "motor" taxi, then tried to call one, but got a 30 minute wait advisory.

Damn! Then a tiny blinking ad caught her eye: "Water Taxi pickup, vanfloat37." Her GPS gave the direction, but when she looked up from the phone she still had to spend long seconds searching her surroundings before she spotted a water taxi sign in faded blue paint nailed to a post beside a battered ramp that descended into the dark underside of the pier. She blipped the vanfloat code. To her relief, she got an immediate acknowledgment. Taxi waiting. Tor was staring back at the catamaran ferry in Berth Four. She grabbed his arm like a doting girlfriend and tugged him toward the ramp, not risking another backward look. Behind her she could hear the quiet swish of the Salish Pride revving its propellers, then a single long hoot.

Later, she promised herself. If Mary Smarch is the pipeline, there will be more deliveries. And next time I'll track her courier all the way to Choi.

# 3

July, 2109
Cortes Island

Tiny claws scrabbled across Toni's cheek and lips, jolting her from sound sleep into terror. She screamed and sat bolt upright. For several seconds she couldn't think where she was, but she knew the feel of rats' feet on her flesh. She grabbed her pillow, glimpsed movement on the hardwood floor, and threw it.

"Fucking rat!"

She scrambled out of bed, looking around for something else to throw and found a handlight. She hurled it across the small room.

"Fucking rat! Fucking rat!"

Feet pounded up the stairs, then Rigo burst into the room.

"What's wrong?"

"It's a fucking rat!" was all Toni could get out. She was shaking so hard she could barely stand.

Rigo stared into her eyes for an instant, then took her by the shoulder and pushed her towards the door.

"I'll take care of it. Go."

The door snicked shut and Toni stood alone in the upstairs hallway in bare feet and a night shirt, choking back hysteria and feeling her terror slowly ebb into humiliation. Floor boards creaked in her bedroom as Rigo walked around, and she heard low muttering that went on for long minutes while she shivered. Then the window slammed and footsteps came towards the door. Hurriedly she wiped her face and tried to assemble some semblance of calm.

The door swung open and Rigo stepped out, the image of doctorly competence in a crisp tunic with evenly rolled up sleeves, and neatly combed black hair, frosted with gray. All he lacked was a hospital name tag: Dr. Amerigo Lau. She glared, daring him to joke,

14

but he didn't look amused. He looked angry.

"It was a squirrel, Toni. It must have come in through the window."

"Oh."

Squirrels were just tree rats. But how stupid. She hated thinking what she'd looked like a minute ago. This would hardly improve Rigo's crumbling confidence in his son's therapist. She'd seen the doubt haunting his eyes lately and could hardly blame him—she had been a highly-regarded professional in her time, but that was old news. Eleven years ago she'd lost her own grip. Dripped, tripped, and emotionally wrecked she'd fled her practice at the Seattle Neurological Institute for the slums of Vancouver and gone on a six month binge she remembered mercifully little of. Beaten and left for dead in an alley, she'd been rescued by a good Samaritan who gave her a job as a bartender when she recovered. And that's all she'd done for the better part of a decade—serve drinks. Hell, she hadn't yet applied to reactivate her ID, so she remained legally dead. On her blackest days she feared all her skills were dead, too.

She got control of her voice and started to apologize, but he interrupted.

"I need you downstairs. When you screamed Simon tried to bolt for the stairs and the restraint kicked in. I can try to calm him, but he's always better with you..."

Shit, thought Toni, heart sinking. She nodded, trying to look calm.

"Make him comfortable. I'll be right there."

She went back into her bedroom and pulled on pants, a shirt and a heavy sweater with icy, shaking hands. The room was cold and she felt queasy from shock. In the bathroom she wiped her face with a wet cloth, catching a sudden glimpse in the mirror of an aging chigger hag, with black smudges under her eyes and lines that etched deeper every day. Eleven years. Had she forgotten too much? Lost her touch?

Sudden pain stabbed her stomach and Toni buckled against the sink, gasping. Damn! She dropped the washcloth, hurried back to her bedroom, rummaging in the bottom of her closet for her old boots. In the left boot, stuffed into the toe, was her private stash of meds. She took out a tube of anti-inflammatories, loaded it into a spray gun, rolled up her sleeve and gave herself a quick shot in the forearm, careful to center the gun over old drug stains so the new spray mark wouldn't show. One good thing about dark skin pigment—it tended to hide minor abrasions. She pulled her sleeve back, shoved the boot away quietly and hurried downstairs, forcing herself to stand tall against the instinct to curl around her aching gut.

Simon lay in a heap at the foot of the worn wooden staircase. Rigo had wedged a sofa cushion under his head and sat next to him on the floor with a portable med unit, checking blood chemistry while he talked soothingly. His calm voice contrasted oddly with the lines of anger and grief in his face. Simon wasn't listening and Rigo knew it. After half a year of patient caregiving, Simon still wouldn't meet his father's eyes. Choi had destroyed most of Simon's early memories, but Toni was quite certain he recognized the father he hadn't seen since the age of seven. He simply refused to acknowledge him.

Toni sat and took Simon's hand. His fingers were as cold as hers and trembling. As she waited for her own meds to kick in, she was grateful for the long minutes it took to calm Simon. As soon as the neural restraint chip released his motor control, he sat up with his arms wrapped around his knees and rocked silently back and forth, tears running down his cheeks. At least he could cry after a fashion, but Simon's owner had shaped him with insane brutality. The only time he cried aloud was under direct stimulus to the pain center.

His altered face further hid emotions. His skin had been pulled tight to his skull like a death mask, and follicle suppressant had left him entirely hairless, with lashless eyes. A burned left ear, and burn scars spilling down onto his shoulder and back heightened the grotesque impression. The alterations erased identity. Toni could find only small resemblances to his handsome Chinese father in the spacing of his eyes and lines of his neck.

"Simon!" She put a hand on his arm and gave her voice a sharp edge of command. "Do you want to stay inside or go outside?"

She saw him flinch a little, then he did what he always did when forced to make a choice—his eyes flicked to her face, trying to decipher what she wanted him to do. Toni kept her face expressionless and waited. She knew what he wanted—he wanted to sit outside where he could smell the fresh air and watch the trees and know that he was no longer a prisoner in Choi's underground bunker. But he had to make that choice himself. Finally, he whispered:

"Outside...?"

"Fine," she told him, putting warmth into her voice and squeezing his shoulder. She stood up stiffly. "Let's go."

Simon rose with smooth grace, unfolding into a tower of muscle. Toni never got entirely used to it. Simon's armpit loomed higher than the top of her head. The cabin had been built in old measurements with eight foot ceilings, and Simon could stand inside, but he had to duck through the doorways. Oddly, it didn't make him look big; instead Simon made the cabin look like a doll house.

She followed him outside to his favorite spot at the end of the weather-beaten porch. A few splashes of sunlight sparkled in long wet grass but the sun hadn't yet risen above the wall of trees encircling the cottage. Toni felt trapped by the trees but Simon loved them. He sat down cross-legged on an old cushion and Toni wrapped a musty blanket around him. Although his face betrayed no expression, he clutched at her hand and wouldn't let go. A Bach fugue began pouring from the porch speakers—good choice, Rigo, thought Toni. Finally, she induced hypnosis and let Simon rest in a trance state. When she felt sure he was calm, she extricated her hand and stood up, feeling queasy and chilled.

Cool air wafted through the kitchen, carrying the smell of burned food. Rigo must have been cooking when Toni screamed. He'd opened the back door to disperse the smoke, cleaned up, and started again. Toni walked past him, scooped cheap pre-ground coffee into a filter and fitted it over her mug. She held the mug and filter under the sink tap, adjusted the temperature to ninety-five Celsius and poured. Pipes whined and the roof cistern chugged. She sighed. The primitive plumbing system was high on her cabin hate list—almost as high as the unsanitary bathroom and the four ancient portable heaters they'd lugged from room to room all winter. She longed to make repairs, but retrofitting utilities into walls built of solid cedar logs was a nightmare. The others seemed to view the wood as bucolic—she found it dark, depressing and grossly impractical.

She took a calming breath and looked over at Rigo.

"I'm very sorry for that scene. But the damned animal woke me up by running across my face."

Rigo had regained the slightly wary composure he maintained around her. He gave a sympathetic nod.

"I understand. We used to get rats on the boat sometimes." He shot her a cautious look, then asked: "Were there rats where you grew up?"

"Yeah. We slept on the floor and they'd come out at night. I was terrified to go to sleep...." She trailed off, suppressing a shudder. She didn't try to hide her past any more, but she hated talking about the Chicago camps, hated remembering the Zone.

"Would you like some breakfast?"

"No thanks," said Toni, trying not to show irritation as she waited for the coffee filter to finish dripping. Rigo knew she never ate breakfast, but he kept fussing, trying to get her to eat more and cut down on coffee. Now he peered into her eyes with a sharp gaze, and before she could move away he reached out and rubbed a curl of her hair between two fingers. He frowned.

"You look exhausted and your hair is brittle. I'd like to check you over."

"You did that last month," she said, fighting to keep her voice level. "I'm tired but I'm fine."

Rigo looked unconvinced, but he didn't push it. Toni rinsed coffee grounds into the composter, then carried her mug to the old green-painted kitchen table and sat down. She sipped cautiously. Hot liquid lit a trail of pain down her gut, making her gasp. She glanced at Rigo, but he had his back turned. Good. She'd asked Doc to send up new meds from Vancouver to keep her stomach under control until she could get to a proper hospital. There was no way in hell she was having her ulcerated intestine treated in that shabby little room over the library that was all this godforsaken island had for a medical clinic.

She had hoped for a half hour of peace, but instead Rigo joined her at the table, carrying a tea pot that trailed jasmine-scented steam. He poured himself a cup and then looked purposefully at her.

"We must decide what to do next."

Toni nodded reluctantly. She'd known this was coming.

"All right."

Rigo waited a beat for her to say more, then started.

"Directed dreaming hasn't worked."

"I know," said Toni grimly. She had been trying for two months to teach Simon to stop his own nightmares. "Simon's too passive. He's been conditioned to do nothing without orders."

"And you still believe that he must start dancing again."

"Absolutely. Dancing is how Simon defines himself. We won't make any real progress until he decides to dance."

"But you won't order him to dance."

"No," she said wearily. They'd been over this. "It must be his choice. He needs more time."

Rigo sighed.

"He also needs repairs to that damaged neural chip, cognitive repathing, and reconstructive surgery on his left hand."

"I know."

"Toni, you're wearing out."

Wearing out and longing to leave this rural pit, she thought bitterly. She'd hoped that sunny weather and long days would help, but she still felt trapped in the cabin, crammed in unbearable proximity with three other people. The fact that she had no other home and nowhere to go was fading into insignificance before her desperation to get the hell off this miserable island.

And Rigo was right—they hadn't made much progress. Simon had arrived in a semi-catatonic state, and was now active—doing chores, exercising, answering questions. But he remained utterly passive, never initiating.

"I'd like to try one more tactic," she said finally. "I'd like to try talking to Simon in his other induced personality state—as Choi. I've been avoiding the dark side of him, but maybe that's a mistake."

She braced for Rigo to argue, but unexpectedly he didn't.

"All right. I agree. But, Toni," she looked up to see his intense frown, "if we don't see any improvement by the end of this month I insist we call in more professional help or take him to the Seattle Institute."

And maybe it's the only choice, Toni found herself thinking, then kicked herself mentally. No! Simon had risked everything when he put himself in her hands. She couldn't lock him in an institution. He'd be too terrified to cooperate and he'd end up catatonic, psychotic, or, at best, an empty human 'bot programmed to mimic normal behavior.

Years ago Toni used to tell her students: the most dangerous thing a therapist can do is to enter a psychotic patient's fantasy world. Well, she'd tried everything else. She gulped the last of her coffee and stood.

"Let's get out the netsets."

Rigo looked startled. "Now?"

"Now."

Toni carried her own set down from her bedroom while Rigo dug out Mary's old set and put it on the kitchen table. Then they brought Simon inside and sat him down in front of Toni's set. He squeezed his knees under the table, face expressionless, as Toni waved on the set and heard it hum to life.

Toni handed Simon the neurolink cables, patted his shoulder reassuringly, then moved to the other end of the table and wiped dust off the battered plastiche case of Mary's ancient Integra. This set started with a rising whine of protest, but it worked, and Toni was able to slave it to the newer unit. She hoped the old set wouldn't crash. Her own unit couldn't handle Simon's high-capacity neural links and Toni's headset at the same time. And she didn't want to use Rigo's set. Simon as Choi was unpredictable, and they couldn't risk losing all their customized medical and diagnostic 'ware.

She checked the screen, nodded at Rigo who had taken up a position behind Simon, then looked at her patient.

"Jack in," she told him.

He moved as if she'd switched him from "pause" to "forward," connecting optic cables to the netset ports. Then he took the other ends of the cables, breathed on each suction cup and pressed it against his bald skull over one of five implanted neural chips. When he finished he closed his eyes and sat absolutely still for a few seconds, then he reached for the command pad with his right hand and, simultaneously, began issuing voice commands in Mandarin.

At his first words Toni twitched, then swore under her breath at her own nervousness and tried to relax. But she was on unfamiliar ground. She had never treated a datashark before, and this aspect of Simon's training hadn't been archived by Choi. Worse, she knew she couldn't control Simon once he was loose in the net. She had to move quickly to establish rules.

She slid goggles over her head, and put in a call to Mr. Choi, using her own netset as the address. Seconds crawled by while waitmusic tinkled in her ears and she began to worry. What if this didn't work? What next?

Abruptly light flared and she found herself sitting in Choi's office facing the old blackmailer across a polished expanse of mahogany desk.

Toni struggled with sudden fear. She hadn't expected Simon to have Choi's sim. He must have pulled it from some data cache on the web—very quickly, too. And she'd forgotten the menacing intensity of Choi Shung Wai.

Mr. Choi's dark eyes shone like chips of hematite in an old parchment face. His Chinese silk jacket was black, as was the porcelain tea set and calligraphy brushes on his otherwise empty desk. His office looked exactly like the real room Toni had once seen, with oriental wallscreens and a polished wood floor, except that the sim showed windows looking out into a courtyard. There had been no garden in Choi's antiseptic underground bunker. And the man sitting behind Choi's desk had been Simon.

The real Choi was dead, Toni reminded herself, and however powerfully he had twisted Simon into this psychotic shadow, it was still Simon behind the sim. Still, she found herself reacting with a raw surge of hatred. She'd watched hours of Choi's sadistic training records. It was hard to look into Choi's face and not feel rage.

"Good morning, Simon," she said.

Choi stared at her expressionlessly, then folded his hands precisely on the desk in front of him.

"I believe, Dr. Almiramez, that you are attempting some crude psychological ruse. However, you know perfectly well that I am Choi Shung Wai."

"Choi is dead."

"Oh, no." Choi's eyes gleamed and he came very close to smiling. "I am very much alive."

His certainty was unsettling and Toni had to work to keep her voice confident.

"Choi is dead and you, Simon, belong to me now. I am your master. You obey me."

One of Mr. Choi's eyebrows rose very slightly, creasing his dry skin.

"No, Doctor. I certainly do not."

Toni felt an instant of alarm, then pushed it back. Simon needed independence and initiative, she told herself. This was good.

"Moreover, the hulk that you persist in calling Simon is organic waste," he added in Choi's flat, precise voice, with a trace of Chinese accent. "The original Simon is dead. I erased every part of him that was not useful to me and tailored the rest to my purposes. If you believe that you can do therapy on slag, you are wasting your time."

Toni shook her head and smiled a little.

"I'm not wasting my time."

"Why this charade, doctor? You could use the neural filaments to re-train him easily enough—make him anything you want. Or if you want a reliable tool you would get better results by starting with a new subject."

Good points, thought Toni as a chilling realization hit her. She should have done this months ago. Simon understood the situation and the dangers. He needed to ask her tough questions and for that he needed "Choi." She had underestimated him again.

"I'm here to help you, Simon. And to do that, I need your full cooperation with therapy."

Choi leaned back in his chair. Had the original Choi's face been so utterly emotionless, wondered Toni? Or was the netset simply translating the mask-like inflexibility of Simon's altered face?

"Why do you think I would cooperate with you?"

"The real Choi was a frail old man and he's dead. You know that. You can open your eyes and look down at your own hands."

Choi sat motionless.

"I don't like this part of you, Simon. Choi created a shadow of himself—a ghost that you're keeping alive. And, as you pointed out, I can use those neural filaments to erase the ghost."

Was "Choi" breathing a little too hard? Challenging his delusion must be upsetting him. Toni realized too late that she had neglected to set up a window in her visual field so she could monitor the real Simon's reactions. Trying to do it now would break her concentration. It was a stupid mistake, amateurish!

22

"But you haven't you tried to erase this 'ghost'," he said.

"I prefer not to because all the parts of you that Choi fragmented are interdependent—Simon the original personality relic, Blade the slave, and Choi, too. With assistance you can reintegrate into one person—with Simon in control, not some twisted shadow of Choi."

"Do you expect me to believe this?" he said contemptuously. "A damaged tool is certainly not worth such an investment of your effort. And you must realize that radical alterations decrease life expectancy. Your tool is already thirty-one years old and will only be useful until forty, if that."

Of course she knew. But Toni felt a pang of sadness that Simon did.

"Simon, you're worth all of the effort I can give," she said quietly. "We're helping you because we love you."

Unsurprisingly, 'Choi' didn't have a response to that. He simply stared at her across the desk.

"I require you to help me review Choi's training records and answer my questions about Choi's implanted directives."

"And what do I get in return?"

Toni took a breath and thought rapidly. What could she offer? It had to be something that he valued.

"You get access to the net so you can search for Choi's assets."

Choi's fingers pressed tighter against each other.

"You should have started searching months ago."

"I don't need the money," she pointed out calmly. "When you triggered the dataspill you also transferred more than enough into my account to pay for your care for the rest of your life. But I thought you might be interested in tracking Choi's other caches, rather than leaving them for treasure hunters."

"Any competent hunters will have traced my accounts already!"

"What, you hid them that poorly?" mocked Toni, then realized that she'd slipped and spoken to him as Choi. Damn, this was difficult! "Also, you can check to be sure that we haven't been tracked here by the tongs. I know our security isn't as good as it could be."

Nothing like appealing to a paranoid's paranoia. His eyes narrowed.

"Your security is farcical and so is this set! Without good 'ware, any search I make would be traced back here within minutes."

"I assume you know what you need and how to get it," said Toni.

"Oh? And what do you want done with these assets you deem so unimportant?"

"We'll decide when you find them," she said, realizing that she had no idea. "Give me immediate reports on anything you locate. But do not make any transactions without permission from both Dr. Lau and I." Hopefully Rigo knew something about finances and data trading. She certainly didn't.

Choi appeared to be staring at his steepled fingers.

"Do you agree to my terms?" she asked sharply.

"No."

Damn! She leaned forward, speaking slowly and very coldly.

"Then I will unplug you now and this is the last time you will ever have net access. We will remove all of your neural filaments tonight."

Choi's eyes widened slightly, copied by the netset's scanner from the real Simon. He was frightened. And when he spoke, Choi's voice, for the first time, sounded shaky.

"You're bluffing, doctor. If this was your intention, you would have done so months ago."

Toni made her voice soft but firm.

"Simon, I prefer not to do anything so drastic, particularly here where we don't have good medical equipment. But we're running out of options. If you won't cooperate with me, I promise we will do it."

There was a long pause during which Toni concentrated on not betraying the tension she felt. Had she pushed him too far?

"I am interested in your motives, Doctor," said Choi suddenly. "Are they professional? Perhaps you intend to present your research on this tool to your former institute in return for reinstatement of your credentials? Or are you interested in the notoriety that such a case would certainly give you?"

"I can't prove what my motives are," said Toni steadily. "You will simply have to trust me."

Silence. It wasn't the answer Simon wanted to hear.

24

Unfortunately, it was the truth. She needed to grab back control of this conversation.

"What is it that you want, Simon?"

"Simon the child?" Choi's voice dripped contempt. "It wants to dance, of course. Choi taught it to crave music."

"That's not true," said Toni softly. "Your musical talent was born in you, Simon. Your mother is a dancer, and you started dancing as soon as you learned to walk—long before Choi bought you." She waited for a reply, but got none. "What about Blade? What does he want?"

"To kill."

Of course, she thought. Blade contained Simon's rage, and he understood that.

"And what does Choi want?"

"Revenge."

Toni's interest sharpened.

"Revenge for what?"

Choi's mouth opened, then he hesitated, seeming uncertain. Probably Simon never knew what motivated Choi. Maybe even Choi hadn't known.

"Do you agree to my terms?" she asked.

He spoke slowly.

"It appears that I have no other option."

"Yes or no?"

"Yes."

Toni felt a wave of relief but she didn't let herself relax. Not yet.

"Good," she said. "But if you break your word, I will remove your neural interface."

"Understood."

"And I have another thing to say." She paused to gain his full attention. "Simon, this office is a sim. It is NOT real, any more than Choi is. The underground bunker is gone. You don't have to be here. You can leave this office at any time. Or you can use it differently. For instance," she said, with sudden inspiration, "you could get up from behind the desk and walk into that garden."

"The garden isn't real."

"None of this is real. It's what you are choosing to see. And

25

you can choose to see something different."

Choi remained immobile, staring at her, thin old fingers laced together on the polished desk in front of him. Toni hadn't expected him to take her suggestion. Not yet. But if she could get into the sim's coding she could put something behind the false door to the garden. Something that would surprise Simon and kick him out of the Choi persona. Of course she'd need expert help, but they had the money.

For the first time she allowed herself a flare of optimism. This had gone well.

"Good-bye, Simon," she said, reaching for the headset jack.

"Not yet, Dr. Almiramez. I have not yet given you my terms."

Startled, she looked over at Choi.

"If you try to destroy Choi," he said, voice taut with hatred, "I will kill Simon."

"You can't," she said coolly, then hit disconnect. Her headset went black. She pulled it off quickly and looked across the table, hoping to catch some hint of expression on Simon's face. There was none. He sat perfectly still, eyes closed, cables trailing from his neural interface cups. Only the hum of the netset suggested that he was doing anything at all.

Dr. Lau stood behind him, looking stunned. He had seen glimpses of Choi in Simon's training records, but he had never witnessed Simon's uncanny imitation of the old sadist. As Toni turned off Mary's old set, he came across the kitchen and spoke very softly in her ear.

"Is he bluffing?"

"Yes," said Toni.

But she was far from certain. Simon had been conditioned never to think of the possibility of suicide. Nonetheless, he had overcome the most extreme conditioning in order to kill Choi, and then again to give himself to her. And she was further eroding that old conditioning through therapy.

In truth, Toni really didn't know what Simon might be capable of. And she had misjudged him before—too often.

# 4

## Wednesday, July 10, 2109
## Cortes Island

Preoccupied with the rhythm of swimming in mirror-smooth water, one arm, then the other, almost in silence, Simon didn't notice the figure on the beach until he had put his feet down to search for footing among the seaweed slippery rocks. He caught a movement out of the corner of his eye, his head snapped up, and he felt the first edges of terror.

"Hi! Hi!"

A slight figure waved and ran down the beach towards him. A child. He'd seen this boy sometimes in the early morning on the neighbor's dock. He must have discovered Simon's route to the water.

Simon closed his eyes and hung motionless, half kneeling, half floating in the water, struggling with his dilemma. Dr. Lau had gone back to the cabin early and he was alone. He could swim away, but he had to return sooner or later to get ashore. Could he just walk past the boy? The boy didn't seem to be a threat, but if Simon's restraint device cut in he would be helpless. He could already feel a warning tingle in his fingers. He took a long, slow breath and concentrated on blanking his emotions, letting himself drift a little away from Blade's body.

Tiny wavelets slurped at the shoreline. A seagull screeched. Be calm, he told himself. Feel nothing.

"Hello!" The voice came again, shockingly close. Simon didn't dare look, but the boy kept speaking. "I'm David Anderson, your neighbor. That's our blue wind rotor, sticking up from the roof over there. Uh...." He had evidently noticed Simon wasn't looking. Would he go away?

"You're staying in Miz Smarch's pan-abode, right? Look, sir, I was wondering... I've seen you swimming out here in the morning. Uh... do you scuba dive, or just swim?"

Simon finally risked a glance through his water streaked mask. The hood of his dry suit and the mask must disguise Blade's face because the boy stood at the tide line looking at him and didn't seem alarmed. He wore scuffed hempen jeans, a green shirt, and a blue backpack. He had an odd squished-looking nose, freckles and shiny blond hair that fell into his eyes. He did not seem ready to leave.

"I swim," ventured Simon finally.

"Oh." The boy sounded disappointed "I hoped you knew about diving. See, I'm not allowed to take lessons until I turn fifteen, which is another two years and three months. Um...."

He gave Simon an apprehensive look and Simon felt a surge of anxiety. He inhaled very slowly, steadily. His face mask was starting to fog up.

"So, I guess you know about ADAT marine monitoring stations, right?"

Simon's breath puffed out in bewilderment.

"No."

"It's part of the University of BC's Amateur Data Collection program," David told him. "I've been running station MB1347 for two years. Actually, it's in granddad's name because I'm not old enough, but I do the work. We have twenty-three ADATs on Cortes, you know—nine marine and fourteen land-based—and we're the most populous island to get class A recovery status under the Coastal Waters Treaty. Uh...."

He paused uncertainly, then receiving no response, started again.

"Look, I monitor inter-tidal organisms. It's a microstudy to gather data for simulations. Here, I'll show you."

The boy shrugged off his backpack, kneeled and rummaged in it, then drew something out. Simon tensed automatically, but it wasn't a weapon, it was only a stiff sheet of plastiche about forty centimeters square.

"I set up collector plates at the two meter level which is about where the tide is right now, and then I monitor them every week for marine growth. I wanted to get one on that nav marker out there, but.... well, I'm grounded, so I was hoping maybe you would do it for me..."

Simon glanced over at the white painted navigation marker which stood about a hundred meters out in the bay and felt his thoughts whirl. He had no idea what to do. Toni had explicitly canceled all his old standing directives. She had instructed him to avoid the neighbors, but it was too late for that. She also said that if he encountered islanders he should not frighten, endanger or offend them. If he refused the boy's request, would he offend him? Should he ask Toni? If he called her for directions he would have to wake her up and try to explain a situation he didn't understand himself. Desperately, he tried to think it through. The boy's request was simple enough. And if Simon complied, the boy might leave.

Very cautiously he knelt and held out his hand.

"Strat!" David's face lit up and he lunged forward ankle deep in the water to pass Simon his collection plate. "There's marine epoxy tabs on the back. Just break the seal and hold it a few seconds. Um, it works best if you can find a clear spot and if you can get the plate flush against a clean surface or jam it between two rocks where the tide won't grab it, right?"

The task proved simple, but when Simon returned, the boy was still there, waiting at the shore. Now what? Dr. Lau expected him back at the cabin by seven thirty. Dr. Lau had also told him to please call for assistance if he saw anyone on the beach, but Toni had said that any sentence prefaced with "please" was not a direct command. And Simon did not like talking to Dr. Lau.

Very carefully and slowly, Simon stood up. He pulled off his swim fins and waded up the beach. The boy gave a startled upward glance at his height.

"Thanks very much. Uh... did you see any otters this morning? There's a den around here somewhere and I'm looking for it."

Simon spoke hesitantly. "I saw a seal."

It had surfaced and stared at him with soulful brown eyes behind a long-whiskered gray muzzle. Simon had floated spellbound, studying its gleaming mottled pelt until it rolled under water.

"There's lots of harbor seals around. The population is rebounding like crazy. Oh, hey, here's a good sample site."

David dropped to his knees. Simon lifted his mask slightly to peer under it. David had pulled out a pocket knife and was scraping at a clump of mussels and barnacles cemented to a rock.

"Acorn barnacles accumulate nutrients and trace toxins from the water at a pretty constant rate, so they're great biodetectors. I still find trace toxins leaching from the old pulp mill site at Powell River and mine tailings from Texada Island. Now I just bag it," he swung off his backpack and groped in a pocket," then I record the precise location." The boy put the barnacle into a small plastiche tub, then unfolded his phone and held it beside the rock. It cheeped—linking to navsat, Simon guessed. "And while I'm at it I always take a look underneath."

David lay the phone down, then put both hands under one side of the rock and yanked. As the rock shifted, Simon heard frantic scrabbling.

"Looks like a healthy population. Good diversity. Hold out your hand."

Without thinking, Simon shoved his face mask up on his forehead, crouched down and held out his free hand. David dropped something small into Simon's palm.

A mottled green-gray crab, about two centimeters across, waved white pincers in the air, then scuttled sideways and tried to shove itself into the crack between Simon's thumb and fingers. Simon put down his swim fins and cupped both hands together, fascinated by the tiny living creature. It scuttled again, feet tickling his palm, and Simon broke into a delighted smile. Then he looked up to find David staring at him.

Simon's stomach lurched as he realized that David had seen Blade's face, but the boy smiled nervously, and then busied himself with the rock.

"I'll just put the rock back. That's important for a stable environment. I always put the crabs back, too, though I guess it doesn't matter—I mean there's about a hundred million of them on this beach and they're cannibals, but it's a good habit."

Simon crouched, frozen, waiting for something terrible to happen. But David was still talking to him. Just as if Simon was a person.

Simon felt stunned. The crab scrambled frantically out of his hands, fell to the beach and scurried between two rocks, apparently unhurt. But David didn't run away.

"Do you watch birds?"

Abruptly Simon remembered the Downtown waterfront. Blade had waited on the wharves motionless for long hours, carrying out Choi's surveillance.

"Seagulls," he said.

David nodded solemnly.

"Most people can't tell the Glaucous-winged gulls from the Herring gulls. They look a lot the same, except Herring gulls have yellow eyes instead of brown and a row of white spots along their black wing tips. The red dot on their beak is for the chicks to peck at. It triggers a reflex so the parent birds regurgitate food. Did you know that?"

"No," said Simon.

"I wanted see them in action, so I took the dinghy over to the gull colony on Mittlenatch Island. I tried to sneak up quietly, but it didn't exactly work. The gulls all flew up in the air screaming and then they started dive bombing me with guano and fish barf. The smell was.... Well, Mom made me stand in the yard while she sprayed me with the hose and then I lost my sea privileges. It's not fair. The weather was fine, and I used a proper navlink so it was totally safe, and the dinghy hardly smells any more."

David stopped, frowning. Simon tried to think of something to say.

"You're very knowledgeable."

David nodded.

"I've been studying ecoscience for years. But they waste my time at school will all kinds of pitless sludge... Well, never mind. Uh..." He brushed his hair nervously out of his eyes again. "Look, I don't suppose you'd be interested in helping me out? I mean, since I'm grounded I can't get to my best collector sites, and it's going to punch holes in data sets I've been working on for two years. I publish all my results on the ADAT hub. If you help out, I'll put your name on as a research associate, of course."

David wanted him as an associate? thought Simon incredulously. He felt a surge of delight, then made himself think carefully. Toni had not forbidden him to talk to people, or to do things for them. But she might forbid it, he thought, with a stab of uneasiness. She might, if she knew. But she didn't know.

"I'd like to help," he said.

David's eyes widened.

"Really? Ferocious! Hey, I'm forgetting my manners, I didn't ask your name, sir."

"Simon."

"Thanks, Mr. Simon!"

"Just Simon," he managed. "It's my first name."

"OK!" The boy looked pleased. "And I'm David, right?"

Simon stood cautiously and picked up his fins. It was getting late. If he didn't return soon, Dr. Lau would call.

"I'll follow you," said David. "There's a short-cut through your yard to the bus stop."

Simon didn't want to be followed, but he couldn't think of anything to do about it. The boy walked up the beach and preceded him into the forest on a foot trail that snaked up between tall evergreens. Slanting fingers of sunlight pierced the dimness, spotlighting fern fronds and the shiny dark leaves of salal bushes. The soft ground felt springy underfoot—a deep layer of leaf litter and humus criss-crossed by roots, which trapped small patches of chocolatey mud. Simon stepped over a yellow banana slug almost as long as his hand and followed the trail as it wound along a creek, passing three small water wheels that churned power to a local grid. It suddenly occurred to Simon that they must belong to David's family.

"Shhh!"

Simon's heart lurched as David stopped suddenly in the path. He reached for his knife as David took two slow steps forward, then pointed. Simon saw a flash of scarlet and became aware of hollow tapping.

"Pileated woodpecker," David said quietly. "I think that's the female that's nesting near our house. She's pretty bold."

Simon clutched at stillness, calming himself. He focused on the crow-sized bird which now perched motionless on a dead tree, its toes digging into the bark. The hunched black body blended with its dim surroundings, but the bird's had an elongated white head with a black stripe like a blindfold across its yellow eyes, and a scarlet crest, brilliant against the tree bark. Abruptly it started hammering with a long chisel-like bill, and the crest became a scarlet blur.

They watched until it flew away, giving a maniacal screech. When David started forward, Simon followed very cautiously, not wanting to be startled again. He floated a little away from his body, letting Blade's muscles propel him automatically up the needle-matted tree-root steps. Consequently, he was alert and calm when a white-haired man stepped onto the path in front of them, rifle leveled, and yelled:

"Don't move!"

# 5

Simon froze, feeling the first warning tingles from the restraint device. No! Don't feel the danger! Inside himself, Simon fled, reaching for Blade's icy detachment.

Blade stood motionless, waiting for his adrenaline to ebb, and watched the old man approach. He wore work-stained hempen coveralls and held an ancient rifle to his shoulder—a local then, not a tong hench. Despite his white hair and lined face the man looked muscular, and he aimed the barrel steadily at Blade's head, finger on the trigger. An amateur, but a smart one, and from this distance Blade couldn't take him. If he boosted, his adrenaline would trip the neural restraint. And without enhanced response he couldn't dive for cover fast enough.

"Granddad, no!"

David stood in front of Blade with his arms up, trying to block the old man's shot, but he was only as high as Simon's waist.

"Get out of here, David!"

"No! This is Simon! He's helping me!"

"Like hell he is!"

The man's cold eyes flared menace and Blade felt a distant thrumming deep in his gut as he remembered the other old man's eyes, how they'd burst and splattered blood when he stabbed them...

No! Don't listen to that music! Feel nothing. Be wood, be stone. Wait.

The old man stepped closer. David's voice took on a shrill edge.

"Please, granddad! It's OK!" Abruptly he spun and grabbed the phone clipped to Blade's drysuit belt. He flicked it to "home" and yelled: "Hello, hello! Somebody answer!"

"David!" The old man shouted furiously, but he couldn't move any closer to Blade. "David, stop that!"

The boy clutched the phone, shaking his head. Abruptly Dr.

Lau's voice responded.

"Hello? Who is this?"

"This is David Anderson, your next door neighbor...."

"But you're calling from.... Where's Simon?!" Lau's voice rose in alarm.

"He's right here. He's, um... fine." The boy floundered, then continued desperately. "My grandfather's here, too. He wants to come up to the cabin and talk to you."

"What?!!"

"We'll be there in just a minute! OK?" He flicked disconnect, hit reset. "Local voice call, Anderson Woodwork."

The phone peeped.

"David!" roared the old man at the same time as the phone said "Hello?"

"Dad! Granddad's got his gun! You've got to come over to the old cabin right now!"

Without waiting for a reply, David disconnected, and for a long second there was silence on the path. Insects flickered through a shaft of sunlight between Blade and the old man. A woodpecker tapped in the distance. The old man glared at the boy, then shifted his gaze to Simon.

"All right. Might as well go up. You! You walk first. I'll be right behind. David, follow me and keep quiet. You are in trouble, young man."

Blade moved ahead with slow deliberation, hearing footsteps behind him; the old man's firm and steady, David's light and uneven further back. He listened for a scuff or a slip, but the man maintained an optimal distance and didn't falter.

When he walked into the overgrown yard, Dr. Lau was standing on the back porch, face worried. As soon as he saw the small party emerge from the trees he hurried down the steps and through the weedy grass toward them. Then Simon heard another voice in the woods to the west.

"Dad? David?"

"DAD!" yelled David. "Over here!"

The man who ran into the clearing wore worn hempen coveralls, but he looked very little like the old man. He had a stocky body, brown hair, balding at the temples, a full beard, and shoulders that were slightly hunched, as if he felt perpetually worried. His face seemed naturally aged, between forty and fifty. He viewed the rifle, Simon, and the old man with alarm.

"Simon," called out Lau. "Did you hurt anyone?"

Blade shook his head, shifting slightly so he could see the gunman in his peripheral vision.

"He was with my grandson!" said the old man furiously. But he lowered the rifle barrel to waist height, hand still on the trigger.

"We were just talking, " said David. "Simon's helping me with my microstudy."

"He's staying the hell away from you!"

David's father looked unhappily at the old man. "He's my son. My call."

"He's MY grandson. And it's MY shoulder you'll be crying on if that ghoul kills him!" said the old man harshly. He turned his attention to Lau. "Dr. Lau, you can talk my credulous son around and you can talk those fools on the Island Council around, but you won't get my heart bleeding for you. I want you and your little therapy project the hell out of here. Keep that killer away from my family or so help me God I'll shoot him dead."

"Dad. Let me handle this."

For a long second the two men locked eyes. It was the older man who broke off, swinging his rifle up to rest on his shoulder.

"I'm not dropping this," he said tightly, and strode away up the path his son had just come down. He didn't acknowledge Lau or look again at Blade. There was a charged silence, then the balding man let out a gusty sigh.

"Well, that was a great start to the day. Dr. Lau, hello." He held out his hand. "Ethan Anderson—we met at the Solstice potluck down at the Firehall. That... ah... that was my father, David Anderson. And this is my son, David Junior. Look, I'm really sorry...."

"No, don't apologize." Lau had been watching Simon, but now he turned his attention to the neighbor. "I must apologize. I should not have left Simon alone, and it's entirely my fault. I'd like to explain. Would you come in for a cup of tea?"

Ethan hesitated, then forced a smile.

"Sure. Thank you." He turned to his son. "David, you're going to miss your bus again. Expedite it!"

"The bus hasn't even been beeped me yet, Dad!" David's words were interrupted by the chirp of a phone in his pocket. "Oh, all right, two minutes." He turned and looked up at Blade. "There's a point nine tide at six eighteen a.m. on Saturday. I'll be down at the beach if you want to come. Thanks very much for your help." He started towards the road, then turned, jogging backwards through the grass and called: "And don't worry about Granddad. He hasn't shot anybody yet. Well, not that we know about."

Through Blade's armor, Simon felt a sudden pang. He wouldn't see David again. They would never allow it. He watched the boy's slight figure as he ran through the yard and vanished around the side of the cabin. Suddenly Simon's stomach ached with tension and he felt weary.

"Mr. Anderson," said Lau, "come in. Simon, go get changed and come down for breakfast. Oh, and knock on Toni's door, please. Ask her to join us."

But Toni was already awake. She stuck her head out from her bedroom when Simon walked past. Her eyes were puffy and her voice rasped.

"I heard voices. What's happening?"

"A neighbor has come for tea."

"Tea...? Neighbor?!"

Simon changed and showered. When he went down to the kitchen, Toni, Lau and Anderson were sitting around the table with mugs, talking. As Simon entered, conversation faltered. He crossed the room quickly, eyes lowered, and sat at his place. The kitchen felt warm and moist, rich with scents of rosemary and cheese. A large glass of blackberry juice stood at Simon's place, and Lau put a steaming plate in front of him—scrambled eggs with feta cheese, peppers and crispy herbed potatoes. Simon could feel Anderson's gaze and kept his eyes on his plate, willing himself to be invisible. The others started talking again, gradually easing into a natural rhythm.

It was hard to eat and listen at the same time—anxiety and the intense flavors of the food kept distracting Simon's attention. He tried not to taste what he was eating and listened. Anderson was explaining that his family had lived on Cortes for six generations. He and his wife had forfeited Guild housing in Campbell

River to stay on the island, and they ran a custom woodwork shop, which Anderson Senior managed while Ethan and his wife traveled to Guild projects. Usually they made ends meet, he said, but last fall they'd taken a big loss on a partly-completed contract for a Vancouver venture that collapsed after the tong war.

"It's been hard on Dad," said Anderson. "He's spent his whole life fighting to keep the property, and now we might have to let it go..."

"He must be very anxious," said Toni quietly.

"Dad's a remarkable man and a true artist. But... he's not the easiest person to get along with."

"Sounds like my father," said Lau. "He was a hard worker, but I never could..." His voice trailed off. Simon risked a glance and saw him staring bleakly into his mug.

In the short silence, Anderson cleared his throat.

"Well, you must of had a time living in this cabin all winter."

"Oh no..." started Lau.

"Yes," said Toni vehemently.

There was a second's pause.

"It was a little...." started Lau, and Toni interrupted again.

"What he means is that this cabin isn't so bad except for the decrepit wiring, plumbing, roof, appliances and heating. Well, there's no proper heat. No graywater system. And the toilet is in the same room as the sink and shower. Archaic and unsanitary."

"We've been meaning to come by and ask if we could lend a hand with some repairs," said Anderson, apologetically. "But my wife and I took a bunch of bonus shifts on the new reprocessing plant construction project in Port Alberni. We haven't been home much."

"No, no," said Lau firmly. "This is Mary's cabin. It's hardly your problem."

The conversation trailed off again, and Simon became aware of Toni looking at him. He put his fork down.

"Simon," asked Toni quietly. "How did you meet David?"

Simon explained, using Blade's enhanced memory to recount their conversation verbatim. For some reason Lau began laughing and Anderson smiled and put both hands against his forehead.

"That's my son, all right," he interrupted, shaking his head.

"Crazy about nature and oblivious to everything else."

Simon stared at his plate, aware of a sick knot in his stomach. He wouldn't see David again. He wouldn't get to be a research associate.

"You like David, don't you?" Toni asked abruptly.

Simon looked at her nervously and nodded.

"Why?"

"Because... he talks to me. Like I was a real person." He darted an uneasy glance at Anderson, who looked away. "He's also very knowledgeable."

"That's an understatement," Anderson's voice was a shade too hearty. "Our daughter's first word was 'ma.' David's first word was 'bug.'"

"Simon was like that, too," said Lau. "But with him it was music. When he was learning to walk we'd hold our arms out, 'come to Daddy' or 'come to Mummy.' He ignored both of us and went straight for my guitar."

Anderson smiled, then his eyes wandered to Simon and the smile vanished. Lau didn't seem to notice. He looked intensely at Simon, smiling. Simon looked at his plate.

"By the time he was three he was trying to play everything. I made the mistake of showing him how to pound on the wok with chopsticks and nothing was safe after that. To get him to do anything I had to put it to music. We had the getting-up song, the toothbrush song, the setting-the-table song, and even the don't-fall-in-the-water song, because we lived on a boat. We set it to The Drunken Sailor and Simone—his mom—taught him the hornpipe. Let me think..."

He paused for a moment, then started beating time on the table with his palms.

"What can we do with a boy named Simon?
What can we do with a boy named Simon?
What can we do with a boy named Simon?
Walking near the water."

Simon felt a sudden sharp sense of vertigo. He'd heard that voice singing those words before. He'd stood on an gnarly old boat with big flakes of paint peeling off the side. It smelled of brine and rotting fiberboard. If he kneeled down next to the rail, he could peek in through the round galley window where Daddy was cooking congee for breakfast.

"Hang on and watch your step now,

Hang on and watch your step now,

Hang on and watch your step now,

Don't go in the water!"

Lau trailed off. "I can't remember... what was the next verse?"

"Stick to the center up the gangplank," whispered Simon. His bandaged hand tingled, then twitched convulsively, knocking his juice glass off the table. It shattered on the tile floor with a crash that rang in his ears. NO! No noise!

Panic grabbed him. Simon started to bolt, his knees buckled and he went over sideways, tangled with his chair. Automatically he tried to sink into the punishment position, but his body no longer obeyed him. The world fell into silent, reeling, terror.

Hands. Toni's hands stroking his face. Simon clung to the sensation. Toni wouldn't punish him. She'd promised. He tasted the familiar tang of bile in his mouth, and felt his stomach heave. Suddenly he pictured the kitchen. David's father sitting at the table. Watching Simon vomit breakfast onto the floor at his feet.

NO!

Go to the mountain, thought Simon desperately. Count. He pictured himself sitting lotus on top of Mount Beautiful, far above fear and pain, then he called up Chinese numerals. The one stroke floated gracefully up from the valley below and circled into the sky like an eagle soaring on the thermals. Two followed. Slowly, gently, he counted ten of them, then he sank back down to the kitchen.

A broom swished across the floor near Simon's face. He felt a pillow under his head and Toni's hand holding his. She was talking.

"...but mainly the result of prolonged torture. There's no treatment that can replace the growth and maturity a normal person would have experienced. Simon's missed half of his life—more, actually. He was around David's age when Choi bought him."

Simon tried moving his foot. It worked. He straightened, shifting weight away from his shoulder.

"Good, Simon!" Toni helped guide him until he sat with his back against the cupboards. Then she wiped his face with a warm, damp cloth. "Excellent. You came out of that very well. In a little while I'm going to ask you about what happened, so I want you to remember it. All right? Now, can you stand up?"

His joints felt watery, but Simon pulled himself up, not looking at the others' faces. He didn't want to see Lau's shame or Anderson's disgust. On Toni's orders he sat in his chair again and took the mug of tea she gave him. His hands shook so hard he could barely hold it, but he tried to sip. Hot tea felt good inside him.

"Dr. Almiramez..." Anderson sounded upset. "Is Simon dangerous?"

There was a short silence. Toni answered.

"You just saw a good demonstration of the implanted neural restraint. It kicks in when he gets angry or frightened. If the stimulus is mild, he gets a warning and thirty seconds to bring his adrenaline down. Under stronger stimulus he loses all motor control instantly."

"Then he couldn't hurt David?"

David? thought Simon. He's talking about David? He wrapped his fingers tight around the mug.

"No," said Lau. "One of us stays with him at all times to supervise. This morning was... well, it was my mistake. I had a sudden, urgent need for the toilet, so I took a chance and came back a few minutes ahead of Simon. I hadn't seen anybody down at the beach for weeks, but that's no excuse. I should have called him in or phoned Toni, or simply gone behind a tree."

Toni leaned forward.

"I'll give Simon specific instructions never to harm the boy— or any of your family. He follows orders. Look... the decision is up to you. But... it would certainly be good for Simon. He's lonely."

"So's David," said Anderson, unexpectedly. "He should have friends his own age, but he's such an odd kid.... All right."

For an instant Simon didn't understand, then his head jerked up and he stared at Anderson in astonishment.

Anderson met Simon's eyes, then looked away again nervously, as if he weren't sure. He pushed his chair back.

"I mean, I'm willing to try it if my wife agrees. And we'll have to talk to my father...." He sighed, then gave a tired smile. I'll call you."

41

He shook hands with Lau, then with Toni, and finally held his hand out to Simon. Simon stared at it uncomprehendingly for a second, then grasped the man's rough, square palm. It felt strange and Simon wasn't sure if he'd done it right. Anderson didn't let go. His eyes bored into Simon's.

"Simon, I want you to give me your word that you will keep my son safe and never hurt him."

Simon glanced at Toni. She gave a tiny nod.

"I promise," he said.

The morning chores passed in a blur. Images kept flicking through Simon's mind. The beach, silent and still on top, but alive underneath with scuttling crabs. Otters. Simon had seen otters on the Anderson's dock and longed to get closer. Maybe David knew how to approach them. He found himself waiting for Saturday. It was in three days, he discovered. And each day would come after the next. He'd never thought about that before, never thought about time, except on the net where there was always a digital read-out. But that was just numbers.

Blade lived in eternity. He had no past or future. He simply existed and followed orders. Simon hadn't cared about time either—only the length of a piece of music, or the timing of a motion that had to be accurate to a tenth of a second.

But now he kept thinking about the future, almost trying to go there like he'd floated up to the mountain top. And for the first time he realized that normal people did that constantly. Toni and Klale often talked about things they looked forward to or dreaded.

In the afternoon Simon went out into the middle of the yard where he'd stamped down a patch of grass for exercises. Toni sat on the porch reading a paper book, her phone by her side. She turned his restraint off when he exercised and stayed nearby. The sun felt warm, so Simon stripped off his clothes and started tai chi, this time thinking about how his motions were anchored in now, but stretched from the past into the future. Trees towered around him, rising from their past to their future.

Saturday, thought Simon. David. Excitement stirred in his gut, breaking his concentration. He stopped in mid motion, suddenly remembering the question Toni always asked him: If you danced it, how would it feel? He closed his eyes, feeling warm sun against his naked skin, and reached for an old dance to make it new.

It felt awkward at first, trying to dance in the grass. The surface underfoot was uneven, difficult to spin or land on, and Simon had none of his accustomed gear—no sim screens or signal reflective suit or frictionless surface. Toni's awkward old earphones shifted against his ears, threatening to slide off. Sunlight flashed in his eyes.

He pushed those distractions away, concentrating instead on the music of the yard—the rustle of grass, rush of breeze in the trees, buzzing insects. Then he called up his favorite Cloudburst song. At the first chords he stretched, spun, and then leaped in the air, flooded with exhilaration. So long! It had been so long! A cascade of flute spilled down his forehead and trickled across his torso. Deep bass notes shivered down his throat into his sternum and spine. His body remembered each note, each beat, each pause, and the music drove him higher, faster, further.

Violins soared to crescendo, lifting Simon with them, then spilling him to the ground, gasping, muscles straining with tension. Then, release! The universe melted in exquisite, excruciating crimson. At some great distance Simon's back arched, his muscles shuddered, and his fingers and toes clenched air as fire seared through him. Tremors of pleasure sang from his toes to his head, arching his pelvis to the sky.

Silence. Simon lay on his back in the grass, muscles melting into damp earth, aware only of his own agonizing joy and the breeze gently licking at his wet face.

# 6

"Toni!"

Toni looked up at Rigo's urgent whisper from the kitchen window behind her, reaching automatically for her phone as her eyes searched for Simon in the yard. But Simon wasn't in trouble. He was dancing!

At last! Thank gods. Tears stung in Toni's eyes as she watched his eerie grace, just as improbable and astounding as in the holos he'd sent her last fall. It seemed like years ago. There had been days she'd been sure he would never dance again.

She couldn't hear his music, but she could see the intensity of the dance building as he moved faster, his body smooth, sexless and sinuous in the dappled light of the yard. Then, abruptly, he collapsed in the grass, and she saw the orgasm ripple through him.

She looked away. She was ready for it this time, but she found it no easier to watch the slamming intensity of a filament-induced orgasm than she had the first time. Simon would lie collapsed for a while, she was sure. He hadn't experienced reward for months, so it would be even more intense than usual.

How intense would it feel after decades? she wondered, then shoved the idea aside. Don't even think about it. She rolled her notebook screen away, got up and went into the kitchen.

Rigo stood at the window, eyes full.

"Finally!" He put an affectionate hand on Toni's shoulder and she pulled away sharply.

Damn, she thought, seeing his hurt. She forced herself to speak.

"Sorry. It's... watching that reminds me too much of my own years as a smut."

Rigo wiped his face with the back of his hand and nodded. He had worked as a medic in the Hong Kong slums. He knew about smuts. Then he looked out at the yard, where Simon lay in the grass. His expression sobered.

"He's addicted to the euphoria, isn't he?"

"Yes," said Toni, firmly. "But its far healthier than an exogenous substance like cocaine, and the dancing gives him mental and physical stimulation as well as sexual release. As coercive addictions go, it's a very functional one."

Rigo looked unhappy.

"It's so lonely."

"Masturbation is always lonely."

"But we have other choices. We can share." His voice became harsh. "Choi took that away from Simon when he castrated him."

"Simon can share," said Toni sharply. "He just can't fuck. And that's no loss."

As soon as the words were out of her mouth, she regretted them. Christ, where was her professionalism? But she knew the answer. Living in this job twenty-four hours a day made it impossible to keep her own feelings and needs at a distance. Lately they hammered at her like a rising storm, and she kept having to put energy into her own emotional stability, instead of Simon's.

When she turned toward Rigo again, she caught him staring at the art on the back of her head. She'd briefly considered letting her hair grow over it before coming to this backwater, but she hadn't felt like investing the time to reverse the follicle suppression. Besides, she liked the my-pain-in-your-face message of that bleeding rose, inked on the site of her old neural plug. She'd hidden her past so desperately all those years in academia, that it still felt good to flaunt it.

"Was it like that for you?" asked Rigo suddenly.

Toni had to gather her thoughts.

"Yes. No. It's...." She found herself floundering and took a breath. "Simon's dancing gives him some control over his sexual response. I had none. My arousals and orgasms were controlled by my pimp. That's far more... damaging."

"Did you get repathing therapy?"

"Some." She'd tried treating herself, not very successfully. Even with the neural filaments removed, sexual stimulus could sometimes trigger old pathways and sequences, and without the controller chip she had no way to stop them—she could only ride it out, or knock herself unconscious with meds. So she'd made it a habit to avoid possible triggers, especially close proximity to men, and she hadn't had a cascade in years. Now that she was past fifty and her hormone levels were dropping, the risk should be much less. With luck she'd never have another cascade.

"What about repathing for Simon?"

She focused again.

"Rigo, if a person is sexually patterned at puberty, those patterns are highly resistant to change. I had ten years of it and Simon's had twenty. His addiction is quite benign, and the repathing process can be risky. I would only recommend it for a patient who was being harmed, or in danger of being coerced."

Rigo nodded, but he looked angry. Toni grabbed for detachment and studied his posture as he leaned against the window frame—a casual pose underlain with rigid tautness. She followed his gaze to the yard. So far Simon showed no signs of being bothered by his castration. Medically there were no issues. Hormone implants maintained his endocrine system balance, and though his sexual response was almost entirely wired to music, he could be aroused by intense touching—as Klale had, with breathtaking recklessness, discovered. But it disturbed his father deeply, and for more than just sexual reasons. Choi had twisted Simon's natural passion for dance to control him. To Rigo it was just another reminder of how profoundly he had failed his son. Nothing he could do now and no amount of regret could recapture twenty lost years.

She took a deep breath, then pulled out a kitchen chair and sat.

"Rigo, this is the breakthrough we've been waiting for."

"I know. It's just... sometimes I realize how impossible a job we've taken on."

"Your son has done the impossible more times than I can count. He killed Choi. He gave himself to me. He survived going berserk. Just yesterday I sat at this table racking my brain for some way to help him re-create the emotional foundation of a secure childhood, and today he turned up with a twelve-year-old boy in tow. He has the most astonishing instinct for survival I've ever seen."

Rigo smiled, tension easing from his tall frame.

"True. Thank you for reminding me." He sighed. "This morning was difficult. I've become so used to Simon that I forgot how other people look at him. They don't see my son, they see a monster."

He turned and looked back out the window. "He's dancing again."

Toni got up and joined him. Simon stood in the clearing, eyes half closed, swaying. As they watched, he began a slow, dreamy dance, his motions so relaxed he seemed liquid. Toni found herself wishing they could hear the music, then it finally occurred to her that they could. Her netset sat on the kitchen table, so she patched in the channel Simon was listening to, and soft tones of bamboo flute filled the kitchen.

She joined Rigo at the window again and watched Simon go into a series of slow, spinning jumps. He landed, jumped again, then his foot slid in the grass and he thudded abruptly onto his buttocks. Rigo laughed, and Toni grinned. Simon lay sprawled in the grass for a second, seemingly perplexed, then he wrapped his arms around his knees and began to rock.

Rigo's face sobered and he stiffened. Damn, thought Toni. There's always one more crisis. She ran out the door and hurried across the grass, circling around to approach Simon face on. The restraint was still disabled, so she stopped about three meters away, dropped to her knees and studied him, growing more puzzled. Simon had his face buried in his arms and he was shuddering, rocking back and forth in silence. It looked like... Finally it struck her.

"Simon?" she asked softly.

He flinched and looked up, his grin fading swiftly to apprehension. Toni moved forward to take his hand and smiled at him.

"That was funny, wasn't it? When you fell down. We saw you and laughed," she told him.

A little boy grin tugged at the corner of Simon's mouth, then he smiled broadly. His mask-like face made it a strange stretched caricature; nonetheless Toni caught her breath at the transformation. She reflected his smile with her own.

"It's OK, Simon," she said. "Laughing is good. Laugh as much as you want to. Any time."

She squeezed his hand, then got up and left, deliberately not looking back.

Rigo hovered at the door, phone in hand, ready to enable the restraint.

"He was laughing," she told him. "Did I say that he does impossible things? There's another one. He shouldn't, according to all the profiles, have a sense of humor."

Rigo grinned crookedly.

"Of course he has a sense of humor. He's my son."

In the distance Toni heard the housecomp beep twice—its proximity alarm—then it chimed as the visitor passed security. A minute later the front door opened and a shout came from the living room.

"Klahowya! I'm home!"

Toni smiled with wry amusement as she heard the loud thump of a duffel bag dumped in the middle of the living room floor, then Klale bounded into the kitchen, red hair in a wild tangle around her head, cheeks pink with exertion, looking closer to fifteen than twenty-five. She wore her usual Fishers Guild work pants, boots, and a sleeveless shirt. She rushed at Toni with a sweaty, ferocious hug, then went for Rigo. He grabbed her and swung her around in a pirouette.

"Simon started dancing!"

"Dancing? Really? Oh, Rigo!"

Klale wrapped her arms around the older man, laughing and bouncing on both feet and Rigo mimicked her. They looked like big kids, thought Toni again, marveling at how they'd instantly begun behaving as if they'd known each other all their lives.

"When did he dance? Why didn't you tell me?"

"Just now and I just did," said Rigo with a teasing grin. "What did you bring us?"

"Oh, presents for everybody!" Klale rushed into the living room and came back hauling her duffel bag. When she unzipped it the insides bulged out like a gashed sausage. She rooted around and tossed a square, foil wrapped package up at Toni. "Here."

"Yes!" Toni snatched the package, twisted the seal open and breathed in the rich scent of fresh coffee. "Blue Mountain! Thank gods. I was reduced to drinking the local swill."

"I sure hope it's deep," said Klale. "Do you know what that sailor friend of yours charges for it?!"

"Worth every dollar," Toni told her. "Were you able to get that other package?

"No smog. It's in here somewhere. Want it now?"

Toni felt a wave of relief. She shook her head. She didn't want to risk Rigo seeing her meds. Klale didn't know what they were, but Rigo might easily figure it out.

"Later's fine, thanks."

Klale dug in her bag again, strewing clothes on the floor.

"Where is that... Ha! This is for you." She turned and tossed a small object to Rigo, who caught it and stared quizzically. "It's a kazoo. Every medic should have one, gives your patients confidence."

Rigo put the thing in his mouth and blew a loud nasal blat. He grinned. Toni grimaced.

"And something very special for Simon." Klale glanced at Toni. "Can I give it to him now?"

Toni looked out the window. Simon lay almost invisible in the long grass, so she opened her phone out and checked his physiological readouts. She didn't do that often—preferring to rely on her own direct observations and instincts—but sometimes monitors were handy. He was just resting.

"Sure," she said.

"Strat!" said Klale. She tucked a package under her arm and hurried to the back door, leaving her duffel and its contents strewn all over the floor. Amazing how one young woman could fill the whole cabin instantly.

"Klahowya, Simon! I'm home!"

Toni almost called out a warning, but Klale had remembered Toni's patient tutoring and she didn't run at Simon. She stopped on the back porch and waited for Simon to sit up and look around, before starting toward him. She gave him a big hug, then took his hand and led him inside.

"We're going upstairs to change," she announced, dragging him past like a child towing an adult although Klale herself was a square-built muscular woman close to six feet tall.

Rigo opened the creaky door of the old methane chest cooler and dug in the bottom of it. He turned around, eyes twinkling, and held up a bottle of champagne.

"This calls for a celebration."

"Absolutely," agreed Toni, taking another deep whiff of coffee aroma before putting the pak away. She dragged Klale's bag into the living room, then helped Rigo dig out crackers, pickled vegetables and paté and arrange them on Mary's old mismatched plates.

When Klale returned with Simon, Toni's eyebrows rose. Simon wore black satin trousers, a cream Elizabethan shirt with puffed sleeves and a scarlet head scarf, tied pirate style at the back. An earcuff dangled jauntily from his undamaged right ear. Rigo turned from the counter and froze.

"Toketie man! That's Chinook for handsome. Isn't he splash?" asked Klale.

"Very," said Toni, nodding. Simon had been watching her covertly and she saw him relax at her approval.

"Lume," managed Rigo. "Clearly he's inherited the ability to wear clothes well." He kept his tone light but Toni heard the roughness in his voice as he turned back to the counter.

As Simon slid onto the bench seat next to Klale, just managing to squeeze his knees under the kitchen table, Toni studied his changed appearance. Klale had hit on a brilliant idea with the scarlet headscarf, she decided. It shifted emphasis from Simon's bald head to his intense brown eyes, and flattered his mocha Afro/Chinese complexion. Moreover, covering the plug sites on his skull might make him feel safer. Another thing they should have thought of sooner.

Rigo served champagne with a flourish, even producing a matched set of champagne flutes that Toni hadn't seen before. They all clinked glasses, then Klale and Simon fell to demolishing snacks while Rigo filled Klale in on their encounter with the Anderson family. Rigo downplayed the old man's hostility, noticed Toni, but she didn't correct his story. She couldn't see any point in alarming Klale.

"So, other than the dancing and neighbors with guns, how were things while I was gone?" asked Klale finally, smiling at Toni.

"Quiet," said Rigo.

Toni snorted. "Quiet, hell. I always heard about the serenity of rural living and I get here to find that the birds start a deafening racket in the trees before daybreak, and deer crash around in the bushes like trucks emptying recycling bins. I can't believe people let those bloody enormous animals run around loose."

"They're harmless," said Klale.

"Then why do they have horns?"

"To impress other deer," said Rigo with a rakish twinkle, and pushed back his chair. "Which reminds me... I have a dinner engagement. I hope you don't mind, but I must go."

Klale giggled. "I'm sure you'll impress her."

"Oh, I shall."

Rigo lifted his high-collared linen greatcoat off a peg by the door and slipped it on, pivoting so the floor length hem swirled around his cavalier boots. He sketched a bow, smiling broadly, and strode out the back door. He'd been itching to do that for the last hour, realized Toni.

Both Rigo and Klale seemed to have slipped into the social life of Cortes Island with scarcely a ripple. Island service tithes were ten hours a week—far higher than in the city—and Klale was working Simon and Toni's hours as well as her own, so she'd met most of the three hundred or so tenured residents. Rigo worked three mornings a week at the health clinic in the back of the library building and he'd also joined the volunteer fire brigade. The locals were only too glad to welcome a trained medic since there were no doctors on the island. Toni had thought about volunteering, too, before she'd realized how unwelcome her brown skin and Afroid features made her on Cortes. On her rare visits to local stores she was the object of uneasy and sometimes hostile stares. It suddenly didn't seem so long ago that white residents of the Gulf Islands had killed American refugees.

"How are you?"

Toni looked up to find Klale watching her with steady hazel eyes set in a broad, freckled face.

"Tired. How's the KlonDyke?"

Klale's expression saddened.

"They've decided to tear the whole building down in September, before Equinox. I moved everything I could from your apartment into storage at Sisters, but it's still awful to think of all that beautiful tile work and parquet you did being destroyed."

"Yeah."

Impulsively Klale got up from the bench seat and wrapped Toni in a soft hug. Toni made herself relax and hug back, conscious of modeling healthy behavior for their silent audience across the table.

They ate dinner promptly at six, sticking to the schedule Toni had set up to help keep Simon stable. Klale made pizza and Simon devoured most of it while Toni nibbled with little appetite. Eating made her nauseous lately, and she couldn't manage more than a few bites. Simon, however, seemed even more ravenous than usual for his accelerated metabolism, and Toni made a mental note to warn Rigo.

After dinner they sprawled around the unlit methane fire-place, Klale watching something on her phone, Toni catching up her notes, and Simon reading one of Mary's dusty old hardbooks. He had begun working his way methodically through the shelves, taking each book in turn and scanning it swiftly page by page, then moving on to the next. Toni couldn't make out whether he was enjoying the books, or simply exercising his new freedom. Choi had forbidden Simon to read or view anything outside a very narrow range of subjects. Toni had lifted those restrictions, except for a few topics related to cognitive therapy. The old paper books were a jumbled accretion of vacation reading—old popular novels, cheap editions of classic fiction, reference books on birds, plants, and local history, and a few volumes from Mary's extensive collection of Native ethnography. Toni hadn't yet seen Simon react to any of it, though his enhanced memory presumably retained everything.

Rigo came back at nine-thirty exuding sexual satiation and carrying a large kidney-shaped case. He opened the case in the living room, unwrapped a layer of silk, and revealed a gleaming wood instrument that looked like a mutant guitar.

"Behold, a five string Appalachian dulcimer!" Rigo beamed at his acquisition, then laid it down gently, grabbed Klale and danced her across the floor.

He'd had a few drinks, decided Toni as he delivered the gig-gling girl into a seat, picked up the dulcimer, and launched into a rousing tune, beating time with his foot and singing in a strong tenor voice. He'd ordered the instrument from an island craftsman a few months ago, after he started playing with a pick-up band down at the cafe. As always, he blossomed before an audience, and Toni had no trouble picturing him thirty years younger, playing in bars in return for a meal and a place to sleep. Simon's eyes lit up with interest and excitement at the first chord, and for the first time in days he looked directly at his father.

As always, the contrast between Simon immersed in music and the blank-faced tool was striking. Simon's whole body took on a confident grace and he rocked to the music like a delighted child, periodically reaching up to adjust the silk scarf on his head.

Rigo swapped his dulcimer for the electronic minstrel Klale had been playing and started into a children's song. Every few chords the song broke into funny sound effects. Klale laughed. Simon rocked faster, smiling.

When the song ended Simon noticed all their eyes on him and buried his face in his arm. Toni leaned over and touched his arm gently.

"It's nice to see you smile," she said, in a warm, approving tone. "How do you feel?"

As usual, any question about emotions confused him. He rocked anxiously, then whispered:

"I don't know."

She tried again.

"Simon, if you were dancing to that song, what kind of a dance would it be?"

"It would be funny," he told her, without hesitation. "Like crows hopping backwards. And looking sideways, trying to fool other crows so they can steal their food."

Directed dancing, thought Toni with a flash of hope. Now that he's dancing again we can use his dances to help him re-connect with his emotions. Across the room she saw the same thought gleaming in Rigo's eyes.

Simon was getting nervous. Toni patted his arm.

"Ten o'clock. Bed time."

They had planned to plug Simon into the sleepware, but Toni wanted to see what effect the day's breakthroughs would have on his nightmares, and Rigo agreed. At least with Klale back, they could sleep in and let her handle the breakfast shift. When Toni went up to say good night she found Simon in bed, still wearing his new scarf. The medical netset sat on the floor beside his futon, trailing neurolink cables and Davidson cups.

She sat on the big cushion on the worn floorboards, where she'd spent so many long nights.

"Simon, I owe you an apology for yesterday morning. I'm sorry I screamed and frightened you."

He stared silently up from his nest of overlapping blankets on two large futons laid side-by-side. None of the beds in the cabin fit him.

"Always answer an apology, Simon. There are various things you can say depending on how you feel about it. 'I accept your apology' is formal, but always correct. Or if you know a person well you might say something like 'I understand' or 'Don't worry about it'."

"Or if you're still mad," suggested Klale mischievously from the doorway, "you could say 'Just don't do it again.'"

Simon took it all in with enigmatic eyes.

"I accept your apology," he said finally, in the soft, childlike voice that always sounded so wildly incongruous in his deathmask face.

"Thank you, Simon," Toni told him. "Have a good night's sleep."

They held a short team meeting in the kitchen to bring Klale up to date on Simon's progress, then the others went to bed and Toni sat in Simon's room reading journal articles. Simon slept peacefully. At two a.m. Rigo got up and relieved her.

Toni had just drifted into a restless sleep when Simon screamed. She woke with a pounding heart, rolled out of bed and ran for his room.

Rigo aborted the spontaneous punishment cycle as fast as he could, but not before Simon received three seconds of full pain stimulation, triggered by nightmares—the worst episode in months. Simon lay hunched and motionless under the restraint, gasping and stinking of terror. Toni used her calming routine for half an hour before he finally relaxed enough for the paralysis to leave. They helped him clean up and gave him juice before Toni put him under hypnosis and asked him to remember his dream.

"Where are you?" she asked.

"I don't know! I'm scared!"

The little boy voice had regressed, sounding even younger, and shrill with terror.

"What does it look like where you are?"

"There's no windows. Just a bed. The door's locked. He hurt me! The man hurt me! I don't know why. He just keeps doing it! I can't get out! He won't let me go! He won't tell me why! I'm all alone!"

"Easy, Simon," she told him. "Easy.... Where's Daddy?"

Simon's voice was a thin, desolate wail.

"Daddy went away...."

Finally! An old memory! Toni turned, but Rigo had already caught his cue.

"Simon, I'm here," he said urgently. "I came back."

There was a long pause, then: "Daddy?"

"It's OK, Simon, I'm here."

"Take me away from here, please! Please, please, I'll do anything! I'll be good! Please come back! I'll fix what I did wrong! I'm so scared, he's hurting me...!" Abruptly, Simon paused.

Toni's instincts blared danger and she grabbed Rigo, pulling him back just as Simon screamed and lashed out. The restraint activated, collapsing Simon half off the futon, his blow just barely missing them. Toni fell backwards into Rigo, then she pushed him off and plunged for her phone, entering the abort code for the pain center stimulus. But Simon kept screaming, veins standing out rigid on his neck. Then she made out words.

"YOU LEFT ME BEHIND! YOU LEFT ME! I HATE YOU!"

Not pain. This was rage, a seething flood, sometimes with words, sometimes incoherent screams that tore at her eardrums. Toni held Simon's left hand and Rigo took the right, staring at his son's heaving chest with a shaken expression. Six months ago he'd seen his son kill four people in a berserk rage and Toni knew he was reliving it. Sitting next to Simon's volcanic fury unnerved her, too, and she found herself praying that the restraint was properly installed. She'd never heard of one failing, but couldn't help a trickle of fear.

After a few minutes she got up and fetched earplugs, then they sat with Simon for hours while he vacillated wildly between rage and terror, with short periods of calm, ending in new explosions. Staying near him so he could feel their reassurance was vital, but also exhausting. Toni overrode the restraint programming and kept it on all the time, but each onslaught still made them flinch.

Finally, when Simon seemed to be wearing out, Toni went downstairs for coffee. Her head throbbed and, as she tried to measure coffee into the filter, she found her hands shaking.

It's the cold, she thought. Then: no, it's not just cold. You're upset.

She managed to use the boiling tap without burning herself, then added a generous dollop of cream. It was a crime to add cream to good coffee, but much easier on her stomach. She carried her mug over to the kitchen table and sat down. Now, what's bothering me?

Well, what's bothering Simon? He was a child abandoned in terrifying circumstances.

And so was I, she thought suddenly. She remembered endless days of her childhood waiting for her mother to come home, wondering if she'd ever come back, and then the time when she didn't and Toni went looking through all the wirehead bars. At one place they said her mother was dead. Toni didn't know if that was true and she didn't know how to find out. She couldn't ask the police— she was an illegal child and she'd always been told that the police took ills away and killed them. So she went back to the apartment. She thought she wouldn't care, after all she was always mad at her mom. But she found herself unable to stop crying. Her younger brother stared at her, so she hit him until he curled up in a wailing ball on the floor.

She was twelve. She had no money, no food, no way to pay for heat. When it got very cold she put on one of her mother's short skirts, pinned tight at the back, and stuffed socks into her shirt and stood on the street with the hookers. They laughed and then yelled at her, and the men ignored her. Finally one man stopped and asked her how much. She didn't know, so she said "ten." He took her into a stairwell. She tried to do it, but he told her that she was stupid and didn't know how, then he raped her on the concrete steps, pressing his hand against her mouth so hard she thought she would choke and die. He didn't pay.

The old analog wall clock chimed softly and Toni jumped. God, she hadn't remembered that in years, but vivid memories had been washing over her lately. Especially the goddamned rats. She kept dreaming about them. It must be the rustling noises that triggered it, like those bloody crows digging in the roof gutters.

She had to quit obsessing about herself. Focus on Simon. They'd had a major breakthrough and she should be ready to move on to the next therapy step. What was it that Graeme had always said about breakthroughs, she thought suddenly, reaching back to her years at the Seattle Institute. That was it. The trouble with breakthroughs is that by the time you get them you're too fucking tired to enjoy it. Yeah, no smog, and lately she was always tired.

Simon had fallen silent upstairs and in the early morning stillness she heard birds beginning to yitter and chirp in the trees. Gray dawn leaked from the windows. Outside something wailed. It sounded like a baby crying. Toni shuddered, feeling suddenly very frightened, then she took a deep breath and stood up, taking her coffee with her.

In the bedroom, Simon lay sprawled in exhausted sleep, his head on Rigo's lap. Rigo's arms were wrapped around his son, and he was crying silently. Toni stood in the doorway thinking she should talk with Rigo about his guilt feelings and warn him that he wasn't over the hurdles with Simon yet, then she felt a sudden stab of unreasoning jealousy.

Why not me? Why didn't my mother come back and put her arms around me and tell me she loved me? Why didn't somebody rescue me?

Suddenly she couldn't cope. She turned and stumbled through the murky hall to her bedroom.

# 7

## Friday, July 12

The ferry whistle shrieked as they approached Nanaimo and Yasmin, leaning against the cool steel rail with a warm breeze stirring her hair, felt a surge of exhilaration. Finally, she was making progress in pursuit of her old enemy, Choi Shung Wai.

"Beautiful!" said Tor, leaning on the rail beside her.

She glanced over with a smile, but his starry-eyed gaze was fixed on the Empress of Vancouver anchored just off the wharf ahead of them. She felt a small stab of irritation, then amusement. After all, she'd told him to take an interest in steam ships.

And, with afternoon sunlight gleaming from white paint and polished brass, the casino ship was an impressive sight. The Empress looked like a clipper ship from an old painting, with graceful lines sweeping from a long carved bowsprit to an overhung stern, except that this odd hybrid of sail and steam had two enormous funnels rising in between three tall sail masts. A radar dish mounted on the wheelhouse and a navsat receiver clamped to one spar added more anachronistic layers of technology.

A floating covered gangway had been strung between the casino ship and the public wharf, and she could see knots of people at the shore end—no doubt gathering for Tommy Yip's party. Excellent timing, she decided. Although she didn't think any of Yip's Kung Lok cohorts would recognize her or Tor, she preferred to arrive in a crowd where she'd attract less notice.

"Do you know why the ship had sails?" asked Tor suddenly.

"No," said Yasmin, looking at him curiously. Tor knew his intellectual limits and rarely ventured conversation, but clearly he couldn't contain his new enthusiasm. She reached up to ruffle his silky blond hair, and he responded with a glowing smile. "Tell me," she said.

"When the original Empress of Japan was launched in 1890, steam engines were new technology. The shipbuilders didn't trust engines, so they put sails on the ship in case the engines failed. They didn't fail, though. The Empress set speed records across the Pacific Ocean running between Vancouver and Nagasaki and Hong Kong. She carried six hundred passengers, plus cargo and paper mail, which was very important back then. This replica isn't completely accurate but it has real nineteenth-century steam engines salvaged from a wreck in the Atlantic." He looked at her hopefully. "Do you think I'll be able to see them?"

"I'll make sure of it," said Yasmin, and he beamed.

As the ferry neared its berth, the Empress loomed larger and larger, making the fish boats around it look like a swarm of grubby beetles. Running that behemoth must drain Tommy Yip's pockets, thought Yasmin. The full scale replica had been built as a casino to cruise the sheltered waters between Seattle and Vancouver, siphoning money from the affluent and pretentious, but it brought in little income now. The surviving remnants of the Kung Lok had used the Empress to flee the tong war in Vancouver. Eight months later they were still shuttling from one penny ante coastal town to another while Yip tried to negotiate terms with the victorious Sun Yee On.

To make matters worse, a giant dataspill triggered by the old blackmailer, Choi, had exposed decades of the Kung Lok's dirty dealings, making them deeply unpopular with the Guilds. Still, the replica Empress remained a draw, and towns reluctantly let her tie up. Yip kept moving along the coast, staying in each port long enough to fleece local sightseers. And his next scheduled stop was Campbell River—the closest town to Cortes Island.

Water boiled from the ferry's propellers and swirled around barnacle-encrusted pilings, then automated docking clamps clanged into place. Tor picked up the suitcases and fell in behind Yasmin to join the crowd at the foot passenger ramp.

On the wharf they veered out of the stream of passengers and doubled back to a ramp leading down to the public float. It was no wonder the Empress lay offshore thought Yasmin—the ship was a full city block long and towered about four stories over the main wharf. Thick hawsers ran from both bow and stern to floats attached to massive anchors. It looked precarious to Yasmin. As they approached, she studied the floating gangway, noting that it led to a modern elevator running up a molecular-fiber cable hung on a retractable arm over the side.

The gangway entrance was guarded by two smiling greeters in antique-style dresses, flanked by two stiff, burly men, who looked hot and uncomfortable in dark nineteenth century suits. Yasmin and Tor joined the line-up.

"Names, please?"

"Yasmin Paroo. Tor Arnnson. We're signing on as medtechs," said Yasmin. The greeter was a strikingly beautiful woman, improbably curvaceous beneath her beaded white dress, and wearing exquisitely understated skin art. One of Yip's smuts, Yasmin decided, studying her green eyes. Slight pupil dilation. Likely an Eros addict. The woman tucked the hard-copy guest list under one arm, and made a call on the jeweled phone pinned to her dress. She wore an invisible earpiece and Yasmin couldn't hear the response but her elated smile never wavered.

"Mr. Chee will meet you on the Upper Deck. Welcome aboard."

Mr. Chee met them at the top of the elevator—young, arrogant, and surgically altered to look Chinese—the very picture of a rising tong junior exec. He met Yasmin's sparkling smile flatly—gay or kinked, she decided—and verified their identity with a hand-held DNA scanner. Yasmin saw Tor tense slightly, but small scanner units only searched for a few key gene sequences, and their newly-manufactured credentials checked. Chee issued security clearances for their phones, told them where to find their cabin and who to report to, then hurried off, leaving them to find their own way. Excellent. Yasmin had plenty to do before starting her new job.

A brass-handled door led inside the ship, onto plush oriental carpet and a surfeit of Victorian decor—mahogany wainscoting, gleaming gas-light fixtures, velvet upholstery and even antimacassars. Chamber music played discreetly in the background. Along a wide public corridor engraved brass signs pointed to the casino, bar, restaurant, gift shop, private gaming suites and first class cabins. The floors weren't numbered, she noted—they were identified quaintly as the Main Deck, Upper Deck, and Promenade Deck.

Tor had studied the ship's plans, so she allowed him to lead her past an iron-cage elevator and through a security-keyed door marked "Crew only," which opened into a steep metal-runged staircase. They went down one level and in a door marked "Lower Deck" to find themselves in a long, narrow, low-ceilinged hallway with a series of doors leading off it at short intervals. Yasmin followed Tor, feeling faintly uneasy. After so many years as a prisoner she didn't like the sensation of being buried inside this ship.

The door labeled "F-2" opened to her phone signal onto a cramped cabin smelling of bioscrub. As Yasmin had expected, it had only one exit and a porthole too small to squeeze through. She tossed her suitcases on the bottom bunk and looked in the bathroom. Tiny, but modern and very clean. Overall, she much preferred this spartan crew cabin to the staterooms she'd seen in the promotional holo, crowded with Victorian bric-a-brac and even pseudo-antique plumbing fixtures. And although she wouldn't have much privacy, she'd be safer with Tor in the same cabin.

Tor was standing in the narrow entrance studying the bunk beds. He caught Yasmin's eye and hurriedly thrust his backpack on the top bunk. Yasmin smiled, amused. Tor was still getting used to her changed appearance, and his new role.

"Tor," she whispered.

She watched his neck muscles and saw the slight quiver as excitement pulsed through him. He turned towards her eagerly, already aroused.

"Please me," she told him.

Tor gave her swift hard sex the way she liked it, and afterwards she showered in the tiny stall, soaping first and then rinsing under the sharp spray. The ship's water ration was generous—about two minutes. As she toweled her thick red hair in front of the foggy mirror, she studied her body with satisfaction. Pale, lightly freckled skin stretched smoothly over taut muscles, and small breasts betrayed no droop. She smiled, luxuriating in the feeling of being young again after all those years of graying her hair, slouching underneath crumpled lab coats, and walking in clunky bad-fitting shoes. With the new face she looked no more than thirty, and unrecognizable as "Dr. Smith." Except...

She pushed back her hair and turned her head, glimpsing a betraying lump at the base of her skull. She hadn't been able to remove the explosive that the Viet Ching had implanted in her spinal cord. All the tong execs who'd known the triggering code were dead now, so the risk was slight, but she would always have this lethal reminder of those years wasted in captivity doing their crude, unsavory work.

And it was Choi's fault, she thought, with a sudden rush of old fury. When she refused to pay the blackmailer, he'd sold her dossier to the Viet Ching. Usually Yasmin ignored past wrongs, but Choi was a special matter. She intended to get her revenge. And a portion of the old bastard's fabled fortune to fund her new start.

According to the netshark she'd hired, Toni, the KlonDyke bartender, had been with Choi's enforcer the day after Choi's "death." The enforcer had gone berserk, but Toni intervened before he could be euthanized. Then both of them disappeared. A week later, Mary Smarch started ordering grocery shipments for her summer cabin on Cortes Island near Campbell River. And Klale Renhardt, Toni's girlfriend, had bought ferry tickets to or from Campbell River four times in the last six months. Yasmin felt sure that Toni was on Cortes, repairing Choi's enforcer. And Toni would lead her to Choi.

Yasmin went back into the cabin and unpacked a new black dress—ankle length, with a split skirt and a high Chinese collar. It was a cheap, premade garment bought from a Downtown stall, but it fitted surprisingly well. The plain hempcloth and low hemline should be modest enough to win approval from even die-hard Guild traditionalists; nonetheless the dress clung provocatively to her muscular body and set off her lustrous red hair. She added gold costume earcuffs and a stylish phone belt that cinched around her waist. At the other end of the cramped cabin, Tor shrugged into a cream turtleneck that flattered his broad shoulders and brought up his Viking complexion. Yasmin checked him over, feeling a surge of satisfaction with her handiwork. The repigmented skin tone matched his new hair and eye color, and his original slim build had been bulked with meds and workouts. He stood confidently, exuding happy pride—an immeasurable improvement from the first time she'd seen him.

On the Upper Deck, Yip's party was in full clamor. Yasmin had no invitation, of course, but she doubted anyone would notice. She told Tor to gather information about the ship—an order he received with delight—then parted from him at the entrance to the Dining Room and strolled alone up a curving carpeted stairway to the Casino on the Promenade Deck. A babble of conversation and clattering roulette wheels engulfed her, muted by clever sound damping, but nonetheless intense.

Yip was hosting a special event for one of the working Guilds, she decided. Citizens crowded around the gaming tables, staring with fascination at the spinning wheels, red-vested croupiers, and gaudy piles of chips. Others craned their necks at the ornate ceiling, the crystal chandeliers, the windows stretching around three sides of the room, and the sweeping view back over the stern towards the wharf and downtown Nanaimo. Yasmin was pleased to note that she attracted many jealous and admiring glances. As she'd expected, her elegant simplicity stood out in the crowd.

Her first priority was identifying tong members and she scanned the room carefully for familiar faces. Clearly, Tommy Yip was as short-handed as she'd heard. Many of the staff running games and distributing drinks had the unnatural beauty of whores. Standing out among them were several awkward men and women in white uniforms who must be engine crew. Then Yip himself brushed past on Yasmin's right—chubby, jovial, and self-important in a nineteenth century suit complete with embroidered waistcoat and watch fob. The woman beaming girlishly on his arm, in an antique beaded evening dress and too much jewelry, had to be his tong-trained Fine Wife. Yasmin watched Yip for a moment as he circulated, joking and shaking hands. He looked very much at ease, using routines he'd perfected in his years as a restaurateur. A few paces away several of his hand-picked henches watched the crowd carefully. Yasmin didn't recognize any of them.

Relaxing, she started to study the rustics. Some Citizens had unearthed family finery for the party and posed self-consciously in ornate hand-worked embroidery and patchwork, some of it no doubt dating back to times when garment salvage had driven fashions. A few younger locals wore new body-tailored faux cotton or ensilk suits. But most were older people, defiantly sporting their Guild-issue hempen work clothes and boxy neck-slung phones. Guild custom frowned on open displays of rank or wealth, but Yasmin found it easy enough to spot those who considered themselves important. Scowls and glares also revealed those traditionalists who disapproved of even mock gambling.

A beautiful olive-skinned girl strolled past Yasmin with a tray of drinks. She looked about twelve years old, with dark hair framing a heart-shaped face, and half developed breasts jutting under a sheer pink blouse, but she walked easily in high heels and maneuvered the tray with confident coordination. A babydoll prostitute, Yasmin decided, no doubt bought from the Viet Ching. With growth and development artificially halted, she would look twelve until she reached thirty-five or even forty. Then the tong would discard her. Yasmin had been forced to work on babydolls, and she despised the senseless waste of human potential.

She pulled her attention away from the girl and started to circulate, introducing herself to local Citizens with a hesitant shyness appropriate to a young medtech. In the next hour she learned about the Master Craftsmen who were being honored at this Building Trades party, and picked up hints that Tommy Yip was trolling for Guild investment, no doubt in hopes of laundering tong money through Guild accounts and blackmailing senior execs. Any Citizen would have to be a moron to traffic with him after all the revelations in last year's data spill, but in time he'd no doubt find someone greedy and short-sighted enough.

Guests were circulating up and down the curved staircase to the Dining Room below where a lavish buffet featured the latest in exotic bio-engineered foods, but Yasmin stayed upstairs where drips and trips circulated freely and the crowd grew more boisterous as the evening wore on. Two hours netted her several sexual invitations but no information about Cortes Island, so she tried a direct approach on a pretty young man who wore gold earcuffs with his Building Trades-issue hempens. He grinned and pointed across the room.

"If you want to know about Cortes, ask Mr. Cortes—the old man glaring at the roulette wheels. He's lived there since forever, pretty much runs the place."

Excellent. Yasmin walked over to the Guildman, sizing him up. He stood stiffly erect, a dozen centimeters taller than her, with a full head of thick white hair. He might easily be in his eighties or nineties, but he looked no more than seventy.

"Excuse me, sir."

He turned and glowered down at her with piercing gray-blue eyes under bushy eyebrows. He had a craggy, narrow face and beaky nose.

"I hope you don't mind if I introduce myself? I'm Yasmin Paroo, ship's crew."

"David Anderson, Building Trades."

They shook hands, Yasmin admiring his strong grip. The people who were born before modern health care and had nonetheless survived the plagues and famines of the last century were often superb genetic specimens. Anderson's coloring suggested Scandinavian ancestry, and she noticed a couple of small scars on his face from the removal of skin cancers. He wore his Guild issue clothes with stern pride, and held his champagne flute uncomfortably.

"I heard that you're from Cortes Island, and..."

The roulette wheel rattled loudly, drowning Yasmin's voice. Anderson frowned. Yasmin looked around for a quieter corner, then made a split second decision and beckoned him towards the stairs. Anderson hesitated, then followed. Below, in the foyer outside the Dining Room, Yasmin spotted signs pointing to private gaming rooms and strode confidently toward them, as if she knew the ship. The first door in a side corridor, had a brass plate inscribed: "Juan de Fuca Salon," and when Yasmin tried her new security clearance, the doorknob turned under her hand. Gas lights flared, illuminating a lavish private gaming room, with a billiard table and fully stocked bar. The air system hissed to life, wafting subtle scents of animal leather, wood, and fresh tobacco that masked a mix of mild disinhibitors.

Anderson took it in with raised brows, then looked at her suspiciously, probably wondering if she was a prostitute. Yasmin gave him a disarming smile and shrugged.

"I was getting tired of the noise in there." She glanced at the bar. "Would you like something else to drink?"

Anderson abandoned his champagne glass with obvious relief.

"Yes, thank you. Aquavit or vodka, if you have it."

"Let me see." Yasmin started searching the glass bottles behind the bar, reading labels methodically from left to right.

"Not a drinker, are you young lady?" observed Anderson, with amusement.

"No," admitted Yasmin. "It isn't courteous, but it would probably be faster if you found it yourself."

"Don't mind if I do."

They traded places, and Yasmin leaned on the bar, watching the old man. He glanced over the shelves, then leaned down and opened the freezer. He pulled out a bottle with a satisfied grunt, got a shot glass and poured a generous dollop. He looked inquiringly at Yasmin. She shook her head.

"No thanks."

He nodded and raised his glass. "Skoal" He emptied the shot in one gulp, then nodded. "Very smooth. Apex."

"Everything on this ship is apex," observed Yasmin. "Did you come all the way here from Cortes Island for this party?"

"Yep. Lot of nonsense, but I got friends in Nanaimo I was meaning to visit anyway." He looked appraisingly at Yasmin. "Been with the ship long?"

"This is my first day."

"And, ah... what's your slot?"

"I'm a medtech."

"Mmm." Anderson looked a little relieved.

"And I'll save you asking—no, I'm not Guild," she added, with a slight smile. "I worked for an independent clinic in Vancouver until it was torched in the tong war. And then..." she let her eyes fall and trailed off with an unhappy shrug.

"No work, eh?"

"No. The City's taken over all the clinics and they won't take medtechs without Guild qualifications. I could pass the exams," she threw Anderson a challenging look, "but I can't afford the fee and anyway it's nearly impossible to get a Guild sponsor. So I was selling spuddies off a cart when I heard about this slot. I don't like the tongs, Mr. Anderson, but they pay me."

"I see." Anderson poured himself another shot, but didn't pick it up. "You worked in a Downtown clinic, eh? Don't suppose you know much about non-consensual alterations?"

Yasmin blinked, surprised.

"A little," she said, making her expression puzzled.

Anderson looked at her doubtfully, seeming to weigh her evident youth and inexperience.

"Know anything about tong enforcers?"

"Well, I've seen them," she said vaguely. Paydirt! Anderson must have seen Choi's tool!

He fiddled with his glass, frowning.

"Can they be cured? You know, fixed to make them normal again?"

It wasn't hard to sound incredulous.

"Cured? Well, hardly. I mean, they're enormous—taller than two meters—and you can't reverse that or the enhanced musculature and emergency responses."

"What about... the mind?"

"I don't think so," she said, sounding doubtful. "There's probably a great deal of neural damage, not to mention that they're trained killers. I doubt any hospital would want to touch one. But I'm not an expert," she lied. She stared at Anderson, who was looking into his shot glass, then prodded. "Why do you ask?"

"Just wondering," he said abruptly, and swallowed his drink.

He wasn't going to talk, she realized with irritation. But she needed details. He was looking at the bottle, so she smiled encouragingly.

"Go ahead. It's on the house."

He gave her a gruff smile. "Well, one more."

While Anderson poured another drink and put the bottle back in the freezer, Yasmin reached into her pouch and silently unwrapped a med patch. The impermeable side of the thin pad adhered to her palm like a second skin, almost invisible.

"What's your position in Building Trades?" she asked him.

"Carpenter."

"Just a carpenter?"

"Distinguished Master Craftsman," Anderson admitted with a gleam of pride.

"Really? Well, then maybe you could tell me about the woodwork on this ship. I've never seen so much real wood before, and I hear some of it's mahogany and teak. Like this bar..."

Anderson nodded, stroking the surface with a large, work roughened hand.

"Mahogany, all right. Farmed, but still it's a handsome wood."

"Really?" Yasmin leaned forward, pretending to study the bar, and put her hand on his arm, squeezing it firmly against his skin. Anderson looked startled but he didn't pull away. "How can you tell it's farmed?"

"Huh? Oh, the grain. See, it's wide and very consistent from year to year, not like wild wood."

"And what about the workmanship? "Would you say this is well built?" she asked, trying to keep his concentration focused for the minute it would take the meds to enter his bloodstream. She had perfected this particular recipe over the years—a potent matrix of hypnotics and protein synthesis inhibitors that blocked long term memory formation. Direct neural hook-ups were far more effective, but this was fast and almost undetectable, and Anderson would remember nothing of the next half hour.

"Well... it's fair," said Anderson grudgingly. "Took a few short cuts, mind you. See, they didn't do a full finishing job underneath. And..." He stared at the wood and blinked a couple of times, then shook his head. "Sorry, lost my train of thought."

Yasmin leaned further forward.

"It must take a lot of polishing," she said softly, making her voice monotonous. "A lot of polishing to finish the wood just right. Real craftsmen do it by hand, don't they? Would you show me?"

She took his hand and pushed it gently back and forth.

"No, no!" Anderson shook her hand off. "Not like that. In circles."

"Would you show me?" said Yasmin. "You said, in circles. Do you mean around and around?..."

Anderson's hand started circling slowly against the wood, almost of its own accord. He stared down, looking faintly quizzical.

"I see," said Yasmin persuasively. "It must take great concentration to do that, watching the grain of the wood, stroking around and around and around. It's a relaxing motion and you flow right into it. Watch your hand going round and round. Concentrate on the motion, just like working in your own shop...."

She studied him carefully. His hand circled on the bar, making strong, even strokes. His pupils were dilated and his blinking rate had slowed. He was under.

"Now, you were asking about enforcers," she said softly.

Anderson's forehead creased.

"I shouldn't talk about that."

"But you aren't talking," Yasmin told him gently. "You're just thinking out loud while you work in your shop. You're polishing the wood and thinking out loud about the enforcer..."

Immediately Anderson scowled. Yasmin braced herself for resistance to the hypnosis, but his circling hand didn't waver.

"They should never have agreed to let him on the island," the old man muttered. "I voted against the permit, but trust Turner and Jantzen's goddamned bleeding hearts and Joy Guthrie has the brains of a cod. And in Mary's cabin of all the goddamned places, but no, they don't live next door, why should they care?" He frowned in silence for a moment, then started again.

"Thought Ethan might have better sense, but he's been talked over too. Stupid fool. Letting young David run around loose at all hours...."

He seemed to be drifting off topic. Yasmin prodded.

"What are they doing in the cabin with the enforcer?"

"Say they can fix him up. Well, I dunno. Don't think Mary knows what she's talking about, nice woman, but always trying to rescue the goddamned world. Can't talk sense to her.... And just the three of them looking after that big ghoul. A Chinese medic. Some American therapist. And that girl. They say they've got some kind of restraint on him, eh? But if he went berserk he could break that little woman in half with one hand. It's not safe! They should take him to a hospital and I'm damnsure gonna find a way to make sure they do it. Never should have sold residency rights on that lot! We could have found the money somehow...."

Yasmin prodded again.

"What does the ghoul looks like?"

"Ugly bastard. Over seven foot tall, bald, face like a Halloween mask. Burned ear. Scares shit out of me."

That was Choi's enforcer, all right, thought Yasmin, with surge of excitement.

"What about the medic?" she tried.

"Dresses real platty, but maybe they all do in Hong Kong. Handsome, smooth manners, big smile. Everybody likes him, bloody fools, just cause he's charming don't mean we can trust him. Coiting his way around the island, too. Women eating him like candy."

That certainly wasn't Choi. But he might have brought in a trainer from Hong Kong—someone the local tongs wouldn't know about.

"And the therapist?" Yasmin asked.

Anderson's scowl deepened.

"Afroid woman... Americans are descended from slaves, you know. Socially impaired, genetically damaged, violent. Had a hell of a time keeping them off the Gulf Islands during the troubles. Lotta people killed...."

Abruptly Yasmin heard voices in the corridor outside. She tensed, looking at the door. Damn, she hadn't locked it behind her! The voices grew louder, then faded. Still, she'd better finish up quickly.

"Well, you don't need to worry about the enforcer now," she told him soothingly. "Just focus on the wood. It looks very smooth now, very polished. Pretty soon you can take a break. See, you're just about finished, going slower and slower. And when you're done you won't remember anything we said. Just brush away the memory. That's right, just like sawdust. Brush it off..... And then when I count down to one, you'll forget. Three... Two.... One..."

Yasmin stepped back and rapped sharply on the bar. The old man started, then looked around, confused.

"What...?"

"You're right, it's beautiful wood," said Yasmin. "And they should take better care of it. Did you see the tables in the casino? They're getting scratched up."

Anderson looked at her and then at the bar, uncertain and faintly puzzled, then he nodded.

"Good wood needs care." He frowned at the shot glass in front of him, and pushed it to one side. "It's getting late."

"It is," agreed Yasmin. She stepped towards the door. "It's been a privilege to meet you, Mr. Anderson. And... well, I've always wanted to visit an island like Cortes..."

"Not much to see," he said gruffly, then seemed to feel guilt at his lack of hospitality. "If you're planning a trip, call ahead."

That was deliberately vague but she gave him a big smile, as if he'd issued an engraved invitation.

"Thank you!"

That smile wasn't feigned. Less than four hours aboard the ship, and she had just moved several steps closer to her revenge.

# 8

Saturday, July 13

The flavor of licorice bloomed on Choi's tongue. He reacted instantly, disabling the satellite link, although he knew it was already too late. His query had tripped a trace. It flashed into existence on the surface of Choi's mahogany desk as a wriggling ferret, then froze and faded out as his defences disabled it. A sheet of rice paper appeared before him displaying a trace analysis. Under a calligraphed Chinese heading, English characters scrolled.

The trace appeared routine—common commercial code, keyed to the name "Choi Shung Wai." The scent had been hacked onto the trace as a convenient marker for neurally interfaced net users. Choi had enough neural ice to taste and smell such signposts, but he couldn't interpret their nuances. Net wizards left their signatures all over, like dogs pissing on posts to tell other dogs they'd been there. Usually they ignored mere datasharks like Choi, and he didn't attempt to understand their convoluted games. He could only hope the wizard signpost had been routine.

Aware that precious seconds were passing, Choi launched a new search, moving as fast as he could manage while covering his trail. He kept his senses hyper-attuned to sounds, smells and tastes while he checked for rumors about Vancouver tongs. His seekers had been collecting data for several days, and flashed up summaries.

Despite tensions between the Chinese tonglords and the American slum gangs, the Sun Yee On/Screaming Eagles alliance was holding in Vancouver. The defeated Kung Lok had fled the city and were trying to regroup, courting survivors of the decimated Viet Ching to bolster a weak position. A familiar name scrolled past and Choi's interest sharpened. Tommy Yip, abruptly risen to a senior position in the Kung Lok, had posted rewards for infor-

72

mation on Choi's holdings. Yip could be dangerous. He knew and hated Toni, and he'd been present when Blade went berserk on Pier B-C so he'd also seen Klale and Lau. Choi aimed more seekers at Yip and the Kung Lok, then followed the link on the Kung Lok's wanted listings.

The warm metallic smell of blood sent a surge of alarm through Choi. He froze, startled, then saw the glowing crimson Chinese characters for "blood debt." He pulled up the icon. Crimson flowed past his eyes, then faded to a holo of a middle-aged woman with graying hair pulled back in a severe knot. The image spun slowly, a double helix below it offering DNA data for download, while English, Chinese and Arabic text identified her as Dr. Smith, former head trainer for the Viet Ching, missing in the tong war and suspected of treason.

Choi allowed a very faint smile to crease his face. He had enjoyed selling that arrogant bitch's dossier to the Viet Ching. No wonder the tongs wanted her so badly. Top skills in neural and behavioral modification were always in demand, and Smith's knowledge of Viet Ching trade secrets would be extremely valuable. The person who located her could start a global bidding war.

A quiet chime interrupted Choi's consideration of this delightful challenge, and he cursed silently at the elapsed time. Wasting no further seconds, he closed his uplink and turned to local data. He'd bugged all the phones and netsets in Mary Smarch's cabin, uploading to his own custom surveillance software. Regrettably, he didn't have vid cameras. He scanned content summaries. The first flag to draw his attention was a conversation between Lau and Almiramez which confirmed something he had suspected. Both of them were aware that Blade could kill in a state of emotional anesthesia without tripping his neural restraint. They had argued over allowing Simon to associate with young David Anderson.

Lau: "Toni, he could hurt the boy."

Almiramez: "He could. But he won't."

Lau: "Well, I'm glad you're so confident."

Almiramez: "Simon doesn't fear David. David is no physical threat, and, most important, he has no kind of power over Simon. So Simon won't hurt him."

Lau: "I hope you're right. But David's just a child. You and I and Klale know the risks. That's different."

There was more of the same, but no new information. Interesting. Almiramez knew that Choi could use Blade against her. She wasn't a complete fool, so she must have other weapons he wasn't aware of.

As he considered the problem, Choi felt a hot surge of fury. He needed access to Dr. Almiramez's journal, but she wrote it directly to a datacube and kept the cube in the front pocket of her pants—a crude system and so far proof against all of Blade's attempts to retrieve it. She had also secured her personal notepad by fingerprint and voice code—hardly unbreakable, but it would take at least ten minutes to circumvent it and she had given him no opportunities. In an attempt to profile her motivations, he had scanned through all of her university records, academic papers, and the professional notes still archived at the Institute. His best hypothesis so far was that she had an obsessive need to prove her therapeutic theories after previous public failures. But this did not tell him what uses she planned for Simon.

No time for speculation! He pulled his attention back to the cabin surveillance log and scanned details of Miz Anderson's visit. Blade had seen David's mother arrive the day after his confrontation with old Mr. Anderson. Almiramez had sent Blade into the yard, out of earshot, and he'd only been able to catch glimpses of her talking with Blue—a compact, muscular woman of about forty-five in workshirt, shorts, and boots, with dark blonde hair pulled back in a ponytail.

Fortunately, the tap had caught the conversation.

Anderson: "...no tea, thanks. Sorry to invite myself over like this, but I wanted to size you up for myself. I talked to the three men in my family and got three completely different stories. And I'm worried about David's safety."

Almiramez: "I understand your concern, but I don't believe David's in any danger or I wouldn't allow it.

Anderson: "Uh huh." A short silence, then: "What I see is a grown man who's immature, had no kind of normal life, and he's taking a big interest in a twelve-year-old boy...."

Almiramez: "You're right, Simon might fit the profile of a pedophile. But he isn't. Part of his conditioning involved..."

As she continued with a clinical assessment, Choi switched to a synopsis. Miz Anderson had asked a number of detailed questions about Simon's condition and received lengthy answers from Almiramez. Then the two women had discussed repairs to the cabin roof.

Blue Anderson held little interest for Choi, but the senior Mr. Anderson did, and Choi had launched a seeker with instructions to tap his net accounts. He opened the seeker, then stared in surprise. Nothing. The seeker had found no traceable telephone, netset or net account in Anderson's name. Evidently the old rustic was much wilier than Choi had anticipated. He wrote a broad query and left it running while he hurried on to check other taps.

Dr. Amerigo Lau had received seventeen calls in the past week and one caught Choi's notice. Simone de la Fontaine, Lau's first wife, had called from a netset registered to the Willamette Dance Company in Eugene. She'd coded the message "don't-reach" so it wouldn't transmit until Lau had switched off his phone. Evidently she didn't want to talk to her ex-husband directly. Interesting.

Choi opened the message and a beautiful Afroid woman flashed up before him. He froze the image to study her. Gold art glimmered against chocolate skin, emphasizing high cheekbones, full lips, and long-lashed brown eyes. She wore a gold embroidered vest over a blue silk blouse, a multi-hued turban, and heavy dangling earrings. This expensive ensemble overlay even more expensive juvving treatments, noted Choi. His records showed that la Fontaine was forty-eight, but she looked twenty-five at most. Focusing on the vid's background he identified a neo-impressionist painting, a steel-framed white chair, and a white fur rug on a red tiled floor.

"Rigo, dear." Simone flashed flirtatious eyes at the vid pick-up and spoke with the mellifluous voice of a professional performer. "Of course, I was delighted to hear that Simon's dancing is going so well. I told you he was born to dance—remember? And I'd give almost anything to see him, naturally, but a small company simply can't spare its director in high season. We've just started our outdoor evening series, and my dear you would not BELIEVE the insects. We have repellent over everything, especially the cast and the first three rows."

She smiled winningly at the pick-up, but Choi saw hints of tension around her eyes.

"Anyway, you must surely remember what a wretched mother I was. You were always the better parent, darling. Give my love to Simon and tell him I'll send vids of the shows. And there's no point trying to talk me into it again because I know you'll both do just fine without me. Must run. Adieu."

Aware of a vague sense of unease, Choi turned his attention back to the rest of Lau's mailbox, but found nothing else of interest. Seven calls were from island ID's, related to Lau's work at the local clinic. Three calls were from local women, all using vocal ranges suggestive of sexual interest. Two calls in Chinese discussed an extension of Lau's leave of absence from the Tai Hang Clinic for a further six months, and there was a brief vid from Lau's second ex wife.

Almiramez's mail log was comparatively short. Her only regular calls were from the KlonDyke in Vancouver, usually the bar manager, Mary Smarch. But one message had been left by the KlonDyke's acting security chief, Pum Saini. Choi opened it.

"Toni, it's Pum. Look, I don't wanna scare you, but I heard from a sailor down the docks that Klale got tailed one time when she left the 'Dyke. Maybe a month or two ago. Two people. Not tong, I don't think. I asked around and waterfront goons saw 'em too, say they followed her to the ferry. I woulda called you sooner but I didn't hear until now. Maybe you better not send Klale back down here, OK?"

Intriguing and also frustrating. Choi sent follow-up seekers, but he knew he was unlikely to get further details. The flots and squats on the waterfront had few phones and avoided creating records that might be pried. Blade's in-person surveillance had been vital to his data gathering activities Downtown and without a similar source he was blind.

His chime sounded again. Two minutes. He abandoned Klale's phone log and returned to his query on David Anderson, Senior. It had turned up nothing except routine Guild records and articles in the Cortes Island archives. Choi distrusted local histories, but seeing no other promising hits, he scanned a summary and found his answer. Anderson had a personal feud against various phone companies and utilities which dated back to the worst years of the Collapse. Many impoverished island families had been cut off from even emergency phone service, and then an underwater power cable had failed in 2053, leaving the islands permanently without power because the utility refused to make costly repairs. Decades later, Anderson still held a grudge, even though the islands had long since become self sufficient for energy. He refused to own a phone or netset.

Incredibly, whenever he wanted to make a personal phone call, the old man got out his velo and pedalled to Manson's Landing General Store. Ah. Choi swiftly located the store's antiquated pay phone and searched its outgoing log for familiar IDs. Mary Smarch's ID appeared two days ago. The pay phone kept no records, but Choi had several taps at the KlonDyke, and he backtraced to a synopsis of the call. Anderson had tried to bully Smarch into evicting Lau from her cabin. When she refused, he had threatened to have the island council rescind her residency permit and....

Ching! The virtual world faded to black. Damn Almiramez! Choi felt a flash of fury, but restrained it, letting no emotion reach his face. With slow deliberation he removed his goggles and reached for the link cables.

"Good morning, Simon."

Dr. Almiramez sat across the kitchen table from him, a cup of steaming coffee in front of her, sharp brown eyes regarding him intently. As he removed the link cups on his skull, the scent of fresh baked blueberry muffins assaulted his nose.

"David's here to take you to the beach."

David! Simon's delight propelled him to his feet so swiftly that he jolted the table with his knees, slopping coffee from Toni's mug. He flinched with alarm, but she just smiled.

"Go on. No harm done."

As he hurried to the porch, Simon felt his heart race with excitement so he paused and took several calming breaths before stepping outside. Klale and Dr. Lau were leaning on the porch railing. David perched opposite them on a battered rattan chair. His open jacket revealed a light green shirt, and blonde hair fell carelessly across his freckled face. When Simon stepped onto the porch he sprang to his feet.

"Hi. Ready to go?"

Dr. Lau and Klale grinned like people who'd just shared a joke. Lau nodded and Klale leaned over to pick up a knapsack. David bolted out to the yard and Simon hastened to follow.

"Hey, you two, don't get out of our sight!" called Lau.

"Yeah, and don't do anything we wouldn't do!" added Klale.

Today, David seemed nervous. He hurried along the trail, not speaking or looking back. Simon tried to think of some way to make Blade's ugly bulk appear less alarming, but it was impossible not to tower over the slight boy. Abruptly David halted on the trail and turned, looking directly up at him for the first time. Simon stopped and crouched down to the boy's height, remembering Klale's exasperated words: "Don't loom!" David didn't seem reassured—he looked startled at Simon's movement and took two rapid steps backward, but he asked:

"Ever see a heron tree?"

"No."

"Come on."

David veered off the main path and started uphill, following a faint trail which traversed mossy rocks, and plunged through bush-choked gullies. Simon followed without difficulty, though he heard muttered complaints behind him. Gray light from the overcast sky made the greens seem as deep as ocean, and the scent of damp, woody earth engulfed him. Slippery leaves brushed his skin, twigs grabbed at his clothes, and his steps cracked down through dead branches and sank into soft pockets of leaf litter between the rocks. A deep eerie thrum reverberated through the trees, its direction oddly difficult to pinpoint. David glanced back.

"Ruffled grouse," he said. Then he clambered onto a log and pointed to the left. "Bush tits."

Simon followed his gesture and realized that the trees were alive with flickers of movement. A flock of tiny gray-brown birds, no larger than Simon's thumb flitted from branch to branch, peeping quietly. David waved at Lau and Klale to halt and put a finger to his lips, while Simon stood transfixed. The chittering birds swarmed closer, clinging upside down to twigs and pecking at branches with odd jerky motions. They paid so little attention to the humans that Simon thought they might even land on him, but they flew past and continued on into the understorey.

Simon noticed David grinning up at him and realized that he had a broad smile on his own face.

"Hear those creaky hinge noises? Heron rookery is just over there. Easiest way to find them is to look for fishy-smelling piles of guano. C'mon, I've got a good observation spot."

Hoarse croaking and clacketing grew louder as David led them to a mossy outcrop of rock. He sat, and Simon copied him, following his gaze up into a pair of large cedars with widely spaced branches. Sloppy nests of twigs, perhaps two thirds of a meter in diameter, rested precariously on high branches. They held tall, long-legged herons with blue-gray plumage, some sitting or standing in the nests and others gripping nearby branches and flapping. Simon counted seventeen, some of them almost at their full adult height of over a meter. Distantly he noticed Lau and Klale settling down on a nearby rock, but his attention was focused on the gawky birds. He'd seen herons poised gracefully at the tideline, standing immobile for long minutes and then darting their long necks into the water after fish, but a long-legged bird standing in a tree looked somehow ludicrous.

David passed Simon a pair of antique passive binoculars, then spoke in a low voice.

"You can see eleven nests from here, and there's more in other trees nearby. The young birds are just about ready to fledge. I really wanted to get a lens up there, had a spot picked out even and I was going to climb up this spring before they started nesting, but Rory told Mom and Mom said no way, it's too dangerous." He sighed.

"See, I can count fledglings from the ground, but to figure out their nesting success rate I need to know how many eggs they laid. Herons were just about wiped out by eagle predation back when the fisheries collapsed and they're still kinda shaky cause of not enough genetic diversity, so ADAT's always looking for good heron reports."

They had been watching for perhaps twenty minutes when Simon became aware of Lau and Klale shifting restlessly and talking together in low voices. David cast them a glance, then leaned over and spoke softly.

"You're good at sitting still. Hardly anybody is, you know.

Dad tries, but he starts thinking about all the stuff he should be doing instead. And the island kids are a bunch of splutzes."

The compliment wakened a glow in Simon. David thought he was good at something—better than real people, even. He cast around for some way to respond, then said cautiously:

"I think a good location for surveillance would be there—that tree opposite, about thirty meters up, above most of the nests."

"Yeah?" The boy craned. "Think you could climb up there?"

"Certainly."

"Strat!!" David's face glowed, then sobered. "But I don't have a weatherproof remote and I spent all my allowance already."

"I could get one."

"Really?! Hey, you could get one with infrared. There's this owl's nest...."

Off to their left, Lau cleared his throat. David looked embarrassed.

"Uh, sorry. Forget it, OK?"

To Simon's bafflement, he said nothing further. What was David sorry for? And why did Lau and Klale grin at each other when the his back was turned? Simon puzzled over the situation as they made their way back to the trail and then down to the beach. He often felt that the people around him were speaking in code and concealing secrets, but it was a revelation to see David treated that way. David had mentioned unfair treatment by his parents—did he have some kind of outcast status that the others all recognized?

The rich smells and sounds of the beach tore Simon's thoughts away from those questions. Klale and Lau seated themselves on a large log, while David and Simon explored the half exposed shore, David delivering rapid-fire bursts of information and conjecture about inter-tidal life and interrupting himself to point out loons, cormorants and, his favorite shorebird, oystercatchers—clownish black birds with oversized red feet and long red beaks. They startled a small group that skimmed off over the water, wheeping loudly. David had several naturalist guides loaded on his phone and he showed Simon how to use the ID function, first on a bivalve and then a rock on the beach. At that, Simon became utterly engrossed. It had never occurred to him before that even the stones under his feet had names and histories. He sat down cross-legged above the seaweed strewn cordon left by last night's tide and started check-ing pebbles, using one of his knives to perform a scratch test, then matching color and texture against the grainy screen on David's cheap phone. Simon's own phone was far better, but the necessity to get permission from Toni for downloads meant he would have to wait.

Klale called him away from a milky white agate for sandwiches and juice, which David and Simon carried to a weathered gray log whose gnarled root mass made Simon think of frozen dancers.

"Didn't take geology in school?" asked David around a mouthful of oatbread and cheese.

"I never went to school."

"Never?" David sounded incredulous. Simon looked away, embarrassed.

"You're lucky," said David, his voice suddenly envious. "School is such greege."

Lucky?

"I thought school would be interesting," he ventured.

"Nah. The Science and Math curriculum is a joke, and then there's all that other sludge like Fiction, Music, Historical Context, and Community Studies."

David studied music in school?

"See, I've always known I want to be a marine ecologist and they're just wasting my time. I guess it's OK for people who don't know what they want to do. My sister Rory says she doesn't, but she'll be a carpenter like Dad and Mom and Granddad. She's just making static." He considered. "Did you always know what you wanted to do?"

"Yes."

"What?"

"Dance."

David stopped chewing and stared, then his eyes flicked away and Simon remembered Blade's ugly face. David couldn't see Simon really, only Blade, he thought sadly, then doubt brought him up short. Could David see Simon? Why had David spoken to him if he hadn't glimpsed him somehow? It was yet another bewildering contradiction in a world grown more and more confusing.

"Uh, look." David seemed uneasy again. "About asking you

to get a remote camera.... I apologize."

For once Simon knew what to say.

"I accept your apology. But... I don't understand."

"Oh. Well. Partly it's that Dr. Lau said not to tell you to do things, right? But mostly, it's money. Things are real thin at home, especially this year. Dad and Mom are all knots about it, scared we're going to have to move into Guild housing in Campbell River and then what do we do about Granddad? So they don't want me acting like I'm asking for hand-outs from anybody, especially somebody who's Guildless and probably can't afford it even worse than us, right?"

He finished in an awkward rush. Simon considered his words and said tentatively:

"But if I can afford it...."

"Oh. Well, maybe that's different." David shot a wary glance over at Lau and Klale. The constant growl of breeze and surf drowned out conversation at a couple of meters. "Do you have lots of money?"

"I don't know. I don't know how much is 'lots'."

"Uh..." David frowned. "Well, a Guild stipend is like two hundred a month and that's sure not much. Dad says our property's worth fifty thousand, if they could sell it." Abruptly he grinned. "For sure a million is lots."

"I have lots," said Simon, then felt a stab of fear. Why had he said that? Simon didn't have money. Choi had money. And Choi's money was under the control of Almiramez and Lau.

David stared at him wide-eyed.

"Seriously? But I thought Guildless people.... Um, how did you get so much money?"

"Extortion," said Choi.

"Hey, you two," called Klale. "We promised to have David home by two, so you've got less than an hour."

"Dredge!" David folded his sandwich bag and grabbed the empty juice bottle. "Let's go. I wish the tide was lower but we can still find limpets and whelks. Limpets are those little cone shells stuck on the rocks. People around here still call them Chinaman's hats. When the tide's in they let go of their suction hold and crawl around, browsing for algae...."

The hour passed swiftly. Then, with Lau and Klale, they walked up the trail, taking a fork which crossed the stream below the water wheels and led to the bottom of the Anderson's yard, emerging between two lichen-encrusted apple trees. "They're old and they don't have hardly any apples," said David, waving at the trees. "Dad wants to cut them down and grow black cherries instead, but granddad planted them when he was a kid and he gets mad every time Dad brings it up."

Climbing up through the yard they passed a door inset into the steepest part of the slope. A bunker, Simon guessed, but David nodded at it and said "root cellar." As they reached the large, white house, Miz Anderson stepped outside to meet them. She shook hands with her neighbors—even Simon—and started talking with Dr. Lau. David fidgeted.

"Mom, I'm showing Simon around, OK?"

Miz Anderson hesitated. When Klale volunteered to go with them, she nodded.

David toured them around flagstone pathways, starting at the raised beds of the kitchen garden, draped with dew nets that funneled condensation into the soil at night. He showed them garden probes for uploading soil composition, moisture, and temperature data to the housecomp, and then opened an insect trap. "We check pest ratios every day so we know if things are getting out of balance," he said. In the outer garden he explained which Native and exotic plant species attracted which kinds of birds, and then pointed out a robin's nest he'd located, low in the branches of a nearby fir.

"What's that weird looking tree over there?" asked Klale.

"Bloodwood—it's a new strain tailored for this climate, kind of an experiment of Mom's," said David. "The wood's supposed to be good for boats. We're licensed to grow non-invasive exotics—they're all around the edges of the garden and on the bluff. My great grandfather started with oaks and maples, then Grandad planted a couple of trees every year. We cut them for special jobs, or sometimes to trade. People bring us wood, too, especially old fruit trees. Grandad used to do a lot of barters—he'd make a piece of furniture with some of the wood and then keep the rest in payment. We don't do that much any more, but the Shaws cut a big walnut in their yard last year and Mom made them a dining table."

He bypassed the greenhouse ("not a real ecosystem") and a weathered shed ("we quit raising chickens cause Mom and Dad are away too much and Rory's going to high school in town"), moving around instead to a large wooden outbuilding next to the driveway. It had wide double doors and a steeply pitched roof packed with solar panels.

"This is the workshop. Granddad's gone over to the cafe to spin with all the geezies, so I can show you around. Too bad the sparrows fledged last week. We have five nests in the eaves."

The pungent fragrance of fresh sawdust met Simon at the door. David waved on lights as he entered, but they were hardly necessary with natural light spilling in from tall windows and skylights. Gleaming hand tools hung in tidy rows above a long workbench on the back wall of the shop. Power tools and a laser imaging system filled a larger bench along the east wall, and shelves on the west wall held a neatly organized array of containers, a sophisticated optical scanner and mixing equipment splattered with old stains. A set of rough wooden stairs led up to a loft in the rafters, where more equipment and supplies were stacked. Klale trailed David and Simon, looking around with interest.

"There's a wolf spider living in the loft," said David, heading for the stairs. "One of my books says they make nice pets but it didn't explain which kind and there's hundreds of species...."

"Hey, I thought you were going to show us carpentry," said Klale, sounding amused. "Come on, walk me through. What happens if a neighbor brings you a walnut tree?"

David rolled his eyes at Simon, but turned back.

"Oh, it's not very exciting. The mill and kiln are back behind the shop. Dad and Grandad put logs through the big scanner and then run cutting scenarios and projections of the finished furniture to see how the grain looks. After they argue forever, they cut, then the wood goes for curing, then it comes here, " he gestured at the workbenches. "Mom and Dad do builds mostly, and Grandad handles the finishing work. He's got all these secret stain recipes, and that spray bot over there handles super high resolution, so he can apply really complex patterns. It takes ages, though, especially for art designs and hand carving...."

"Hey..." he brightened, "I can show you. Granddad did some incredible pieces years ago."

He crossed the shop to fetch a ring of metal keys hanging on a nail behind the door, carried them to a large free-standing cupboard and started trying the keys in the lock one at a time. Simon felt himself tense. Even Klale looked dubious.

"Are you sure....?" she started, then David got the door open and reached inside the cupboard for a heavy inlaid chest, which he carried carefully to the nearest workbench.

"They're always asking Granddad to bring this to Guild shows for display but mostly he doesn't bother. Mom says it belongs in a gallery, but he won't do that either."

David undid the brass latch, and opened the chest to reveal a velvet-lined interior with chess pieces nested inside. Each piece was as large as the boy's fist.

"There's an arbutus table goes with this, too—it has an inlaid chess board, and drawers in each side for the chess men, and it's polished up like silk, but it's up in the loft behind a lot of stuff."

Simon was only half listening, his attention grabbed by the chessmen David was setting up on the workbench. Each was a detailed, lifelike bust of a person, hand-carved in dark or light wood. And each was unique—the large pieces were adults; the pawns were children.

Klale picked up a cinnamon-hued portrait of a woman and held it reverently. Subtle shades of stain gave the skin an eerily life-like texture, and the woman's hair flowed red-gold with the wood's grain.

"This is beautiful!"

"That's my great grandmother—she looked a lot like Rory. All these are real people from the island—people who died. See, those two little pearwood boys are Luke and Jam. They were granddad's friends when he was in school and they died during a superflu epidemic. That old lady is Miz Francis who burned up in her house in Squirrel Cove. Granddad says all the kids were scared of her, used to call her D'Sonqua—you know?"

"Sure!" said Klale. "The wild woman of the woods."

A few of the chess pieces smiled, but most faces were sad, thought Simon, studying them. Three pawns in particular caught his attention. They were carved in a blackish-brown wood and had Afroid features—a young man and woman with bony, haggard faces, and a terribly thin child, maybe two years old. Their eyes stared out with a blind desperation.

David was still talking.

"Granddad says this is his insurance policy. No matter how bad things get there will always be rich people somewhere who pay good money for art. Of course, mom says don't believe it, he'd never really sell the chess set, he'd probably starve first and..."

"David!"

The roar made all of them jump. Anderson Senior stood in the doorway, his furious old-man eyes focused on Simon. Simon stepped back slowly, fighting down a rush of terror. Blade!

"Uh, hi granddad. I was just showing Simon and Miz Renhardt around...." David stuttered to a stop, seemingly taken aback at the intensity of his grandfather's anger.

Klale stepped in front of the boy.

"Hello. Klale Renhardt, Fisher Guild," she said, holding out a hand. The old man glared at her.

"You can leave now and take that thing—" his smoldering eyes grazed Blade "—with you. Don't come back. David! Put my chess set away. And you stay here."

Anderson's frosty hair contrasted with the red rage in his face and the veins bulging in his hands. He would punish David like Choi had punished Simon. Simon had sometimes begged and groveled to delay even for a second the screaming wall of pain that slammed him against Choi's hardwood floor. It had always been in vain. Even through Blade's detachment, the memories woke fear and fury.

No! No adrenaline. Think. How could Blade incapacitate Anderson before he harmed David?

"Simon. Come with me." Klale's order was given in a soft voice, but she stood stiffly, face flushed with annoyance. She beckoned and turned to the door.

Blade followed, then stopped and faced Anderson. He used his full height to stare down at the old man and found a voice—Choi's voice.

"I advise you not to hurt David."

Anderson's eyes flicked towards something in the shed—a gun locker?—but he held his position.

"Of course I won't hurt him. I'm his grandfather," he snapped.

"Simon's grandfather sent him to beg in the streets and took all the money to buy jolts. When Simon couldn't beg enough, his grandfather sold him to a meat merchant for three hundred and fifty dollars."

He turned, glimpsing Klale's wide eyes, and strode into the yard. She came after him, talking, tugging on his arm, but the swelling chord of Blade's rage drowned her voice. His steps began to soar into glorious crimson crescendo, then his knees buckled and he pitched forward to the grass.

Chaos. Voices in the distance. David calling out, Klale and Anderson arguing, Dr. Lau's calm tones near his ear. Simon fled.


Much later, as dusk fell among the trees, he heard David's voice and the gentle swish of grass as the boy walked to the cabin porch where the ugly tool sat.

"Hi, Miz Renhardt. I came over to see if Simon's OK."

"Klahowya, tillicum," came Klale's voice from a nearby chair.

"Uh... what?"

"Klahowya is Chinook for hello, and tillicum is a person or a friend. I hate to ask, but are you supposed to be here?"

"I'm supposed to be doing homework. See? Homework. I brought it. I'm doing it." Light footsteps mounted the stairs and approached. Then a hesitant voice. "Simon?"

"It's all right, David. He sort of retreats inside himself until he feels safe. We just wait him out. Have a seat. What's the book?"

"Shakespeare." David's voice oozed disgust. A dragging noise, then creaks as he sat in a rattan chair. "Miz Matsumoto assigned The Tempest at school. So I get to learn words like prythee and abjure and doth from a teacher who calls beetles and spiders bugs!"

A long silence, then Klale spoke.

"Now that's a humm opoots—stinky tail."

Simon couldn't resist peeking out to the forest edge and saw a flash of white waddling along.

"Skunks aren't native to Cortes, you know," volunteered David. "Back during the Collapse this guy brought them here to raise for fur and food. Granddad says he was a 'suburban twit with his head up his ass.' It didn't work out, and some skunks escaped, spread all over. We're supposed to be eradicating them—we're returning the island to indigenous species, right?—but there's still a few around. They have a den under this cabin."

"Under here?!"

"Well, not this year—I guess all your noise scared them off. I had it all planned to set up an infrared camera in the crawl space and watch the kits being born—visible light disturbs them, you know."

"Yeah, well, please don't tell Toni—Dr. Almiramez—about it, OK?"

Heavy footsteps from the door.

"Hi, Dr. Lau."

"Evening, David. I'm glad to see you. I'd like to talk to you for a minute."

A brief silence, then Klale said: "Uh, I'll go clean up the kitchen. See you later." More creaking and footsteps as Lau took her vacated chair.

"I want to explain more about Simon. I should have done it earlier, but it's complicated."

"Look, sir, you don't have to dumb it down for me."

"I wasn't planning to, David, but Simon's condition is unusual. And... it's difficult for me to talk about. You see, he was tortured for a long time."

"Oh."

"Beaten, burned. Altered without his consent."

"Oh. Is that why...?"

"His face, yes. He needs a place to feel safe and time to heal, and this island is good for him. So are you."

"Oh." Pause. "Granddad said the restraint cut in this afternoon because Simon wanted to kill him."

"Well... That's possible, but it's more likely he was scared."

"Scared? HIM?!"

"It's a traumatic response. He panics very easily. And he's probably afraid of your grandfather."

"Um...." A hesitation, then careful words. "Simon said that his grandfather sold him for three hundred and fifty dollars. Is that true?

This time there was a long silence. Simon almost peeked to catch the expression on Lau's face.

"I hadn't heard that. I... I don't know, David. I hope not... Choi—the man who owned Simon—told him a lot of vicious lies." Lau took a deep breath. "Anyway, when Simon's withdrawn like this we keep him company until he's ready to come back. Talk to him if you like. He knows you're here. And if you're ever worried at all, you've got me or Dr. Almiramez on your phone priority. Never hesitate to call even if you feel stupid about it, OK?"

"OK."

Another long silence, then Klale's muffled voice from inside. "Hey, tillicum, are you doing that homework?"

"Yeah!"

A soft chuckle from Lau, then creaks as he rose.

"I'll be right back, David. Klale, I'm coming in."

Footsteps moved away, joined other footsteps by the door and there were low voices. Then Simon heard a soft rustle as David moved closer.

"Look, Simon, I've been thinking. If you're really interested in bioscience you could get some field gear for yourself, right? Like an infrared camera. Or scuba gear. And then we could share resources, Guild style. Ummm... I mean it's just a thought. You don't have to say I mentioned it. 'Kay, I'm doing that homework...."

# 9

## August 17

Returning to the Empress of Vancouver from a Saturday morning trip to Campbell River, Yasmin discovered that all her elaborate plans to reach Cortes Island had been pre-empted. There, sitting stiffly in a canvas chair on the polished teak Promenade Deck, was the old Guildsman, David Anderson. Waiting for her! She almost let loose a whoop of delight. And he'd brought a bonus. In the chair next him, hunched in concentration over his phone screen, was a blond preadolescent who must be the grandson listed in citizenship records. Yasmin didn't need to feign pleased surprise as she strode along the deck to meet them—indeed she damped it down a little, so as not to seem too eager.

"Mr. Anderson! It's nice to see you again."

"So you remember me, eh? This is my grandson, David Junior. David, Miz Paroo. I hope our dropping in this way isn't inconvenient."

"Oh, no, not at all!" She smiled warmly at the boy as he stood and shook her hand. "So David, are you interested in ships?"

"No."

A certain ramrod stiffness in the set of his shoulders caught Yasmin's eye and she suddenly saw how closely young David was going to resemble his grandfather. The boy stood slightly turned away from the old man—an almost snub, nicely calculated within the limits of acceptable manners. His grandfather glowered at him.

"Of course he is," he snapped, then cleared his throat and tried to sound more friendly. "All the local kids have been talking about the Empress since you tied up. And since we were in town for our regular shopping trip, we stopped by."

It would have made a plausible story if the boy had cooperated, thought Yasmin with amusement. She gave a thoughtful frown.

"The regular tour isn't until two, but... You know, my friend Tor is learning the docent routine. I bet he'd love someone to practice on. If you'll just wait here another few minutes, I'll get him."

As she hurried off to make preparations she felt a rush of exhilaration. Finally, the break she needed. The Empress had dallied in half a dozen tiny coastal ports before finally tying up in Campbell River, where Yasmin had run headlong into roadblocks. Incredibly, old Anderson didn't have a phone. Not wanting to call through his family, she'd tried to pass a personal message through his Guild. They told her to phone a General Store, where instead of a messaging service she'd found herself talking to the live proprietor. "I'll tack a message up on the bulletin board," the fat cow had said, smirking as she waved an actual pencil and piece of paper, "and he'll get it when he gets it. We run on island time, dearie—what was your name?..."

Posting her name for public view in a store was hardly an option and, worse, it showed that her fallback plan—travelling to the island to find him—would be hopelessly conspicuous. The island didn't have street addresses or even a public list of property owners. So she'd been cultivating a Guild contact from nearby Quadra Island, maneuvering for an excuse to visit Cortes. And now, unexpectedly, paydirt!

She called Tor from the Casino, finding him, as she expected, in the engine room. Although he'd signed on with her as a medtech, his obvious interest in steam engines and the short-staffed ship's crew meant he now spent most of his work shifts (and spare time) in the boiler room. Yasmin had feigned displeasure, but this suited her plans admirably and she was more than capable of handling Sick Bay herself. Finishing her call to Tor, she had an inspired afterthought and hurried down two decks to the lavishly upholstered "Hospitality Suites" where she banged on the door of Cin-Cin's cabin. As she'd expected, the babydoll was sleeping in and greeted her with a groggy pout, but a twenty dollar card and the promise of more money won instant cooperation. The Empress's wide menu of sex services had to be kept very discreet in straightlaced Guild towns, so the hookers were bored and broke.

Back on the Promenade Deck the Andersons sat side by side glowering silently at the scenery. The towering Empress gave them a panoramic view south toward the inland sea and east over Seymour Narrows, where wind and rip tides kicked up whitecaps in the treacherous passage between Campbell River and Quadra Island. Hidden behind Quadra lay more small islands, including Cortes, and beyond them were the steep mainland mountains, with black rain clouds hanging above the entrance to Desolation Sound. On the opposite side of the ship lay the town of Campbell River, with the Vancouver Island mountain range behind it. A few puffy white clouds crowned the Island range, and the skies over the strait were blue. It was a stunning view, though neither Anderson seemed to be enjoying it. Yasmin spent a minute chatting with them before Tor arrived in a clean shirt, eagerly gripping his phone with the docent notes. They started the tour.

Although Tor was no expert, he conveyed a guileless enthusiasm that stirred even David Jr.'s reluctant interest. They began by climbing up to the bridge and admired the big oak wheel, gleaming brass engine room telegraph, and the antique compass stand. Yasmin knew the ship had a full modern nav array, but she still had to look carefully to locate the discreetly camouflaged consoles. Then they descended deck by deck touring the Casino, Dining Room, private gaming rooms, first class staterooms, and even the main galley—one of the few areas entirely free of smothering Victoriana. Catching Yasmin's head shake, Tor bypassed the brothel, leading them instead to a discreet crew elevator. Perhaps he might learn a little subtlety yet.

The elevator opened onto the main engine room floor where antique machinery towered three storeys overhead. Here Tor's enthusiasm truly caught fire as he described how the two-century-old steam engines had been salvaged from a wreck and restored to working condition. He spent more than ten minutes pointing out features of the machines, even showing them steam valves called "stops" and explaining the phrase "pulling out all the stops".

Yasmin had to curb her impatience and fix a smile on her face as they climbed along catwalks, touring the four steam boilers that ran the engines—each boiler nearly as large as a house, even though these were new and hydrogen fuelled, rather than coal-fired. One was in operation, running the ship's electrical plant. Yasmin always expected the contraption to emit a deafening roar, but instead it hissed and whirred quietly, with only an occasional clang echoing through the maze of machinery. It radiated a lot of heat though, and an intense smell of lubricating oil. There weren't many crew around—only a weary-looking technician who ignored them. Just how short-handed was the Empress? she wondered suddenly. Many crew members had deserted in the first few weeks after the tong war, and they were almost irreplaceable—at least, Yasmin couldn't imagine where Tommy Yip would find experienced steam ship engineers in twenty-second century Cascadia.

Anderson Senior seemed interested in all the gizmos, but after a few minutes of scrambling up and down ladders to admire valves, gauges and pistons, she noticed young David's attention flagging, so Yasmin dropped casually back to where he'd draped himself on a safety rail.

"I hope you're not missing anything important for this tour." She got a cautious glance.

"Well.... I had some plans. But granddad wanted to come."

Yasmin made a sympathetic noise. "I'll bet he keeps you on your toes."

David grimaced.

"Yeah. He's my Guild mentor, too. Usually they don't let family mentor each other, but we're the only Carpenters on Cortes, and he's a distinguished master craftsman, so..."

Yasmin knew that already from questioning a Building Trades bureaucrat over drinks. But she asked ingenuously: "That's a small island, isn't it? Do they even have a school?"

"Sure. Well, elementary. Then we go to high school in Campbell River. I'll be starting there in the new year, like my sister."

Unhappiness shadowed his face. The boy was guarded and seemed intelligent, but he had no experience at hiding his emotions.

"Is that a long commute?"

"You don't commute. You come home on weekends."

He kicked at the post of the guard rail.

"You'll meet more people your own age," she probed.

"Sure. I'll get to 'mesh with my generational workteam'," he said sourly.

Yasmin let herself smile.

"I didn't like school either. But things improve when you get to university."

"IF I ever get there!" The bitterness in the boy's voice snared Yasmin's interest, but David thrust himself away, embarrassed at his outburst, and joined his grandfather.

Intriguing. Guild gossip labeled young David as a "lobe loner"—an epithet in Guild circles, but potentially useful to Yasmin. She'd have to get access to his school evaluations. Rural Guilds were leery of sending their children to the city for university. It was an insular prejudice, but not completely without foundation. David was just coming up on the prime age for imprinting and deep cyber-interface modifications. The tongs bought or stole children with high potential and rebuilt them as wizards—profoundly altered constructs who could manipulate cyberspace in phenomenal ways, while hooked into data and nutrient flows so that they didn't eat, sleep, shit or touch another person. But a boy that age wouldn't understand the danger—might not even know about it.

After fifteen more minutes of triple expansion steam engines, Yasmin was fuming with boredom and even the senior Mr. Anderson looked restive, so Yasmin reminded Tor that he needed to report for his docent shift, and then led the Andersons back to the Promenade Deck. Cin-Cin was there as arranged, lounging in a folding chair, with her pet kiwi bear in her lap. The baby doll prostitute wore white shorts and a pink shirt with a peter pan collar, its sheer fabric perfectly calculated to betray her small pointy nipples and highlight her cinnamon skin. She even wore her favorite pheromone-laced perfume—bubble gum scent. Yasmin had to smother a smile.

She had intended to introduce the youngsters, but young David got there ahead of her.

"Excuse me, is that a real kiwi?"

"Uh huh." The girl flicked her eyes shyly upward. "This is Cocoa. And I'm Cin-Cin."

"David Anderson." He offered his hand automatically. "Is that a male or female?"

"Female. Well, neuter. Here Cocoa, say hi to David," the girl cooed.

The gray-furred miniature koala was no larger than a small cat, with enormous black eyes that melted the hearts and pocketbooks of wealthy matrons in big tree enclaves. No doubt it had been a lavish gift from a well heeled pedophile. Cin-Cin smiled, tilting her head so that her hair framed her heart-shaped face, but the gesture was completely wasted on David whose attention was fixed on her gene-tailored teddy. He sat on the next deck chair and reached for it. Cin-Cin detached clinging paws from her arm to pass it over and he cradled it gently.

"Wow. I've never seen a kiwi. The gene alterations for these are very tweaky. They aren't really bears, you know. Koalas are arboreal marsupials. How long have you had her?"

He wasn't watching Cin-Cin's face, but Yasmin caught the girl's flinch, quickly hidden.

"Oh, ages," she said.

Tommy Yip gave his baby dolls memory wipes every year. They acted twelve most convincingly when they didn't remember thirteen, he'd joked to Yasmin, but that maintenance had been neglected lately along with everything else. Cin-Cin was overdue for treatment, and with so much enforced leisure she'd clearly had too much time to think. Tommy wanted Yasmin to give behavioral boosters to his increasingly restive whores, but so far her pose as a nervous, inexperienced medtech had allowed her to fob him off.

She cleared her throat and introduced David Senior, then led him to a table a few meters away. Old Anderson viewed Cin-Cin with narrow suspicion, but with his grandson seated in broad view of Campbell River's busy main wharf, he could hardly object.

"She's the daughter of one of the croupiers," said Yasmin, hoping she wasn't overplaying her innocence.

"Mmph. That Tor—he's your partner?"

"Oh, no. Just a friend."

"Nice enough fellow. Little... naive."

"Well...." Yasmin feigned hesitance. "He had some cognitive therapy, you know. I hear..." she leaned forward confidingly and lowered her voice. "I hear he used to be a gang member—violent, addicted. But he got treatment and turned his life around. He's a different person now."

"Ah. Hmm." Anderson clearly didn't know what to do with that. But Yasmin's tone invited confidence. He responded by leaning a little closer to her and speaking very quietly.

"Miz Paroo. I know this ship is tong-owned, and I hear they sell most anything. I'm looking for an seven millimeter scan-transparent automatic handgun."

Yasmin didn't have to fake surprise. She blinked and raised her eyebrows.

"That's a very restricted weapon," she said, making her tone doubtful and a bit disapproving. "Are you sure that's what you want? I mean, what do you want it for?" In fact, she could guess. A handgun that size was easy to conceal and it might stop even a bio-enhanced enforcer.

Beneath his sternness, the old man looked uncomfortable.

"I have a need, but I'm afraid I can't discuss it. You'd have to take my personal word of honor that I'd only use it in case of extreme necessity. Self defence, of course."

"Well..." Yasmin frowned unhappily, while suppressing glee. She couldn't have scripted this better. "Well... I could ask around...."

"You line it up and I'll pay you a commission," said Anderson.

"But how would I get it to you? I mean, I assume you don't want anyone to know..."

"No!" He looked alarmed, and no wonder. He could have his Guild citizenship revoked for trafficking restricted weapons.

"I think I have an idea...." she started, then a sudden wail, like a baby's cry, caught her attention. The kiwi was pawing at Cin-Cin, mewling. The girl tried to shush it, then gave the pet an exasperated swat. Yasmin saw young David glare. The kiwi bawled again, louder, and Cin-Cin scowled. She reached into a pocket, pulled out her phone, and said "Cocoa sleep."

The tiny koala stopped in mid-mewl and blinked, then swayed. It blinked again, collapsed and closed its eyes. Cin-Cin smiled and scooped it into her arms, stroking its back. Yasmin was just looking away when she heard young David's choked voice.

"You use neural controls?!"

"Well, yeah."

"That's inhumane!" The boy jumped to his feet, taut with indignation. Cin-Cin scowled up at him.

"Hey, they all come with them. I can't watch the little poop every minute, can I? I mean, I leave her in my cabin, she chews on things and pees and tries to climb the curtains. They sleep a lot anyway—it says so in the owner's manual."

"That's bent! How would you feel if..."

His grandfather interrupted in a commanding voice.

"David!"

The boy whirled, face flushed.

"It's not right, granddad! And it's banned under the Animal Welfare Treaty!"

Yasmin intervened before the battle could escalate. She touched Anderson's arm and spoke quietly.

"Let me talk to him."

Anderson hesitated, annoyance warring with embarrassment. Before he could make up his mind, Yasmin got up and steered the boy across the deck to the ridiculous bowsprit—a carved wooden statue of a woman leaning out over the water. When they were safely out of earshot, she spoke.

"David, she doesn't know any better."

"Any splutz ought to be able to see...!"

"And yelling at her won't make change her mind."

He vented an explosive sigh and shoved his hands in his pockets.

"Yeah, I guess I know that. I just... I just got mad. That's so mean! How would she feel if somebody did that to her?!"

"She doesn't understand," said Yasmin. "But I see you do. You seem very interested in animals. Are you studying biology?"

"Well... yes."

It was easy enough to draw David into a discussion of science. He got more and more animated as he described his ecostudies, and his detailed answers to Yasmin's questions impressed her very much. This boy didn't simply have a good memory, he had an excellent mind, already on the way to becoming disciplined. And judging from his outpouring, few people around him shared his interests. She decided to probe and beamed him one of her most winning smiles.

"I hope your parents appreciate what a gifted son they have."

David looked away.

"Yeah."

A hit.

"Brilliant people are this planet's most valuable resource," said Yasmin seriously. "Are you qualified for university fast track?"

The boy's face revealed desperate unhappiness.

"My parents don't want me to go."

"Oh. I thought...." She put on a puzzled expression. "I thought all the Cascadia Guilds were signatory to the Pacific Justice Pact."

"Uh... Well, yes." He looked puzzled.

"Well, then they have to take education seriously. After all, you're over ten, so you have the right to apply for alternate custody. And withholding education is grounds."

David looked stunned.

"Uh... Well, I never.... Um, I don't think...."

"I wouldn't encourage you to do that for a minute," she said hastily. "I was just thinking of that case a few years ago where a girl left her Guild—Miners, I think—to attend UBC. She applied for admission and alternate custody."

"Ummm.... did she get in?"

"Yes, she won the case. But the circumstances were unusual. I think she was a musical prodigy. I don't remember the details."

"Oh."

She let him contemplate that in silence for a minute. He'd be searching out the details of that decision on his phone before he got home, she bet.

"Do you think you'll be visiting the Empress again?"

"Pardon? Oh, no. I mean we don't come over very often..."

"That's too bad." Yasmin put on a disappointed frown. "I thought you might be company for Cin-Cin. There's nobody else near her age on the Empress, and I'm worried. She's bored and this ship... well, it's easy to find trouble. I know it's none of my business, but I thought a friendship with someone her own age might be good for her."

David's gaze flicked back towards the baby doll and the tips of his ears reddened. Ah ha, so he wasn't immune to those nipples or that perfume.

"Do you have a phone?" she inquired cautiously.

"Sure." David pulled a boxy Guild-issue phone from his

pocket. "It's only granddad living in the Stone Age."

"OK, here." Yasmin exchanged IDs. "Give me a call if you can come back over. Or..." She paused as if inspiration had struck. "I can book one of the ship's launches and take a day trip with Cin-Cin." She waved towards the gulf. "You could show us around, take us to some interesting marine spots."

"Sure!" His eyes glowed.

Perfect. And she had leverage with old Anderson now—she could force his cooperation if necessary.

Young David's apology to Cin-Cin held hints of his grandfather's stiff dignity, but overlain with a boyish sincerity that might have charmed the girl even if she wasn't being paid to like him. She smiled shyly up from under long lashes.

Yasmin was just about to sit down next to Mr. Anderson again, when she spotted bad news—Tommy Yip himself heading their way, his oily smile beaming straight at her. Today he wore a white Captain's uniform, amply decorated with gold braid and topped off with a visored cap. As he approached sunlight flashed off the sextant hanging from his belt. Yasmin felt a flash of disdain. She doubted Yip knew what to do with a sextant, assuming that the device wasn't a fake.

"Miz Paroo. Cin-Cin, my dear."

Cin-Cin notched her voice up half an octave.

"Hi, uncle Tommy."

"And this is...?"

Yasmin introduced the Andersons. The old man stood and greeted him with stony politeness.

"May I offer you a drink?"

"We're just leaving," said Anderson. "David..."

"Oh, so soon? We're opening in a few minutes, you know."

"Thank you, we had a tour."

"And did you like my Empress?"

"Beautiful ship," said Anderson, unbending just a fraction. "Very impressive."

"And this is a fine town. We'd like to make it a regular port of call."

Anderson didn't actually say "when hell freezes over," but his face conveyed it eloquently. He turned to his grandson. "Time to go.

We've got lumber to pick up."

"Let me see you off the ship...." began Yasmin, but Tommy intervened. He waved at Cin-Cin to escort the two Citizens, then turned to face Yasmin.

"Did you invite him here?" he asked, as soon as they were out of earshot. Yip's smile was still in place, but his blanched knuckles betrayed underlying tension, and there was a faint flush of sweat around his chubby brown neck.

"No, sir, he just turned up. He seemed interested in the ship, and you said to put out the welcome mat for important Citizens, so I had Tor show him around. I hope that's OK..."

"Pompous Guild bastards!"

Yip radiated anger. Yasmin met his glare with concerned sympathy.

"Your meeting didn't go well?"

"Uptight suspicious fuckers backed out on the cost-sharing contract. Somebody got to the Guild Council before I did and they weren't having any, didn't even look at the tourist numbers. Pissant shitheads! I've had enough of these armpit towns. I'm pulling out tomorrow. We'll head for Seattle, see if we can pick up some real trade."

Tomorrow!

Yasmin wrinkled her brow and looked worriedly at Tommy. He stood slightly below average height for a man, so she'd taken to wearing thin-soled shoes and now she slouched subtly to get an upward angle into his eyes.

"Mr. Yip... Sir, did you take your stress meds?"

"What? Yes. Why?"

"You just look.... Well, I'm sure it's nothing, but if you have time for a check-up..."

She saw him waver as business priorities battled with hypochondria.

"It would take half an hour to check your electrolyte balance, and give you a massage."

"All right. I'll see you ten minutes."

"Yes sir." She resisted the urge to salute. Tommy loved salutes, but it was too obvious.

The door to Sick Bay was a Victorian oak door with a large

brass doorknob and plaque, but inside the furnishings were entirely modern. The clinic held two beds and equipment to handle almost any emergency. Guild citizens under fifty rarely needed treatment for anything except injuries, since they'd received prenatal gene-screening and broad preventives during childhood, but older Zits with money to spend at the gaming tables were another matter. They wanted top notch medical support. And since the crew were mostly Guildless, they had enough chronic ailments to keep Yasmin busy a couple of hours a day. She had treated everything from migraine headaches to tooth decay.

She just had time to unfold the massage table, mix a medical tea, and set it to steep in a china pot before Tommy huffed in. She sat him down and started her routine health questions: How did he feel? Any shortness of breath? Indigestion? Stiff muscles? As usual, Yip loved talking about himself and he detailed every ache and pain. Then she had him strip to undershorts—a tedious process with all the authentic buttons and zippers in his outfit—and lie face down on the massage table.

Offering Tommy medical massages had been a calculated risk. Predictably, he'd demanded sex, but Yip had a critical crew shortage and he needed a medic. Even without dropping her ingenue role, she'd been able to refuse and make it stick. She slipped on vibra gloves, poured massage oil into her palm, then started with firm strokes along his fleshy back, allowing herself a tiny smile. Stupid ass. He analyzed every med she gave him, but he hadn't thought to test the massage oil, which she'd laced with a subtle hypnotic. The drug was detectable for up to six hours, but it was her own formulation and Tommy's off-the-rack diagnostic equipment was set to search for more obvious poisons and euphorics. That kind of oversight was why Yip had been stalled as a mid-level exec in the Kung Lok. If it hadn't been for heavy losses in the tong war he'd never have risen this high.

As she worked she talked soothingly, slowly inducing deep hypnosis until he began humming a pre-arranged tune. Then she asked the question that had been bothering her most.

"Why Seattle? And why now?"

"Can't run forever," muttered Yip. "Need allies. There's some Viet Ching down there—left Vancouver in the war, no tong to go back to. They need slots, I need firepower. And I gotta start making trafficking contacts again, grease the net. Lotsa demand, always lotsa demand, gotta bend some key players. If my sons were here... Damn flots kill my sons, nothing but daughters left and..."

He was whining now and Yasmin had heard this story too many times. She shushed him, thinking furiously. Damn him for courting the Viet Ching and damn him for wanting to leave. But how far could she maneuver Yip? He hated Campbell River—no suggestion to stay here would stick very long. And bending him in a major way could be dangerous.

She gave him a mild suggestion that he would feel happy and relaxed for the next two hours, then brought him out of it and spent another ten minutes working on muscle spasms and an old shoulder injury that triggered headaches. Afterward she sat him in a chair and offered him tea, which he carefully tested with the diagnoster he carried everywhere. Moron!

After he left, she stayed in Sick Bay, running a meds inventory while she considered her options. The David Andersons were her key to Cortes, she decided. The old man was playing straight into her hands, and the youngster might be even more useful. An intelligent boy could hardly help but be curious about mysterious new neighbors. He could nose around without arousing suspicion.

She had no doubts now about who those neighbors were. She'd identified the Chinese medic as Amerigo Lau, on leave from a tong-run clinic in Hong Kong. Even better, she'd finally ID'd "Toni" as Dr. Antonia Almiramez, former hotshot researcher in behavioral neuromodification who had dropped out of sight several years before Yasmin was captured by the VC. She must have gone into the training business. So who was she working for? Choi? And was she working for him willingly? She might even be a potential ally. Certainly Yasmin's future plans had room for a top therapist with the skills to enhance humans instead of maim them.

Whatever Almiramez was doing in that cabin, she'd been at it for months. Still, that made sense. Choi's enforcer was likely a messy piece of work—nothing worse than a tool trained by an amateur. Could she be waiting for Choi? If he was still alive, what would the old bastard be up to? Enhanced rejuvenation? He had to be ninety at the very least, but with good genes and assuming he'd kept up medical treatments he could live another twenty, even thirty years.

Whatever was happening, Yasmin needed to stay here in Campbell River. She could jump ship, but as a Guildless drifter she'd risked being escorted out of town. So she needed the ship. And if she couldn't persuade Tommy to stay, she would have to find another way to make sure he didn't leave.

Time for Tor to prove his skills with steam engines.

# 10

## August 10

Simon woke to the touch of cool snakes against his scalp—optic cables leading from suction cups on his skull to a netset on the floor. He quelled an instinctive rush of fear and sat up, detaching them.

His room. He was in his bedroom in the cabin. He looked around, soaking it in.

The walls were tongue and groove wood, faded with age to a dull gray-brown but still smelling very faintly of cedar. Thick new curtains hung at the window, in a shifting pattern of primary colors. On the far wall a large scale satellite photo showed Cortes Island in natural color. Tacked up around it were pix that Klale had taken—Dr. Lau playing his dulcimer; Toni savagely whacking a post with a sledgehammer; David with purple-stained fingers eating salal berries. A big paper calendar hung nearby with colored pens dangling from strings below it.

He rolled to his feet and went to look. Each night before bed he crossed off the old day, so today was 10 August 2109. There were notes written in, too, and stars beside the nights he'd slept naturally without a nightmare (three in a row last week). Toni's notes were briskly penned in blue, Klale's were sloppy splashes of color, and Lau sometimes used Chinese characters. They often wrote on the calendar at night when they checked on Simon. Today's box said "Forecast: sunshine" in Chinese, then "special dessert surprise!" in Klale's loopy scrawl.

He turned back to his bed, coiling the optic cables in his hand, then saw a note flashing on the netset screen by the futon: "Today is Mary's visit."

Sick fear welled up in his gut and he dropped to his knees struggling for control before his restraint triggered. Mary Smarch was coming as a representative of his parole committee. He had killed Citizens. They would want vengeance.

"She'll punish you," came a gloating whisper.

He clapped his hands over his ears and kneeled for long moments before he could ease his trembling. His hands fumbled the sheets as he made the bed. He stopped in the kitchen to drink juice and then went out to dance on the low platform he'd helped Toni and Miz Anderson build. It was five meters by five—small for a dance floor, but sturdy and a far better surface than grass. The familiar task of mopping dew off the low-friction laminate helped calm him, then he began with tai chi, moving into dance when he felt centered. Sometimes Dr. Lau joined him for tai chi, but this morning he only saw Lau's face in the kitchen window. He stayed with familiar routines and danced well, but a tiny thread of fear would not stop worming in his gut.

After showering he picked out clothes from his closet, stroking his favorite fabrics first, then selecting a practical blue t-shirt and a yellow cotton head scarf. When he looked in the mirror, he blurred his eyes to erase the ugly tool face, but he could still see how brown the sun was turning his skin. It was much darker than Toni's now, making his eyes and teeth look very white.

Klale had left early to catch a low tide in Smelt Bay where her community service shift was husbanding clam beds. Simon ate breakfast with Dr. Lau, then took Mary's netset out to the porch and ran a quick review of the last 24 hours of bird nest surveillance. He expected David to stop by at seven-thirty, but it was almost eight when the boy rushed up to the porch, pink-faced and panting.

"Sorry, I can't stop or I'll be late for school. I was talking to someone on the phone and I ran out of time. Can we do this later?"

He seemed distracted, and started to leave even before Simon said yes. Then abruptly he turned back.

"Simon..." He looked around, then stepped closer and lowered his voice. "Uh, do you know much about girls? Real girls, I mean, not like my sister... You know, more like, well Klale, right?"

Simon found himself with his mouth open and no idea what to say. Girls? David's sister wasn't a real girl? Klale?

"Sorry, I didn't mean to be too personal. It's just, um, you're pretty much my best friend and, um...."

The boy trailed off into an embarrassed shrug. Simon barely noticed, transfixed by a flare of sudden delight that boiled in his chest and rose into his throat. Friend? David had called him "best friend?" He was trying desperately to think of something to say when David's phone beeped.

"Sludge! Gotta go! We'll talk later, OK?"

David bolted for the bus, waving over his shoulder, and leaving Simon in a welter of delight and perplexity.

He was almost grateful for this latest mystery, since it gave him something to ponder while he worked on the roof with Blue Anderson. Toni had bought new roofing a month ago, but when they started ripping off old tiles they discovered rot in the ancient plywood sheathing, so they were replacing everything down to the rafters with treated bias hempboard. The cabin had been under tarps for the four days it took to get twenty sheets of hempboard shipped from Campbell River, and Blue wanted to get the job finished before she left for her Guild shift. Simon knew that David's mother felt uncomfortable near him, so he kept his distance, passing up tools and heavy sheets from the ground as she needed them. Once she had the first couple of boards down, the job went quickly.

A little after ten Lau left on his velo for a shift at the Island Clinic and Toni joined them on the roof in her paint-splattered work clothes, blinking and sipping at a lidded mug of coffee which she set down on top of the chimney.

"It evades me," she growled, "why anybody would build a house with solid log walls. They're murder to run services through and gloomy as hell inside, and there's not even a flat wall you can paint."

"Actually it makes sense in this climate." Blue spoke around a mouthful of nails. "Western red cedar is naturally resistant to rot, it's a good insulator, and if you don't have plaster walls you can leave the cabin unheated without worrying about mildew. This cabin's holding up pretty well for a hundred and fifty years of neglect—even made it through the earthquake fine."

"Huh." Toni didn't sound convinced.

The two women worked together smoothly until eleven, when Mary Smarch drove up in a boxy little electric sharecar, and Simon suppressed a rush of fear.

She climbed out of the vehicle looking just as Simon remembered her—a plump Native woman in her sixties who'd let her hair and face age naturally. Yet seeing her here gave Simon a small shock as he realized that she was real. Simon had seen Mary as often as twice a week for more than a decade in the KlonDyke bar, but those memories felt like shadows of another world. Nobody Downtown dared approach a bioaltered enforcer or look one in the eyes, and Blade, in turn, had known faces only as visual datapoints for Choi's blackmail business. He had not seen people.

Reviewing Choi's old records on Mary, Simon knew that she had been born in 2045 in Teslin, a small town just north of the 60th parallel. Hardbooks on Mary's shelves gave the history of her Tlingit ancestors who had lived near Teslin Lake for ten thousand years—a stretch of time he couldn't imagine. The Smarch family was influential, with connections throughout Cascadia, but he had few details on Mary's early life—only her certification as a lay mediator by the North American Native Council and a short marriage. After she moved to Vancouver in '73 she joined Sisters' Residential Co-op and SisOpp Ventures, helped found the Downtown Residents Association, and became an advisor to the Vancouver Council of Guilds. She lived modestly on her salary as Manager of the KlonDyke bar, and had given most of an inheritance from her grandmother to charity.

Choi had rated her a poor blackmail target. Simon, he realized uneasily, didn't know her at all.

Mary called good morning to the workers on the roof as she walked around the cabin, lugging a perforated carrier box, which she opened on the back porch. A black cat poked its head from the carrier and stepped out cautiously. Toni, climbing down the ladder, groaned. Mary grinned.

"Pauline Johnson will be staying with you until the new KlonDyke is built. I couldn't keep her around the Co-op—she keeps getting out of my apartment and scaring the chickens. So I got a temporary pet permit from the Island Council and a wildlife alert collar. She sure doesn't like it... do you sweetie?"

The cat ignored Mary's attempt to pat her, and padded straight over to strop Toni's legs. Toni glowered and pushed the cat away with her foot. Mary laughed. Simon watched, fascinated in spite of himself. When Pauline Johnson sniffed at his feet, he bent down and touched her gingerly. He'd never stroked cat fur before. It felt silky and warm.

Mary hugged Toni. "I brought some things from your apartment." She looked at Toni closely and frowned. "You're so thin. I thought Rigo's cooking would fatten you up."

"Would you like coffee?"

"No thanks. First things first."

Then they were both looking at Simon. He fled inside himself, into the cold void of Blade.

Mary took Blade down to the beach. He'd expected Toni or Dr. Lau to accompany them, but Mary walked alone, carrying a big cloth coat over one arm. The tide was very low, revealing rocks coated with barnacles the color of old teeth, jet black mussels and lime green sea lettuce. When they got there, Mary put on the coat, which was decorated with images of birds in red and black and white applique, embroidery, and sewn on shells. A large eagle spread its wings across her back. She gestured at him to sit next to her on a log in the breezy sunshine, then she took his hand in hers and stroked it. Her broad, warm palms felt smooth with age and the backs of her hands were wrinkled, like the creases on her brown face. Her touch drew Simon out from hiding, out into the sound of surf and wind and the briny smell of low tide. They sat in silence for long minutes, then she surprised him by reaching up and caressing his face, snaring him with her dark eyes. She wore a bone medallion on a leather thong around her neck. Simon recognized it from the past.

Eventually she spoke softly.

"I'm here alone speaking for the parole committee because you know me and I think you will believe me."

Simon tried to flinch away, but she reached out and laid a warm hand against his face. Fear writhed in his gut.

"I need your full attention, Simon. Don't leave me." She waited before dropping her hand to his shoulder.

"Now, I know you can't talk about this without being frightened, maybe angry. So Toni gave me the code and I'm turning off your neural override. OK?"

She waited until he gave a little, startled nod. When she reached for her phone he felt nothing, but he heard a chime.

A papery voice rustled at his ear.

"You can kill her."

No!

"She has the codes. She can punish you...."

Fear rose inside Simon. Mary's voice seemed to echo through a long tunnel and he had trouble focusing on her words.

"Now I'm going to explain the terms of your parole to be very sure you understand them. You are not a Guild Citizen, Simon, but you committed a violent crime against Citizens so you've come under the jurisdiction of the Vancouver Council of Guilds, which acts under provisions of the North Pacific Criminal Justice Pact. You are charged with killing Harbour Patrol Officers Baljit Dhillon, Neil McCaskill, Adam Fung and Nasir Bahi, and assaulting Citizen Rill Clarke on October 28, 2108.

She was watching him steadily. He pulled his eyes away and studied the rounded stones on the beach, barely able to breathe.

"Normally pre-sentencing release isn't granted for murder, but your father petitioned the Court for a medical parole until you are mentally competent to stand trial."

"There are seven people on your parole committee. Five are relatives of your victims. And three of us are acting as your personal guarantors: myself, your father, and Ron McCaskill. It's very compassionate of Ron to stand for you after you killed his grandson, but he knows you are a victim, too, and he feels he failed you as a child when you needed his protection. We have given our personal pledges for your conduct, and if you commit another crime we all face possible felony charges." She paused.

"Are you with me so far?"

Simon nodded.

"Do you understand what the parole committee has sent me here for?"

"Vengeance," he whispered.

"No! No, Simon, this is not about vengeance, it's about responsibility. And remorse. And rehabilitation."

"Blade killed, he must pay."

"YOU are Blade, Simon. You must accept that part of you."

"Tools are killers. They cannot be changed."

"You are a free person and you can choose to change."

Simon kept his voice toneless and stared at the beach.

"There was a time. Blade delivered Choi's note that if a man could not pay in one hour his child must die. Choi thought the man had sources of money but he had none. After one hour Blade took the baby from its mother and beat it against the wall."

Gulls shrieked into the silence between them. Then Mary spoke softly, sadly. "If you were the court, what would you do?"

"Kill Blade."

"Killing you would not bring back the dead."

"Blade wouldn't kill again."

"But it's wrong, Simon. Killing is always wrong. Always. Listen to me."

She squeezed his hand tightly, trying to draw his eyes.

"If you burn down an ugly house without healing the hearts of the people who built it, they'll build another house just as ugly. Healing is slow. But it's the only way to build a better world."

Her voice resonated with passion and certainty.

"All things and all people are a part of the whole. Your death would diminish all of us. Your healing will enrich all of us."

Simon said nothing. Mary waited a long time, then shifted on the log.

"Enough parole talk for now. I wanted to ask you something else. Can you tell me about your father?"

The query took him off guard.

"About... Dr. Lau?"

"Yes. You live with him. Tell me what you think about him. As a person."

Simon groped.

"Dr. Lau is intelligent and a capable medic.... He plays music and sings and cooks very well. He's handsome. He wears beautiful clothes. He is respected and people like him."

"So why won't you talk to him?"

Simon swallowed. Words rose, like tar in his mouth. He spat them out.

"His son shames him. His son makes him vomit!" A pause, then a whisper. "Toni didn't vomit, but she got very angry."

Mary's voice was steady and calm.

"When did he vomit?"

"When he watched Choi's training records. When he saw his son's failure."

She let a silence fall before she spoke again.

"Simon, Choi must have taught you about interrogation. Did he?"

"Yes."

"Tell me, how many people can withstand expert torture?"

"None."

"How many children.... How many boys like David could resist the kind of brutality Choi used on you?"

A pulse throbbed in Simon's throat, and he felt suddenly dizzy.

"How many, Simon?"

David was so small. Sometimes he seemed as fragile as a spider web.

"None," he whispered.

"Rigo knows that, dear. He was crying for you. He vomited because of what Choi did, not because of you."

Simon felt vertigo. Mary's hand tightened on his.

"Your father loves you Simon."

The scream rose suddenly, from nowhere.

"He'll leave me!" Simon bolted from the log and turned on her, screaming. "He'll leave me! He'll go away to Hong Kong! He'll leave me!"

Mary just sat and watched him with that old gnarled face and said nothing. Simon paced in urgent circles, struggling with the rage that thrummed a rising chord in his chest. Abruptly he remembered something he'd seen David do. He reached down for a weather-rounded rock, spun and threw it far across the beach into the water. He picked up another heavier one and another, heaving stones until his arm ached and the howling rage eased. Then he sank back on the log and wrapped his arms around his knees. Mary touched his shoulder very gently and spoke.

"You have all of us now, dear. Toni. Myself. Ron. Klale. And your father. You have five people to keep you safe."

Choi's voice: "She's lying."

"You're lying," whispered Simon.

"No," said Mary. She touched his cheek with gentle fingers. "I give you the oath of my heart. I will stand by you. And..." She rummaged in a pocket. "I brought you a gift. Here. Hold out your hand."

He had to unwind his arms and sit up. A leather thong coiled in his palm, then silver flashed—an engraved disk.

"This is a talisman, made by my cousin who's a silversmith. On the front is a Crow. That's the symbol of my clan. And on the back is a Tlingit healer performing a medicine ceremony. There isn't another talisman in the world like this. My cousin sang your name as she shaped the disc and etched the design. When your heart is sad, hold this and feel our love."

Simon turned it over in his hands. The etched healer stood in crane position and the shiny disc sat warm in his palm—warm from Mary's body. He closed his fingers and clutched it tightly.

After lunch Mary left for a meeting with the Island Council and Simon helped again on the roof. Blue and Toni, both wearing wide-brimmed sun hats, had finished the sheathing and were nailing down strips of composite tile. It was simple work and Simon fell into the rhythm of it under the hot sun. He wore a cotton cloth knotted on his head, but sweat still ran down his face and leaked salty into his mouth. He hammered with his right hand. Dr. Lau had removed the bandage from his left, but his broken fingers had healed stiff and clumsy.

At three he went down to the yard for his scheduled workout. Soon after, Klale arrived home in a filthy "Weed Warriors" t-shirt, reeking of tidal mud flats, and she jumped up on stage with him, mimicking his moves. He mimicked her back, and they got sillier and sillier until Klale was laughing too hard to dance and Simon had to fall down and roll with silent giggles.

They both needed showers and they bumped into each other on the upstairs landing, carrying towels. Before Simon could react, Klale said "The water table's low. Let's share."

It seemed sensible but the shower stall was very small for two. They wet themselves down, then turned off the water and soaped.

Simon found himself fascinated by the smooth slickness of Klale's skin pressing against his. Then she stood up on her toes and kissed him.

Memories flooded back. Klale's hot mouth in a cold, dark, freighter hold. Klale's body pressed against him on a warm bed, her hands playing a Bach fugue along his rib cage. He felt excited. Confused. Dizzy with the delight of touching so much, being so close. He wrapped his arms around her.

"Klale!"

Toni's angry voice. Simon pulled back, banging his shoulder on the shower nozzle. Klale turned around.

"Toni, we're just..."

"No, you're not. Get out of there now! Simon, finish your shower. I'll talk to you later."

Her tone of command sent him automatically for the taps and he sluiced off, but beneath the practiced motions his mind raced in confusion. Why was Toni angry? What had he done wrong? Under the noise of the shower he heard voices in heated discussion, but he could not make out the words.

Choi's voice whispered: "Fool. You're not one of them. You're a tool. Or a pet. They'll use you and discard you."

Fear clutched at Simon, then his hand brushed the wet leather thong, heavy around his neck. He clutched his silver pendant.

"Go away! Go away!"

Klale passed him in the hall, wrapped in a wet towel, and gave a forced smile, but she said nothing and neither did Toni. Then Dr. Lau came home with Mary, and Simon shelled peas from the Anderson garden and set the table for dinner. Lau opened a bottle of Okanagan Riesling and poured glasses for all of them, then passed around crackers and smoked salmon that Mary had brought.

While Lau and Klale cooked, Simon sat in the corner at the kitchen table, hulling strawberries and trying to puzzle out the meanings beneath the words and gestures around him. In trying to research touching rules he'd found thousands of studies analyzing touch according to power, status, age, gender, relationship, propinquity, culture, setting and many more factors, but the papers he'd read were contradictory and inconsistent with his observations. As Simon watched, Klale slapped Dr. Lau with a dish towel. He lunged over and yanked her hair. Lau was an unrelated older male, so Klale should keep a formal distance according to Simon's reading, but she touched Lau often, slapping his shoulder or giving him hugs. And he touched her back, even tickling her sometimes. And yet Simon didn't think Klale showered with Lau...

The rules seemed different for David, too. He didn't initiate touch with the others, and they rarely touched him. Mary touched everybody, most often on the arm or hand, but also on the leg or head. She was careful with Simon, never touching unless she was sure he saw her coming, but she touched him too. And Mary seemed to affect people strongly—their faces lit up when she touched them, even Toni, who Simon found the most complex. Toni touched others when Simon was watching, but when she thought he didn't notice she would pull away. And she didn't like to touch Dr. Lau—only when necessary. But sometimes, especially after his nightmares, she would stroke Simon's face and cup his cheek in her soft palm.

Did it mean she loved him? Or did it mean she owned him?

Dinner was almost ready when a rap sounded at the back door, and Ethan Anderson stepped in. He said hello to everyone and shook hands with Mary, then cleared his throat and spoke awkwardly.

"I just came to say: don't take my father to represent the whole Anderson family."

"Oh!" Klale turned to Mary. "I meant to ask: how did the council meeting go today?"

"Well..." Mary looked rueful. "Mixed. My residency permit was sustained, but things got ruptive, and I'm afraid there were hard feelings afterwards."

"What she means," said Ethan, "is my father shouted and threatened and then stomped out of the meeting with a few of his cronies. Look, I really want to say I'm sorry, but I'm not going to start apologizing for my Dad. I mean, where would it ever stop?"

Mary gave him a warm smile.

"He's afraid of Simon and he's worried for his grandson. It's understandable."

Ethan nodded, but didn't look directly at Simon. David's parents rarely did.

"And he's used to getting his way around here. Sometimes I

wish I'd pulled up stakes and left years ago. Never mind. You spoke very well, Miz Smarch, and Dr. Lau and Miz Renhardt have made a good impression on the island. I don't think there was really any danger."

"Stay for dinner?" offered Lau.

"Oh, no thanks. We've got dinner cooking at home. Just wanted to catch you when I had a moment."

"That reminds me," Mary said after he left. "Did you know that the Empress of Vancouver is tied up in Campbell River?"

Simon snapped alert.

"The Kung Lok casino ship?" asked Toni. Mary nodded.

"I heard that down at the Clinic," said Lau. "Lots of locals are going over to see it. It's quite the tourist attraction."

"Well, I'd suggest you stay well away. There's an old acquaintance of ours on board—Tommy Yip."

"So he survived the tong war," said Toni grimly.

"And rose in the ranks. He's a senior exec now, and he's running the Empress."

"Scum floats to the top," observed Klale.

Mary looked at her seriously.

"I wanted to remind you that Yip is dangerous. It's important he doesn't get wind of Toni. Or, especially, Simon."

"Everyone on the island must know he's here by now. It's an open secret," said Toni unhappily.

"People around here know, but they don't know much, and Rigo and I keep spreading misinformation," said Klale with a mischievous twinkle. "Also, we've tried to make it a kind of an insider conspiracy—like islanders can know but outsiders can't. I think it's working."

Dr. Lau looked over at Toni, frowning. "I remember Tommy Yip, but I didn't know he had a grudge against you."

"Mmm." Toni shrugged. "Well, I might have called him a 'shit-licking pimp.' Loudly. In a crowded room." Behind Toni, Klale grinned. "But we'd better be extra careful to keep Simon hidden. Yip only knows him as a deaf-mute enforcer, but if he heard we were working on him, he'd start to wonder."

"So," added Mary firmly, "All of you stay away from the bright lights of Campbell River until the ship leaves."

Rigo and Klale nodded and Toni muttered very dryly: "However will I manage?"

As they ate around the dining room table, the cabin seemed very full although there was only one more person than usual. Mary gave a dinner blessing, then she raised her glass and offered a toast to the KlonDyke bar, "which is being demolished even as we speak." Toni drank, but her face was shadowed, and she said little during dinner while the others shared funny stories.

Later, Simon stepped out to the porch to watch the last turquoise glow of sunset above the trees and nearly tripped over Dr. Lau's tall cavalier boots standing beside the back door. They needed cleaning and oiling, he remembered Lau saying. Simon peeked back into the living room where the others were talking, then went quietly to the pantry and took out a cloth and the leather oil.


At two-thirty a.m., Simon woke in his dark bedroom to a flashing light from his netset. He had modified the sleepware to wake him. He padded into the hall and listened at the bedroom doors for deep, regular breaths, then moved very cautiously downstairs. By screwing down the risers and then mapping the remaining creaks, he'd made it possible to descend almost without noise. Mary, asleep on the fold-out couch in the living room, snored softly.

The netset in his room had its uplink transmitters disabled, but Mary's old cabin set didn't. He carried it silently into the dark kitchen, and used his sense of touch to jack in....

The familiar mahogany desk blinked into existence before Choi. He slid swiftly into his routine, uplinking to the market indexes...

WHEEP! WHEEP!

The warning caught Choi by surprise. He unlinked fast and slammed his defenses in place before checking the security log. The Cortes node was being probed by a high level search. Worse, there was evidence of previous probes. He could only hope he'd reacted fast enough to avoid a full backtrace to Mary's ID.

Acting on a hunch, he set up a millisecond uplink and blipped a tracer via the nearest weather satellite. A minute later another microlink returned paydirt—an active path between the Cortes node and the S.S. Empress of Vancouver. It could be coincidence, but Choi's experience in blackmail had taught him the rarity of coincidence.

Most inconvenient. He wanted to set a ferret on Mary's phone to see if he could retrieve the neural restraint override code Toni had given her. But he couldn't risk further uplink activity from this ID right now. In the morning Simon would rediscover the security breach and inform the others, then establish a different communications route. But the longer he waited, the higher the odds that Mary would purge the restraint code from her phone, or that Toni would change it again.

He felt a sharp wave of fury, but fought it down. Anger was a waste of time. Only vengeance counted. Meanwhile, he had local surveillance logs to review. And his bugs had caught several interesting conversations from yesterday.

Toni: Klale, your behavior is inappropriate!

Klale: Why? He's not a kid, he's a 31-year-old man!

Toni: He's a psychiatric patient under my care! And emotionally, he is a child. A vulnerable child. You're exploiting him.

Klale: I am not! I care for him. And he wants to be touched.

Toni: Klale for christsakes!... You can't have an adult relationship with Simon. The most you'll get from him is an adolescent crush. He is not legally or cognitively or ethically capable of making his own decisions. Don't you dare start making them for him!

Later, from the kitchen monitor:

Lau: Would you please talk to Toni? She's obviously ill, but whatever the problem is she refuses to tell either of us. Damn it, Mary, she's worse than Simon! I'm supposed to be her colleague and she treats me like the enemy!

Smarch: Try to be patient with her Rigo.

Lau: I've tried! But it's no wonder Simon won't trust me when she doesn't trust me!

Smarch: She's hurting terribly, I can see that. I'll ask her what's wrong, but I'm afraid I won't get an answer until she's ready.

Lau: She better get ready. Soon.

Only of marginal interest, except to confirm that Lau had still not diagnosed Toni's ulcerative colon. She was most adept at distracting his attention by annoying him. Choi searched for references to Simon and found that Mary Smarch and Toni had talked on the verandah after dinner.

Smarch: You were right about Simon needing an outsider to talk to, but that was one wild ride! He changes so fast! One minute I felt a torrent of emotion pouring from him, the next minute it was like talking to stone. No wonder you're tired, dear. After an hour with him I felt like I'd swum a rapid.

Toni: What did he say?

Choi skimmed her answer, noting only that it was unusually factual and precise for an anecdotal account. He slowed again.

Toni: Have you reported to the parole committee?

Smarch: Not yet, but you don't need to worry. I'm delighted at his progress. He still has a very long journey ahead, but you've put his feet on the path. You're doing a wonderful job, dear.

(silence)

Smarch: We cleaned out your apartment. What do you want me to do with the rest of your things?

Toni: Give them away.

Smarch: No. I won't. You're not thinking straight. What's wrong? (a long silence) Toni... Please promise you'll tell me when you're ready, all right?

Toni: All right.

Inconclusive, all of it, except for the implication that Smarch and Almiramez had planned Smarch's conversation with Simon—and Choi had no record of it. He had been tapping the team meetings his housemates held after he went to bed and that plan had not been mentioned. Did Almiramez suspect his taps? Had she found a method of messaging around him? He would have to search all the Island phone logs carefully.... yet another thing he couldn't do without an uplink.

He found himself tapping the polished mahogany desk in front of him. The impact of his fingernails made no sound in the virtual office. In the real room the rapping of Choi's long nails had echoed along the polished hardwood and off the ricepaper screens, a rhythmic counterpoint to Simon's screams. And the other, older screams. Choi had had tools before Simon.

Simon found himself breathing fast as the walls of his nightmares closed in. Frightened, he rose from the chair, grabbing for his headset, then his eyes fell on the carved lattice windows leading into the bamboo garden. In the real office there had been a blank wall there. Toni's words echoed in his memory: "You could get up from behind that desk and walk into the garden."

In the sim he circled the desk and moved in silent strides across the room, his feet remembering the cold, hard feel of the floor he'd scrubbed and polished so many times. He reached for the lattice windows and pulled them open....

Mountains lay at his feet—row after row of blue peaks stretching out to the horizon. He stood on a bare rock outcrop, a sheer cliff before him and wind-twisted pine trees behind. He'd hiked up here one astonishing day, from Buntzen Lake to the summit of Mount Beautiful. As he watched, he heard a whisky jack screech, then he spotted the graceful soaring glide of an eagle rising on the thermals.

He sat watching until the chime of his timer brought him back to the dark kitchen.

# 11

## September 1

An eagle soared high in the afternoon sunshine over Cape Mudge, and Yasmin leaned over the stern of the steam launch to watch it, then dropped her gaze to the water where a smooth white wake cleaved the randomized chop of blue waves. She turned to look forward, and wind whipped her hair as she glimpsed a white flash in the distance—the upper decks of the Empress coming into view as the launch rounded the south tip of Quadra Island. The big launch handled the waves smoothly and quietly. Tor sat at the helm, steering it with a wide, delighted grin. Even Cin-Cin, sprawled in a recliner chair in the cabin with the kiwi in her lap, had an excited flush on her pouty face.

A perfect day, thought Yasmin. The trip to Cortes couldn't have gone better. They'd borrowed one of the Empress's two launches, its biogas-fired steam engines making a quick half hour trip of the twenty-five kilometer crossing. David had rushed up to the launch hastily, a nervous backward glance over his shoulder confirming her hunch that he hadn't told his family about this trip. With luck they wouldn't find out. Not wanting to be seen at the Anderson's private dock, Yasmin had picked David up at a decrepit float tied to old concrete pilings in Cortes Bay.

A pair of small, uninhabited islands in the strait just south of Cortes had proved an ideal, discreet spot for her to work. She smiled satisfaction at the memory of David—so sweet and refreshing after the damaged goods she'd been forced to deal with for years. Boys like this were exactly the genetic material needed to build a better human race. He'd been easy to open up with a combination of hypnosis and anti-inhibitors, and he'd provided a jackpot of data, including some very unexpected insights about Choi's slave, Simon, who turned out to be anything but the simple, mindless tool he resembled. Devious old Choi had camouflaged his data shark as an enforcer—a move that was either completely mad or brilliantly subtle; Yasmin still hadn't decided which.

Originally she'd planned to target Dr. Almiramez, but Yasmin now knew that Simon was the key. If she abducted Simon, Almiramez would follow. Moreover, if she took Almiramez, she'd be leaving an angry, intelligent bio-enhanced killer loose to follow her—something she didn't care to risk. Capturing him wasn't a task to underestimate, but she had the element of surprise, and the extraordinary fact of his friendship with David made it possible to bait a trap.

Briefly she wondered again what Almiramez was up to. The sentimental bullshit she'd peddled to Mary Smarch and the island residents was a cover, of course. Was she working for Choi, or did she have her own uses for Simon? Yasmin wanted Almiramez, too, of course. Although it would take a while to gain her cooperation, she'd be an invaluable asset in Yasmin's new lab. But that was for the future.

As for the present, she'd finished David's session with subliminal encouragement to resent and distrust his parents, and hypnotic triggers that would allow her to plant suggestions via phone. She didn't bother reinforcing his interest in Cin-Cin—it wasn't necessary.

The bow sank as Tor reduced speed, then the launch bobbed up as their own wake overtook them. Tor tossed bumpers over the right side of the boat and steered it alongside the enormous white bulk of the Empress. Yasmin smiled in satisfaction. The ship had now been tied up in Campbell River for almost two weeks, waiting for replacement parts for the engine.

The faulty parts had been an unexpectedly clever idea of Tor's. In reading through the engineering logs, he'd noticed that critically fatigued water injectors had been replaced last year. Acting on a hunch, he'd gone down and searched the Chief Engineer's office. The Chief had fled the ship after the tong war, but he'd been a pack rat, and sure enough, he'd kept the broken parts. And all three crew members who had participated in the engine room overhaul eighteen months ago had also deserted, so when Tor deleted their log entries, no one knew better.

Yasmin had helped Tor distract the on-duty crewman one night while he replaced new injectors with the old faulty ones. Then she'd blanked his conscious memory and placed a suggestion to check the injectors, so that he could discover the dangerous parts with unfeigned dismay. Tommy Yip had been furious, but since almost every component in the Empress's engine rooms was custom-built, he had no choice but to wait for replacements to be fabricated and shipped from Britain.

As the steam launch bumped gently against the Empress, Yasmin got up and walked to the launch's bow to snare a cable hanging from davits over the side of the big ship. She grabbed the thick cable and lifted its heavy shackle into a ring bolt mounted in the deck. Tor had left the helm to secure the rear cable. He checked both cables and shackles, then returned to the pilot's seat, shut down the engine and remote-activated the davits. Five stories above them a motor whirred to life, cables pulled slowly taut and the launch began to lift from the water.

Preoccupied with making plans for Simon's capture, Yasmin didn't notice two men lounging against the rail on the Promenade Deck until the launch settled into its cradle and the whole contraption slid across onto the deck. When they straightened and walked over to intercept her, Yasmin felt a nasty shock of recognition.

Identical black ferret eyes glittered over high cheekbones and identical lank black hair fell to shoulders left bare by identical black muscle shirts. Thirty years ago monozygotic twins had been popular—reaching almost forty percent of births before the fad subsided—and the Nguyen brothers, Kicks and Fix, were an unsavory souvenir. They'd risen fast in the Viet Ching, genuinely Vietnamese by ancestry and savage even by tong standards. They looked like a couple of scrawny, luckless roamers, but they had turboed reflexes and a flair for brutality, and Yasmin had discovered to her cost that they were not stupid. Damn Tommy Yip. These must be the Viet Ching he mentioned and they had evidently decided to travel here from Seattle, rather than wait for the ship's repairs.

The twins stood beside the steam launch, casually clenching and unclenching their knuckles to make their demonic skin art writhe. Their eyes were fixed on Tor, so Yasmin squeezed his shoulder and stepped off the launch first. A twin accosted her.

"You the medic?"

"Yes."

"We hear you worked in a Downtown clinic, that right?"

Yasmin feigned indignation.

"Who are you?"

"Which clinic?"

"The Davie," she said.

"Yeah? Well, that's real interesting. Because there weren't ever no 'Yasmin Paroo' working at that clinic." Fix—she recognized him now by the very faint pull of scar tissue on the left side of his mouth—moved closer, staring aggressively into her eyes. He was shorter than Yasmin, but radiated menace. Yasmin stepped back, feigning surprise and alarm.

Kicks had his eyes on Tor. "There wasn't no 'Tor Arnnson,' neither. Nobody looking like you two."

Tor tensed, ready to fight, but Yasmin gave him a tiny head shake. The twins hadn't recognized them, so best to bluff.

Fix stepped forward again, mashing Yasmin against the launch. His breath stank, and she felt his penis stiffening against her.

"You feel like changing your story, Miz Medic?"

"Hey, look..." She let her voice crack, then stiffen with resolve. "Look, I don't know who you are, but I report to the boss. Tommy Yip. I'll talk to him, not you."

For two long breaths Fix kept staring in her eyes, then he glanced at his brother and stepped back. Good, they were new here, not willing to step on Yip's toes. So far. Kicks made a mock bow and gestured along the deck.

"OK, Miz Medic, let's all go talk to Mr. Yip."

The hint of disdain in the way he said "Mr. Yip" caught Yasmin's ear. These two wouldn't like the pudgy, vacillating Tommy. And Tommy wouldn't be able to control them. Yip had made another mistake, and a very big one. The Nguyens had only been reliable—just barely—because their Viet Ching bosses had implanted explosive "fish hooks" at the base of their skulls. The hooks were undoubtedly still in place, as hers was, but the trigger codes were probably lost. Certainly Tommy wouldn't have them. Damn Yip for a moron!

As they started along the deck, Cin-Cin tried to slip away,

but Kicks stepped back and grabbed her, ignoring her squeals of protest. Damn! Cin-Cin was a liability—she hadn't heard Yasmin's interrogation of David, but she'd seen enough today to raise questions. They marched in tense silence down one level and through passageways; a parade that attracted speculative looks.

Polished wood and brass gleamed in the Captain's office, and oil paintings of ships crowded the wood-paneled walls. The room was four times as large as Yasmin and Tor's crew cabin but still very small, and cluttered with Yip's Victorian desk, a glass-fronted bookcase, leather armchairs, and an upholstered settee by the window. With three people seated in front of the desk and the Nguyen twins standing at the door, it felt crammed.

Tommy, wearing his Captain's uniform again, greeted them with an unctuous smile which faded to a suspicious squint as Fix barked accusations at Yasmin and she admitted that she had never worked at the Davie Clinic. She had worked in a massage parlor next door, she told Tommy. In the chaos after an angry mob set fire to the clinic, she'd stumbled across a dead lab tech and stolen her ID, then taken it to a data shark and had the gene scan overwritten. She gave the story her best delivery, knowing it would be impossible to verify since a Guildless rub in Downtown would have no net records and the massage parlor had burned with the clinic. Fix asked the name of the data shark. She gave a name she'd heard and held her breath—for all she knew the man had died in the riots—but Fix merely grunted.

Yip looked furious.

"You're telling me you're not a real medic!"

"I am! I studied the whole curriculum!" protested Yasmin, allowing her voice to rise. "I just couldn't get a slot without a sponsor. Look, I'm good, I'm apex. I can do the job!"

"Bitch is lying," said Kicks. "You give her to us, we'll get the truth."

"No!" Yasmin didn't look at the twins, she kept her attention focused on Tommy. "You can test me on MedNet! I'll take any exam you pick!"

Despite his anger, Tommy's eyes showed a flicker of interest. Yasmin would be hard to replace. He also liked having power over people, especially women.

"Don't believe the bitch!"

"Don't believe them! Mr. Yip, I worked Downtown and I heard about these two. They got banned from all the smutshops, even the VC ones." Then inspiration struck. "There's even a rumor...." She stopped dramatically, looking frightened. Tommy went for it.

"What rumor?"

"Uh...."

"Yeah, bitch, why don't you tell us?"

Yasmin bit her lip and looked pleadingly at Yip.

"Spit it out!"

"It's just.... I heard the Viet Ching were betrayed by insiders, that's how all the senior tong execs were killed."

"You calling us traitors?" She didn't see which twin had spoken, but his voice had turned silky.

"I'm just saying, how do you know you can trust them?"

Yip didn't trust them, of course. But he certainly wouldn't say so to their faces.

"I heard those rumors," he said slowly.

"Yeah, you heard them," said Fix, stepping forward. "And this here's the traitor." He reached for his phone, flipped up the screen, and displayed a photo of Yasmin taken two years before. She didn't flinch, confident that her new face made her unrecognizable as the severe, gray-haired 'Dr. Smith.' Voice and movements were much tougher, but the twins hadn't twigged so far.

"When we find this bitch, she's gonna wish she died in that fire a thousand times over."

Tommy sat forward and frowned at the photo. Playing for time, Yasmin decided. He was scared of the Nguyens, probably unnerved by their identical menace. Few people could tell them apart.

"What'd she do exactly?"

The twins exchanged a glance, then Kicks spoke.

"Two VC enforcers went berserk. At the same time. In the safe house. Execs all had their fishhook codes, but nothin' went bang. Smith worked on both those tools. She had to of sabotaged them."

"Then she vanished with a lotta VC business in her head," added Fix.

Yasmin made a show of glancing at the photo.

"You recognize her?" asked Tommy.

She shook her head.

Fix started to speak, but Yip turned his attention to Tor and interrupted.

"What about you? You lied to me, too?"

"No, sir."

Tor recited his original story—he'd been an aide in a Seattle clinic, fired last fall for stealing meds. That story would stand up to a net search and Tor sounded genuine, especially when he explained how he'd fallen in love with Yasmin, cleaned up his junk habit, and followed her north. He looked at Yasmin with glowing eyes while Kicks and Fix sneered. They seemed to be dismissing him. Good. The less attention they paid to Tor, the less likely they were to recognize him as a former Viet Ching hench who'd been caught double-dealing his own tong, and given to Dr. Smith for "readjustment"—a punishment no tong member would forget.

Tommy had moved his attention to Cin-Cin, who stared back at him with big, moist eyes.

"And why are you here?"

"Little candy cunt was on the launch with them," said Fix.

Tommy beckoned. Cin-Cin hurried around the desk to sit in his lap.

"Now, honey, are you tight with these two?"

"Oh, no, Uncle Tommy!"

"Yeah? So why were you with them?"

"They asked me for a picnic. I thought it would be fun!"

"But you didn't ask me if you could go, did you?"

"No, Uncle Tommy. I'm sorry!" Under the childishly abashed tone, Yasmin caught real fright in the girl's voice. Tommy caught it, too, and his eyes gleamed.

"Bad girls get punished, you know." He stroked her narrow ass.

"I'm sorry, Uncle Tommy, really! I won't do it again."

Yasmin risked a glance from the corner of her eye and saw a telltale bulge at Fix's crotch. The Nguyens were spoiling for rape, and Yasmin couldn't afford to be their victim. Quite apart from the risk of discovery, it would lower her status; make her open game aboard the ship. She leaned forward.

"Give me a test!" she urged Tommy. "You pick it, and I'll do it right now. I'll prove I can do the job."

Fix leered down at her. "We got a test for you, bitch." He grabbed for her neck and Yasmin ducked sideways, before he could feel the betraying lump of her implanted fishhook.

"Hey!" Yip dumped Cin-Cin off his lap and stood up. "You don't give the orders on my ship, get that?"

"Bitch is too smooth. She's lying." Kicks spoke this time. "You don't rake her down, you're a fool."

Bad choice of words, thought Yasmin with satisfaction as Tommy's face flushed red.

"I'll decide what to do with her. You can get out!"

Neither twin moved. They watched Yip with predator eyes. His gaze flicked from one to the other, then fell on Cin-Cin.

"Here, take her with you."

He shoved the girl roughly towards Fix, and Yasmin saw her eyes widen in alarm. Fix reached over and grabbed the girl around her shoulders, all the while keeping an eye on Tommy. His brother kicked a chair aside and opened the office door.

"Your funeral, Yip. That one reeks like Atlanta."

Tommy glared, then turned his scowl on Tor.

"You can leave, too."

Tor stood uncertainly, his eyes going to Yasmin. And Tommy didn't miss it.

"It's OK, honey," said Yasmin, putting a quaver in her voice. "I'll be fine, don't worry."

When the door finally thumped shut, Yasmin sat alone before a furious Tommy Yip. She concentrated on looking small and scared while he paced the tiny space behind his desk, passing back and forth in front of his framed Captain's certificate in the bookcase. The certificate was fake. Abruptly Yip slammed into his padded leather chair and Yasmin braced for recriminations, but he surprised her.

"You ever meet those two before?"

"Well... yes. I saw them around. They don't remember me, though."

"I'm surprised."

"I stayed out of their way," she said in a heartfelt tone. Yip grunted. He looked like he was already regretting bringing them aboard. Then he straightened and looked at Yasmin.

"OK, here's how it's gonna be. Tomorrow you take the tests I give you. You score eighty-five percent, you stay as medic. You fail, then you join the cleaning crew and I give you to the twins."

Yasmin spoke in a low voice.

"Yes sir."

"And if you pass as medic, you'll do what I tell you. Exactly what I tell you. Or the same thing happens."

"Yes sir."

"Now you get to your cabin and stay there. You get caught anywhere else before tomorrow morning, the deal is off."

"Thank you, sir."

Yasmin rose from her chair, started for the door, then turned back, wiping her palms nervously on her trousers.

"Sir..."

"What?!"

"I just.... Look, just in case you don't know—those two, they're really bad smog when they're crazy high. They used to shoot Bone and Orbit and go on rape sprees Downtown. If they go out in Campbell River and hit the bars...." She let her voice trail off. From Tommy's face, his imagination was filling in the details very well.

"OK, I heard you. Out!"

"Yes, sir."

The cabin door closed on a very frightened man. Good. She could keep playing on his fear of the Nguyens, keep his attention distracted from her. That shouldn't be too difficult. Kicks and Fix were their own worst enemies here—far more overtly frightening to the cowardly Tommy than a simpering young medic. The exam certainly posed no problem. But—and she felt herself scowling—the twins were very serious trouble. They wanted Dr. Smith more for revenge than money. And even if they didn't recognize her, they'd be watching, restricting her movements severely. She needed to get rid of them, and soon.

Tor waited anxiously at the end of the corridor. She told him loudly, in case anybody was listening, that she was confined to their cabin and then followed him below decks, her mind racing.

Her meditations were interrupted two hours later by light tapping at the cabin door. Tor answered, and let in a disheveled, tear-streaked Cin-Cin. The baby doll limped over the sill, waiting until the door shut to loose loud sobs.

Yasmin sprang down from the upper bunk, all shock and concern, and helped Cin-Cin to the lower bunk, then sent Tor to Sick Bay for medical supplies. While he was gone, she closed the small porthole window, turned up music, and activated a jammer. So far as she knew, none of the crew cabins were bugged, but she didn't want to take chances, so she'd set a jammer signal that mimicked random commercial interference. When Tor returned she had him pass the med kit in through the door and then gave Cin-Cin a private exam. The twins had been careful not to visibly damage Tommy's merchandise, but they'd raped her roughly and terrorized her with vivid threats. Yasmin sponged her down, administered analgesics and a mild sedative and made sympathetic noises while she waited for the sobbing to ebb. Cin-Cin calmed quickly—another indication of her real age. Abruptly she sat up and shot a defiant look at Yasmin.

"I didn't tell nothing about today. I just said it was a picnic, the three of us."

"Oh?" said Yasmin, keeping her voice casual.

"But they kept asking and I could of told. About David. I could still tell...."

Yasmin let her face harden.

"What do you want?"

"Meds," said Cin-Cin tensely. "Meds to make me grow up."

So she knew. But she didn't realize that the implant in her arm was a hormone pak, not anti-virals as she'd been told. Take out the implant and she'd be in full blown puberty within days.

"There aren't any meds on the ship," Yasmin improvised. "I'd have to order them in without Tommy finding out. And it's expensive."

"I could sell Cocoa for lots!" Under her bravado the girl was clearly terrified.

Yasmin hesitated. Cin-Cin knew too much; she was dangerous. On the other hand, she might still prove useful. Most of the crew ignored and underestimated the girl.

"Do you know how old you are?" Yasmin asked gently.

Cin-Cin paled.

"No. But... I heard a couple of the big girls when they thought

I wasn't listening. One of them said I've been here longer than any of them." She fastened desperate eyes on Yasmin. "Is that true?"

"Could be."

In fact, she'd checked Cin-Cin's medical records. The girl had been aboard the Empress less than six years, but she'd worked several tong whorehouses before that, and Yasmin guessed her age at 27 or 28. There were already subtle hints of age around her eyes.

"Look, if you took meds to restart puberty, it would happen very quickly and people would notice," she pointed out.

"So I'll run away!

In truth, the girl couldn't escape. She was almost certainly booby trapped with subs and meds that would plunge her into suicidal depression if she left the Empress. But she wouldn't know that—it was a Viet Ching trade secret.

Yasmin lowered her voice. "I want to get off this ship, too," she admitted. "So does Tor."

"Yeah! We can all run away! Right now!"

Cin-Cin's eyes gleamed with desperate hope.

"We can't just run without a plan. I have to make arrangements. And it's got to be a secret."

"I can keep secrets. Like, I didn't tell about today even when they hurt me."

Yasmin gave an approving smile.

"Smart girl! Look, it'll take several days, maybe a week. It's important that you stay away from me and Tor—the twins will be watching us. Keep your phone on and be ready to leave any minute, OK?"

The girl scowled anxiously.

"How do I know you won't leave without me?"

"I can't give you a guarantee. You'll have to trust me."

Cin-Cin bit her lip.

"A week?"

"At the most."

When Cin-Cin left, Yasmin let Tor back in the cabin. He had begun shivering, and fixed her with a distressed, longing look. Damn, she couldn't put off working on him. It had been a week since their last thorough session, and today had been very stressful. She locked and bolted the cabin door, reset the jammer, and then ordered him into the lower bunk while she prepped.

Tor's face lit up. He stripped naked, folded his clothes and then lay down eagerly. Yasmin started by stroking his face with a cloth impregnated with a tailored chemical matrix overlain by her regular perfume. She stuck a couple of small sensor pads on his forehead, so she could monitor his reactions on her netset, but she kept her attention on his face while the first level of euphoria and disinhibition took hold, and then began debriefing him in a soft, even voice.

At most of their recent sessions, Tor had had little to say, but tonight anxieties poured out. She had encouraged Tor's interest in the Empress as being useful, but he had developed a deep, irrational attachment to the ship and sabotaging the boilers had distressed him, even though he no longer consciously remembered doing it. He babbled on about water injectors and level glasses and scotch boilers until she ran out of patience.

Kicks and Fix had scared him too, and she spent more time pursuing that avenue, trolling for any hint of old memories. Sure enough, he'd retrieved something—fascinating how the brain could retain fragments of memory even years after a complete wipe. She saw the anxious, indirect flick of his eyes that betrayed him when he tried to hide something, so she smiled and stroked his throat, using the friction of her gloved fingers to warm the oil and speed the release of psychoactives.

"It feels so wonderful when you cleanse ugly old memories," she told him softly. "See, you're frowning. You have thoughts that make you feel bad, don't you? So I want you to gather up all those black thoughts to tell Yasmin and then we'll make them go away."

She picked up a small medspray with her left hand and shot a tracer into his upper arm. She used a lot of it in her work—a biochemical tag that bonded with the neurons activated by memory retrieval. Tracers were used to flag specific memories and could be followed up with DNA methylation inhibitors that locked onto the tracer and wiped the memories. When administered by an expert on a thoroughly mapped patient like Tor, memories could be expunged with pinpoint accuracy.

She reached over to the compact netset she'd placed on a chair next to her, and opened monitor windows.

"Now tell Yasmin the bad thoughts."

Tor grimaced, and his voice came out shrill with confusion. On the screen spots of intense activity flickered in his medial temporal lobes.

"There's a girl, a little girl. And... I'm burning her with a cigarette on her legs, inside her legs.... I like it, I like hurting her. The man, the twin, he's holding her hair and he has a lighter. He says he's going to set her on fire and she's screaming..."

Interesting. Yasmin prodded, getting as much detail of the memory fragment as she could. Then she injected the inhibitors and had Tor go over it again to reactivate and sever the synapses. When he finished, she turned off the set, removed the sensor pads, and cleaned his face again, telling him "Wonderful, Tor, wonderful," and watching for the programmed euphoric response to her voice. His pupils dilated at each keyword, and he sucked in breath.

"There, Tor, we're wiping away all that pain and filth. Forgetting feels so good. Forgetting makes you clean. And obeying Yasmin brings joy. You feel warm and safe with Yasmin now, don't you?"

He nodded, eyes glowing ecstatically up at her, erection stiffening at his crotch. She'd go back next week and check to make sure the memory fragment was entirely wiped, but right now it was time for their cleansing ritual. She smiled down at him, enjoying the moment.

"Begin," she whispered.

"I belong to Yasmin, I love Yasmin," whispered Tor, shuddering with programmed euphoria. His penis was rigid now, but he wasn't allowed to touch himself. Yasmin used vibra gloves to masturbate him, and he kept his gaze locked on hers as his arousal peaked. After his first ejaculation, she simply sat back and let the orgasm continue for its programmed two minutes, while Tor moaned and thrashed, always keeping his eyes open and fixed on hers.

Afterward he lay in a regressed infantile state, whimpering quietly. She let him suck on her finger while she considered her options.

She could count on no more than a week before the new boiler parts arrived. So she had to take Simon from Cortes as soon as possible. And to do that she must eliminate the Nguyen twins.

# 12

## September 14

Finding a gift for David's thirteenth birthday gave Simon a whole new set of social perplexities to wrestle with. He'd never given a gift before, and the advice he received was unhelpful. Dr. Lau grinned and told him that Chinese children traditionally celebrated their birthdays by giving their family gifts, as a thank you. Simon couldn't see the point of this datum, since David wasn't Chinese, so he tried Toni who gave him a blank look and referred him to Klale. Klale enthusiastically explained the derivation of the word "potlatch", then told him that she listened to people to find out what they needed or wanted, and finally warned him not to spend "too much" and to consider David's parents. Reviewing recent conversations, Simon knew that David wanted a submersible boat, a university scholarship, fifty infrared and waterproof smart surveillance cameras with a hub to run them, and a platinum net account. However, since the cost of any one of those items exceeded all of the Andersons' annual stipends added together, Simon felt relatively sure he could eliminate them as "too much."

Finally, in desperation, he took up Mary Smarch's invitation to call her any time about anything. Mary listened to him, then quickly and methodically helped identify possibilities, and volunteered to ask David's parents for their approval. Enormously relieved, Simon was then able to turn his attention to other birthday customs, such as gift wrapping, cards, cake, and parties.

His curiosity unleashed a flood of stories from the others, and Simon made the discovery that adults also received gifts, but he had failed to give anything to Toni and Klale on their birthdays in April. This worried him, but Toni simply rolled her eyes and said it didn't matter, while Klale suggested that he give them two presents next year. Dr. Lau's birthday was in November and Simon decided he would solicit Mary's help again.

The Andersons invited them all over for a birthday barbecue on Saturday afternoon, and after some discussion, Lau and Toni accepted. So at three o'clock on a sunny Saturday Simon found himself in his finest clothes walking along the path behind Dr. Lau, carrying a carefully wrapped birthday gift.

They had all dressed up, and Simon found it fascinating to see how differently they looked and moved in their festive garb. Klale ran downstairs and twirled, laughing, as her multi-colored Mexican skirt billowed around her. She wore it with a loose yellow ensilk blouse, a matching headband and a gaudy biolume necklace. Lau strode down, erect and graceful in a tailored blue ensilk suit, with ruffled shirt cuffs, cravat, and matching silver earcuffs that accentuated the silver strands in his shiny black hair. Toni's was the most startling transformation. She wore a scarlet seacrepe robe and a brilliant African head scarf tied into an elaborate sculpture. She'd even put on make-up that accentuated her long-lashed eyes, cinnamon skin tones and her striking, high cheekboned beauty, and she walked with a regal elegance that made her seem taller. Simon caught a flash of surprise in Lau's eyes and a look of satisfaction from Klale.

On their arrival at the Andersons' front verandah, Lau shook hands formally with each family member in turn. Simon followed, copying his motions. Ethan and Blue shook his hand firmly, and David's sister Aurora grasped it nervously. David leaned forward while he shook and whispered: "This is SO embarrassing. Can you believe, balloons!?" Simon nodded, though he had no idea what David meant. The rainbow-hued balloons tied to the white rails of the verandah looked pretty to him.

The Andersons had dressed up also, and Simon studied them with interest. David's mother usually tied her blonde hair in a pony tail and wore neat, practical work clothes, but today her hair fell loose over her shoulders and she wore an heirloom patch-work dress, sewn in a traditional Guild pattern. Aurora wore a sari sheath with smartweave that changed color and designs every few minutes, and Ethan had traded in his perennial baggy overalls for an embroidered tunic, vest, and trousers that suited him well. David looked handsome, if ill at ease, in a purple z-shirt and pants.

His grandfather was not in evidence, but Simon assumed he was watching nearby. Several times during the summer he'd caught distant glints from the old man's binoculars and knew he was being followed by the rifle. He had not mentioned it to anyone.

There were seats on the verandah, and also folding chairs in the sunshine on the brickstone patio. A table on the porch held bowls of snacks and a decorated birthday cake. Bottles of Ethan's home-made wine protruded from individual solar-cooled sleeves—currant, salal, oregon grape, and honey. Ethan poured a glass for Rigo, then gave Simon an uncertain look.

"It's fine," said Toni from behind him. "I don't know exactly how much alcohol it would take to intoxicate a muscular one hundred and thirty kilo man with an accelerated metabolism and raised tolerances, but believe me, it's a lot."

Ethan gave a slightly uncomfortable smile and poured Simon a glass of the honey wine. It smelled wonderful and tasted even better.

David opened his gifts on the patio. Lau and the others had given him birthday cards, one containing a phone credit chip, which he pocketed with a pleased grin. Simon sat nervously while his friend tore off gaudy wrapping to reveal an underwater remote camera with infrared and autotargeting. To his immense relief, David looked delighted. "That's the best present I got this year!" he told Simon, adding in a sour undertone, "Mom bought me clothes!"

As they picked up shredded wrapping paper—he now understood why Klale had called it "worthwhile waste"—Simon caught sight of David's grandfather coming out of the workshop. The ramrod straight old man wore neatly pressed work clothes and carried a folding chair, a glass, and a long wrapped bundle—the rifle, Simon assumed. He marched down through the terraced rockeries to the bottom of the garden and set up his chair under the gnarled apple trees, facing Simon. Simon watched this maneuver over his shoulder, then stood and moved his folding chair around sideways so he could watch Anderson, placing it a meter distant from David, where a stray shot would be less likely the hit the boy. Ethan and Toni both observed this, their gazes moving between Simon and the old man. Ethan looked unhappy, but Toni gave

Simon one of her rare smiles. He glowed.

So far a birthday party seemed to consist of people sitting around squinting into the sun and talking. Klale was describing Toni's beautiful, now demolished apartment to Blue. Toni interrupted roughly.

"Klale, it was just wood and concrete."

"It's something you built," said Blue. "I always hate to see something I built torn down. It's part of me."

Toni nodded, eyes downcast. Lately, she seemed to be only half there. She walked slowly, was easily distracted, and Simon had noticed her several times staring into space with a shadow of black desperation in her eyes. But she didn't share her hurt with anyone.

Tires crunched in the driveway and Simon looked around as a sharecar pulled up. As the soft whir of the electric engine died, a woman looked out the window and waved.

"Oh no!" muttered Blue, standing abruptly. She looked at Simon, then at Lau. "It's Miz Guthrie. I certainly didn't invite her. I bet she's come around to get a look at Simon."

"She knows about him?" asked Toni.

"She's on the Island Council. I'll try to head her off." Blue hitched up her skirt and hurried for the opening vehicle doors.

"That woman never drops in by accident," said Ethan darkly, stroking his beard. "And she's impossible to get rid of. If you want to duck out quickly now...."

"I think not," said Lau. He looked at Toni. "He's got to meet these people sooner or later."

Toni looked at Simon.

"Can you handle it?"

Simon considered his gold silk shirt, Caribbean blue pants and matching head scarf, and David's pleading look.

"Yes."

When Blue returned she was accompanied by two women— one young and blonde, carrying a baby. The latter turned out to be Miz Guthrie's excuse for a visit—her niece and six week old grandniece. She introduced the young woman around, but her gaze kept flicking to Simon who was, in turn, fascinated by her. He knew Miz Guthrie to be Mary's age, but she'd had a facial sculpt that gave her the girlish features of a popular vid star. A fuchsia robe flowed over her chubby body, matching pink hair was piled on her head like an ice cream cone, and she towed a small tubby dog with satiny fuchsia fur and enormous eyes. As they approached, David stood behind Simon and kept up a low-voiced commentary.

"Great, she even brought the 'muttant.' She's not supposed to have a dog, she lives adjacent to a fragile wetland, but she got a permit because she's on council. It's the stupidest animal on the island, too. She calls him Bobo. Everybody else calls him Bozo."

While David's mother talked to the niece, his father made introductions, barely able to get a word in edgewise over Miz Guthrie. Simon watched closely as Lau took a graceful step forward, shook her offered hand, then stepped back, bowing slightly. When Simon's turn came he copied the moves precisely. Miz Guthrie gave one white-eyed upward glance at his height and his face, but shook hands defiantly. Behind her, Klale flashed Simon a thumbs-up.

"Well, Mr. Lau, how are you enjoying your stay on Cortes Island?

For the second time that day Simon realized that he was "Mr. Lau."

"Fine. Thank you," he managed. "It's very beautiful."

"You know Miz Smarch, don't you? How did you meet her?"

"At the KlonDyke bar."

"And what were you doing there?"

"I was... assisting." He wasn't sure what he should say, but that seemed safe.

Fortunately Miz Guthrie's sharp eyes had been distracted by the sight of old David Anderson sitting at the bottom of the garden. She waved at him. He waved back, but didn't get up. She frowned.

"What's Davy doing down there all by himself?"

"He's stationed himself so he can shoot me," said Simon.

Ethan Anderson interrupted hastily.

"Of course not. Simon's not dangerous."

Simon shot him a puzzled look.

"I'm on probation for murder," he pointed out.

"Would you like a glass of Mr. Anderson's wonderful wine?" asked Dr. Lau. He put a hand on Miz Guthrie's arm and steered her towards the verandah.

The other women had gathered around the baby. Blue cuddled it, then gave it to David's teenaged sister, who passed it hastily to Toni. Toni, taken by surprise, fumbled and the baby let out a high-pitched wail. Simon caught a flash of panic on Toni's face, then the mother stepped in, apologizing, and took the child back. Toni edged away.

Miz Guthrie had intercepted David at the steps with a birthday greeting which ended "...and I'm sure you'll do much better at school next year." David muttered something inaudible and backed away, but didn't get far. "Oh, and David. I know you're fond of animals, dear. Would you mind very much keeping an eye on Bobo? Thank you."

David stalked past Simon with the dog in tow, and plunked himself down in a lawn chair, scowling. His sister followed, and Simon joined them as soon as he could, sitting a cautious distance away from both.

"...worst birthday ever," David was complaining.

"You are such a douse lately! It's not forever. She'll leave."

"I hate it here, Rory!"

"Well, it's no wonder if you act like a total loner retro. You even flunked Community Skills! Nobody zilches that!" She got up, flicking her sari dramatically. The smartweave sensed the motion and sent patterns shimmering across her slim body. "You've been a creep for weeks. If it's adolescence, call me when it's over. I'm going to find someone nice to talk to."

Simon listened uneasily. He still didn't understand the relationship between David and his family. David and his sister seemed to dislike each other, but Klale said their arguments were "normal." He also complained about his parents and sometimes seemed nervous or frightened of his grandfather, but Toni and Lau both assured Simon that the old man didn't hurt him, and Simon had seen no evidence of it. Still, the old man emanated a sense of menace and Simon thought the others were naive.

When Miz Guthrie waddled down the garden to talk to Anderson, Simon watched intently. The slanting afternoon sunlight illuminated them nicely, and Blade's lip-reading skills came in useful. Miz Guthrie had her back turned, but he could see Anderson's replies.

"Well, Ethan isn't handling the boy well. David's as single purpose as a locomotive on rails, hasn't got the smallest interest in building trades and he's not going to get any."

Pause.

"You heard about that, eh? I found out this spring that the little bugger's been using my net account at the store. Went in early one week and found mail from a Dr. Srivastava at UBC. I thought he must have me mixed up with somebody else, so I phoned him back and discovered that David has been writing articles about the ADAT station and sending them in with my signature. Fellow had no idea he was only twelve."

Pause.

"No, I didn't bother. No harm done. If he can fool some certificated bighead, more power to him."

Long pause.

"Well, I don't know about that, Joy. I just think Ethan should ease off on David and pay more attention to Rory. That girl's smarter than she acts, steadier too. She'll settle into the Guild just fine."

Blade didn't see any more because David started talking about where to deploy his new camera. This was inconvenient—Simon wanted to know what Anderson and Guthrie said about him—but talking about possible underwater sites cheered David up. They strolled down through the terraced rockeries and leaned on the warm wood railing of the dock.

Below them the water lay glassy smooth, giving a clear view of sea life on the rising tide. Purple, ochre and brown sea stars crawled in slow motion across barnacle-crusted rocks. They spotted half a dozen varieties including a huge orange sunflower star, some stick-limbed mottled stars, and a small brown star unusual for having six legs rather than five. Schools of tiny fish darted between fronds of olive rock weed, neon sea lettuce, and reddish-brown sea brush, and by watching very closely they could spot the lurching progress of hermit crabs, dragging their snail shell homes behind them. Down on the mooring float, pale green sea anemones clung to the submerged sides—long tubes as fat as Simon's wrist with a spray of waving tentacles, like a wild hair-do, at the end. David began strolling to the end of the float, but hesitated at the sight of Toni, seated on a coil of hose, staring moodily out across the strait.

They backtracked instead and climbed up through the yard where shade edged across the terraces, and a low murmur of voices blended with piping chickadee chatter in the still air. This peaceful scene was disrupted by pitiful howling from the woods in the direction of Mary's cabin. David stiffened and looked around.

"Oh, hell. Bozo!"

He pelted up granite steps and ran around the house to the cabin trail. Simon followed as far as the house and glanced urgently at Klale, who jumped up and joined him. They started onto the trail, but before they could catch up with David they heard his expostulations over the dog's approaching howls.

"Oh, YEUCH! Oh no, you stupid.... Stop, Bozo! I mean Bobo. Come back here!"

The dog plunged around a corner towards Simon, skidding to a halt when it saw its path blocked. David hurled along the trail behind Bobo and grabbed him by the collar, then he sat down, trying to hold the struggling dog at arm's length. It reeked of skunk.

"Whoa, we're outa here," announced Klale, tugging on Simon's arm. "That's one hyas humm kamooks."

David ended up behind the workshop with a hose and detergent, trying to clean the whining, wriggling pink dog while his parents plied a furious Miz Guthrie with more of Ethan's wine. Simon offered to help, but David said not to scum his clothes, so he held the hose while David scrubbed. Anderson Senior busied himself in the workshop and watched them through the window, while Simon used reflections from the house windows to discretely return his surveillance. At one point Anderson crossed the workshop, and Simon caught a glimpse of what looked like a compact automatic handgun silhouetted against a far window. He felt a stab of worry. A Guild Citizen like Anderson shouldn't own a handgun. What was the old man up to?

"OK, spray now," called David.

It took over half an hour and the results were not optimal—Simon could still smell skunk, though he didn't say so. Miz Guthrie did, however—loudly—and departed with her embarrassed niece and a backward glare over her plump shoulder.

David watched her leave, wiping wet hair out of his eyes, and muttering angrily at Simon.

"She didn't ask if she could come to my birthday party, she didn't ask if she could bring her stupid muttant, and whose fault is it? Mine!" His voice was choked with fury, close to tears. "I've had it. I'm leaving, getting off this stupid island, going to enroll in fast track on my own. I can do it, there's been three cases, I looked them up. And I've got friends who will help me, not like any of the splutzes around here." He stopped abruptly and shot a glance at Simon. "Well, not you, I mean—the rest of them."

Dr. Lau walked up, giving David a sympathetic look.

"How are you managing?"

He held out glasses of lemonade. Simon took one, but David ignored his.

"I'm going to change my clothes," he said blackly, and headed for the back door.

"That was unfortunate," said Lau. He began walking around to the verandah and Simon followed, pondering whether he meant the lemonade, the dog or everything. Lau looked up at him. "We're starting dinner, finally. How's your blood sugar?"

"Fine." He'd been eating snacks.

It seemed like a good time to talk, but Simon hesitated, still very wary about asking questions, even though Toni had assured him repeatedly that all questions were permissible. Choi's unpredictable rages at 'wrong' questions had been brutal.

"I wonder... I wonder how you tell when somebody's 'acting strange'," he tried.

Lau stopped and raised a bemused eyebrow.

"Well....if it's somebody you know well, you look for behaviors that are out of character. For example, I'm sure you'd notice if Toni was acting unusually for her."

"Like this evening?"

"What?" Lau looked around. "Where is she? Did she go home?"

"No. She took a bottle of vodka and went down to the dock. But that isn't out of character for her, because she used to get drunk often."

Lau stared at him, startled.

"Toni's drinking? Is she drunk?"

"Well, the bottle was half empty."

141

"Oh, hell!"

Now Lau looked worried. He walked briskly toward the dock and Simon followed, bypassing the others, who were sitting on the verandah. Ethan, tending the barbecue on the patio, gave them a friendly wave.

Toni sat in a brooding huddle on the weathered float beside Andercraft, the family's dilapidated workboat. She'd taken off the headscarf, and an empty mickey lay on the fabric heaped beside her When Lau started down the rolling ramp, the float lurched under his weight and Toni whirled.

"Lea' me alone!"

Lau stopped part-way down and held out a placating hand.

"Toni, why don't I take you home?"

She screamed.

"Gedda way! Gedda way! Fuck off!"

She reached for the bottle, tried to get up and got tangled in her robe. She fell down, still screeching.

Lau stayed where he was, emotions flitting across his face—anger, embarrassment, alarm. The commotion attracted attention and Simon saw old Mr. Anderson hurrying down through the garden, Blue behind him.

"I could talk to her," said Simon.

Lau looked back at him in surprise, then nodded. He retreated up the ramp.

"All right. I'll head off the Andersons. You try."

Toni had stopped yelling, and now she was blinking, swaying slightly. Simon recognized that expression from old times.

"I'll need a towel," he said, and stepped onto the ramp.

Toni flinched again as the float dipped, but when she saw Simon she didn't yell at him. He walked down and sat silently next to her. She put a cold, unsteady hand on his knee and he held it.

"Got drunk," she slurred. "Didn't help. Fuck!"

Her face crumpled and she began to cry, then she put a hand to her mouth. Simon helped her lean over the edge of the float to vomit, supporting her head gently and tucking her beautiful clothes underneath so they wouldn't get scummed. When Lau tossed a towel down, he cleaned her face the way she had cleaned his so many times. He felt proud to be able to help her.

When she seemed better, he tried to help her up, but she couldn't stand, so he lifted her into his arms. Lau watched with an odd expression on his face as they came up the dock, then followed them back to the cabin. Along the trail Simon had to stop for Toni to throw up again, but by the time he entered the cabin she was falling asleep against his shoulder.

She woke as Simon put her in bed, grabbed his hand, and wouldn't let go. He held her hand while Lau checked her blood alcohol level and grimaced at the read-out, then coaxed two cups of rehydration mix into her and administered a medspray of anti-oxidants. When Lau left, Simon sat waiting for Toni to doze off, but every time he tried to move she woke and grabbed his hand again. Finally he stretched his legs out on the bed beside her.

"We'll have to watch her anyway," said Lau softly from the doorway. "Keep her on her side so she doesn't choke if she throws up again."

Lau relieved Simon for an hour so he could eat dinner with the Andersons, but he wanted to watch over Toni and Lau agreed to let him sit up late. So Simon sat next to her in the dim room, reading a little, but mostly looking at her. He liked feeling useful, liked being able to help her for a change, liked being so close.

Around one a.m. she reached for him. At first Simon thought she was sick again, but she crawled over top of him, stroking his arm and his chest, panting hot stale breath in his face, whispering "Fuck me, please fuck me, I need... oh god, it's a cascade. Got to fuck me, you got to help. Now! I need it!"

Simon knew about smuts, knew all about cascades, and understood. Something had triggered old neural pathways, and she was in hyper-arousal, out of control, the way the pimps had programmed her years ago. She needed him.

He removed their clothing before her desperate, clumsy fingers tore it, then with her skin warm against his, he let her demonstrate what to do. The part with his hands was easy, but the things she wanted him to say were ugly: phrases like "stupid cunt" and "chigger bitch". He felt reluctant at first, then realized that these were trigger words, so he whispered harshly in her ear while she slammed against him, stifling agonized whimpers against his chest. He knew he'd got it right when spasms started shaking her thin body. She jerked violently again and again, finally collapsing into sobs, and he knew what to do then, too. He held her gently against his chest, stroking her soft, woolly hair while he glowed with happiness. He wanted his own release, wanted to dance with her, wanted to feel her hands touch him with saxophones and symphonies and crying woodwinds, but for now it was enough to have helped.

Her final whisper as she fell asleep filled his heart with impossible, bursting joy:

"Don't let go! Don't ever leave me!"

When he got up the next morning Simon felt more buoyant than he had ever imagined. He went outside right away and did all his favorite dances, reaching a rare, gasping intensity and yet still longing for Toni's soft skin against his. He waited impatiently until long after breakfast to take her coffee upstairs, but she was asleep, and when he tried to wake her she slapped his hand away with a grunt.

He hesitated, then leaned over and kissed her lips. She flinched and opened her eyes.

"Wha the.... No! Simon, no!"

Simon felt sudden fear in his gut, in his throat.

"But.... last night."

"What...?" Toni rubbed a hand over her forehead, then a dawning look of horror crossed her face. "Oh no! Oh no! I didn't...."

Simon couldn't listen any more. She had only been drunk. She'd never wanted to touch him, not him, she'd made a mistake. And now... all he could see in her face was revulsion.

Choi's old words echoed in his head. You are not a human, you are not a person, you are nothing. You are a slave, a tool.

She didn't love him. She couldn't love him. She'd used him.

Simon stumbled downstairs, desperate to lose his own twisted ugliness in hot pain.

# 13

## September 15

Toni woke to hands shaking her, a swirling world of pain, and an ominous sense of disaster. Rigo's voice, harsh and furious, knifed through her throbbing head.

"Get the hell up! I don't care how bad your hangover is, I want to know what you did to Simon!"

Toni made a feeble attempt to sit, and sank back instantly under a roiling wave of nausea. Stabbing pain in her gut loosed an involuntary moan and brought tears to her eyes. Her gorge rose. The smells made it worse—a stale whiff of her own vomit and another horrible odor in her nostrils, for all the world like burned flesh.

Curtain hooks screeched and a wall of light fell on her.

"Get up!"

Not gonna happen, fool, she thought, then an irresistible upswell of nausea hit, and she rolled to the side of bed to puke onto the floor. Spasms wracked her, then she could only lie gasping, heart pounding in her ears, praying for the terrible pain to ease. In the distance she heard Rigo walk around the bed and then mutter "Oh, shit!" The sudden alarm in his voice prodded her to open her eyes and look down into a pool of scarlet blood.

Fucked up big this time, she thought and passed out.

Someone was squeezing her hand, calling her. It was Rigo, using his calm doctor voice now. Pain and nausea tore at her. She felt too hot, too dry. She wanted to be unconscious, but she forced gritty eyes open.

"Toni, I've started an IV and called for emergency equipment from the clinic - it'll be here in about ten minutes. But first I need some medical history."

She sucked in a breath, every movement sending fire from her sternum all the way through to her cunt.

"Hurts," she gasped.

"I'll start painkillers, but can I trust the dosage profile you gave me?"

"Yes." She hadn't altered that, just lost most of her records and kept them lost.

She shut her eyes and concentrated on breathing very shallowly in, out, in, out, trying to hold nausea at bay. She heard the familiar sounds of Rigo taking out a med capsule and clipping it into the IV tube. In the downstairs distance she heard Klale talking urgently—on the phone, perhaps? The pain eased back fractionally. Rigo squeezed her hand again and she opened her eyes.

"That's as much as I can give you right now. You have intestinal bleeding. Do you know what the cause is?"

She forced words out.

"Ulcerative colitis. Been treating. Meds in my old boot. In the closet."

Rigo hurried to the closet, not bothering to ask why she'd hidden her illness. Maybe he didn't need to. Guild-born people her age didn't contract colitis—the genetic susceptibility was screened out prenatally, and broad-spectrum preventives given to children made them resistant to most common viruses. In her years at the institute, Toni had gone to great lengths to ensure that no give-aways of her slum childhood showed up in her official records—like repaired tooth decay or cholera antibodies. Or H. pylori. intestinal bacteria...

Rigo was back.

"How long have you had this condition?"

"Years. Recurs. Flared up after Christmas."

"Ever had symptoms this severe?"

"No. Oh, damn...." Nausea welled up. This time, Rigo helped her roll over and vomit into a bowl. She rolled back, tears sliding down her face, ears ringing, trying to hold on but it all slipped away....

When she came to again she was still in her bed, but it was dark outside the curtains and the bedside lamp was on. The fire in her gut had eased. Thank gods. She felt terribly weak, her head ached, and her foul-tasting mouth was dry-glued shut. A med monitor peeped softly. Moving her head gingerly, she glimpsed an adhesive sensor patch on her hand and felt another on her chest. An IV trailed from her arm. Footsteps came to the door and Rigo looked in.

"Good, you're awake." Without asking he reached for a bulb of water and a bowl. "You can rinse, but don't swallow. Spit in here."

He held the nipple to her mouth, then braced her while she spat. Two rinses eased the foul taste, but made the sore spots in her mouth and the raw ache in her throat more noticeable. She'd had a surgical snake down her esophagus, she realized. Rigo took the water away, then pulled over a chair.

"Toni, I know you need rest, but we have to talk."

She nodded, feeling a terrible rush of shame. She didn't want to face it, didn't even want to think about what she'd done. But she had to.

"OK, I went in to cauterize the worst of the mess in your intestine. I repaired a couple of perforations and sprayed an anti-inflammatory coating. You're stable now, but you'll be on fluids for a few days. And you need a proper work-up in hospital."

She nodded again. This wasn't news.

"I need to know why you got drunk."

She grimaced.

"I'm sorry, Rigo. Truly sorry." She cleared her scratchy throat. "It was so stupid. I know better. But I don't know why I did it. I really don't."

She risked glancing at him. Lau's face was closed and rigid. Angry, but holding himself in control.

"Then we need to figure it out. Walk me through it. What happened at the party?

Toni took a cautious breath, trying to gather her thoughts. She started talking, beginning with their arrival at the party, and adding everything she could remember: watching old Anderson sit like a malevolent troll at the bottom of the garden; sampling a glass of Ethan's syrupy salal wine, thinking David looked oddly miserable for a kid having a birthday party, feeling pleased with Simon's behavior and amused at the way he mimicked Rigo so very accurately. Then those awful people had arrived and she was hauled over to admire their howling spawn....

"I remember suddenly looking at all those people around me—all those white smirking Guild faces—and I just went completely tilt. I don't know why, it doesn't make sense. But I had a mother of a panic attack. I used to get those sometimes when I was drinking, or on bad trips. But I haven't had one for a long time."

"Had you been drinking?"

"A glass of wine, that's all. Then.... All I could think was to get away from those people before I started to scream. I had to make the fear stop, drown it. I didn't have any tranqs, and I wasn't thinking straight enough to go back to the cabin and get some, so I grabbed a bottle from the kitchen—old Anderson's vodka—then I went down to that little dock and started chugging. I don't know why there—I hate water. Uh... things get fuzzy after that."

"Do you remember coming home?"

Rigo's tone was so flat, it set off alarms in Toni's head. She concentrated, sifting through nightmarish neon flashes of yesterday and then it hit her again.

"Oh shit!" She put her hands over her face.

"Tell me." Rigo's voice was sharp with anger now. Toni couldn't look. She took a breath, continued unsteadily.

"I woke up having a neural cascade. It's that old smut wiring, still burned into my brain chemistry...."

She remembered the bed, the heat of Simon's body lying beside her and his pungent male smell, the hot slam of overwhelming need, utterly out of control. Now! Fuck me now!

Shame burned in her face. She took a ragged breath.

"I think it was an olfactory trigger. I usually keep a distance from men; that's why I've been avoiding you so much. If I hadn't been drunk, I'd have had the sense.... Well, it doesn't matter. I ordered him to fuck me, showed him how."

"What did he use?"

"Ah.... What?"

"You've got vaginal lacerations and internal bruising all through your pelvis. You were lucky not to sustain kidney damage."

"Oh that. His fist."

"Christ!" Rigo looked shocked.

Toni's bitterness flared.

"I'm programmed to want it rough! No, I'm programmed to fucking beg for it rough! Endorphins kick in. I don't feel any pain—not until after. I...." Her anger ebbed into misery. "Rigo, I'm sorry. All I can say is that it's been years since I had a cascade. I didn't think...."

"No you didn't! And what the hell did you do next?"

"Next?"

"This morning."

"Uh..." It was very foggy. "Simon tried waking me up. Then he kissed me. I said no, I said I made a mistake."

The implications started dawning before Rigo's next words, but it was far worse than she'd imagined. Simon had gone downstairs and begun burning himself on the stove. Luckily, Rigo had found him and pulled him away, but he had second degree burns on both arms, and now he'd retreated to a semi-catatonic state.

As Rigo filled in details, Toni wished she could pass out again and never wake up. She didn't want to listen, didn't want to feel like a monster, a failure, a pussing smut. Her own lecture to Klale came back in horrific detail—and she'd done far worse than Klale. In any clinical setting she'd be fired, maybe permanently disbarred. Certainly this was the end of her involvement in Simon's therapy. Rigo wouldn't trust her again. He'd bring in outside help, probably take Simon to the Seattle Institute. And right now that felt like a relief, an escape. She lay waiting for him to say the words, but he stopped talking.

"I'm sorry," she said finally. "It's not enough, but that's all I can say."

"You can do a lot better than that. You can tell me what's wrong with you."

"I don't know!"

Rigo persisted.

"If you had a patient with your symptoms, Doctor, what would you suspect?"

She winced. She'd been through this in her head a hundred times.

"Repressed traumatic memories from childhood. Working with Simon has been kicking up old ghosts for me. There are a lot of parallels between our experiences. And I don't remember very much of my childhood, especially my mother. I suspect it's something to do with her. But that's too vague to be useful, and I don't know any more, really I don't."

"So what treatment do you propose for yourself?"

She was shocked into staring straight at him.

"What?"

"You heard me."

"Well... I was putting it off until I got Simon stabilized."

"That sure as hell didn't work. Now what?"

Toni found herself flummoxed. Rigo prodded.

"What's the usual procedure?"

"Most often... memory enhancing meds and controlled regression. But..."

"No! No 'buts.' You nearly died this morning. This is killing you."

Toni lay silent, unable to find anything to say. Lau shoved his chair roughly against the wall and paced.

"You know what I really want to do right now, Toni? I want to hit you. Then I want to fire you as Simon's therapist and get another therapist who isn't as sick as her patient. But the truth is that I don't have that option. Simon is completely dependent on you and he's not going to transfer his attachment to somebody else just because you can't handle it. So I need you back on your feet. I need you to treat own your wounds, so you can go on treating him.

"Now, are you going to do that? Or are you going to give up and abandon my son?"

A voice in the back of Toni's head screamed "No! Don't touch me! Go away!" She lay in rigid silence, unable to talk through a smothering waterfall of panic and denial.

"I called Mary. She tells me she's a registered personal mediator, as well as a Tsimshian healer. That's not as good as a therapist, but she's your friend and she thinks that trust is the most important thing. So... will you trust her? She'll come the minute you call, but it has to be you who makes the call."

Another long silence stretched out. Then Toni forced an anguished whisper:

"I can't do it."

Rigo stopped pacing and turned on her, his handsome face twisted with fury.

"Tell that to Simon!"

He slammed the door behind him.

# 14

It had become hard to hide inside himself. Something kept Simon chained to the ugly body that rocked on the porch, trapping him so he couldn't dance above the grass or fly among the trees.

Instead he hid behind Blade's deafness, ignoring people who tried to talk to him, refusing to look at them and see their words. Finally, in the evening, the pressure in his bladder sent him to the toilet, then he returned to the porch, fleeing the scent of Toni on the second floor.

Toni didn't come.

When he wouldn't go to bed, wouldn't hear anything, Dr. Lau got some cushions and covered him with a blanket, then stayed beside him in a chair, watching something on his phone. In the welcome dark Simon eventually crept out from Blade's emptiness to listen to the soothing swish of wind in the trees and, towards morning, the patter of rain on the roof. Some time in the night Klale replaced Lau, and the cat came and curled up in his lap—a hot, soft weight that eased his bleakness.

In the morning, Klale brought a plate of breakfast and left it on the chair beside Simon. Simon tried to ignore it, but sweet, warm pancake steam wafted past his nose, overwhelming the musty scent of drizzle in the grass, and waking his stomach. It growled and suddenly he felt ravenous. Abruptly he also noticed pain—his burns flamed under their bandages, as if his arms still lay on the stove. Finally—resentfully—he reached for the plate. The cat woke, stretched, and stalked away. Simon ate.

Afterwards, Lau brought him a cup of tea, then sat and talked quietly. He said Toni had been very ill and couldn't come down, but she would want to talk to Simon when she woke up. Simon said nothing, but his thoughts whirled. Lau's voice sounded tense, strained. Was he lying? Was Toni truly sick? Very vaguely in the background of yesterday he had an impression of hurried footsteps on the stairs, raised voices. What if Toni was dying? Fear hit him—

and then a thrumming, screeching tornado of rage that flung him paralyzed to the porch boards.

Much later when he was calm, Lau checked the burn dressings on his arms and put pain patches on his skin. Then Klale came and sat beside him, huddled inside a hooded sweatshirt against the cool damp of the rainy day. Gray misery pooled in Simon's gut, swelling until it became unbearable. He felt trapped. Finally he couldn't sit still any more, so he got up and went to the stage. Klale turned off his restraint and watched in silence. His movements were clumsy, his timing bad, and he slipped often on the wet platform, but he persisted in long sets of exercises and tai chi sequences until he was soaked, aching and so tired he could barely stand. He drank the fruit shake Lau carried out for him, then showered and ate dinner with Lau and Klale in a tense, silent house.

He went to his own bed that night and plugged himself in. He didn't look at Toni's door.

After breakfast Tuesday morning, Lau ordered him to go to Toni's room. She was sitting up in bed, sipping milky tea as pale as her haggard face. She talked to Simon but he called up a symphony and drowned her words with the music. After a while she stopped and sat watching him with eyes he wouldn't meet. When she tensed, he thought she was going to reach out to touch him and his gut clenched, but she only shoved the cat off the bed and then waved at him to leave.

David came over late that afternoon and they went down to the beach with Klale and Lau. The weather was blustery and overcast, but the tide had dropped to one meter leaving a wide expanse of beach. At the lowest tide in summer, David said the beach was exposed almost to the twentieth century high tide line, but Simon had never been able to spot any trace of the former beach, perhaps because of the extensive reclamation work the islanders had done to reestablish intertidal zones during the six meter sea level rise. "Kind of hard to imagine Granddad toting slimy rocks up the beach, but I've seen the vids," David had told Simon.

David led them over slippery, seaweed draped rocks to the water's edge and then started hunting for chitons, snails and sea squirts. Lau and Klale looked dutifully at the first couple of gray, gooey blobs, then picked their way precariously back up the beach.

"Finally," exclaimed David. He looked up at Simon urgently. "I need to talk to you."

For the first time that day, Simon focused on his friend and realized that the boy seemed nervous and unhappy. He gave the bandages on Simon's forearms an uncomfortable glance, and Simon at first thought they disturbed him, but it soon became clear David had other things on his mind. With the others out of earshot, he explained that he wanted to test out his new underwater camera by taking a night-time research trip on the family boat—without telling his parents. And he wanted Simon to come.

Three days ago, Simon would have asked Toni's permission, but he no longer wanted to take her orders, no longer wanted to hear words that burned his heart like acid. So he listened to David's proposal, determined to make his own decision. David wanted to observe phosphorescent plankton in the strait. He needed assistance with his equipment and he pointed out that he would be safer with Simon along in the unlikely event of an accident. Best of all, they should have plenty of time to return before dawn without getting caught.

Despite his rapid-fire talk of plankton, David seemed oddly downcast, almost brooding. Simon prodded cautiously and got an angry outburst about his parents. "There's no point asking them permission because they always say no! They won't let me do anything that counts! They don't care about science, or about anything I care about! I can't do real research if I can't take some risks, but they treat me like a moron, like a little kid! They won't even let me apply to fast track—they want me to improve my overall school performance and go for a scholarship in a few years, but that's a total waste of my time studying sludge I'll never need!"

David's anger worried Simon, and he noticed that the boy repeated himself verbatim twice—he must be very distressed to do something that unusual. There were also flaws in David's reasoning, but no mistaking the boy's intense urgency.

Still, Simon had explicit orders never to be alone with David. He couldn't break those orders.... or could he?

The thought gave him a surge of excitement that set off warning tingles in his fingertips so Simon closed his eyes and blanked his thoughts, concentrating on the sensation of sea air buffeting his face, and the piercing cries of gulls along the low tide line. In late summer some of the full grown juvenile gulls were still following their parents around, mouths agape, demanding food. As Simon listened, an escalating series of shrieks ended abruptly in strangled gulp.

Calmer now, he concentrated on the problem. Toni herself had told Simon that he'd broken Choi's commands last year. He didn't remember how he'd done it, but he could think of several approaches. It was possible. And then... would Toni punish him? That idea threatened to wake old terrors, but Simon clung to calm. If he was careful—very careful—Toni would never find out.

He opened his eyes cautiously and looked at David. Accustomed to Simon's sudden retreats, the boy had crouched down to wait for him, arms wrapped around his knees, blond hair blowing across his freckled face. Simon would be taking a great risk, but this was important to David. And David was Simon's friend.

"What time do you want to leave?" he asked.


Simon slept under induction again that night. With Toni ill, only Lau and Klale were available to sit watch, and they were both tired. This was convenient—otherwise Simon might not have been able to slip away. He went to bed at ten as usual, surreptitiously setting the sleepware to wake him at two a.m.

He woke to the gentle patter of rain on the cabin roof and spatters against his bedroom window. Simon had done some reading on phosphorescence before bed and he felt doubtful about their chances of success in this weather, but he had agreed to meet David, so he dressed silently and left his room. His rain cape rustled when he tried to put it on, so he carried it folded under his arm.

In the hallway Toni's door stood open, with faint light shining from it. Simon listened for a minute, then stepped very quietly over and looked in. The light came from a medical monitor display on a table by the bed. Toni lay asleep, a tiny silent lump under the covers. The room smelled of her skin and her breath and her hair....

Simon fled.

On the verandah he nearly tripped over Pauline Johnson, whose black fur blended into the dark. She meowed and rubbed against his ankles. He stopped to don his rain cape and his night goggles, one of the few pieces of customware he had brought from Choi's bunker. The flexible strap that held the goggles in place rested directly over his occipital chip, and an embedded signal receptor allowed him direct neural access. Adjusting his view to infrared, he started into the rain, across the yard. He took the beach trail, which branched up to the bottom of the Anderson's property, rather than the direct trail that led to the back of their house beside the workshop. It was a longer route, but more discreet. He found that his rain cape brushed noisily against bushes, making it difficult for him to hear anything else, so he shrugged it off again and made quieter progress along the muddy path.

He stopped between the lichen-covered apple trees at the bottom of the yard and lifted his goggles briefly to check his calibration of visible light. He could just make out the gray shadow of the house, but no lights showed. He replaced the goggles and accessed infrared. This time the house showed as a warm rectangle, with brighter windows leaking heat. He started towards the dock and glimpsed a white flare through the trees that lined the beach. He'd expected to find David there, but that light was far too hot for a body or even the small electric engine on the dinghy.

Feeling the first edges of alarm he continued silently toward dock. He couldn't get a clear view until he reached it, then he saw something utterly unexpected—a big launch moored at the end of the Anderson's float, opposite Andercraft. Automatically Simon triggered Blade's old surveillance software. Three human figures flashed green. A small person stood on the float by the launch. Amber text scrolled: "MATCH: DAVID ANDERSON JR." Two larger figures were aboard the launch, one of them busy at the stern, facing the Anderson's workboat. The goggles gave sex, height and mass, but no ID.

Run! thought Simon instinctively. But... was David in danger? He froze in sudden indecision. What could he do? He was unarmed and unprepared. He hesitated another crucial second. A tall figure on the bow of the launch raised a shadow to his shoulder and...

WHAP!

Something sharp bit Simon's shoulder and an instant later he heard the distant chuff of an airgun. Blade!!!

Blade whirled and started to run, not risking an adrenaline

boost that would certainly trigger his neural restraint. He took three accelerating strides even as a strange tingle started down his arm, spreading swiftly through his veins. Then his right foot failed to swing ahead properly and he fell forward. He was only just able to throw his weight aside to avoid a rockery wall. His right knee slammed into dirt, then his jaw and shoulder. He rolled and tried to rise, but his muscles were spasming now, out of control, and he felt himself fall back into a bed of scratchy thyme. Even as poison pulsed through his body he knew what it was—a paralyzing neurotoxin. His raised tolerances were no defense against this. In a few seconds it would seize his lungs and stop his heart.

In the distance David called out, then his voice was abruptly stifled. Heavy footsteps thumped up the ramp, along the dock, and onto the path.

Blade's face pressed into wet leaves, filling his nose with the pungent scent of crushed thyme. His breathing slowed. He felt the edges of panic, but fought it back. If he triggered the restraint he would have no chance at all. While he struggled to suck air into leaden lungs, he felt his arms grabbed from behind and shackled together. Then someone pulled his legs straight and strapped his ankles.

More footsteps approached, lighter than the first. Blade's lungs ached and his ears rang. A woman's low voice said:

"Is he secure?"

She didn't wait for the affirmative answer from a male voice before removing Simon's head scarf. She retied it tightly around his mouth as a gag, and then pulled up his right sleeve. Her voice whispered near his ear, soft and strangely happy.

"It's all right, sweetie. Yasmin won't let you die." A medspray hissed against his skin. "That's the antidote. It'll take half a minute."

His lungs were on fire, and the pounding of his heart in his ears was labored, slowing. Dizziness. Hard to focus.

Long seconds passed before a ragged gasp shuddered through Simon's body. Two sluggish heartbeats thudded. He inhaled, and felt cool sweet air in his lungs. Relief. He managed another breath, then tried to flex his muscles. They didn't respond. The woman spoke again, her voice low but commanding.

"I'll stay here and watch him. You get the hand truck."

Footsteps receded down the dock, then a slim cool hand touched Blade's neck, pressing against his carotid artery. Blade listened for any sound from the Anderson house or any hint of pursuit from the water, but he heard only lapping waves and wind. Belatedly he thought of the emergency beacon on his phone, but it was much too late.

"Excellent. Pulse strong, breathing better. Now, let's remove that neural restraint...."

Blade flinched involuntarily as hands explored his neck. They moved closer to the recessed thalamic plug—the one Choi had used to punish Simon—then brushed right over it. Panic slammed him, shredding Blade's control, destroying any semblance of volition. Simon tried to scream against the gag and started to thrash in terror, then the heavy numbness of restraint grabbed him, freezing him into utter helplessness.

Reeling terror. He heard the buzz of a surgical blade behind his ear, then felt a sharp pain.

The voice talked to him, but Simon couldn't hear through churning panic. A medspray hissed, then blackness...


He woke to the sensation of tight straps binding him rigidly to a frame, and the sight of a paneled ivory ceiling, elaborately edged with molding and gold-painted curlicues. A polished mahogany wall stretched down to his right and he could glimpse another wall just two meters away on his left. Blade tried to see more, but his head was secured, so he couldn't look down at his right arm, where he felt hands expertly changing burn dressing. He flexed his leg muscles cautiously. They responded but the restraints were expertly fastened—he felt no give.

"Ah, you're awake." It was the woman's voice again. Peripherally, he glimpsed movement, but his field of vision was limited to the peculiar ceiling and an ornate frosted glass light globe.

"Poor thing. Look what they've been doing to you."

A hand reached out and adjusted the arm of a surgical spotlight that reminded Simon suddenly of Choi's medlab. He felt the edges of panic, but blurred, distant. He'd been given a sedative, he guessed. He slid into Blade's detachment and tried to focus.

"Damping your fear response, I see. Now that is an interesting neural pattern.... But don't worry, I won't hurt you. I'm just treating the burns on your right arm. You fell on it and tore the artificial skin, so I had to put some more on. Never heals as cleanly the second time, I'm afraid—you'll have some scarring.... Tor, pass me that tape. Good.... And then, I'm going to run an external neural scan, see how you look when you're awake."

He heard the clatter of implements on a hard surface, then a woman moved into his field of vision and looked down at him. She was white, young and strikingly pretty, with hazel eyes and long red hair, brighter than Klale's, tied back over a green sweater. Blade did not recognize her.

"Hello, I'm Yasmin. And this is Tor." She gestured at someone beyond Blade's vision. "Will you say hello?"

She waited, then continued.

"I understand you're frightened, Simon. So I'm going to explain something. I won't burn you. I won't punish you. I will never use thalamic stimulation to inflict pain on you. I'm not a sadist or a barbarian."

She gazed watchfully into his eyes. Blade stared back.

"I just checked your hormone levels to make sure your implant is adjusted within normal parameters—it's fine—then I gave you a high nutrient injection, and now I'm going to do one more search for locator beacons. I removed the restraint, of course, along with its locator chip. The beacon in your fishhook doesn't seem to be working—damaged or disabled, is it? But I'd expect a backup somewhere...."

She passed a handheld scanner over his body, methodically starting at his head and moving down. Her movements were precise and practiced, and as her hands passed his face Blade noted a network of very fine wrinkles, characteristic of someone much older than her superficial appearance. He caught a strong whiff of spicy-sweet perfume.

"No secondary beacon. Very sloppy!"

She moved back into his field of vision.

"Nasty burn scars from childhood, I see. And old Choi certainly made a mess of your face."

Choi. The name woke some sleeping part of him, snapping him into focus, sharpening his thoughts.

Where was he? On the wall to his right he could see blue velvet curtains—evidently drawn over a window—and up on his left there was a gilt edge that looked like a picture frame. He could hear the soft hum of air recirculation, and smell faint odors of leather, wood, and salt water. He'd never been on a big ship, but it seemed likely this was the Empress of Vancouver. That meant he was in the hands of the Kung Lok.

He rejected fear and focused on analysis. Who was "Yasmin?" Probably not her real name but he had maintained dossiers on prominent tong members and did not recognize her. And how did she know about Simon and Choi? He thought back, reconstructing events. David Anderson. The boy must have betrayed him, led him into a trap. He almost let anger grab him, but quenched it. Not now. Focus on the situation: what did Yasmin want with Simon?

Treasure hunting seemed the most likely answer. No doubt she sought Choi's hidden fortune, vastly inflated by rumor. And she could succeed. An expert would eventually break the coding on Simon's neural chips, or simply rewire, adding new filaments and junctions to retrain him. But even without expertise she could find a way to activate the thalamic chip and torture the information out of Simon. The ugly weakling would buckle easily.

She was studying something out of his vision, a monitor probably.

"Well, well, Simon. How delightful! Six neural interface chips! Our young friend David didn't tell me that but it explains a great deal. Lots of odd pathing, too, and some singular development in your post cingulate cortex..."

David was not a friend, he was a traitor, thought Choi icily. Simon had been a fool to trust him.

"He's very gifted, young David—and observant. He's going to be a big help to me. Hmmm.... Well developed neural connectivity, good synaptic rate. It'll be interesting to test your intelligence, but I'm sure it's very high."

She looked down and smiled, showing even white teeth.

"You are quite the find. Unique. I'm going to enjoy working with you. And you..." She reached down and cupped his face with her hand. Like Toni. Like Klale petting the cat. He lay rigid under her soft touch, straining to pull away, but he could not move.

"You are going to be happier than you ever dreamed. You're going to feel such joy when I touch you—you'll long for it, miss me when I leave the room. You're going to love me, Simon. And I'm going to wash you clean, and then make you a beautiful new person."

She's like Toni, thought Simon through burning rage. She would touch him and give him joy, then shove him away like a pile of steaming feces.

"Interesting." Yasmin glanced at the monitor. "You're angry, not scared. I expected fear." She studied the readout a few seconds more, then smiled. "I very much want to start working with you, Simon, but I've got other problems at the moment. So I'm going to use sleepware to put you down for a few hours. It'll be just like what you're used to. I'm starting the sequence now."

He heard a ping as the three minute sleep sequence initiated, then Yasmin leaned down and kissed him full on the lips. A jolt of surprise shocked him even through his anger. She pulled back, smiling into his eyes as if she knew exactly his reaction.

"When you wake up we'll talk again."

She walked away, footsteps muffled on carpet. Simon loosed his pent fury and tried the restraints again. Still futile, but the neural restraint didn't kick in. It must truly be gone. He heard the rattle of a door handle.

"Tor. Wait a minute, then follow me. Lock the door behind you."

A male voice answered: "Yes, Yasmin."

The door shut, then a handsome blond man stepped into Simon's field of vision. He put his hand gently on Simon's hand and gazed at him with solemn blue eyes.

"Hi, Simon, I'm Tor. I bet you're scared right now, but you don't have to be, really, it's OK. Yasmin will help you like she helped me. I used to be horrible, all twisted and mean, but Yasmin fixed me, made me good." His voice grew husky. "I love her more than anything in the world."

His eyes shone down at Simon, then suddenly he grinned.

"She even made me handsome! So don't worry."

He patted Simon's hand once more, pulled a blanket up over him, then switched off the overhead light and left. The door latched with a solid click, leaving the room dark, and Simon felt grogginess settling over him. He tried desperately to think while consciousness remained, but his thoughts were floating off, disconnecting, falling away....

# 15

Yasmin left the first class cabin smiling. Simon was a tremendous find—unique and far more valuable than she'd ever suspected. No wonder Almiramez had snatched him. However, before Yasmin could work on him she had to implement the next part of her plan. She hurried through the empty corridor from the cabin to Sick Bay.

Getting at Kicks and Fix had proved very difficult. She hadn't at first realized that they'd come aboard the Empress with five other Viet Ching thugs—a worrisome addition to the ship, since Tommy Yip had only nine fully armed Kung Lok henches on board. The rest of the Empress's staff were ship's crew, entertainers, and hookers—not tong members, not loyal to Yip, and next to useless in a fight.

Inevitably the Nguyen twins would wear out their welcome with the Kung Lok, but Yasmin couldn't wait for that. She laid plans and searched impatiently for an opportunity. On Monday when the steamship boiler parts arrived her time had run out, so she'd opted to snatch Simon first and kill the twins second in an elegant one-two move. So far things had gone perfectly.

Last night a large party of Viet Ching and Kung Lok henches had gone to town for drinks. Evidently impressed by Yasmin's warning, Tommy had ordered Kicks and Fix to stay aboard ship, giving her the chance she'd been waiting for. She watched the sullen twins retreat to their cabin, then sent Cin-Cin down to visit them with a bottle of absinthe, a pocket full of subtly tampered Orbit peels, and instructions to keep them inside until dawn. They had stayed out of the way during Yasmin's trip to Cortes, and now she intended to finish them off. The adulterated drips and trips she'd given Cin-Cin would leave them unconscious and the additional drug in her medspray would deliver a fatal overdose—hardly an unexpected fate for anyone with their habits.

She was just preparing the medspray cartridges in Sick Bay when her phone rang. She reached for it, noticing it was almost six am. Where was Tor? she wondered suddenly. He should have followed her to Sick Bay ten minutes ago. It wasn't likely he'd been waylaid to run an errand. Most of the crew kept casino hours and she'd rarely seen them up before mid-morning.

But it was Tommy Yip. Not only was he up, he wanted to see her in his office immediately. She replied in an eager-to-help voice, then snapped the phone off, annoyed at his bad timing. Still, she couldn't risk disappointing him, so she slid the medspray and cartridges into her pants pocket and left Sick Bay at a fast walk.

The first thing to meet her eyes when she opened Tommy's office door was Tor, bound and gagged, slumped on the leather settee. Standing over him were Kicks and Fix. They were smiling. Yasmin whirled, but Fix darted like a snake, jerking her through the door and twisting her arms behind her. Tommy watched malevolently from behind his Victorian desk. He wore his white uniform, but his hair was uncombed and his eyes were puffy. He'd posted a Kung Lok hench in the corner behind him, cradling a bulky automatic handgun. The beefy hench looked hung over.

Fix's warm, foul breath brushed the back of Yasmin's neck and she felt a wave of revulsion and then anger.

"Well, if it isn't the ship's medic! We just called you up here to thank you for that little baby doll and her party supplies. Funny thing, you know, we was just revving up for a good time when we got a call from a guy in Seattle, does data forensics. He autopsied some genescan records from an old VC clinic. Seems like your scan matches a certain Dr. Smith."

"But I...." started Yasmin.

Kicks crossed the small room in one stride and struck her hard across the face. Pain exploded in her left cheek. She felt a surge of fury, but made herself sag helplessly. Fighting back now was futile—she'd have to wait for a better opportunity. Tor looked on with stricken eyes and struggled, but he was efficiently trussed.

"Shut up, bitch! And keep it shut!"

Behind her, Fix groped at the base of her neck.

"Now, lookee here." He shoved her forward a step and bent her down over Tommy's desk, banging her forehead on the glossy wood. He shoved her hair up to give Tommy a clear view. "That sure looks like a fish hook to me...."

"Got the code?" asked Yip.

"Nope. But we don't need it. And you know why?"

He pressed gloatingly up against Yasmin, his penis hard against her buttocks.

"You know what we're gonna do, bitch? We're gonna sell you. But first, we're gonna teach you about loyalty. And takin' orders. We don't need no wizzy medtech either. We're just old-fashioned guys. We're gonna burn you and cut you and fuck you and beat you and we're real good at it."

Abruptly Fix raised her up and shoved her across to Kicks who started a strip search, tearing her clothes off and poking roughly in her mouth, ears, vagina and anus. Yasmin took it passively, feigning fear even though it fed Kicks' excitement. She could hear his urgent breathing, see those ferret eyes fastened on the tears of pain that rolled down her left cheek. Tommy Yip watched in silence as Kicks finished the search and tossed her phone, medkit and the medspray on his desk. Tommy picked up the kit and opened it.

"You should of checked her out better," said Kicks.

He wasn't saying "Mr. Yip" any more, noted Yasmin, trying to keep her mind off discomfort and anger. The Kung Lok hench behind Tommy stared at her naked body with cool appraisal as Kicks gagged her and tied her hands behind her back. Tommy flicked a glance of distaste at her, then turned his gaze to the twins.

"Yeah, well don't mess her up too much, or you won't be able to sell her."

"We know what we're doing," said Fix ominously. "Hope you didn't let the bitch touch you. No telling what she can do."

Yip kept his expression bland, but his fingers tightened on the medkit. He gestured at Tor.

"So who's this other one?"

For the first time Fix looked uneasy.

"Not sure." He glanced at Kicks. They knew, thought Yasmin, but they didn't want to tell Tommy—didn't want to explain that the childlike blond man sobbing on the settee used to be a ruthless VC soldier.

"She worked on this one a lot," said Kicks. He shot Yasmin a venomous glare.

Tommy tossed the medkit back on the desk.

"We'll sail for Seattle. We can be there by tomorrow, unload her."

"No way," said Fix.

Yip looked up, eyes narrowed, and spoke slowly, dangerously. Having the armed hench behind him gave him confidence.

"What do you mean, 'no way?'"

Kicks spoke.

"We go down there, the Yakuza gonna grab her. They got that city tight. Even with your guys along we don't have the lube to get our price."

Fix joined in.

"Yeah, we need to sell her to the triads. Our tongs got juice with them. And the best place is Honolulu."

"Hawaii?!" Tommy glared incredulously. "How do you plan to get there?"

"What the hell do you think we're standing on? A boat!"

"This is a casino! We can't take this thing across the Pacific!" As he got angrier, Tommy's face reddened. The twins, in contrast, grew ominously pale

"Like hell we can't," said Fix. "We took your fuckin' boat tour. This is exactly the same boat as made hundreds of trips across the ocean before they even had navsat. And there's lots of food, water and fuel—more than enough."

"That was another ship two hundred years ago! This ship's never been in open water! And I've only got half a crew!"

Yasmin, standing a little behind Fix caught his tiny gesture—a finger wave behind his back. Kicks reacted, grabbing Yasmin and thrusting her forward as a shield. The movement distracted Tommy's hench just enough. As he swung his gun towards Kicks and tensed to fire, Fix nailed him in the chest with three rapid bullets from a silenced pistol. Blood spattered the glass-fronted bookcase. The hench stared incredulously at them and collapsed with a deflating grunt. Tommy looked back over his shoulder in horror.

"We got five guys waiting outside. We're leavin' for Hawaii right now."

Yasmin saw Tommy draw a shallow breath. He turned to face the twins, face ashen, a spray of crimson across his snowy uniform shoulder.

"We can't leave right now." His voice came out high and shaky.

"If you took the tour you know it takes four hours to get up steam."

"OK, then we leave in four hours. Get on it!"

Kicks shifted his grip on Yasmin, pinching one breast and then shoving a rough hand between her legs.

"Four hours," he whispered in her ear. "That's lots of time."

But Tommy hadn't picked up his phone. He looked up at the twins, frightened but stubborn.

"You can't take over this whole ship with just seven of you."

The words were still leaving his mouth as Fix's pistol coughed. Tommy jerked backwards, grabbing at his left shoulder and swearing in a high, terrified voice. Blood blossomed on his white shirt.

Fix cradled his gun thoughtfully, and looked at him.

"Now shut up, asshole, and listen or I kill you right here. What you got here, Yip, is a boat full of broke, pissed off people that want to be the hell outa here. And a few henches so outa practice they can't take down a guy at three meters with a gun in their hand. But we don't need lots of shit. So here's a deal."

"When we get to Hawaii, we're gonna give this little present to the triads and pledge with them. You and your people cooperate, maybe they'll take you, too."

"This ship won't make it to Hawaii!" wailed Tommy.

"It better, cause you're on it and that's where we're goin'."

In the silence that followed, and during Tommy's subsequent call to the engine room, Yasmin stood in bare feet on plushy Indian carpet trying to ignore the cold air against her skin and the still warm barrel of Fix's gun stroking her breasts. She needed a plan, but all she could think of was that she'd been made a prisoner again, and the medspray she needed to kill these vermin lay out of her reach on Tommy Yip's desk. Damn them! She felt the gun push between her thighs and bit down on a surge of raw fury.

Gathering all her self discipline, she made herself concentrate on logistics. How long was a boat trip to Hawaii? She vaguely remembered Tor saying that the old Empress had crossed the Pacific in ten days. Well, Hawaii was about halfway, so say five days. The Nguyens would hurt her, of course, but they wouldn't risk major injury or brain damage—not if they wanted to sell her.

So she had five days to retrieve the situation. And she had a few cards left. The twins didn't seem to know about Simon. Under sleep induction her new acquisition would be fine for two or three days before his condition began to erode seriously. His accelerated metabolism was a deficit there—a normal person would last longer without nutrients.

David, for instance, had a drinking water tap and emergency rations in the empty crew cabin she'd locked him in, so he would be fine. And five days was a very long time for Kicks and Fix to hold this entire ship against a crew that loathed and feared them even worse than they hated Tommy Yip. So she had time—time to find an opportunity to turn the tables.

# 16

Another bad awakening. Not a rat this time, though, it was Klale leaning over Toni's bed and shaking her shoulder gently. The girl's freckles stood out against her pale, anxious face.

"Toni, Simon's missing. I didn't hear him get up at six, so I went to his room. He's gone."

"Oh hell," breathed Toni, trying to gather her thoughts. She heard heavy rain on the roof, felt the brush of a draft against her face, heavy with the smothering odor of wet vegetation and moldy rugs. "Is Rigo....?"

"He went down to check the beach. Look, maybe Simon just woke up early...."

"Not plugged into sleepware he didn't," said Toni grimly.

Leaping out of bed was not an option. Toni pried herself up in gradual stages, wincing as each new position wakened different bruises. Klale offered to help, but she shooed the girl out and then dressed slowly, leaning on the dresser when she felt woozy. She managed to get into a loose old pair of work pants, a t-shirt and an oversized wool sweater, then headed for Simon's room. Dr. Lau found her there, kneeling over the netset beside Simon's futon.

"He hacked the sleepware, didn't he?" Rigo said from the doorway. His gray-streaked hair was wet, and his long greatcoat dripped water on the floor.

"I wasn't careful enough," said Toni bitterly. "He's a god-damned data shark, and of course he had opportunities alone with this set. It looks to me like he's been getting up regularly in the middle of the night, probably jacking into the net as Choi. He set it to wake him at two this morning."

She braced to rise. Rigo came over and took her arm with a strong, cool hand. Toni hated assistance, but she let him help her stand up. No point threatening their fragile truce.

Faced with Rigo's ultimatum she'd finally made the call, and Mary was coming up on the weekend to start therapy. Rigo and

Klale were relieved. Toni, no matter how hard she tried to be logical, felt like a condemned prisoner awaiting execution.

"I checked the yard and the beach," said Rigo. "No sign. No answer on his phone."

Damn, damn damn. This wasn't a coincidence. Toni had let her own problems wreak havoc with Simon's therapy, then he'd burned himself and now he had run away. She couldn't meet Rigo's eyes when he spoke again in a tight, angry voice.

"We'll have to call Mary and Ron."

"I'll do it," she said tersely, biting back apologies. She wouldn't shirk this call, no matter how unpleasant.

As she walked very slowly down the staircase an ugly thought whispered at her—if Simon was permanently gone, she'd be off the hook. She wouldn't have to face Mary, face any of it.

No! She shoved the idea back in its dark niche.

Down in the kitchen Klale had dialed the tap to boiling and was filling a teapot. Toni longed desperately for coffee, but instead she slid onto the bench seat behind the scarred kitchen table and tried to make her groggy brain work. The old dial clock on the wall showed five minutes to seven. Simon had been missing five hours. If he'd stolen a fast boat, he could be in Vancouver by now. She watched Lau hang up his coat on a peg by the door and then go to stare miserably out the kitchen window at the gray wall of rain.

"We better check the locator beacon on the neural restraint," he said.

"Right," said Toni. She didn't move.

Klale looked from one to the other in puzzlement, obviously wondering why they didn't rush to do it. 'Because we're afraid of the answer!' Toni felt like yelling. She massaged her temples, avoiding Klale's worried eyes. She was overdue for an honest talk with Klale about that disastrous drinking binge, but she didn't feel up to it.

"I'll get Mary's netset." Klale put the teapot on the table so fast it sloshed and went hurrying out.

Rigo's phone cheeped. He grabbed it from his shirt clip.

"Lau here."

It was a woman's voice but Toni couldn't make out the words. She sat still, feeling her heart thud in her chest.

"No. Is he missing?"

Rigo listened intently.

"Simon's missing too."

Another pause.

"Where?"

This response took much longer.

"We'll be over in a few minutes."

He clicked off the phone, then looked over at Toni.

"That was Blue Anderson. David didn't come down for breakfast and she can't find him anywhere. He's not answering his phone. She did a trace on it, and the signal's coming from somewhere out in the gulf."

Shit! thought Toni.

"Good!" came Klale's voice. The girl walked into the kitchen carrying the netset. "That means they're off on some harebrained research thing of David's."

"Simon knows better than that."

"Yeah, but he's impressionable. And David's devious."

She beamed a relieved grin at Rigo, who forced a smile. He didn't look reassured. Neither was Toni.

Toni pulled the netset over and tried to remember how to run a beacon search. She couldn't focus on the screen, and her brain was full of sludge. She rubbed her eyes.

"Rigo, I need coffee. I'll drink it tepid with lots of milk."

Rigo had started preparing something at the counter. He looked over his shoulder.

"No, you'll eat breakfast. Klale can run the search."

"But.... Oh, damn!" Toni gave up and slid the netset across the table. She didn't return Klale's grin. A few seconds later Rigo placed a steaming bowl of congee in front of her. She picked up a flat-bottomed Chinese spoon and took a cautious sip of the savory rice soup, then another, surprised to find it both tasty and soothing on her abused stomach. Rigo put a bowl down beside Klale, then sat down with one of his own.

"Found it! But what the..." Klale stared at the netset. Rigo looked over her shoulder and she pointed at the display. "It's a fuzzy signal, lots of interference, but he's out there in the strait just southeast of Cape Mudge. That's a bad place to be in this weather.

It blows up very rough."

Rigo's expression lightened. "That's where David is."

Toni frowned, trying to figure out what seemed wrong.

"How far away is that?"

"Oh, just a few kilometers. It's about half way to Campbell River."

"Then why the poor signal?"

Klale shrugged. "No idea. Was it like this when you tested the beacon last?"

"No." Rigo answered. "Mary tested it on her way up here. She got a good signal from fifty kilometers out."

A tense silence fell around the table, and Toni finally broke it, her eyes fixed on Rigo.

"Do I call the parole committee?"

Rigo's spoon halted part way to his mouth.

Toni continued grimly. "Once we make that call, they'll issue an unrestricted warrant on Simon and every trigger happy cret on the west coast will be gunning for him."

"I know," said Rigo quietly. He fixed his gaze on Klale as he said: "I'd like to hold off another hour," and it took Toni's brain a long muzzy second to realize why he was staring at the girl with such significance. Failure to give immediate notice of Simon's absence was an offense under the Justice Pact and a breach of conditions they'd all agreed to. But Toni was Guildless and consequently hard to prosecute and Rigo could always evade retributions by returning to Hong Kong. Klale, with her future hanging on a Fishers Guild university scholarship, had the most to lose.

Klale's answered with uncustomary gravity.

"I'm OK with waiting. I don't believe Simon is dangerous, especially if he's with David."

"Toni?"

Toni grimaced and tried to get her thoughts together. Of course she wanted to hold off, but was she letting sentiment cloud her judgment?

"We should let Blue decide," she said finally. "Her son is out there, too." She started to stand, but Rigo tapped the table in front of her.

"Finish that bowl and take your meds. I'll get your coat."

Toni felt much shakier than she wanted to admit and she was afraid of slipping on the path up to the Anderson's house, so she took Rigo's proffered arm and held onto him tightly all the way. The rain had eased off, but foliage dripped and slapped wetly against them, and the ground underfoot had turned slimy with mud. Slugs crawled everywhere. Why anybody thought nature was idyllic, Toni couldn't imagine. It took all her strength and concentration to stay on her feet even with Rigo walking slowly.

Blue met them at the door. She wore clean work clothes, and had tied her blonde hair neatly back, but her expression was tense and frightened.

"Our boat's missing."

"The dinghy?" asked Rigo.

"No, AnderCraft. The work boat. The navcomp must be have been wrecked or removed, because we can't locate it."

Toni vaguely remembered sitting on the float next to the boat— a retrofitted fiberglass antique five or six meters long. The coast was full of 'resails' like it, Klale said—mostly small sailboats abandoned or sold cheap during the Collapse and rebuilt with hydrogen or biogas inboard engines. They weren't fast, but they were reliable and seaworthy in rough weather if you had to make an emergency trip. Toni took her word for it. Personally she'd rather die on firm land than embark across churning waters in some makeshift tub.

The Anderson's kitchen smelled of toast and tea. David's older sister, Rory, sat on a stool at the old-fashioned island eating breakfast. She muttered "hi" and kept her attention on her unrolled phone screen. Blue took out a jar of chicory-laced coffee mix and scooped some into a mug, adding hot water and then handing it to Toni. It smelled vile, but Toni felt like kissing Blue's hand. She took a stool at the other end of the island and added a generous dollop of milk before trying a small swallow. Right now she didn't give a damn if it ate a dozen new holes in her gut.

"...same location." Rigo was saying.

"I called Campbell River Search and Rescue. They say it'll take them forty-five minutes to launch a boat and get there."

The back door banged shut and old Anderson strode in. He stopped at the sight of Toni and the others, and his ice blue eyes narrowed with fury. Toni saw Blue grimace.

"So the ghoul's missing, too, is he?"

"Yes," said Rigo steadily.

"Recognize this?" Anderson took a yellow bundle from under his arm and shook it out. Rigo stepped forward and touched it.

"That's Simon's rain cape. Where did you find it?"

"Bottom of the yard, lying under some bushes. And there's signs of a struggle." Anderson planted himself in the middle of the kitchen and glared belligerently at Toni from under bushy white eyebrows. Toni kept her eyes on her coffee.

"Struggle?" said Rigo, alarmed.

"Damn straight. That ghoul took David and God knows what he's done to him."

Rigo's face stiffened with anger and Toni tensed, ready to retort, but it was young Rory who looked up from her toast and spoke impatiently.

"Granddad, that's tilted. Simon could pick up David with one hand and shove him under his arm. Besides, David would follow Simon anywhere. He sure wouldn't struggle."

The old man shot her a startled scowl, then focused on Blue.

"You call the Coast Patrol?"

"No."

"Then I will." The old man started to cross the kitchen towards the living room. Lau stepped in front of him.

"Mr. Anderson. We have no reason to believe that my son would hurt David. If you call the Patrol out after an enforcer, they'll go in frightened and ready to shoot. You'll be putting David in real danger."

"He's already in goddamned danger!"

"We don't know that!"

"STOP IT!" shouted Blue. "This isn't helping!" She glared at her father-in-law until his gaze dropped, then turned and spoke to the everyone. "OK, Dr. Lau, would you please call Search and Rescue and tell them about Simon—tell them to be cautious and not to go in all Yankee. And meantime, Dad, I want you to show me where you found the cape."

"I want to see that, too," said Rigo.

"I'll phone," volunteered Klale. Rigo hesitated, then nodded. Klale had marine search and rescue experience from her years working fish boats out of Prince Rupert. She'd know how to talk to them.

"Good. Dad?"

Anderson looked at his daughter-in-law, and for the first time Toni glimpsed the desperation underlying his anger.

"Blue, you're risking the boy's life!"

"If you want, I'll call Ethan and ask what he thinks."

"Damn it, he'll only agree with you!"

"Probably."

"If David gets hurt...." The old man looked at Rigo, then Toni, threats clearly stated in his eyes. Toni kept her mouth clamped shut. No point making things worse.

Klale spoke to Blue.

"Look, I'm Fisher Guild. If you give me David's phone code, I could ask for a Marine Satellite fix. You never know, it might help...."

"Sure." Blue nodded, clearly grateful for any constructive suggestion. "Here..." She pulled out her phone and messaged Klale, then she turned to the others. "Let's go."

She, Rigo and old Anderson went through the front of the house, where Toni remembered double doors opening onto a porch and wide steps down to the garden. Klale followed as far as the living room, pulling out her phone and sticking the audio plug in one ear. "Check Simon's phone location too, would you?" Toni called after her. Klale gave a surprised backward glance, but nodded.

Toni stayed where she was, sipping tepid bad coffee and trying grimly to figure out what to say to Simon's parole committee, or—worse—what to do if they asked for the trigger code for the explosive implant at the base of his neck. Toni had the code, but there was a problem she hadn't told anybody. She didn't think it would work. She suspected that either the implant receiver was malfunctioning, or Simon had given her the wrong code. Simon didn't know himself and there was no way to test it without risking his life.

Abruptly she realized that Rory was watching her. Throughout the family drama, the girl had kept her eyes fixed on her phone screen, feigning aloofness, although her posture vibrated tension. The girl had dark blonde hair in a dandelion cut and wore semi-perm skin art that Toni knew from experience must have taken hours of painstaking effort to apply. A flashing ear cuff dangled from her left ear, and a tight white shirt showed off her honey complexion. But under the elaborate window dressing was a frightened fifteen year old.

"Uh, Dr. Almiramez..." She stumbled over the name and flicked Toni a nervous sidelong glance.

"My students used to call me 'Dr. A'," said Toni dryly. "Easier."

"Yeah, thanks. Um... You don't really think Simon would kidnap David, do you?"

"No." She felt fairly sure of that at least. "Do you think David might have persuaded Simon to take your boat out on some research mission?"

Rory rolled her eyes before fixing them back on her screen.

"Oh yeah. He does the craziest stuff. One time he decided he wanted to find out about brain hemispheres, so he taped one eye shut and walked around for days, bashing into stuff until Dad told him to quit already."

"Where is your Dad?" said Toni, realizing suddenly that she hadn't seen Ethan.

"He's out on a job. Left Sunday. I would of gone back to school in Campbell River, too, but we got a home study week." She lowered her voice. "You know, I think it must have been David for sure. He's been so weird lately, all miserable and grouchy. He kept going on and on about how everybody was against him and he wanted to run away where people would understand him and let him do marine ecology all the time. But I didn't think he'd do it. And I sure didn't think he'd take Simon."

Toni frowned, remembering her vague impression of David at the birthday party as subdued and unhappy. Damn it anyway, she should have been paying attention. She started to frame another question, then heard boots scrape the back door mat, and the others tramped in through the mud room in a gust of cool, rain-smelling air. They all looked unhappy.

Rigo came over and leaned on the counter.

"It looks like there might have been a struggle, but I can't tell for certain. What worries me more is the whitecaps out there. Neither

David nor Simon knows anything about running that boat."

Toni looked at Blue. She didn't like to betray Rory's confidence, but this information was too important to ignore.

"Rory says that David was talking about running away. Maybe you should search his room."

Blue shot a startled look at her daughter.

"David said that?!"

"Yeah."

"I'll look," said old Anderson. He started upstairs, followed hastily by Blue. Toni turned her attention back to Rory, who was pushing toast crumbs around her plate.

"Rory... Would you say that David is normally an unhappy person?"

Rory shook her head.

"No. I mean, sure he complains about stuff, but five minutes later he's off looking under a rock or something, and he's fine."

That agreed with Toni's impression of David as good tempered and cheerful.

"Can you think when his behavior changed?"

"Um... He was okay at Solstice holidays... A couple weeks, I think. I remember when he and granddad took that tour on the Empress, he met some lady who told him how brilliant he was and afterwards he couldn't stop talking about it. But he wasn't a total douse then, not until later."

"The Empress?" Toni exchanged alarmed glances with Rigo. "Wait a minute. Your grandfather visited a tong casino ship?"

Rory gave an 'adults are crazy' shrug.

"Was that David's idea?" asked Rigo.

"No way. He said granddad wanted to go, even though he'd already been on the ship once before, and he dragged David around looking at engines. The only good part, David said, was that he saw a kiwi bear and this woman who was really smart told him he should go to university early."

Toni stared at the girl, thoughts whirling. What could old Anderson have wanted on a casino ship? She could only think of one possibility: that he had sold information about Simon to Tommy Yip.

Two sets of footsteps descended the stairs, and Toni twisted

176

on her stool to watch Blue and her father-in-law returning to the kitchen. They both wore grim expressions.

"David's backpack is gone," said Blue. "And his netset, his collecting bags and his new camera. I don't think any clothes are gone, but he wouldn't pack clothes...."

A shrill cheep interrupted her. She grabbed her phone from the cord at her neck, answered, and then switched it to broadcast so everyone could hear the gruff male voice.

"We're off Cape Mudge now and I'm sorry to report there's no sign of your boat, Miz Anderson...." The man hesitated and Toni heard the crackle of wind and ocean in the background. "Your son's phone signal and the other one your friend gave me are originating from underwater."

Toni thought she'd feel numb, but the news dropped her into black reeling horror, as bad as anything she could remember. As she struggled for self control, one distant corner of her brain kept analyzing, noting her own panic, noting that she'd become as dependent on Simon as he was on her, and as crippled by her own abandonment fears. No wonder she'd slid into professional disaster.

Distantly she noticed that the Patrol officer was still speaking.

"...sonar blip about the right size for AnderCraft, but we'll keep searching the strait and nearby shoreline. Please don't panic, eh? Just because the phones are down there, doesn't mean the boy is. He coulda dropped them overboard."

Toni couldn't move, couldn't breathe. I let Simon become my whole life, she thought sickly. Long seconds later Blue spoke, her voice choked with anguish.

"It must have been an accident! David must have gone out there collecting...."

"Accident, hell!" snarled old Anderson. "David has more sense than to go out at night in weather like this with the navcomp off! Besides, he's always on about tidal zones. If he'd taken the boat on some damnfool thing of his you can bet he'd be around Marina Island or Twin Islands or Mittlenatch. It was that damned ghoul took him and killed him!"

Beside her Toni saw Rigo stiffen, but a flash of welcome fury snapped her head up to meet Anderson's glare.

"Like hell it was! You sold information about Simon to the Kung Lok when you went to the Empress, didn't you? You wanted to get him killed, but when they snatched him, they took your grandson, too!"

"Toni!" Rigo clamped a hand on Toni's shoulder, but she shoved it off. She didn't want to calm down, didn't want to slide back from this soaring rage. She strode over to Anderson and looked straight up into his face. "What did you tell them you son of a bitch?!" she yelled.

"Nothing!"

"Then what were you doing on the Empress?"

Anderson flinched guiltily and backed off a step, his gaze flicking toward Blue, who had her arms wrapped tightly around Rory. He hadn't told her, thought Toni with savage satisfaction.

"I was finding out about enforcers and how to stop one, in case he went berserk around my grandson!"

"A Guild citizen asking questions like that on a tong ship?! You might just as well have taken out an orbital billboard. And on top of that, you paraded your prime pup of a grandson around meat-market traders!"

"You took David?" asked Blue, shocked.

"I was with him the whole time!" snarled Anderson.

"And he hasn't been right since!" snapped Toni, then she saw the stricken look in Blue's eyes and felt a stab of shame. She didn't know that—she was just hurling hurtful guesses at old Anderson.

"Toni?" Blue was looking at her. "What did you mean 'prime'?"

Toni swallowed and fought for calm.

"Blue... I shouldn't have said that."

"But you did, so tell me."

No point trying to bullshit this woman. Toni took a long breath, then spoke steadily.

"Gifted kids like David are targets for the underground cyber market. I'm sure you've heard rumors. They don't usually snatch Guild kids, but it sometimes happens. The Empress is a Kung Lok ship, and the Kung Lok don't do alterations work themselves, but they sell merchandise to others when they can get it."

"That's soap vid crap!" snapped Anderson.

Toni spoke between clenched teeth.

"Then get on your goddamned trike and go to your goddamned store and phone somebody you believe! Call Coordinated Coastal Treaty Enforcement or the Criminal Justice Clearing House!"

"You think the tongs might have snatched David?" asked Blue, horrified.

"Well... it's not very likely. They'd be far more interested in Simon."

"What would they do to Simon?"

Toni found she couldn't answer. It was Rigo who spoke, voice gravelly, his eyes on old Anderson.

"They'd torture him for the secrets they think he has, and then kill him."

In the silence that followed, Toni saw Rory clutching her mother tightly. She was almost her mother's height.

"Rory, maybe you should go over to the Thibodeau's place for a while."

"No!" The girl pulled away, tears in her eyes. "No, this is my family! I'll be earning my full Guild membership in less than a year and none of you pay any attention to me, it's always David this and David that..." Her eyes abruptly went wide and she put a hand over her mouth.

Blue took a long breath, visibly gathering self control, then spoke to the room.

"Look, please, everyone sit down. We need to decide what to do." She gestured to the dining room table. The others went and sat, Toni trailing. Old Anderson stood watching, then finally dragged a kitchen chair toward the table, stopping several meters away. He sat backwards on it, crossing his arms over the backrest. Blue sat at the head of the table, maintaining her calm with obvious effort.

"We're yelling at each other over things we don't know. We need to find out what happened for sure. So—what can we do?"

Klale leaned forward.

"We know that the phones are underwater, but we don't know David and Simon are. So we need a search."

You're forgetting that Simon's neural transmitter is down there, too, thought Toni miserably. But she couldn't say it. She leaned back in her seat, shaky and ill, holding herself together with effort.

"Aren't Search and Rescue doing that?" asked Rigo.

"Not underwater, not yet," said Klale. "The strait's deep there—around three hundred meters. I doubt they're equipped for deep water SR in Campbell River.

"They're not," grunted Anderson.

"So they'll have to call in a divebot with vids and sonar or even a small sub. It could take a while."

"And we need to know now," said Blue.

"Right," said Klale. "So we do some expediting on our own. Or even chase down one of those deep water tourist subs from Jervis Inlet. Ummm..." she looked at Rigo. "We'll pay, right? Simon can afford it?"

"Certainly. Order whatever you need."

"I'll get on it," said Klale. "Oh, and here's another thing. If anybody snatched Simon or David and scuttled AnderCraft at Cape Mudge, they had to have another boat."

"Our boat has a life raft," said Rory.

"It's a survival pill, right? They've got a maximum speed of two knots, and the neon orange is totally conspicuous." She looked over at David's grandfather. "Mr. Anderson, could you call around Cortes, see if there's another boat missing?"

Anderson glowered. "Phone?! I'm not goddamned...." he started, then intercepted his daughter-in-law's gaze and dropped his eyes. "All right, then, it's a waste of time, but if that's what you want."

He got up and strode stiffly toward the back door, heading for the workshop.

"Check rentals, too," called Klale.

Futile, Toni was thinking. We're just doing forensic reconstruction. But she wanted that evidence—wanted to prove the old bastard's accusations against Simon were wrong. And as long as she focused on that, as long as she stayed angry, she could hang on.

"Toni?"

She looked up to find Blue's eyes on her.

"I didn't want to ask this while Dad was here. But, you told us that you gave Simon orders not to be alone with the David. Orders he couldn't break."

Toni felt a sick knot in her gut, but tried to keep her voice steady.

"I can only see three possibilities. Simon left against his will. Or he and David worked out some convoluted way around my orders. Or Simon decided to disobey."

Brittle silence fell around the table.

"You said he was conditioned to obey orders."

"And we're dismantling his conditioning," said Toni grimly.

Rigo leaned forward, intercepting Blue's gaze.

"Miz Anderson, we knew eventually Simon might rebel against orders. Saying no, making his own decisions is part of his recovery. But we weren't expecting it so soon. Maybe not at all."

Blue looked furious. "You're telling me that he might really have taken David?"

Toni answered as levelly as she could.

"It's not impossible, but I don't believe it. Simon might do a lot of things, but he wouldn't hurt David for the world."

Blue stared in her eyes for a long moment, then nodded, the motion almost a shudder of deflation.

"OK, so let's get to work and find them."

# 17

It required every bit of self control Yasmin could summon to feign helpless terror while Kicks and Fix took turns raping her on the settee in Tommy Yip's office. Intelligence, discipline and savagery makes humans strong, she reflected as she lay limp under her tormenters. The Nguyen twins had broken many weak women. But Yasmin never let herself be crippled by fear or sentiment, and she'd survived pain and degradation before. She knew how to stifle her anger and wait for opportunity. And then she would turn the tables—show these two sons of bitches what torture could really do.

They were rough, but not as brutal as she'd feared. They took quick, almost perfunctory turns—one twin raping, while the other searched Tommy Yip's terminal, using the personal code they'd bullied out of him. For once, they weren't concentrating on sadism. They had a bigger problem—controlling a one hundred and fifty meter ship with only seven Viet Ching.

The twins had sent Tommy Yip and Tor to Sick Bay under Viet Ching escort—Tommy to be bandaged by Tor, and Tor to be checked by the twins for weapons implants. They'd also checked Yasmin thoroughly for biologicals before dragging her back to Tommy's office for the rape session. Around the time she started hoping they might finish up and lock her in the office alone, they jerked her to her feet and paraded her, naked and bloodied, along the short corridor to the ship's bridge. Yasmin focused on the clamor of pain in her body, and stumbled forward in a beaten posture, eyes fixed on the carpet, wrists strapped tightly behind her. She let tears spill down her face.

Kicks led the way through a crew door, up a flight of stairs, and into the wheelhouse and Fix followed, shoving Yasmin ahead. She stumbled over the door sill and found herself facing an expanse of tall windows that gave a sweeping view forward and to both sides of the ship. The lone Watch Officer turned around with an exclamation of dismay that he choked off with the appearance of Fix's handgun. Yasmin took a careful glance around through wet eyelashes and confirmed her memory of the room's layout. In addition to the door she'd come through, doors on either side of the front of the bridge led to outdoor bridge wings. At the rear of the bridge another small door led into a low-ceilinged Chart Room, reproduced in painstaking antique detail.

The twins stood Yasmin against a wall at the back of the bridge and used a small canister of riot glue to cement her shoulders to the wood panelling. Modesty didn't especially bother Yasmin and sporadic blows could be endured, but the increasing chill in her extremities was worrying, especially her bound hands. The wood panelling behind her was fake—some kind of finish on a cold plasteel surface, the room felt unheated, and raw gusts of wind blew in each time an outer door opened. The weather had closed in—heavy rain, wind, and an oppressive gray cloud cover that made it seem more like evening than morning. Torture seemed a less immediate problem than hypothermia.

The rear door of the wheelhouse opened again, and the Second and Third Officers entered, followed by a Viet Ching escort—a burly man with chiselled features popular in Asian action vids. The officers, Mr. Quero and Miz Lizares, were a trim, silver-haired couple in their seventies, on special secondment from the Mariner's Guild to pursue their passion for ancient steamships. Now they looked as though their worst nightmares had come true. They glanced around the bridge with apprehension which turned to open horror when they saw Yasmin. She dropped her eyes, feigning humiliation, and listened attentively.

"Got all the phones?" asked a twin.

The big VC hench answered. "Most of 'em. And Trinh's runnin' a sweep."

"Good." A cabin door opened and banged shut, and Yasmin heard the squeak of shoes on the floor as one of her captors turned to face the uniformed officers. "You the captain?"

It was Fix speaking, Yasmin decided. He was the dominant twin, though she doubted many people could tell them apart well enough to guess that.

"I'm the highest ranking officer on board," said Quero stiffly.

"Then you just got promoted to captain. And that makes you first officer, Ma'am. Congratulations. Now it's time to get this museum outta here."

There was a long pause, then Quero spoke cautiously.

"We haven't received instructions from Mr. Yip."

"Mr. Yip," said Kicks, "is indisposed." She heard the smirk in his voice.

"Yeah, we're giving the orders from now on," said Fix. "And you can call me 'sir.'"

There was a very brief pause in which Quero no doubt considered the weapons the twins wore in plain view and the spectacle of Yasmin shivering against the wall.

"Yes sir. What course should we lay in?"

"See, now that's smart of you to cooperate, Captain," said Fix with satisfaction. "You can head for Port Hardy. And you won't be using NavLink."

Miz Lizares spoke up, her voice shocked.

"Turning NavLink off is a violation of shipping regulations! And we need navigation!"

Yasmin heard motion and peeked through her eyelashes. Fix had just laid an arm over the woman's snowy uniform shoulder. He rotated her to face Yasmin, who dropped her gaze again.

"Now, you see what it says on that door back there? It says 'Chart Room.' And it's full of paper charts for the whole Pacific coast. We checked. And we ferreted both of you, too, and you know what? You both graduated in chart reading and you both been up and down this coast a shitpot fulla times. So we got full confidence. In fact, we got so much confidence that we already offlined the NavLink receiver and the autobeacons."

Yasmin didn't need to see the officers' faces to surmise their dismay.

"Oh yeah, and, I'll take your phone."

The third officer spoke again, voice shaky.

"But... Sir... I need to call crew up to the bridge."

"There's three of you here already," said Kicks from the other side of the wheelhouse.

"We need another crew member, now, and then we'll need relief crew to cover breaks."

"You tellin' me it takes four people to turn this wheel?" demanded Kicks.

Quero spoke up.

"Some of the controls on this ship are modern but the rest are fully mechanical. We need one person on the engine room tele-graph, one at the wheel, one at the systems console, and one com-manding."

"We might need a fifth, also, in the Chart Room," added his wife.

Yasmin wondered if the woman was bluffing. She doubted that any of the rest of the crew would know what to do with a paper chart.

"Well, I tell you what," said Fix. "This here ship has old wire telephones and a PA system and you know how to use 'em. So use 'em. And if you still think you need a real phone, you just ask me or my brother, right? Now, how long before we can get out of here?"

Yasmin heard a quiet hum and click, and risked another glance to see the heads-up display unfolding from above the front windows. Even with enhanced 20-10 eyesight, Yasmin couldn't read all the text from the back of the wheelhouse, but she saw color-ful status graphs along the top of the display and six vidpanes on the sides. Two vids showed overhead views of the engine room, and the others gave views from navigation cams at the bow and stern, starboard and port sides of the ship. In one pane she saw crew members dismantling the floating gangway and loading sections through a cargo hatch by crane. The screen's centre was dominated by a blank rectangle where NavLink data should have been. The two officers studied the display under the twin's suspicious gaze.

"We should be ready to leave within half an hour," said Quero, finally.

"Good," said Fix.

Yasmin wondered if Quero would try delaying tactics, but he and his wife seemed to work efficiently, using antique wall telephones to relay orders to engine and deck crew to prepare for cast-off, while the twins paced the wheelhouse behind them. Kicks feigned a blow at Yasmin and laughed when she flinched. It took everything she had to look frightened and tearful instead of furious. For a long moment she indulged in plans for revenge. She wouldn't kill the twins, oh no. She'd take Kicks first—twist that smelly jackal into a whimpering lap dog. And she'd let Fix watch, then use Kicks as his tormenter....

The rear cabin door banged open and three new crew members arrived. They took their posts while the original watch officer went off duty. One man took the helm—an oak steering wheel nearly as tall as he was—a woman stood at the shiny brass ship's telegraph, and another woman walked to the port side of the bridge and gave a voice command that caused a console to lift up from beneath faux wood panelling. The twins didn't like being outnumbered, noted Yasmin. They slouched against the windows on either side of the bridge, their posture relaxed, but guns in their hands and eyes roving sharply from person to person.

Captain Quero spoke to the nearest twin.

"We're ready to cast off. I have to notify the port that we're leaving."

"They'll figure it out," said Kicks.

"Sir, I need to ask them for tide flow figures since we don't have NavLink. The Seymour Narrows runs up to sixteen knots— that's nearly thirty kilometers an hour. Normally we'd time our departure for slack water or a north-running ebb tide...."

Kicks straightened, suddenly alive with menace.

"Don't hand me that shit! Get moving!"

They shouldn't have called Quero "Captain," realized Yasmin suddenly. A lifetime of inculcation in heroic Mariner tradition had given that title mythic importance to the Guild man, visibly puffing him up. He stood looking down into Kicks' eyes for two measured seconds before turning to the woman at the engine telegraph.

"Ring up standby," he said.

"Aye, sir." She pulled both handles. A loud ringing echoed through the bridge, startling Yasmin.

Quero turned and flipped a switch on a bulbous antique microphone.

"Ready fore and aft moorings."

She heard his voice echo along the decks outside. He strode to the front window, hands folded behind him.

Lizares joined her husband at the window and they conferred for a moment, then she crossed the bridge to the Chart Room, giving

Yasmin an anguished glance as she passed. She left the door open, and Yasmin heard a wooden drawer slide open, and then the eerie crackle of big sheets of stiff paper.

The ship's telegraph rang again.

"Standby ready," called the crew woman.

Quero grabbed an antique telephone handset, pushed buttons and then spoke into it.

"Let go stern mooring," he said, then out the window. "Slow ahead, both engines."

Yasmin didn't feel any motion but the vidpanes showed water boiling at the ship's stern and a space opening slowly between the ship and the wharf. At the edge of one camera's view, she glimpsed a small crowd of locals on the wharf, gesturing angrily up at the ship.

"Quartermaster sound one blast!"

The woman at the telegraph reached up and grabbed a line hanging down from the ceiling. A deafening hoot made Yasmin flinch and the twins jump.

Quero spoke alternately into his wire telephone and to the bridge crew. "Let go bow mooring. Standby bow thrusters. Bow thrusters one quarter port. Steersman, ten degrees starboard. Ahead one quarter."

As they pulled slowly away from Campbell River, Yasmin's view out the real windows showed frustratingly little. On a clear day she might have seen distant mountains, but driving rain obscured the landscape and big windshield wipers did little to help. The vidpane view astern showed a bleak seascape dotted with white caps, and the town of Campbell River fading into gray mist. On sunny days Yasmin had seen dozens of small boats in the channel; today the waters were empty.

The ship moved into the strait without any problems Yasmin could see. Once in the middle of the passage, Quero ordered half speed, then full speed. They seemed to make very slow progress and the Nguyens barked suspicious questions at Quero, who responded that the tide was running against them at eleven knots while the ship's best speed was sixteen knots. From the Chart Room behind Yasmin, Lizares called out marker locations and courses to her husband, and Yasmin felt vague amazement to see him lean over the binnacle and use an ancient gyro compass to set the ship's course.

SECOND CHILDHOOD

But she soon lost interest in the monotonous routine. Shivers
racked her body, her shoulders ached, her wrists hurt intensely
where they were bound behind her, and cramps were moving down
into her feet, where she had to stand slightly on her toes to keep her
weight off the glued skin of her back. Her bladder was painfully
full. Sooner or later she'd have to urinate and then the twins would
beat her again—part of the ancient humiliation game. Yasmin knew
the game well and knew that she was better off to let go now and
get it over with, but it was vital to stay in character as a frightened,
naive young woman. Kicks and Fix knew better, of course, but her
appearance was deceptive and they might yet be lulled into making
a fatal slip.

Heavy footsteps approached and Yasmin flinched, banging
her head against the wall, before she realized it was the captain. He
shrugged his coat off and draped it over her shoulders, warm from
his body. She gave him a tremulous, grateful look.

"Hey, get away from her!" yelled a twin, but Quero turned
and bellowed back.

"This is MY bridge! And there are some things I will not toler-
ate on my bridge, ever!"

He wasn't going to back down this time, judged Yasmin, and
the twins saw it too. They hesitated.

"Bitch is staying right there where we can see her," said Fix
finally.

"But she's not going to freeze and I won't stand by to see her
abused," said Quero firmly. As he spoke his wife emerged from the
Chart Room with a tartan blanket that must have been a prop. She
wrapped it around Yasmin's waist and whispered very quietly:

"I'll get a container you can pee in. I'm sorry not to help more,
but you're probably safer here on the bridge where we can see you."

Idiot, thought Yasmin. The least she could have done was find
some riot glue solvent.

"Thank you," she whispered faintly, then as a quick afterthought: "Could you put something under my heels?"

The woman looked down at her trembling shins and nodded,
then went back into the Chart Room and returned a minute later
with a container which she held for Yasmin to piss into, and a paper
booklet. With the booklet wedged under her heels, Yasmin let her

weight down with intense relief. The wool blanket was scratchy but she could already feel warmth starting to return.

With the immediate physical relief came a wave of exhaustion and then hunger. The twins ignored her. They muttered into their phones and one of them left the bridge several times, but one twin was always present, watching the officers.

In mid afternoon two VC henches arrived with Tor and Tommy Yip. Tor was limping and bruised—evidently he had put up a fight. He shot a desperate, horrified look at Yasmin, which she didn't return. She couldn't use any of his coded voice commands here. Tommy's white uniform was rumpled and stained, with the right shirt sleeve torn off where his arm had been bandaged, and he looked scared. The twins herded Tommy and Tor to the rear of the bridge on Yasmin's left, then ordered them to remove their shoes and socks, and riot-glued their bare feet to the floor. Kicks grabbed Tommy's gaudy gold braided captain's hat and stuck it on Quero's head. Quero, silently furious, removed it.

Gray afternoon faded into night. No lights were turned on in the wheelhouse—the only illumination came from the dimmed-down display screen up front, the system console, and a tiny glow in the binnacle. One of the onscreen panes showed a swirling green read-out—apparently that antique radar dish on the mast actually worked. The officers watched that and their compass instead of using headsets, and moved between the chart room and the windows, peering out at the scenery through zooms and tensely discussing tides, wind velocity, nav markers, and deviation. At eight o'clock the bridge crew changed over again, but both Quero and Lizares stayed on duty, eating meals sent up from the galley. Kicks and Fix ate too, first making the officers sample the food on their plates. They allowed Lizares to give Yasmin water but no food.

In the quiet darkness Yasmin found herself dozing off, jerking awake each time her knees gave out. Groggy with exhaustion she missed the twin's next orders to Quero, and tuned in part way through his outraged response. She raised her head and stared, trusting the darkness and distraction to cover her interest.

"....impossible! This ship isn't certified or outfitted for ocean-going, and neither is the crew. Most of them have never sailed any further than Seattle. And I don't hold a deep water ticket for a vessel this size!"

"Well, this is your big chance to get some experience," said Fix, in the silky tone that made Yasmin's flinch involuntarily.

Lizares interjected.

"Sir, I don't think you understand..."

"I understand fine. The Empress was designed to cross the Pacific Ocean and that's what it's going to do.

"There's a storm blowing into Queen Charlotte Sound, and this ship isn't seaworthy! We don't even have proper emergency gear!"

Kicks moved up on the other side of him.

"Then you sail her nice and careful and hope we don't have an emergency, right?"

"It's suicide!" shouted Quero.

"No," said Fix. "Suicide is staying here, because we'll shoot you. But first we'll take your wife and glue her to that wall over there and rape her and beat her to death in front of you."

They had him, thought Yasmin with annoyance as Quero gave his wife an anguished look. The man wouldn't risk his wife, even though he must know the twins might kill her anyway.

"We need time to secure equipment," he said finally. His hands were shaking.

"You don't..." started Kicks.

"YES, WE DO!" Quero shouted, then controlled himself with obvious effort. "We're going into rough water and nothing on this ship is bolted down. If there's an accident in the engine room and we lose steam, we're sunk. Literally."

The twins exchanged frowns.

"How long?"

"Three or four hours. And we need every person who can drill a bolt into a deck. Then there's the galley, the furniture...."

"You got an hour."

"But we need...."

Fix overrode him. "We'll send a couple of our guys down to the engine room to help. We'll give 'em some riot glue. It works pretty good."

He looked up into Quero's furious, frightened face and smiled.

# 18

In fact, it was more than two hours before Fix and Quero returned from the engine room and when they arrived Yasmin studied Fix carefully. The stringy little weasel had dark smudges under his eyes and he looked tense. When Kicks tossed him a med-spray he shot up with obvious relish—probably some cocktail of street drugs like smudge and boost; maybe even old fashioned amphetamines. The twins hadn't slept last night. Neither had she, she thought bitterly, longing for a dose of sleep suppressant. Her strength was being sapped by injuries, hunger, and simple age. Despite extensive rejuvs, she had thirty years on the twins. She had to stay alert and find a chance to act soon, while she still could.

When the ship started underway again its progress seemed much the same, but soon Yasmin felt big swells rolling underneath them. The roar of the storm grew louder, too, and when Quero stepped briefly onto the outer deck, salty wind shrieked through the cabin door. She was just thinking that the sea had gotten very rough, when they left the last shelter of Vancouver Island and the full force of the storm hit. Inside the wheelhouse it felt like riding a crazed, slewing elevator. Yasmin had nothing to hang onto, and fought desperately to keep her weight on her feet, but each time the ship rolled it felt like all her skin was going to rip off her shoulders and back, and she was terrified the ship wouldn't be able to right itself. The captain's coat fell off, the blanket slipped from her waist, and the paper book slid out from under her heels.

Quero seemed calm, but Yasmin heard retching to her left and caught a glimpse of Tommy Yip crouched on the floor. The sour smell of vomit dribbling across the deck made her own stomach churn, though there was nothing in it. The woman at the engine room telegraph was sick, too. Yasmin saw her heaving into a bag while she held desperately onto the brass stanchion.

The people on the pitching bridge were mere silhouettes, occasionally bathed in dim green or amber console lights, and as Yasmin fought for her own footing, it was hard to keep track of what they were doing. When she caught a flash of fear on a twin's face, then glimpsed the twins next to Quero, screaming in his ear, she thought it might be over—surely they were telling him to turn back. But the nightmarish ruckus went on. And eventually, as the ship climbed another towering wave, she deduced the problem. To go back they would have to turn the long, narrow ship broadside to wind and waves. The storm would swamp them.

She lost track of hours. Time was measured in wavelengths, each accompanied by a cycle of agony, brief respite, and suspense: would they survive the next one? It seemed to have been going on for hours when Yasmin suddenly glimpsed a flash of light and realized it was a gunshot, inaudible in the storm. She cursed her own helplessness—unable to fight and pinned to the wall as a target for any stray bullet. The bow rose, letting her lean back for precious seconds, and she peered uphill into the struggle, trying to identify figures. Tor! He'd got free!

Bodies rolled past her and crashed into the rear bulkhead. A scream pierced the storm noise. The ship started to level and heeled left. Another figure blundered past her and joined the struggle. Yasmin braced against the ship's roll and the pain, worsened by uncontrollable shivering. She could feel a trail of sticky blood down her back and buttocks. Then strong arms grabbed her around the waist and she heard Tor's voice shouting: "It's OK, I've got you."

She heard a hiss, then riot glue solvent burned like fire in her open cuts. She cursed while Tor braced her for the thirty seconds it took to loosen the glue, then she slumped to the floor, shaking and unable to stand, arms hanging heavy and lifeless from her shoulders. Tor untied her numb hands, then clung to her, pouring out a stream of anxious questions and reassurances, oblivious to their surroundings. She cleared her throat and swallowed, then managed to croak:

"What's happening?!"

"Yasmin! Yasmin are you OK?" He was crying.

"What's happening?!" she barked furiously.

Finally he looked around, but by then Lizares had come over. She kneeled, bracing herself, and held out the coat Yasmin had lost.

"Are you OK?!" she yelled.

"Twins?!" demanded Yasmin hoarsely.

"Shot one. The other one got away. You're safe now," she said, squeezing Yasmin's shoulder.

Safe, like hell, thought Yasmin as the ship slammed into a wave and shuddered, and spray smacked the wheelhouse windows.

"Take her below," Lizares told Tor.

Yasmin managed to get her arms into the sleeves of the captain's coat, but Tor had to close it up in front. As he helped her towards the rear cabin door, she glimpsed a crew member trussing one of the twins with tape. She felt a burst of fury. She felt like kicking the bastard in the head, but she had bare feet and could barely keep her balance anyway. Later, she promised silently. The rear cabin door banged open and two new crew members rushed past. She caught a snatch of Quero's bellowing voice.

"...safety line. See if you can get NavLink up! Hansen, did you find those phones?"

Tor grabbed her and half carried her down a flight of stairs to the Casino lobby, down another flight to the Upper Deck, and then along the gyrating corridor towards Sick Bay. Where were the rest of the Viet Ching? wondered Yasmin urgently. But the first priority was medical treatment.

She'd expected a crowd at Sick Bay, but the door was locked and a hand-printed sign had been taped to it: "First Aid in cabins 4A, 4B and 4C." What? thought Yasmin. Then Tor opened the door and she saw why.

Her neatly organized room had become an utter shambles. Everything on the counters had spilled to the floor, the contents of the cupboards had emptied out, and the whole mess tumbled back and forth as the ship heaved. Examining tables rolled and crashed on their castors, and drawers slammed in and out. Fortunately most meds were stored in unbreakable containers, but delicate equipment and instruments had been wrecked and the room was almost unusable. She felt a new burst of fury. Damn those VC vermin!

Tor waded in, vials and packages crunching underfoot. He set the brakes on an examining table and jammed the wheels with bandages, then carried Yasmin over to sit on it. She braced herself awkwardly upright, and gave Tor instructions while trying to massage circulation back into her hands. Tor found and heated thermal pads and strapped them to her torso and feet, then located a container of rehydration mix. She held it with difficulty between her forearms and drank all she could hold, ignoring nausea.

She needed clothes, so she sent Tor below to their cabin. When old Anderson had asked her for the gun, she'd used his money to buy two, and with luck her weapon would still be where she'd hidden it.

The wait for Tor seemed very long and she had time to consider that he might be captured again, or the VC might come to Sick Bay. She rummaged in a half empty drawer and found a scalpel, but it was a poor weapon and she was in no condition to wield it. Though she could move her fingers now, agonizing stabs from returning blood circulation brought tears of pain to her eyes. Working clumsily, she swabbed off the worst of her injuries and sprayed them with disinfectant/sealant. The shallow knife cuts on her breasts and stomach had scabbed over and she could see bruises blooming. That sight and a whiff of stale semen sparked a new flash of rage.

The door rattled and she grabbed a scalpel, but it was only Tor returning with weapon and clothes. It took her long, awkward minutes to dress. When she finished, she saw Tor staring at her desperately, shaking with distress and dopamine starvation.

"Yasmin, they hurt you!"

"No shit! she snarled.

"I'm so sorry, Yasmin. It's my fault! I'm so sorry!

His utter patheticness was the last straw and she lost her temper. She slapped him clumsily across the face.

"That's for fucking up!" she yelled.

Tor grabbed his cheek, whimpering, then lost his balance and went down on his knees in the debris, grabbing at his stomach. His hand came away bloody and Yasmin felt a start of surprise, as she realized he was wounded. She hadn't seen the blood against his black clothes, and he hadn't told her! Idiot!

The examining table threatened to overbalance under Tor's weight, so she had to examine him standing, braced in a corner. His coat and shirt were wet with blood dribbling from an abdominal knife wound. The entry was small, but it looked like a deep thrust and from the smell she suspected colonic perforation. Normally she would have used a surgical explorer to make immediate repairs, but it wasn't possible, so she cleaned the area thoroughly, sprayed it with sealant/disinfectant foam, and then taped it up. She had trouble finding enough supplies—most must have been moved out. Finally she gave him pain meds and then used her warmest voice:

"Good job, Tor. Good boy."

Tor's pupils dilated and he gasped with cued reward. She let him slide down until he was sitting against the wall, and gave him thirty seconds of reward. His color improved and his breathing steadied.

"Where did you get the riot glue solvent?" she asked.

"The helmsman passed it to me. I think Captain Quero had it all planned."

"And the wound?"

"One of the twins. I knocked his gun away, but he had a knife."

Tor was getting upset again. She patted his shoulder.

"Tor! Look in my eyes. Byzantium. Now calm down. You are feeling calm. Good, Tor, good. Feel calm and happy. Very good."

The keyed voice commands and sensation of her hand on his arm worked instantly. Tor's face twisted into a beaming smile of relief and joy.

A particularly large swell heaved the floor under them, sending a fresh avalanche of broken equipment careening around. Something whacked Yasmin's ankle and she swore.

"In real ocean ships, all the furniture is bolted down and the cupboards have latches," Tor volunteered happily.

"I could guess that!" she snapped, but he kept talking.

"The original Empress of Japan rolled a lot and passengers got sick, so they installed stabilizers. But this ship only has little stabilizers to keep the gaming tables steady in protected waters. And it was never properly certified anyway. The tong bribed the inspectors. Those windows in the casino are eight millimeter marine glass instead of twenty millimeter. Also, storms are bigger now than two centuries ago because of climate change."

He gave her an eager smile, like a child showing off a new trick. He was happy. He had Yasmin, he had his reward, and he was on his favorite steam boat. In his childlike state he didn't think further.

But Yasmin did, and despite pain and fatigue she had to make plans. First, she must make sure the twins were eliminated. Too bad she couldn't use Simon as a weapon against the Nguyens—the possibilities in that scenario made her smile—but she had no control of

Choi's tool yet.

A readout on the wall told her it was 3:08 a.m., so she'd been up almost forty-eight hours, but she had no time for sleep. She found an undamaged vial of sleep suppressants and administered one dose to herself and another to Tor. That should be good for six hours, she estimated. She put the rest in her pocket.

An antique speaker on the wall crackled to life.

"Attention! This is Captain Quero. All ship's crew are to report to the Chief Engineer immediately to help with damage control. If you are unable to assist, go to the Upper Deck and stay fully dressed. Repeat. Remain on the Upper deck and stay fully dressed. Familiarize yourself with the lifeboat drill. Captain out."

Well, that was useless, thought Yasmin with annoyance.

She straightened up, tucking supplies in her pockets, and nearly fell over. It wasn't just the ship, she realized suddenly—she needed food. Damn. She briefly considered a nutrient pak before remembering that she'd stashed most of them with her hidden prisoner. She hesitated a minute, tempted to go down and check on him, but other priorities were more urgent.

She disabled the pistol's safety, then sent Tor ahead into the corridor. As a last thought she grabbed a red & white first aid bag—waving that would legitimize her presence anywhere on the ship.

Carpet squelched underfoot, and in the metal-decked service passages rivulets of water sloshed back and forth. As they neared the galley, Yasmin heard a new throb over the storm. She stopped, tensing, then realized that somebody had cranked up a popular blatt album.

A half dozen hookers sat on the Galley floor, tripped to the eyeballs, singing along with pop lyrics in a howl of sitar, drums and voices. Fortunately someone had taped cupboards shut and cleared away loose objects, and a pile of fresh sandwiches sat in a box taped to the counter top. Yasmin and Tor braced themselves in a corner and ate ravenously. Someone offered luke-warm coffee made in condiment containers, but Yasmin declined. Instead she found a large mug and got hot water from the beverage tap, spilling almost as much as she managed to drink.

She looked at Tor and noticed him frowning up at the ceiling. "What is it?" she shouted.

He leaned down to her ear.

"We're still sailing into the wind," he shouted. "I think we should of turned around by now."

Probably couldn't, thought Yasmin, then an alarming idea struck her. What if the Viet Ching had retaken the bridge? Well, she was armed now and she could turn the tables. She smiled wolfishly as her mind raced. Entering the wheelhouse through the inside door meant going in blind, but nobody would expect an outside approach.

The wakeups and pain meds had taken hold and Yasmin felt a soaring sense of exhilaration. She beckoned Tor and set out, slinging the first aid pack over her shoulder. They climbed a narrow crew companionway with salt water dribbling down metal treads. At the top Tor led her through a corridor, then stopped at an outside door. The sound of the storm was much louder up here and he had to shout.

"This is the lee side!"

Yasmin tucked her gun into an inside pocket of the captain's jacket, closed up the front, and stepped out into the storm.

Inside, the wind had been a muted howl. Outside it shrieked. The deck vibrated under her feet. Spray flew at her, rain battered her, and biting gusts sucked the air from her lungs. In the sheer excitement of it all she opened her mouth and screamed delight, then stopped to look at the foaming mountains of water illuminated by the ship's lights. As the Empress crested an especially large wave, the full force of the gale slammed into them and only Tor's quick grab kept Yasmin from losing her grip on the rail.

Tor waited until the ship dropped into the next trough, then led hand over hand along the railing. Yasmin followed, feeling at one moment as though she would pitch head first over the side, and at the next as though the ship was going to roll back on top of her. They passed through a "Crew Only" gate and climbed a set of steps to the bridge door. She'd hoped to be able to see in through the windows, but the low lighting inside, and turmoil outside made it impossible.

"Go in!" she yelled.

Tor nodded and grabbed the door handle. It took much of his strength to pull it open against the wind, then he stepped over the sill and it slammed shut behind him.

Yasmin clung to the rail for long seconds wondering if the

bridge crew or the VC might shoot him, then the door opened again and Tor beckoned. She judged the motion of the deck underneath her and ran at the open door.

Pale faces turned toward her in semi-darkness. The door slammed shut, muting the storm's scream. Captain Quero stepped forward, looking disheveled and exhausted. His eyes focused on Yasmin's face, and he raised his eyebrows incredulously.

"Miz Paroo?"

She waved the first aid bag and shoved wet hair out of her eyes.

"I came up to see how you were," she shouted, looking around. She counted seven crew members, plus Tommy Yip still glued to the floor, huddled miserably under the tartan blanket. She almost laughed. Quero must hate him more than she had guessed.

"I can't believe you came back!" It was Quero's wife, Lizares, teary-eyed with admiration.

"Any injuries?" yelled Yasmin, assuming the role of resolute heroine.

"One broken arm but we sent him below."

"What about Nguyen?"

"I glued his hands to the floor," shouted Lizares with savage satisfaction. "In the Chart Room."

"No sign of the other twin?"

Lizares shook her head. Tor leaned forward.

"Why hasn't the ship turned around?"

Lizares moved her gaze to him.

"Can't get NavLink up, can't get a usable phone fix. If we turn around and run back blind, there's a thousand rocks we could pile up on."

"We're hoping to keep our nose into the wind and ride it out," added Quero.

Ride it out? That could take days, Yasmin realized with horror. She couldn't spend days stuck in the middle of the bloody Pacific Ocean. She had a mission.

"You have to turn around," she said decisively.

"We'll see in the morning when we have daylight," said Lizares, putting a hand on her shoulder.

Yasmin shook it off, thinking urgently, then put on a distressed expression.

"But what about my patients?! I've got two seriously injured people in Sick Bay.

As she'd hoped, Quero looked worried.

"How bad are they?"

"I've done what I can, but my equipment is damaged and I can't operate in these seas."

"Damn!" The captain rubbed a hand across his stubbly face. "I got a call through to the Coast Patrol, but they can't medevac in this, and there's another twenty-four hours of it coming. You sure you can't keep them stable?"

Yasmin shook her head.

"Six or eight hours is the longest I can hope for."

Lizares gave Tor a puzzled look.

"Who's in Sick Bay with the patients?"

"A volunteer," said Yasmin. Damn the woman's nosiness. Fortunately Quero distracted his wife by turning to her.

"What's your best guess at our position?"

She shrugged wearily. "I think we're about one hundred kilometers northwest of Cape St. James. I've been steering well north to keep us away from the Triangle Islands, but all I've got is some tide tables for Sandheads so I can only guess at currents and drift."

"How long would it take us to make Milbank Sound?"

"Four, maybe five hours."

"It'll be light by seven," said Quero. "But hell, it's a crapshoot going in there—worse!" He looked anxiously up at his screen as if expecting NavLink to reappear, then ran a shaky hand through his gray hair while hanging onto a stanchion with the other hand. He looked exhausted, and every bit his age.

Unexpectedly, Lizares weighed in, her voice decisive.

"Manny, we're taking on water. I don't think we can keep her afloat another twenty-four hours. And I don't know about you, but I can't hold together that long. The guys in the Engine Room can't either."

Quero met his wife's eyes for a long moment, then took a deep breath.

"All right, work out a course for Milbank Sound."

# 19

## September 19

Simon struggled slowly to consciousness, throwing off sleep to enter a nightmare. The surface under him vibrated and tilted down hill toward his head, yet he didn't fall. His mouth was dry, his head hurt, and noise roared in his ears. He gasped, fighting to open gluey eyes.

David. His friend stood beside him, tugging at the buckles on a wide restraint strap that held Simon's right wrist to a padded surface. Then memory and horror washed over Simon. David had betrayed him. His breath came in shallow, panicked gasps and he felt vertigo. He fled into Blade....

Calm. Silence. Blade lay back and concentrated on breathing. As he forced his leaden lungs to suck in air, dizziness and nausea eased. But his orientation still felt wrong. The room underneath him heaved sickeningly. He opened his eyes again.

David stood braced against the bed, jerking at the restraint. He wore rumpled clothing and a heavy jacket much too large for him, open at the front. Behind him, a young, brown-haired girl clutched a lamp bracket with her right hand and watched David sullenly through a bruised and swollen face. With her other arm she hugged a furry toy.

David spoke and Blade watched his words.

"Help me with this, will you?!"

"No way!" The girl nodded backed toward the door. "Come on, let's get out of here!"

"No, I told you, this is Simon!"

"That's a tool, you lobeless cret! He'll kill you!"

"He won't...."

"I'm outta here!" The girl turned and fled. David looked after her then turned back to the straps, tears in his eyes. Abruptly he

200

noticed Blade.

"Simon! You're awake! I'm getting you undone, OK? Just having trouble with these pitless things."

As he spoke, the wrist strap came loose. David shifted position and began working on the strap on Blade's upper arm. Blade watched his movements closely in case the boy attempted to trick him again. In his peripheral vision he noted the room. It appeared to be the ship's cabin he'd fallen asleep in, with polished wood wainscoting and an old fashioned globe light in the paneled ivory ceiling. And it was definitely in violent motion

"Cin-Cin unlocked my cabin and let me out," David said. He looked pale and agitated, and his hands were clumsy. "Then I went looking for you. It's total craziness around here. We're in the middle of a big storm and almost everybody's sea sick and Cin-Cin says there's gang members with guns fighting over the ship. She said she thinks we're going to sink and we should find a lifeboat, but I had to find you first. Are you OK?"

Blade met his gaze without expression. The strap parted and Blade flexed his arm and fingers, then reached for the belt restraining his shoulders.

"Simon?... Simon, are you OK?..."

The boy kept speaking but Blade did not watch his words. He found the quick release clamp on the shoulder strap, then unfastened the other restraints in quick succession. He sat up, reaching for leg straps, and pushed the blanket off. Cool air brushed his naked skin. When he swung his legs over the bed and stood naked, David stumbled back a step, looking wide-eyed at Blade's scars and his sexless crotch.

As the boy hastily averted his eyes, Blade grabbed him, bound his small wrists together, and secured him to the bed, noting that it had a wood frame, retrofitted with tie-downs. Then he examined the swaying cabin, hunching slightly to keep from banging his head against the low ceiling. His clothes lay on the floor and he searched them, finding his night goggles and handlight but not his phone. He had to brace awkwardly to use the toilet, get drinking water from the potable tap at a small porcelain sink, and dress. A search of the slamming bedside drawers yielded a selection of medical instruments and drug paks, and six pouches of nutrient mix. Aware that he felt shaky and weak, he opened two immediately and drank them, then put the others in his pockets. In another drawer he found a silver talisman on a leather thong. A crow flashed on its polished surface....

Simon shoved the disk in his pocket, suddenly aware of wood and metal groaning around him and a constant background roar. He pulled aside the velvet curtain and glimpsed movement outside—something large and white in the darkness beyond the ship. Water slammed against the window. Simon flinched back, letting the curtain fall. The tiny cabin closed in around him. He must find a way out, but his thoughts were fogged by rising panic. His eyes brushed David and dizzy horror grabbed at him. No! He had to think! Choi!

Choi closed his eyes for three calming seconds, then turned to examine the cabin's desk and found, as he expected, that the polished wood surface lifted up to reveal a retractable netset, defaulted to the Empress of Vancouver's directory. When he woke it, the screen flashed a red emergency notice and lifeboat drill instructions. Conveniently, they included a holographic model of the ship with a blinking yellow dot at his location—cabin 3B on the Main Deck. A yellow line traced the most direct route to a life raft station one deck up, and red triangles marked all the other life raft locations. He magnified the Promenade Deck and also noted two large steam launches near the stern. These looked far superior to life rafts. The further he could travel from the Empress, the better.

Now he needed to know the ship's position. Switching screens, he tried the NavSat link, but it didn't open, nor did the data uplinks. His requests produced only the date and time: Thursday, September 19, 6:43 a.m.

The boy might know.

"Where are we?"

David looked up at him, face ashen with fright.

"Uh...."

"Where?!" Choi snapped.

"I don't know! Cin-Cin said we went north and now we're somewhere out in the ocean. ...Simon...?"

"You betrayed Simon," said Choi icily. "Who did you sell him to?"

David's eyes went wide.

"I didn't!"

The ship heeled suddenly, forcing Choi to grab at the desk for balance, then the entire cabin slammed backward and he was thrown across the room onto the floor. The desk flew with him, its edge smashing into his rib cage. Thunderous noise filled his ears and the ship lurched to a steep angle, then stopped moving. The lights died.

For long seconds nothing happened. Choi levered the desk off his chest and sat up painfully in pitch darkness, unable to tell at first whether the ship was still moving. Shudders pounded through the hull and when he took a deep breath, pain flared on the left side of his chest.

"Owww!" Somewhere nearby David wailed, a piercing, high pitched noise.

Choi found Blade's night goggles and slid them on, adjusting to infrared. He immediately saw David hanging by his bound wrists from the bed, which was bolted to the floor. As the boy scrambled frantically for purchase on the steep polished wood floor, Choi felt a momentary flash of pleasure. Revenge would be most satisfying....

But no. Regrettably, there was no time. He must escape quickly, and the boy could not help him. He started toward the door, then another thought struck him. The boy was not useful now, but he might make a valuable hostage later. And if not—he could always be killed. Punished for his betrayal. Made to scream as Simon had screamed....

He had to brace the boy with one shoulder to unbind his wrists, and found his left hand fumbling, so he switched to his right. Released, David lost his balance, and Choi grabbed him by the shirt. He didn't want to lose his hostage, so he took one of the longer restraints, opened it out, and fastened it around the boy's waist, under his shirt. He secured it tightly at the back and added another restraint as a crude leash. His captive trembled, but blinded by the darkness he did not struggle.

The passage outside the cabin stood empty. Studying the angle of the corridor, Choi decided that the ship lay canted uphill towards its bow, listing to the left side. It must have run aground. And judging from the shaking around him, it could break apart or sink at any moment. He must leave quickly. Every movement sent flaring pain across his rib cage, and he breathed shallowly as he finalized a plan. He formulated commands and called Blade.

Blade started down the sloping hallway toward the stern, towing the stumbling boy. Numbered cabin doors lined the corridor on both sides. He passed a glass-fronted cabinet mounted on the wall and flicked his handlight at it. An antique fire axe. He punched through the glass and hefted the axe—dull-edged and cheap, but better than nothing.

Light flickered from an intersection ahead. He spun and started back up the corridor but it stretched too far before him. He couldn't reach the other stairwell in time. He grabbed the nearest door handle and twisted. It opened inward. He shoved David inside and dove in after him, pulling the door shut just as a hand-light beam swept the corridor.

This cabin stank of vomit, but infrared showed no occupant among the mess of tumbled furniture and bric-a-brac. It was an interior room, opulently furnished, but with no windows and no other exit. He positioned himself beside the door and waited, watching the door handle. Long seconds passed. It didn't move. The door's tight seal admitted no light or sound. Anything could be happening outside. Blade flipped open one of his goggle lenses to release a microcam, then took out the tiny device, eased the door open a crack and extended the camera into the corridor.

To his right: an empty corridor stretched down hill. To his left: two figures stood outside the cabin he'd been imprisoned in. Blade had anticipated seeing Yasmin and Tor, but these were two unknown men. Blade zoomed on their faces and used full spectrum enhancements to create portraits in the periphery of his vision. Even before the ID scan finished he recognized them: veteran Viet Ching henches, Nguyen and Trinh. This was a Kung Lok ship, but the beleaguered Kung Lok might have easily have made a Viet Ching alliance, and the VC certainly kept trainers like Yasmin. They were armed, too, carrying live semi-automatics in their hands.

Blade made a second fast scan of the other end of the corridor, enhancing infrared and searching for a hint of warm breath. Nguyen had a twin and they were rarely apart. But there was no sign of him.

The henches conferred by the closed cabin door, then Nguyen tried the handle. He seemed surprised to find it unlocked. He nodded at Trinh, who flattened himself beside the door, then he shoved the door open and went in fast, gun ready. Trinh followed.

Blade snapped the microcam back into his goggle, reached back to grab the boy, and pulled the cabin door open.

The corridor stood empty in both directions. He tucked the boy under one arm, boosted adrenaline and ran seven long strides to a plain, unmarked door which the map showed as leading to a service stair. Light flickered behind him. He wrenched the door open and entered.

Water spattered down steep, metal grill stairs, and the reflections of red emergency signs flashed from enameled metal walls. Draughts of air brushed his skin, cold and pungent with salt water and marine lube. Picturing the map he'd seen, Blade knew this stair shaft reached from the Engine Deck all the way up to the Promenade Deck. He put the boy down and started up, his speed hampered by the angle of the ship which slewed the steps to one side and made alternate flights lethally steep. The boy scrambled behind him, sometimes grabbing the taut leash for support.

They were one flight from the top when light flared through the grillwork above. Blade changed direction instantly, hauling open a door marked 'Upper Deck.' It led into a service corridor where a set of double doors gave access to the main dining room.

Blade cautiously edged a door open into pitch blackness. After checking infrared he risked his handlight. Crystal chandeliers sent sparkles of light cascading across an empty expanse of carpet and a heap of tables and chairs, snarled in white tablecloths. It was bitingly cold here, and wind swayed the chandeliers. The ship gave a massive shudder and foam poured in through an expanse of broken windows. Blade crossed toward them, waterlogged carpet squishing underfoot. He waited for water to pour back through the windows, then peered out onto the windward deck.

In infrared, the ship was a ghostly shadow with glowing smokestacks, surrounded by gray. Blade tried a motion overlay, and the scene erupted in flaming streamers of wind, rain and spray, underlain by great burgundy mounds of ocean. The horizon heaved and he ducked back, grabbing a brass lamp bracket just as a new wave broke on the deck, spraying him with salt water so icy that it sucked the breath from his lungs. The leash tugged sharply against his stiff left hand—the boy falling or trying to flee. He kept a tight grip, forced a deep breath, and leaned out through jagged glass, cycling through enhancements to get a good view of the Promenade Deck. The ship's stern sagged beneath pounding waves, but the launch davits one deck above him still looked accessible. And just a few meters away, an outside staircase led up.

He used the axe to clear remaining shards of glass from a window, waited for another wave to subside, and stepped through, lifting the boy behind him. He'd intended to run for the stairs, but a hammer blow of wind knocked him sideways. The boy fell and slid flailing along slick teak planks until the leash jerked him to a stop. Blade braced and pulled until he could grab the boy by the seat of his pants, then he lunged for the stairs, just ahead of the next foaming surge. At the top he crouched to reconnoiter.

A steam launch hung from davits less than ten meters ahead of him, but the full brunt of the gale was smashing it wildly from side to side. It looked damaged and impossible to launch.

Small hands clawed at his arm, then grabbed his shoulders. Blade tensed to strike out, then realized that the boy was trying to crawl onto his back. He hesitated, hating the sensation of someone behind his neck, but realizing that it was an efficient carrying solution. The boy wrapped his legs around Blade's chest and arms around his shoulders, and clung tightly, forming a tiny island of warmth on his back. Blade ignored fresh stabs of pain in his ribs and stood, bracing against the rail, then hunched forward and ran across the exposed deck to a passage behind one of the giant smokestacks, heading for the launch on the lee side of the ship.

As he rounded the corner behind the funnel, the wind dropped abruptly and he stumbled forward into a wash of emergency lighting and people. Fortunately, they had their backs turned—all attention focused on the portside steam launch, descending from its davits toward surging waves. A few meters away two crew member struggled with manual controls on the housing of the davit motor while several others waved frantically at the launch, beckoning it to return. Infrared showed that the launch held only three people—two seated inside and a third small figure huddled on the floor between the seats. Blade zoomed, instantly identifying the first two people as his captor, Yasmin, and her assistant. She was fleeing the ship, abandoning the other passengers.

Muzzle flashes came from his left and Blade dropped to a crouch, bracing the axe. When running steps pounded past, he realized the shots had not been aimed at him. His goggles ID'd the sprinting figures as two Viet Ching henches. They were shooting at the steam launch. Other men moved to intercept, all of them clumsy on the rain-slick deck. Two went down grappling, and there were more muzzle flashes. Were the Viet Ching fighting the Kung Lok? No matter. Any of them would shoot Blade once they noticed him.

Blade rose from his crouch and ran uphill toward the bow, trying to focus on his memorized map of the Empress. Both launches were out, and he could see people standing by a large lifeboat ahead—what else? The map showed symbols for inflatable boats, stored in chests along the both decks. There was one behind a companionway on the starboard Upper Deck, almost directly below them.

He had almost reached the next companionway when a man ran out of a doorway and shone a light in his face. Blade's goggles compensated, cutting the glare and enhancing the man's face, but he was already swinging the axe, slamming its flat side into the man's left shoulder and bowling him off his feet. An instant later he had an ID—one of the Nguyen twins. The wiry hench scrambled to his knees, firing wildly from a gun in his right hand. Slightly off balance from the weight of David on his shoulders and the precarious footing, Blade elected for brute force. He ran at Nguyen and slammed into the man with both fists, knocking him backward and sending the gun skidding across the deck. Blade didn't bother going after it—the safeties would be fingerprint-locked to Nguyen.

Instead, he kicked Nguyen full in the chest as the man tried to rise, then stomped down hard on his right hand, feeling knuckles break under his foot. The man's face contorted with pain even as he tried to roll away. Blade pursued, connecting a savage kick with Nguyen's knee.

Hands beat at his shoulders and abruptly he heard a reedy shriek near his ear "Simon! No! Don't kill him!"

Kill? He had no orders to kill. He was simply disabling his

opponent. More shrieking pierced the wind—no, it was screaming, coming from the man writhing on the deck. Simon stared at this agony, breath catching in his throat. Suddenly he felt sick, frightened. Why? He'd done this and much worse hundreds of times....

"Simon! No!"

Simon labored for breath, ribs throbbing with pain, ears ringing with storm static and animal shrieks, and felt the familiar onset of panic. No! He made a desperate grab for control. Not here! Not now! Blade! He needed Blade!

For several long seconds the world churned in chaos, then focus returned. Blade drew in deliberate long breaths and checked his surroundings. Preoccupied with the steam launch, and deafened by storm noise, nobody had noticed his fight. He turned, and jogged five meters forward to a companionway. Down one level waves were washing up the teak deck from the stern, but the boat chests stood in the locations shown, unopened. He dumped the boy off his shoulders and used the axe to bash off a lock on the first chest, then lifted the lid. It was half empty, containing only packages labeled "thermal rain gear." He moved further astern and broke open the second chest. This held a large rectangular bundle—the life raft.

Icy foam swept around his feet as he studied a faded set of instructions on the inside of the chest lid. Simple drawings showed two men lifting the bundle out, but he was able to grab the handles at each end and heave it out by himself. He dumped it on deck, loosened the packing straps, and pulled the red trigger tab. At first nothing seemed to happen. Then the bundle bulged and began unfolding in segments, each section ballooning after the next. A large wave swept up the deck, ankle deep this time, and Blade grabbed a corner of the boat, realizing it could be snatched away. As the wave sucked back, he returned to the chest for the motor and fuel cells. He heaved them into the stiffening craft, then as an afterthought returned to the first chest and threw in all the survival gear.

He had just turned away from the empty chest when old instinct flared, telling him that it wasn't deep enough. He smashed down with the axe and broke through a false bottom. Below were two compact duffel bags. He took them as well.

Mentally consulting the instructions, he worked his way

around the boat, snapping sectional pieces of alloy frame into place. The motor slid neatly into a clamp at the stern, and the fuel cells snapped into place on either side. He found the motor's fuel line and plugged it into a recessed socket on the nearest fuel cell. It was a simple task but it took two tries. His hands were growing numb with cold, especially his left. He had to use his right hand to stow loose objects in equipment pouches and clip the boy's leash to a tie-down.

A flash of light caught Blade's eye and he turned to see hand-lights in the distance, approaching from the bow, with the blue out-lines of hand guns behind them. He grabbed the boat and dragged it sternward, wading into oncoming surf. As a large wave rolled at him he boosted adrenaline, shoved the boat forward with all his strength, and then jumped after it.

He barely managed to roll inside before the surf shoved the boat backward, almost flipping it. He got to his knees, fighting clumsily for purchase, and flung himself at the starter switch. A green light flashed. The outboard motor coughed and shook, then died. Another wave grabbed the boat, driving it at the Empress's side. Blade hit the starter again and this time the motor caught. He grabbed the tiller and gunned the motor, wiping an arm across his rain-streaked goggles as he tried to orient himself. A retreating wave sucked them sternward and he aimed away from the Empress's superstructure. An instant later the full screaming force of the gale hit them, skidding the inflatable sideways.

The next moments were churning chaos. Blade clung to the engine, trying to turn the boat into the wind, but a large wave raised the propeller out of the water, then a gust caught the under side of the boat, nearly flipping them. Blade threw his weight on the rising side of the boat, then reached back for the tiller again, and maneu-vered to get the wind behind them. For a moment he almost had control, then they pitched violently into a chaos of foam. Breakers. Blade braced, expecting to be smashed against a rocky shore but the boat hurtled through churning water and into suddenly lower seas.

Again, Blade wiped his goggles and tried to find a visible landmark. On maximum pickup his goggles showed faint gray light to the south, but daylight was still a half hour away. He switched

209

through spectra and frequencies, then tried motion detection and found himself able to distinguish between calmer and rougher water. A dark shadow stood out—an island? With no other visible options, Blade aimed the boat for it, steering his course over the fetal curl of the boy, huddled in fading infrared near the bow of the boat.

# 20

Thursday passed as a painful hell of waiting for bad news while rain pattered incessantly on the roof of the cramped old cabin. Klale multitasked on her phone at the kitchen table, locating a mini-sub and then persuading a series of people to expedite it to Cape Mudge before nightfall. Toni listened for a while, then realizing she had nothing to contribute, retreated to the sofa and pretended to update her notes. Rigo paced, then started cooking.

Around four Klale called them over to the netset to watch vid feed from the sub as it dived. The descent was a long monotony of inky static, ending with a gray blur that resolved into Andercraft resting on its side at two hundred and sixty-nine meters. The sub's waldos retrieved David and Simon's phones from the sea floor nearby and the operator even managed to locate Simon's tiny restraint implant inside the boat. Despite a lengthy and widening search, there was no sign of bodies.

Toni greeted the news numbly, aware that she didn't want to have her hopes raised and then killed again. But fear leaked past her attempted anesthesia as they talked the situation over. Simon might have removed his implant himself—difficult but not absolutely impossible if he had tools and assistance—and then fled with David as a co-conspirator or hostage. Or, and Toni found this far more plausible, they'd been snatched by some of Choi's old tong enemies.

The Empress seemed the obvious place to start, but when Klale phoned Campbell River she discovered that the steamship had pulled out that morning without port clearance, and was running at full speed up the inside passage. No phone calls were getting through.

With this news, Toni needed to make some ugly calls of her own—the kind she couldn't expect Rigo to make about his own son. Besides, it was her responsibility as the closest thing they had to a practitioner of record. She trod grimly upstairs to her bedroom, carrying her netset.

She started with Mary Smarch, who took the news somberly, saying only that she would notify the rest of Simon's parole committee, and would Toni please call the Coast Patrol to give them a detailed rundown on the situation. So she called North Island Patrol headquarters in Port Hardy where an officer took her report with surprising equanimity—surprising until Toni realized that the woman had no idea what a bioenhanced enforcer was and knew nothing about tongs. Toni unleashed the full force of her caustic tongue and started climbing rank. Two angry officers later she was switched laterally to a senior crime specialist with the Canadian Forces Pacific Region in Vancouver—one of the independent military units that had survived the fall of nationalism fifty years ago, and now provided security services on contract to organizations like the Vancouver Council of Guilds.

Major S.B. Kim had an oval, flat-planed face, and antique round-framed eyeglasses that made him look like a student, but he required only one sentence to grasp the seriousness of what Toni was telling him.

"Photo?" he snapped.

Toni sent it and saw his face tighten. The eyes behind those owl glasses were cold and very sharp. Fifty at least, she estimated, looking at subtle creases around his mouth.

"Choi Shung Wai's enforcer. That would make you the KlonDyke bartender who reportedly accompanied the construct and Dr. Lau to Hong Kong for therapy."

"That's right," said Toni, trying to keep the shock from showing on her face. She hadn't realized the CFPR had a tong expert, and certainly hadn't considered how much he might know.

"But you said your name was...?"

"Dr. Antonia Almiramez."

He reached offscreen and checked a readout.

"Formerly from the Seattle Neurological Institute?"

"That's right," said Toni, chilled at his efficiency.

"I assume you have no objection to a sanctioned official taking a genetic sample?"

"No. But I'd prefer it be kept off the record."

"Who's looking for you?" he asked bluntly.

Toni grimaced.

"Ten years ago it was the Yakuza. Maybe others. I'd still be worth something on the training market."

He studied his screen, before turning to meet her eyes. "You've been in hiding?"

"Yes," she said steadily, meeting his gaze. "I hid so I wouldn't be forced into training for the tongs."

She didn't expect him to simply accept that, but she was far from prepared for the expert, detailed and coldly furious interrogation that followed. She gave him basic details about Simon's therapy and even—with great reluctance—surrendered his fishhook code, but then she found herself blocking and evading, suddenly afraid that she might have delivered Simon to an enemy more deadly than the tongs. Even in their short conversation she'd noticed Kim's enmity for bioaltered humans, so she portrayed Simon as a simple tool with personality remnants. That profile wouldn't stand up to much scrutiny, but if Kim realized the full extent of Simon's abilities and knowledge, he might be tempted to kill Simon outright.

Tired of being on the defense, she eventually interrupted with a question of her own.

"Do you think Tommy Yip took Simon?"

"Not Yip's style."

"He hates me," pointed out Toni. "Personally."

The Major gave her a very hard look, then asked: "Do you believe he'd target a boosted tool instead of you?"

Hell no, thought Toni, her heart sinking. Yip was a renowned coward, and if he'd been able to snatch Simon he could surely have taken Toni. She closed her eyes wearily, then opened them to find Kim staring at her.

"However, Yip is rumored to have invited Viet Ching survivors to join the Kung Lok."

"On the Empress?"

Kim hesitated, then nodded.

"Damn," she muttered. "They'd be interested." More than interested if they realized what he was. Kim leaned back in his seat and spoke icily.

"Doctor Almiramez, I don't know how you and your friends managed to convince a jurist to approve medical parole for a psychotic, bioaltered assassin, but if one soldier or Patrol officer is

213

harmed trying to retrieve it, I will personally make the rest of your life a living hell. Do I make myself clear?"

"Take a number," snarled Toni and cut him off.

She was just massaging her forehead when a call came in from someone on her personal priority list. She waved the screen on and a familiar white-haired old man looked out at her. Ron McCaskill. Toni's stomach clenched. Ron, the compassionate elder Citizen who had persuaded his Guild and his grieving family to parole his grandson's killer. Ron, her friend, who had risked his life to help smuggle Simon out of Vancouver, and staked everything on her passionate assertion she would prevent Simon from harming anyone else. Looking into his worried blue eyes she felt like the lowest piece of shit on Earth.

Afterward she had no idea what she said, only that she found herself staring at a blank screen, wondering distantly if she was going to throw up, wondering if Rigo still had that bottle of cognac in the sideboard, thinking that one more bottle and a couple of tranqs for good measure would take her away from having to deal with consequences....

It was Rigo's hand on her shoulder that roused her. He closed the set and led her down to the kitchen where he brewed medicinal tea and stood over her while she drank two cups. Then he set a bowl of herbed winter melon stew in front of her. She chewed mechanically, tasting nothing, but too numb to argue even when ordered to bed.

She slept heavily until the meds wore off, then found herself awake and restless. She felt miserable, but the worst of her black depression had lifted. Finally, unable to sleep, she did the unthinkable and got up before seven a.m., only to find Rigo and Klale already in the kitchen, huddled tensely over Mary's netset. They'd been up all night, Toni discovered, and Klale filled her in.

Unable to get information from official sources, Klale had logged onto TideTalk—a big Fisher/Mariner board—where the Empress was hot news. At first the situation had simply aroused interest. Credible postings confirmed that the ship had only junior officers aboard, but those officers were experienced enough to navigate a large vessel up the Inside Passage to Alaska, even without NavLink. The trickiest part of the route was where it left the shelter of Vancouver Island and crossed the open waters of Queen Charlotte Sound before ducking back into Fitz Hugh Sound—a fifty kilometer fully exposed crossing that was notoriously treacherous in bad weather. With a very large system blowing in from the northwest, Mariners figured the Empress would anchor somewhere in the vicinity of Port Hardy and wait the weather out. The Coast Patrol's big cutter, Quatsino, stationed in Port Hardy, would almost certainly investigate.

At first it seemed TideTalk had called it right. Satellite tracking showed the Empress slowing near Malcolm Island and stopping in Cormorant Channel. Boaters in Hardy Bay posted vids of the Quatsino casting off. Then events veered. Instead of intercepting the Empress, the cutter answered a distress call from a troller taking on water off the Scott Islands in hurricane force winds. And a few hours later, the Empress started north again and steered west through Goletas Channel into open ocean.

Traffic on TideTalk hit new records, and even with smartsifting Klale couldn't winnow credible analysis from speculation. Many Mariners alleged that the replica steamship was not seaworthy. And rumors of mutiny and tong war abounded, though nothing could be confirmed with the ship's uplink disabled.

Rigo and Klale had followed TideTalk all night as the Empress headed west, then unexpectedly changed course to the northeast, apparently running for Milbank Sound. At 6:45 a.m. a data station at McInnes Island reported an SOS, and twenty minutes later the Coast Patrol issued a terse announcement that the Empress had run aground. Weather conditions were too severe for Patrol vessels or air support to approach.

Klale and Rigo looked distressed, but Toni found all this talk of storms and steamships as unreal as a ficvid. Besides, far worse things could happen to Simon than drowning—assuming that he actually was on the ship. So far they had no reports of David or Simon.

Rigo made another of his special teas, then went back to the netset. Toni sniffed her steaming mug. It smelled like composted garden clippings. She made a show of sipping it, then with a cautious sideways glance, she poured it down the sink and made coffee, drinking it defiantly on an empty stomach while Rigo sat oblivious at the kitchen table. It helped, but what she really wanted, she realized, was a mother big hit of Black Lace. Abruptly the thirst hit her, as intense as it had been ten or twenty years ago, and she found herself doing a mental inventory of Rigo's medkit, obsessively working out how much of what she could steal and how much of a trip she could load without getting caught. When the housecomp bleeped she flinched, then hastily swallowed the last dregs of coffee while Klale jumped up to check perimeter security and then went to the back door.

Blue Anderson stood on the porch in her work clothes, carrying a tool box. Behind her, rain drizzled against a gray-green wall of trees.

"Morning," she said, stomping her boots on the mat.

"Morning." Klale waved her inside, and faced her anxiously. "Heard the news?"

"Yeah, and I'm sick of it." Blue looked directly at Toni. "I need something to do, so I thought, what the hell, why don't we rip up the kitchen floor?"

For the first time in days, Toni felt her face stretching into a grin.

"Good plan," she said. "Give me a minute, I'll get changed."

"What?!" Rigo looked up in confusion.

"Hey, it's a ferocious scheme," said Klale. "Here, you take the set into the living room and stay with the news. I'll move the cooker and the cooler onto the verandah, no smog."

When Toni came back downstairs in her work clothes, Rigo was carrying dishes into the dining room while Blue and Klale disconnected the antique stove and dragged it out to the porch, leaving behind a rats nest of ancient spills. Toni picked up a pry bar and started in with savage satisfaction on a peeling, discolored section of floor near the back door. Digging down she found two layers of laminate flooring, then a sheet of crumbling particle board, then a layer of vinyl tiles that must date from the mid twentieth century before she finally hit floor boards.

"What do you think?" she asked Blue, who was leaning down to look.

Blue gave her a mirthless grin and handed over a wrecking bar.

"Go for bedrock."

Much as she enjoyed destroying the floor, Toni had little stamina. After an hour she left the heavy work to the others and made herself useful passing tools or piling debris into totes and emptying them onto a tarp in the yard. When she leaned against the living room doorway to catch her breath, Rigo joined her, looking down on the demolition site with bemusement.

"News?" she asked.

He spoke quietly near her ear.

"Coast Patrol says the ship hasn't sunk, but they can't get near it before tomorrow at the earliest. There's not much point in my staying by the set." He frowned at her. "Did you eat breakfast?"

"Toast," she lied. "Blue, what supplies are we going to need?"

Blue spoke without looking up from where she was pulling rusty nails.

"We'll have to replace a stringer near the door. Got lots of lumber in the shop for that, and I think there's enough flooring underlay, too."

A nail screeched as she yarded it out.

"For the surface, it's a choice between troweling down some kind of faux stone finish, or going for laminate or dura-tiles. I don't recommend ceramics—floor's way too uneven."

"What option gets me my kitchen back soonest?" inquired Rigo.

"Laminate," said Blue without hesitation. "Call Building Supply in Campbell River and look for commercial grade roll laminate. I'll get you the measurements in a minute. If you order before noon you can get it on the weekly boat that's coming tomorrow."

Klale looked up, shoving unruly red hair out of her face and leaving a smudge behind.

"Yeah, you pick it out, Rigo."

"Flooring?!" Lau drew himself up, for the first time looking like his usual self. "I'm not qualified to prescribe floors. Anyway, I'm going in to take my shift at the clinic."

"Call Ethan, would you?" said Blue. "He got in late last night with a sharecar. He can give you a lift into Manson's. Ask him to pick up a kilo of number six flooring nails and some cutter blades from the store."

Rigo saluted.

The floor was a godsend, Toni decided. It kept them all occupied, and whenever she had a particularly bad moment she just picked up a tool and hit something. Blue said little and wielded her crowbar savagely. Klale worked quietly and kept a close eye on Toni. She even took bathroom breaks at the same time. Another time Toni might have found that amusing or annoying. Today she couldn't care.

Around noon Ethan and Aurora came over with sandwiches and the workers straightened up with relief. As he greeted everyone and cleared a place on the dining room side board, David's father sounded like his usual gently ironic self, but Toni saw shadows of exhaustion around his eyes and rigid tension in his stooped shoulders.

Klale logged in and relayed the latest news as she ate. TideTalk's consensus was that having weathered one high tide, the Empress was unlikely to slide off the rocks and sink. Marine satellite was tracking two lifeboat beacons, but most passengers were still aboard. There was no passenger list available.

After lunch Toni went back into the kitchen where Blue was using a laser level to check the surface. Rory, who had eaten in silence, sidled up next to Toni.

"How are you doing?" asked Toni.

"OK."

Teenagers were always OK, but the girl's voice sounded steady. Not surprising. Fifteen year old Guild kids never expected bad things to happen. Not for real.

"Want to help?"

"No thanks. Uh..." She gave Toni a significant look. "I'm kind of keeping an eye on Granddad."

Toni raised an appreciative eyebrow.

"Good plan."

Blue kicked at the floor near the back door. "Got to tear up a lot of floor to get at that beam," she muttered.

"Why not go in through the crawl space?" said Rory. "You know, where David had his cameras on that skunk family."

Her mother looked at her with sudden anguish.

"I didn't know," she said.

218

Rory flushed and looked down. Klale stepped in.

"Better hope the skunks aren't still living down there." She glanced at Toni. "Oops. You didn't hear that, right?"

Toni had, but at the moment she didn't give a damn. Still, she didn't volunteer to go into the crawl space even though she was the smallest person. It was Blue who rolled up the living room rug, lifted the trap door, and went down with a hand light into the musty, spider-webbed cave. Toni passed tools from above and held boards in place while Blue sawed and drilled. Ethan shuttled supplies over from the Anderson's workshop and Klale chiseled up recalcitrant bits of old flooring.

By the time Rigo arrived back from the clinic with a case of beer, Toni needed another rest. She picked up a beer and viewed the label with a raised eyebrow:

"Rising Gorge Ale...?"

"Family on Gorge Harbor started making it last century," said Blue shortly, taking one for herself. She and Klale went back to work, but Toni made coffee and slumped on a chair in the corner of the dining room. Ethan and Rigo sat drinking beer on the sofa—Rigo with his long legs stretched over the coffee table, and Ethan perched on the edge of his seat, elbows on his knees, hands wrapped around his bottle. There was a long silence before Ethan unexpectedly asked:

"What's Simon's mother like?"

Toni's attention sharpened.

"Simone. Hmm..." Rigo looked thoughtfully at the ceiling. "Talented. Stunning. Impossible. We met in an amateur revue in Vancouver. She was trying to make it as a dancer, and I thought I could sing. I was twenty and she told me she was eighteen, but when she got pregnant I found out she was sixteen."

He gave a sad smile.

"She wanted an abortion, but I was young and in love and I convinced her to have the baby. She told me the child would be my responsibility, and I said fine—never really believing it. I thought she'd change her mind once the baby was born. She didn't though. Never a trace of maternal instinct that I saw."

"David tells me that she's a dancer."

"She was," said Rigo. "These days she runs a dance company

in Eugene, been sending Simon vids of their performances. He's quite fascinated—must have watched each vid a dozen times."

"But she hasn't come to see him?"

Not a chance, thought Toni sourly, recollecting her one conversation with the woman.

Rigo stared somberly at his bottle.

"I don't think she wants to face what happened to Simon. And when Simone doesn't want to do something... stubborn doesn't begin...."

No, it didn't. Manipulative, self-aggrandizing, narcissistic and opportunistic, maybe.

Ethan's first bottle was empty. Rigo fetched more beer from the porch. Toni roused herself enough to check her mail. She found a three second message from Major Kim: "Nothing yet. Will call when I have news." Thanks for nothing, she thought, waved her netset off and slumped back in her chair.

"How's your father taking this?" asked Rigo, sitting down and handing Ethan a new beer. Ethan rolled the bottle between his hands.

"He's in the shop, of course. Won't tell me what he was doing at the Empress, won't say a goddamned thing!" Abruptly his calm facade broke. "He's always the fucking sphinx!"

He took a deep breath.

"Sorry. I didn't mean...."

"I understand. It was like that with my father, too."

Ethan peered at Rigo, small eyes half hidden in his wild-bearded face. Good camouflage, thought Toni. People often overlooked Ethan.

"What was your father like?"

Rigo frowned.

"Hard-working. Never said much. He grew up in northern China during the Collapse. In some ways things weren't as bad there as other places. Climate change made farming hell, but that wasn't new and they got by until the pandemics hit. Then it was the old story. Millions died. Dad lost all his family. He headed for the coast and managed to get a job in a factory in Fuzhou. That's where he met my mother."

"I don't remember her very well. She died when I was small.

220

And my father was always at work. I was ashamed of him—embarrassed at his old clothes, his country accent, his lack of education. I had big plans, I was going to be a doctor. I studied very hard at the factory school, even took English. Then when I was fifteen the factory closed and there were no more scholarships. That's when we left. Dad bought an old junk and we sailed it across the Pacific to find a better life, but there was nothing here for us either."

Toni listened with interest. Rigo had told her some of this, but only the outlines. Pain shadowed his face.

"As a teenager I was always angry at him—I thought everything was his fault. But it probably killed him, working in that factory to support me. There were no safety standards, no protective gear. I know he used toxic cleaners to scrub biomass tanks, without even a mask. There were a lot of accidents, and many workers died of autoimmune disorders and cancer. After we came to Vancouver he started behaving oddly, but I didn't really notice, I just thought he was fed up with being crammed on a tiny boat with me, Simone and a baby. But when I researched it later, I realized he had all the symptoms of neurotoxin-induced dementia. I think that's why...."

He took a long, shaky breath.

"I thought it was safe to leave Simon with my father when Simone and I went looking for work. Even when the tour company folded and stranded us in Singapore, I missed Simon of course, but I didn't worry. I never dreamed.... I keep hoping it's not true that he sold Simon to Choi.... I know he couldn't have done it if he was sane, but....!" He stopped, then forced a grimace. "It's surprisingly hard to forgive the dead."

"I understand," said Ethan quietly, then added forcefully. "It's no picnic forgiving the living either."

At five-thirty a sharecar dropped off Mary Smarch. Toni had forgotten she was coming and had utterly forgotten her promise to undergo therapy. She felt a new wave of dread and guilt.

Mary greeted them all with warm hugs, but any risk of an immediate tete-a-tete was postponed by Aurora, who phoned to invite everyone for dinner. Downing tools, they walked to the Anderson's house in the dripping dusk.

Warm smells of fresh baked corn bread and lasagna wafted through the Anderson's house. The visitors sat on comfortable old furniture in the living room while Blue washed up and Ethan helped his daughter serve out the meal. Twitchy with stress and cravings, Toni paced, looking at the accretion of family knickknacks piled on bookshelves, and the crowd of photos on the wall next to an antique wood-burning stove that had probably heated the house through much of the last century. Here was a real family—each generation layered on the previous one, right back to sepia-toned chemical photographs in wooden frames. Everything spoke of permanence, casual acceptance, assumed belonging.

How could I have been crazy enough to think I could recreate something like this for Simon? she wondered bitterly. I've never had anything like it, don't understand it, have no idea even what "normal" is. I'm a fraud—nearly as damaged as my patient, but old enough and smart enough to have known my own limitations.

A hand touched her shoulder. She flinched, even as she recognized Mary's faint lavender scent.

"You look sad."

She shrugged tense shoulders.

"I always feel like an intruder in people's homes."

"Because you never had one."

"Yeah."

"Was it hard to fake a normal background?"

Toni felt a twinge of surprise, then nodded, forcing herself past instinctive reticence.

"Always. I watched all the vids I could find, read texts, listened, and I lied well enough to pass the psych profiles, but every day was another test. There was always some detail that would trip me up and I'd get strange looks."

"Nobody caught on?"

"I built a reputation as a spoiled bitch—made a great smokescreen. But it was a constant strain, keeping track of the lies, worrying somebody would check my fake ID or re-examine the admission tests and I'd lose my position."

She fixed her gaze on an ancient wedding photo, feeling cornered by Mary's gentle sympathy. It was a relief when old Anderson Senior stomped in the back door, glowering. With him, at least, she could get back onto familiar ground—being angry at some son of a bitch who flacked her.

Despite young Aurora's efforts at playing hostess, no one had much to say at dinner. Toni sat silently, pushing food around her plate. When Ethan's phone rang next to her, she flinched. He snatched it out of his pocket.

"Hello? .... "I'm sorry, David isn't available. Who's calling?" His face took on a puzzled frown as he listened. Finally he interrupted. "Look, I'm sorry I don't know anything about this. David isn't in university, he's entering ninth grade." He listened further. "Sir, this is a bad time. If you'll just post a callback, I'll phone you when I can."

It took another minute to discourage his determined caller, and as he put his phone back in his pocket he frowned at his father.

"Dad? What's this about? This Dr. something-or-other said you told him to call me."

"Oh, that," said Anderson gruffly. "Some bighead from the university. Turns out David's been posting his research from my ID down at the store. Now this guy's all excited—something to do with teredos. I told him if he wanted to contact the boy he'd have to go through you." His voice took on an edge. "I seem to remember that he's your responsibility."

For a second Toni thought mild-mannered Ethan might actually blow up. His muscles went rigid and he glared furiously. Blue put a restraining hand on his arm. Then Rory spoke hesitantly:

"Dad... why don't you just send him to that early university thing?"

The adults froze. Finally Blue spoke.

"Rory, thirteen is too young to live that far away from his family."

"He only has to wait three years," said Ethan, with exasperation. "He can get a full Guild scholarship at sixteen, but if he goes early we have to pay half ourselves. We don't have that kind of money."

"We should send him anyway," grunted old Anderson suddenly, putting his fork down. "I know it's your call, Ethan, but you're making a mistake. David'll never be a craftsman and we might as well face it. The boy knows what he wants, we should let him go for it."

"You know we can't afford it!"

"Times have been worse."

"Yeah, and we've heard about it!" snapped Blue.

Old Anderson gave her an uneasy glance but bulled on ahead.

"OK, so you've heard it, but it's true. Anyway, there's always the chess set. Guy offered me four thousand for it once, but I figure I could get a lot more these days, get it appraised and listed for global auction. Ten thousand, maybe more if I write it up right. Big market for Collapse heirlooms these days. That should buy him a couple of years."

The Andersons looked stunned. Rory stared wide-eyed at her grandfather.

"Granddad... your chess set?"

Anderson put his napkin down and shoved back his chair.

"You can't live in the past." Abruptly he looked over at Toni. "You live in the past, you make mistakes."

He stalked out.

# 21

The island was little more than a rock outcrop with a few hunched shrubs, but it created a windbreak for a small patch of water. Blade steered the inflatable into the calmer shallows, then had trouble peeling his frigid fingers off the motor so he could remove his goggles and empty the water that had leaked in. He shook them out and slid them on again to orient himself. Time: 7:17 am. Status... A simple infrared sweep of his legs showed diminished body temperature. And his hostage, with a small body mass, was cooler.

He fumbled awkwardly to unpack thermal rain gear, but found the first suit's power was dead. So was the next one. In the end he found power in only four of nine suits, and the cells were all low. They were also all one size: "large." He wrestled the limp boy into a suit, then tried to put one on himself. He managed to squeeze his legs into the lower half of one, then by removing his coat he got his arms into the top half of another, though he couldn't close it up the front. He put his coat back on over top and wrapped the excess material awkwardly around his midriff, then stuffed the other suits into one of the raft's storage pouches.

Currents kept sweeping the boat out from behind the islet, and Blade had to run the motor to hold his position. It was growing light—a dim gray luminescence filtered through three thousand of meters of storm cloud to light a monochrome seascape. Using his goggles to layer spectra helped, but his view was still obscured by heavy rain and flying spray. Nonetheless, he found what looked like land shadows. He checked the engine's fuel cells. One showed half full—two or three hours of power, he estimated—and the other was full.

Warmth from the suits had begun to penetrate his wet clothes, but when he accelerated back out into the weather, the biting maelstrom of wind sucked that heat away. The suit gloves didn't fit so he had to leave them dangling from his wrists and his hands quickly lost feeling. Amid driving wind and heaving ten meter waves, the motor felt almost powerless. Blade could only catch glimpses of his surroundings and steered by keeping the wind behind his left shoulder. He pulled up the thermal hood, but stinging needles of rain pelted his face.

Lost in the storm he fled into remoteness. Be wood. Be stone. Endure....

He woke to a small hand prodding his shoulder.

"S-Simon?"

He smelled brine, tasted it in his mouth, felt it crusted around his eyes. Pain throbbed in his ribs. He sat in the stern of the inflatable in a pool of water, clutching the motor. Waves moved under him, but these were small jerky motions, not mountains of water. The rain beating against his suit came in drops, not bullets.

"Simon? Simon, p-p-please talk to me! ... Are you okay? C-c-come on, answer!"

The boy kneeled in front of him, shivering, wrapped in flapping folds of the much too-large thermal suit. He looked up at Blade with a face bleached of color. The boy....

...had betrayed Simon. Had let Simon start to believe he was a real person, then had treated him like a tool.

Rage fountained inside him. Choi would make David pay. Choi didn't need meds or neurolinks—he had studied the old ways, too. He knew the nerves of the hand and face, the terrible pain that carefully applied pressure could bring. He would watch the boy spew and scream and beg—torment him, twist him as Choi had tormented and twisted Simon. The desire hit him with a force stronger than the storm, stirring him so deeply he could barely breathe.

Distantly he heard David's shaky, high-pitched voice: "Simon, remember, Toni said...."

"Choi does not obey Toni," he hissed hoarsely.

And realized he was out of Toni's reach. Free to start again, build a new bunker, start a new business. He could take David with him, train the boy to obey him...

"But... I thought you s-s-said Choi is d-d-dead!"

Choi could never die. Then a sliver of doubt crept into his

mind—an echo of a voice that had once told him: "You are not some twisted shadow of Choi, you are Simon!"

The world lurched. Simon blinked and looked down at his long, square, brown fingers. Those were Simon's fingers, not Choi's. Choi's fingers had been pale, thin as spider legs, and tipped with long nails. This hulking, ugly body was his, not Choi's. And not Blade's. He was Simon.

But he could be Choi. Permanently. He studied the idea carefully. Being Choi was easier—stronger. Choi was clever, confident, invulnerable. But... If he became Choi, then Choi would win. Choi would have stripped everything from Simon, even his name. Even his music....

"Please, Simon. I'm sor-r-ry for what I did, but I c-c-can't go back and fix it, all I can d-d-do is say I'm sorry."

"You sold me!" he yelled.

David cringed back, terrified, crying.

"I m-m-made a mistake! It was a terrib-b-ble mistake. Haven't you ever made a t-t-terrible mistake before?"

Reluctantly, Simon nodded.

"I d-d-didn't know what was going to happen. I th-th-thought I was running away with them—with Miz Paroo," he spat the name out, "to go to univer-r-rsity. She said why didn't I invite you to c-c-come and say good-bye to me before I l-l-left, to show you I was OK. I can't believe I was that s-s-stupid..."

Simon's grasped at the problem, trying to understand. Deliberate betrayal could not be forgiven. But a mistake....?

"You didn't mean to?"

"No! And I'm sorry! Will y-y-you please forgive me?"

Choi never forgave anything. But Simon wasn't Choi. He spoke slowly, feeling his way around it.

"You made a mistake,"

"Yes." The boy nodded desperately, water dripping through his wet hair and down his face. Simon met his eyes, then finally spoke.

"I accept your apology."

When Simon offered his hand David edged forward and took it nervously. Simon shook, unable to feel David's small fingers. David moved back and silence hung between them. The wind roared in Simon's ears, but it didn't shriek. Waves splashed into the boat. Simon's short burst of adrenaline ebbed into a fog of exhaustion and pain...

David was shaking him again.

"Simon! W-w-where are we?"

Simon blinked and fumbled his goggles off to rub his eyes. They were drifting in the middle of a wide, wind-whipped passage, he realized. He could just see shadowy humps of land to either side.

"I don't know where we are."

"Your goggles aren't uplinked?"

"No." Toni and his father had disabled the link, he recalled bitterly.

"I think we n-n-need to get out of here. Before we f-f-reeze. Or starve."

Emergency rations, thought Simon abruptly. The boat instructions had mentioned emergency supplies. He crawled forward to the nearest storage pouch, sloshing through water and triggering fresh stabs of pain in his ribs. The compartment contained a pair of disassembled alloy oars and an inventory list.

The list described all the supplies that marine regulation required, and that weren't there. There were no rations, no thermal blankets, no flares and only one of three coils of rope. Four of ten life jackets were missing. So was the first aid kit and the emergency beacon. They did find a knife, a tarp, four collapsible water containers, a saltwater filtration unit and a package of fire starter with an igniter. The two duffel bags Simon had taken were not useful either. One contained a long-barreled, high caliber air rifle, and the other held pieces of disassembled alloy frame and a phone. He tried the phone immediately, only to discover it was a fake—an electronic device retrofitted into a standard phone case. Smuggling gear, he guessed. He threw it back.

The reverse side of the inventory list proved equally unhelpful. It gave instructions on how to rig the tarp as a sail, using ropes which weren't present. It also showed how to rig the tarp as rain tent over the boat, also using rope they didn't have.

Simon noticed David struggling to fill a narrow-mouthed water container. He was trying to drain the deep pool inside the flat bottomed inflatable and empty it over the side. Simon sawed the container in half with the hunting knife, producing two usable bailers. Then he helped bail. The vigorous work ignited new pain in his ribs, twinges of returning circulation in his hands and feet and an ache from the half healed burn on his arm. Without Blade's anesthesia, he found the clamor of discomfort hard to ignore. And he was so hungry....

Belatedly he remembered the nutrient paks in his pocket. He passed one to David and drank one himself. It didn't begin to sate his appetite and left him thirstier than ever.

Abruptly he noticed David looking at him with white, fearful eyes. Shivers racked the boy's body. The suit's power indicator was red.

"W-w-we don't have a beacon or a phone. What are we g-g-going to do?"

Simon had no idea. He knew nothing about surviving in the wilderness. He put his goggles back on and studied the landscape. "I think we came from that direction," he said finally, pointing. He slid his goggles up on his forehead. "We must be on the west coast of Vancouver Island, or up the north coast. I don't think there are many towns here."

"It's the total sticks," agreed David miserably.

Simon frowned, trying to work through the unfamiliar problem. He still wanted to gain distance from the ship. If the tongs had valuable cargo aboard, they might try to salvage it before Guild rescue teams arrived. They would not hesitate to kill or kidnap Simon, and David as well. Other rescuers were equally danger-ous. The Coast Patrol were liable to shoot if they glimpsed Simon's deathmask face.

"I think we should continue moving inland, away from the storm. Then... find a place to stop and make a fire," he said.

David nodded.

"Sounds g-g-good,"

One fuel cell was empty. Simon switched to the other cell and started the motor.

They continued for hours through the rain. Simon steered in a direction he hoped was inland, though he swiftly became lost in a winding maze of fog-shrouded passages. Rocky bluffs loomed out of the mist, and seaweed-festooned skeletons of drowned trees poked out of the water. A few days ago Simon had thought the coast was paradise. Now it seemed hostile and empty. He saw no birds or mammals in the storm, not even a sea gull. After nearly hitting a snag, he steered farther away from shore and started watching carefully for deadheads and driftwood. Although the sea level rise had stopped a decade ago, this area did not appear to have been salvage logged—perhaps because the dead trees were small and spindly.

Dave wrapped himself in the tarp and lay down near the bow of the boat, trying to stay warm. Simon shouted over the roar of wind and waves, asking if David knew what direction the tides were running, but the boy shook his head and said they were too far from Cortes.

By the time the orange fuel warning light came on, Simon had been searching for a beach for some time, with no success. The shoreline was rugged, dropping straight into the ocean in most places. He'd hoped to find a cove with a stream and beach, but high tide, dense foliage and mist hid any watercourse smaller than a river. The few coves he found were steep, and the streams were waterfalls spilling down cliffs. Finally, as the fuel cell light began blinking red, he spotted a small patch of cobblestone and gravel wedged between two rocky bluffs. He steered the boat in, crunching the bow ashore, and then staggered clumsily forward and jumped off into shallow water. As he dragged the boat up the beach, David looked up blinking.

The cold was Simon's biggest concern. He and David were both soaked and shivering. Then there was food. Simon's accelerated metabolism required five thousand calories a day and he lost stamina quickly without food. He felt ill and weak.

Simon helped David roll up the legs of David's suit so the boy could walk, then while he hunted for fire wood Simon searched for a camping spot amid the tangle of debris on the beach. Half way along he discovered a tree-shrouded creek which poured into a small pool above the high tide line and then flowed underneath the gravel beach. He moved well away from the stream and tried to drag some weathered logs apart, but their waterlogged weight was more than even he could shift. Finally he piled smaller logs against a larger one, dug a shallow pit to create space out of the wind and flipped the inflatable upside-down over top, lashing it to the logs with their one length of rope.

David had accumulated a pile of twigs and was using the knife to cut shavings from small pieces of driftwood. He hunched under the boat muttering blackly:

"'Look underneath trees for d-d-dry branches,' the survival vid said. What a b-b-bunch of slag. Everything's soak-k-king. First thing I ever learned in school that I try to u-u-use and it's c-c-crap."

David knew how to build a fire pit from stones, but even using fuel bricks and the igniter they had to feed twigs and shavings one by one into the flames slowly to build a steady fire. Simon rigged a tarp to block the wind, anchoring the edges with stones, and David piled wet branches near the fire to dry. Water from the stream tasted pure, but it was very cold, and Simon didn't dare chill himself further by drinking much. He dug through all their supplies looking for something he could use as a pan, then he finally pulled off part of the engine casing and propped it between stones to heat drinking water.

By this time it was growing dark and they were both exhausted. They shared lukewarm ash-specked water and another pak of nutrient drink. There was no hope of getting dry so they wrung out their clothes as much as possible, then lay down on a bed of life jackets and arranged the remaining thermal suits across them as crude covers. Gusts of wind found crevices and blew smoke in their eyes. David curled up between Simon and the fire, creating a tiny bundle of heat in a world of bone chilling damp.

Simon worried about sleeping. What if he had a nightmare and woke in a rage? He tried to stay awake, but found himself dropping into an uneasy doze in which faces and voices swirled through his mind. Toni. Nguyen. Yasmin. Mary. He pulled himself awake and groped in his pants pocket for Mary's talisman.

The Tlingit dancer flashed reflected flame. He watched the silver disk spin slowly, then wrapped his fist around it and put it back in his pocket, clinging to its promise of safety.

Pain and cold woke him several times in the night. Each time he reached over David and put more wood on the fire before falling into an uneasy slumber. No nightmares came. Finally, he awoke to see two tiny circles of white-gray light in his boat ceiling. Bullet holes, he realized suddenly. Another half meter and the shots would have punctured one of the boat's air bladders.

The fire had died down to embers and rain still poured ceaselessly from low clouds. A chorus of drips plinked all around, waves growled across gravel, and a gull's eerie shriek echoed across the inlet. Simon tried to get up without waking David, but stabbing pain in his chest brought an involuntary groan. He lay back and groped under his clothes, feeling his ribs for breaks.

David sat up. "Are you OK?" His voice was squeaky with anxiety.

"Ribs," grunted Simon, poking gingerly. The bones seemed to be in place. He tried applying pressure to see if anything wiggled and got more pain for his efforts. He lay back gasping, waiting for the nausea to ebb.

"Is that bad?"

As David's frightened eyes stared down at him, Simon had a sudden revelation. David was only thirteen. He'd known that all along, of course, but it hadn't meant anything to him. Now he realized that David was a child looking to Simon for adult guidance and Simon didn't have any idea how to be an adult.

"Simon!"

"Uh, I don't think they're broken, just cracked," he said, racking his brain desperately. What was he supposed to do? What would his own father do? he thought suddenly. Well, Dr. Lau would reassure his patient.

"Cracked ribs are painful, but they heal. It's... it's not a severe injury."

"Oh." David looked relieved. He wrapped his arms tight around his knees and forced a tremulous grin. "Sorry, I just got this picture in my head of you dying and leaving me here. I mean I love intertidal ecosystems, but I don't want to become part of one." His voice cracked.

For the first time Simon considered David's vulnerability. The boy was small and not strong. He couldn't row the inflatable; possibly he couldn't drag it off the logs. Left alone he would die. And even with Simon's assistance, things looked bad. They were cold and lost, and Simon had only one pouch of nutrient drink left.

"Is there anything on the beach we could eat?" he asked.

"Oh, sure." David pushed damp blond hair out of his eyes. "Mussels and seaweeds, of course." He looked over his shoulder. "Oysters, if there are any, but the tide's not far enough out. And there's lots of other edible bivalves, but they're small, like acorn barnacles. There might be plants we could eat, too, but I don't know anything about them."

"Mary had some books in the cabin about native plants," said Simon. He concentrated for a moment, picturing the brittle, dog-eared pages of Plants of Coastal British Columbia including Washington, Oregon & Alaska. "Most berries are past their season. I don't see other broad-leafed plants here. Ferns... Sword fern and bracken fern roots are edible."

"With a net or a line we could catch fish or crab. Let me look through our stuff. Maybe we could pull some heat weave out of a suit or something."

While Simon carefully rebuilt the fire, David searched through the gear piled between the logs. Suddenly he called out in an excited voice.

"Ferocious! You know what this is?"

He was holding out a duffel bag.

"Smuggling gear?" offered Simon.

"Uh uh. These are poaching kits! I've never seen one before, but I heard about them. The rifle's for sport hunting, and this is fishing tackle. It's got handheld sonar, a collapsible rod, and a morsel lure with sim-sensory bait!"

"That's unsanctioned?"

"Unsanctioned?! You can get revoked for taking marine life without a Fisher permit!" For a second David's enthusiasm faded. "Umm. I guess this is an emergency, huh?"

"We need food," said Simon firmly.

"Yeah." David's eyes lit up.

No instructions came with this gear and they struggled to assemble sections of rod which had been designed to mimic innocent objects scattered through a tourist's luggage. Only the handheld sonar imager was entirely straightforward—designed for inexperienced amateurs who wanted to get their illicit money's worth in a hurry.

The assembled rod was very long, so Simon carried the rod

and let David take the imager. They walked out to the nearest rocky point, stepping carefully on the slippery rocks. David lowered the sensor into a meter of water, then crouched nearby on a barnacled boulder and unrolled the holographic projection screen. Despite raw gusts of windblown rain, he was grinning. Simon watched over his shoulder.

"Four hundred meter range on this locator and look at the resolution! Oh, this is so icy! I want one of these! You can search by size and species—look that's a rockfish and here's another one. Good eating but spiny. Lots of sculpins. And—whoa!—a dogfish. You know they have venom on their backs? No way we're gonna catch a thirty kilo shark anyway. Hey, salmon! That's a three kilo tagged chum! Let's go for that!"

Simon let David direct his casts, trying to ignore the blustering wind and constant pain. His left hand had stiffened until it was almost unusable and his casts were clumsy, but he found that having a task to concentrate on made physical discomfort easier to endure. It took them a long time to land their first thrashing silver fish, then they caught another almost immediately. David slit open their stomachs on the beach, pausing to examine the internal organs and poke guiltily at a bulging pouch of roe.

After some experimentation they spitted a salmon over top of the hissing fire. It took a very long time to cook and was still half raw when they lost patience and pulled it down. David mumbled something about parasites, but Simon didn't care. He ate ravenously, chewing blackened skin and sucking wet pink flesh from the backbone. Then he spitted the next fish, and left it cooking while he and David searched for fern roots near the creek. They washed roots, wrapped them in leaves and placed them among the coals as another one of Mary's books had instructed.

Then they hunched under the boat, rain pattering above them, eyes streaming from sporadic billows of smoke, while Simon trying to figure out what to do next.

"Simon..." Beside him David spoke with sudden intensity. "How come Miz Paroo.... I mean... was she just using me to get you?"

"She probably wanted you as well. To train." said Simon shortly.

"What does that mean?"

Simon's attention was torn between stomach cramps, and immediate problems, but he couldn't ignore the urgency in David's voice. Reluctantly he refocused.

"Trainers take children your age. They implant neural chips and use torture and memory wipes to erase identity and personality. Then they build whatever they want—shape you with reward and pain." He'd tried to speak calmly but found his voice shaking with old rage.

"Is that... Is that what happened to you?"

"Yes." He'd seen pictures of himself, but he couldn't remember, couldn't imagine being so small.

"Would she have...." David stumbled, flushing, but forged on. "I mean, all your scars...." He gestured toward Simon's stomach.

"The burns were from obedience training. Choi taught Blade... me... to withstand pain."

"And uh, the... the other?"

Simon puzzled for a moment, then understood. "The castration?"

David nodded, cheeks flaming, not meeting Simon's eyes.

"I don't know. It's done to enforcers, but I don't know about other constructs. They'd probably train you as a wizard."

"You mean a net wizard? But I'm not good at systems stuff."

"You're smart and they would try because wizards are worth millions. Even if you weren't wizard quality, you could still be used as a datashark. Or a sleeper—a person of normal appearance who can be planted back into the Guilds, and who doesn't remember being trained but will obey orders without question. They sell for fifty thousand and up."

"Oh." The boy sat in silence for a long time, then spoke bitterly. "I was really stupid, wasn't I?"

Simon looked at him, recognizing a shadow of that terrible shame Choi had burned into him.

"Yasmin is a trainer and she used you. Trainers twist your memory, and plant ideas and emotions in your mind so you think they're yours." Abruptly it occurred to Simon she might also have implanted subdermal beacons—on both of them. He felt a lurch of sick fear and fought back the impulse to search his skin. Futile. She could have planted microchips without leaving a trace, and only

235

specialized surgical equipment would retrieve them.

David looked very pale.

"Rory said I was acting strange."

"You seemed out of character," confirmed Simon.

"Then.... Then it wasn't just me."

"No," said Simon.

"It wasn't my fault."

"No."

And a revelation struck Simon. What Choi had done to Simon was not Simon's fault either. Truly. Simon felt a sudden lightness, found an unbidden smile on his face.

David glanced up, looked startled, then smiled back with relief and Simon suddenly realized how frightened the boy had been. How afraid of him.

Abruptly he remembered the feel of David's father's hand, rough and square in his own hand. Ethan had said: "give me your word that you will keep my son safe and never hurt him." And Simon had promised. Then he had forgotten and almost broken the promise. But he understood it now and felt overwhelmed by the magnitude of his responsibility. He must get David to safety.

How? Should they leave here to seek help, or wait to be found? A satellite might pick up their fire—if somebody looked. And Simon had used up almost all the fire starter getting this one fire lit. He doubted he could make another if they had to camp again elsewhere. Best to eat and rest today and try to dry their clothes. If they were not found by tomorrow, they would seek help.

They huddled under the boat cooking and eating fish, then went to catch more. David ate part of the first two salmon and watched in awe as Simon finished two more by himself. The fern roots never cooked—they seemed half burned, half raw, and even Simon abandoned them, but David concocted a briny mussel and seaweed soup that gave welcome heat. Nothing helped their icy feet.

The second night seemed very long and neither of them slept much, starting awake at odd noises and listening for sounds of rescue in the distance. No rescue came. At first light they ate the last of the cooked fish and broke camp. The wind had eased and changed direction. Showers were interspersed with drizzle. The sky seemed lighter. Simon checked his goggles and noted an eighteen percent increase in ambient light since the previous day. He hoped it was a good sign. He still couldn't establish any coordinates, so he opted to put the wind behind the boat rather than trying to row against it.

Rowing hurt. With each pull his ribs screamed pain. Automatically Simon began to flee into Blade's remoteness, then he pulled himself up short, leaving the oar blades dangling, dribbling seawater down over his hands. If they encountered people, Blade would be dangerous. And if Simon slid from Blade into Choi....

Simon had to stay in control. He gritted his teeth and started rowing again. For a while he tried getting David to talk to him but the boy eventually ran down. Each time Simon caught himself blurring into deafness he stopped and rested, drank water from the containers. Each time he got chilled faster when he stopped moving, and it was harder to start again.

He found his thoughts turning to Toni, and anger helped him focus. Had she been twisting him with love, using him like Yasmin threatened? He couldn't trust that she hadn't changed his memory, hadn't set up subroutines in his sleepware to alter his thoughts and feelings, wouldn't use his music to burn some new pattern into his mind. He couldn't trust her—or any of them.

But what other choice did he have? Choi had marked him indelibly. Citizens would kill him on sight. The tongs would use him and then kill him. Even if he could somehow reach Mary Smarch, she would return him to Toni.

His only other option was death. And perhaps that was the best choice. After he'd seen David to safety.

"Simon! Did you hear that?!"

Simon shipped his oars, panting. Breeze crackled in his ears. For several long moments he heard nothing, then the wind dropped and he caught a distant wail.

"I think it's a fog horn!" said David.

The blustery wind confused sound, so Simon simply kept rowing in the direction he'd been going. Twenty minutes later the sound was distinctly louder. And the sky had grown brighter. Simon leaned into the oars, redoubling his efforts despite exhaustion and pain. If the weather lifted, the fog horn might stop.

# 22

Toni kneeled on the torn up kitchen floor, taking measurements for underlay and baseboards, knowing she should wait for the leveling compound to dry, but needing something to do. The instincts said fight or flee were ingrained in every fiber of her body.

And what a body. She smiled grimly as she recalled the morning's medical consultation with Rigo. Last week he'd used portable equipment from the clinic to run a full body scan, and this morning he'd done another for comparison. He'd also taken time to map old injuries so he could start rebuilding her medical history. The look on his face as he'd viewed the results had been a classic. Toni's scan was a diagnostic crazyquilt—red lines for healed bone breaks, orange for muscle and tendon damage, green ghosts of deep scar tissue hidden under regrown skin, and beneath it all the blue shadows of juvenile malnutrition in her bones. Old surgery showed, too—the sloppy oophorectomy, repaired tooth decay, subtle traces of cosmetic repairs, and even the tiny calcified recess in her skull where her neural chip had been. A neurochem overlay revealed old binge evidence: everything from Eros and Black Lace to bourbon, and the bloodwork showed antibodies to viruses no self-respecting Guild member would ever encounter.

Too old to peddle this ass on the street, but I could sell it to medical schools as a text, thought Toni blackly.

Low, tense voices floated in from the living room. At lunch the families had received another bitter disappointment. Rescuers boarded the Empress of Vancouver, but neither Simon nor David was there, and they could get no confirmation they had ever been present. One launch and several survival rafts were still missing. More worrying, a private copter had reached the Empress an hour before the Coast Patrol. It had picked up a few passengers—presumably key tong members, like Tommy Yip, who'd been notably absent. There was a small chance Simon and David had been with them. In desperation, Toni had phoned Major Kim, but he hadn't called back.

While Rigo, Mary and Klale talked endlessly in the living room, Toni measured floor and Blue repaired cabinets. When Toni's phone finally rang she flinched, then grabbed it like a scorpion.

"Yeah?"

"Major Kim here. We've spotted some survivors in a lifeboat. I'd like an ID."

"Hang on."

She stood, knees aching, and limped stiffly to the dining room where Klale had set up an old bigscreen she'd found behind a bookcase. The picture was streaky with age, but four times the size of any other display they had. Toni pulled up a chair and patched Kim's call in, waving the others to gather around. Gray haze coalesced onscreen. At first Toni thought they'd lost the signal, then she realized she was looking at a foggy expanse of water, and a treed shoreline obscured by low clouds. It took her several seconds to locate a tiny boat near the shoreline.

"Major?"

"Here."

"What am I looking at?"

"This feed is from a vid pick-up at the top of Sarah Island near Boat Bluff in Finlayson Channel. It's an old light station, now staffed as a biomonitoring site. They called five minutes ago to report someone rowing in their direction from the south end of Tolmie Channel. The inflatable looks like a life raft, but its beacon is missing or disabled. It has too small a wake to trigger the sonar detection grid, and it's below satellite monitoring thresholds as well. Visibility is poor. We're trying to enhance."

The camera view zoomed into fuzz, sharpened, enhanced, then zoomed again. Toni could now make out a human figure in a hooded orange suit, rowing with slow strokes. Abruptly the scene switched color. The figure turned crimson and another small red figure appeared, huddled low in the boat.

"Two persons. Approximate masses fifty kilos and one hundred twenty-five kilos."

Toni's breath caught in her throat. She concentrated, forced herself to swallow and breathe. Think!

"Where are you, Major?"

"Vancouver," he said coldly. "But there's a response team on standby in Port Hardy."

A bunch of rurros with guns, she thought grimly. Kim anticipated her.

"We can't expect the station keepers to handle this. There are two couples there and all they have is a couple of old rifles."

"Are there weapons in that boat?" asked Toni sharply.

"Unknown," said Kim. "The lighthouse isn't equipped for weapons scans."

And it wouldn't matter anyway. The tongs routinely carried scan-transparent ceramic, plastiche and bio weapons, and that possibility gave Kim an excuse to shoot Simon dead, just in case. She glanced back, beckoned Blue and dragged a second chair into range of the set's vid pick-up. Toni called up an inset window showing Major Kim, while Blue sat down.

"Major, this is David's mother, Miz Anderson."

She caught a flicker of unhappiness in Kim's eyes as he gave a formal nod.

"Citizen."

Distant oars dipped, rose, dipped, rose. The boat didn't seem to move. Toni turned around.

"Klale, where is Boat Bluff?"

"It's on the Inside Passage north of Waglisla, near Klemtu," said Klale promptly.

Toni sighed and gave her a blank look.

"Uh, that's about halfway between Port Hardy and Prince Rupert...? Here."

She ran over to the couch and brought back another set, then busied herself calling up a map. After a minute she pointed at a pinprick on an island amid a lacework of narrow channels. Goddamned nowhere, thought Toni, appalled. No cities or even towns that far north—nothing but a couple of tiny villages amid hundreds of kilometers of coastal rainforest. And if Kim's vid feed suddenly "failed", no witnesses.

Abruptly Mary spoke:

"Major Kim? This is Mary Smarch, convenor of Simon's parole committee. Could you give me the names of the station keepers at Boat Bluff?"

"I'm sorry, I don't have that information."

Toni heard a quiet snort and turned to see Mary walk out to the verandah, phone in hand.

The minutes dragged on. Ethan and Rory arrived and crowded around. They were followed by old David Anderson who took up a position against the wall with his arms crossed. Toni fumed. Who ever invented the asinine idea of rowing backwards? Turn around, damn it! Then a bundle in the bow of the boat stirred. A head bobbed up and a face looked up toward the bluff. The camera zoomed and enhanced, producing a poor image, but it looked like David.

Klale cheered. Other voices joined her. Toni ignored the ruckus and studied the rower, willing him to turn around. Come on, look! David stared straight at the camera, mouth moving, arm pointing. Then the rower turned around and a skull-like face stared out from under a dark hood. Simon.

Toni felt her throat constrict with sudden emotion, found her hands shaking. She crossed her arms tightly, fighting for control. Simon was alive, but he wasn't safe. Not yet. She swallowed twice before trusting her voice.

"Major Kim, we can confirm that ID. That's Simon Lau and David Anderson. Now what?"

"We're determining that. Please stand by."

Kim had blanked his personal vid feed so she couldn't see him or guess what he might be saying to others. She looked around. Ethan had a hand on Blue's shoulder and his other arm around his daughter. Rigo was hugging a jubilant Klale. Only old Anderson looked grim. His eyes met Toni's and she turned away, but not before she found herself thinking that at least one other person in the room had some grasp of reality.

"Major Kim?"

She waited, hands clenched on the table. Seconds ticked past. On the other screen, Klale had called up a tourist pic of Boat Bluff. Toni had expected to see a tall lighthouse on bare, windswept rock, but the real light station looked more like a white clapboard church huddled precariously on a steep, slope, barely above the tide line. To its left stood two red-roofed white cottages, connected by wooden stairways to a wharf built on high stilts. Probably a fifty year old photo, thought Toni cynically, then reached for the set. Surely there must be more vid channels.

Yes! The station had two full monitoring arrays with multiple channels and Kim had left access open. Their original view was coming from a tower on a steep mountain behind the light station—at least a thousand feet up. Toni opened new windows and got eagle's eye views over two mountain-hedged channels. The light station had been built at the south end of an island, marking a narrow passage that connected two parallel channels.

Simon's boat was now making visible progress around the point and across the passage in front of the light station. Toni tried more monitors, then one labeled "Hoist". This showed a boat hanging from the arm of a crane. There was no floating dock. Apparently boats were hoisted rather than tied up.

Kim's voice made Toni start.

"The station keepers are going to ask the boy to come up. They'll talk to him and decide what to do next."

"And your response team?"

"Still on standby."

She wished she believed him.

"How is he supposed to park?" she muttered, trying other monitors.

"You just tie up to a piling, and then climb a ladder," said Klale behind her. "There's no beach at Boat Bluff and the tides are wicked. The keepers use a boat winch."

Another eternity passed with the clumsy life raft inching along one slow stroke at a time. Finally it approached the dock and bumped clumsily against a pillar. David lunged, grabbing onto something, called up, listened, then climbed onto a ladder, disappearing from the vid view. Simon slumped over the oars and Toni studied him, trying to decide whether he was exhausted, or hiding his face. Probably both. The boat drifted, Simon unmoving. Then:

"Mom? Dad?"

"David! Are you all right?"

"Mom! Look, I'm trying to explain to these people about Simon. He didn't kidnap me and he's not going to hurt anybody! He's got cracked ribs and he's so tired I don't think he can even climb up, but they won't help him! Can you talk to them, please?!"

Blue sighed. "I'm glad you're alive and I want to strangle

242

you," she said, then looked over at Toni. "Handle this, please?"

"Let me," said Mary unexpectedly from behind them. She leaned down over Toni's shoulder. "David, it's Miz Smarch. I have to ask you an important question. Did Simon take you away from home?"

"NO! It's my fault. We were kidnapped and... well, it's complicated, but none of it was Simon's fault. He saved my life!"

"Good, that's all I need to know right now. Would you please pass the phone to Miz Starr?"

"Uh... sure." Toni longed for a vid view, but all she heard was static, then David's distant voice asking: "Excuse me, who is Miz Starr?"

More fumbling, then a soft, doubtful: "Hello...?"

"Hello, this is Mary Smarch. I'm a friend of Simon and David's. Tira, I heard your name and I remembered meeting Colm Starr at a potlatch in Bella Coola—would that be your father?"

Mary's Tlingit accent, normally very faint, had inexplicably thickened.

"He's my great uncle."

"Well, you can tell your uncle that I'm Just Smarch's daughter from the Crow clan, the one who left Teslin for the Big Smoke. I hope he's well?"

Toni did not need vid to picture Major Kim fuming at his desk during the subsequent chat. Mary was brilliant. In three minutes she identified half a dozen mutual acquaintances and then persuaded two station keepers to hoist Simon up in a cargo sling. Toni saw them flinch when they lifted Simon to wharf level and glimpsed his appalling face, but David's lack of fear reassured them, and then it became evident how exhausted Simon was. Rising from the sling he swayed and almost fell.

Rigo wanted a medical report, so Toni let him take her seat at the table, then she took her own phone into the kitchen to make a private, secured call to Major Kim. He answered almost immediately and wasted no time on pleasantries.

"Doctor, you'll get nothing from me until you quit lying. You told me he was a simple tool."

Shit, thought Toni. She closed her eyes, trying to pick the right words.

"I told you he was Choi's enforcer. That's true. I told you he's in danger from tongs hunting Choi's caches and that's true."

"He's far more than an enforcer, isn't he? What did Choi really use him for?"

"He was Choi's datashark."

"And is Choi really dead?"

"Oh, yes." On impulse she added: "Simon killed him."

She heard Kim's intake of breath. Killing a master ought to be impossible. It made Simon doubly dangerous—a bioaltered tool whose conditioning was faulty. But Toni was gambling that it might make him more sympathetic to Kim.

"This must be kept secret," she urged. "He's a slave who rebelled and won. If word leaks out, the tongs won't stop at anything to make an example of him."

"It's far too late for that, wouldn't you say?"

"We don't know. The Kung Lok didn't have him long—they might not even have realized what they had. So I need to find out what happened—fast."

"And I suppose you want to meet him at Boat Bluff."

"Yes."

Silence. She held her tongue, hating the game, hating being powerless.

"We'll fly your patient and the boy to Port Hardy first thing tomorrow morning. You can arrange your own transportation and meet us at CPHQ there."

No! thought Toni as the connection went dead. Instead of gaining Kim's cooperation, she'd given him even more reason to get his hands on Simon and keep him.

She stuffed the phone back under her shirt with shaking hands and walked into the living room. Klale, Ethan and Rory were laughing together while Mary talked quietly to Blue over by the window. Rigo looked up from the netset, smiling.

"They're both suffering from exposure, but there's no serious damage."

Toni nodded, aware of her own strained face.

"Major Kim says we should meet them in Port Hardy tomorrow."

Unexpectedly old Anderson spoke.

"And you don't think he'll be there."

Silence fell as the others looked around.

"David will. Simon...." She hesitated, reluctant to dampen the Andersons' happiness, then dropped her eyes. "Simon will be long gone. They'll take him to a high security facility and start interrogating him."

"But he's under a Treaty parole order," protested Klale.

"He's in violation," Toni corrected. "They can do what they want."

"So we need to show that he didn't intentionally violate his parole," said Mary calmly, stepping forward.

"Like hell they're going to listen!"

Mary put a hand on her shoulder. "City people don't run the coast, love. I can manage this." She turned to Klale. "How long does it take to get to Klemtu from here?"

"Uh...." Klale bounced over to her map and ran a query. "Well, it's about four hundred kilometers by air...."

"Air traffic is regulated," growled old Anderson. "You lease a plane, they track where you came from, where you went, who you took, and where you come back to." He shot Mary a challenging look.

"That's a very good point," agreed Mary serenely. "What about a fast boat?"

Of course it would come down to another goddamned miserable boat, thought Toni as Klale studied the map again.

"Well, it's closer to five hundred kilometers by water. We'd need something really fast, like a skimjet or a foil."

"Call Ron McCaskill, would you, dear? Tell him we need to get to Klemtu very fast—before morning."

"Uh...." Klale looked startled. "How many passengers?"

"Six at least," said Mary. She looked at Lau. "I know Toni shouldn't be traveling, but she will have to take this trip. You, too, of course. Blue?"

"I'll go," said Ethan.

His wife exchanged a long glance with him, then sighed.

"Yeah, I'm probably safer hammering the floor."

Mary turned to Klale.

"Now, Klale...."

"Don't tell me, let me guess. You want me to stay here and hold the fort, right?"

"Right.

"Damn!"

"Thank you, dear. So that's four of us going and six returning, plus any other members of Simon's parole committee who choose to come. This must be open to them. Ron can work out the details."

Old Anderson spoke again. "You're not bringing one of those turbo toys into our dock. Might as well set off a fireworks display."

"I'm sure you can find a suitably discreet place and get us there, David," said Mary. "Now I have some other calls to make."

She strode regally out of the room, leaving Toni and the others staring after her in bemusement.

They ate dinner and then rode to Campbell River in the back of a dilapidated cabin cruiser—a clammy, bone-jarring forty-five minute trip that left Toni desperately regretting having eaten. Mary talked continuously on her phone. Old Anderson tied up at a decrepit wharf in Campbell River, then led them to a work tram that stank of fish but hummed quickly along a shorefront track to a boat ramp somewhere north of town. As they arrived, a shiny yellow contraption floated in through the night, looking to Toni's eyes like a collision between an ornithopter and a ski sled. She climbed aboard with dread, but summoned a smile for white-haired Ron McCaskill, waving from the cockpit. He sat next to another old man, both of them looking boyishly pleased with themselves.

"What do you think, Toni?" Ron's grin shone in the dim light from a bank of nav displays. "StraitShooter hydrofoil yacht, limited edition, 2053. Graphine foam core hull, twin turbines. Broke the mold after they made these beauties!"

"Wonderful," mumbled Toni, thinking: 'shit, it's old, too.' Still the inside looked pretty—all polished wood, leather upholstery and cushy carpets. Down a half flight of steps and through a tiny galley she found a neat sleeping cabin. She sat on a bunk and dosed herself with sleeping meds, then lay down and pulled up a blanket, trying desperately not to think about small rooms with windows that didn't open, or water closing over her head....

The meds knocked her out in less than a minute and she slept deeply until Mary woke her to gray daylight. It took a few seconds to fight off grogginess and orient herself to the strange jolting sensation and the swishing noise, like loud static.

"Uh.... Where...?"

"Just coming into Klemtu."

She'd expected rain, but when she stumbled up front she discovered a cloudless dawn sky with gusty wind kicking up whitecaps. The boat stood up out of the water on skis or pontoons or whatever they were called, cutting a surprisingly stable path across heaving seas, but the dizzy blur of speed and the expanse of water made her feel panicky. She sat on a seat next to Mary and focused on her friend, who looked calm and fresh in a beaded leather vest over a cableknit sweater, and a pair of feathered earrings.

"Why are we here instead of Boat Bluff?" Toni asked.

"David and Simon needed medical attention, so they were shipped to the clinic at Klemtu last night. We're meeting them."

Mary sounded smug. Toni viewed her suspiciously.

"Does Major Kim know they're in Klemtu?"

"Well... communication has been strained. People around here don't much like being shouted at."

"Major S.B. Kim," came Ron's voice. He sat down next to Toni, running fingers through his thinning white hair. "Widely rumored to stand for Sonofa Bitch." His smile crinkled up his whole face, then it faded and he sighed. "He's been a big help to the Vancouver Foundation, Toni. A hard man but straight, very anti-tong, willing to go the extra distance to help us rescue kids from the meat trade. I don't like to play games with him, but unfortunately he hates tools in a big way."

"Well, that's not unreasonable," said Toni ruefully.

"Yes it is," said Mary. "It's not right to hate anybody, especially not the victims."

Ron raised an eyebrow and patted Mary's arm with his gnarly, old man's hand.

"Did I ever tell you you're a very smart woman? That's exactly the thing about Kim. He'll help us with kids who haven't been hurt yet, but once they've been altered, it's a different story. He doesn't seem to consider them human any more."

Abruptly the seat under Toni sank, and the craft plunged down, then lurched backward, bobbing. She grabbed a window ledge in panic. Mary put a hand on her knee.

"It's all right, dear. We're just coming in."

Ron glanced over apologetically.

"Sorry, should have warned you."

Toni ignored them and stared through the window while she calmed her pounding heart. They were heading into a bay where roofs and windows protruded from enveloping rainforest. The setting reminded Toni of docuvids of prehistoric America, and as they pulled up at a floating wharf, that impression grew stronger. Everything seemed pristine—clear sparkling water, clean sharp air. It felt like the beginning of time. And the man standing on the wharf in faded hempens and a Cowichan sweater had a wide brown Native face, much like Mary's. He might be Mary's age, Toni guessed, but he'd kept his hair dark and his face was mostly unlined.

Mary stepped off the boat first and shook hands, then Ron followed, cane in hand but remarkably spry for a man of ninety. Toni hurried after, anxious to escape the floating contraption. There were six visitors in all—Toni, Rigo, Mary, Ethan, Ron McCaskill, and Amin Bahi, a slim young man who was also on Simon's parole committee. He seemed ill at ease, and small wonder—Simon had killed his brother. Ron's friend stayed with his boat. The Klemtu man, who Mary introduced as Colm Starr, led the party up the wide, sloping ramp of the modern wharf toward a scatter of houses and buildings.

Toni couldn't help staring around her. She knew many of the surviving Nations were wealthy—hell she'd served enough tables of spendy Natives back at the KlonDyke—but somehow she'd visualized a coastal village as a bunch of shacks in a mud hole. Instead she saw beautiful homes with soaring roof beams, carved and painted. Starr led them past a longhouse fronted with huge totem poles, and up a walkway to a home built from whole tree trunks. Mary grinned and poked Toni's arm.

"Not what you expected, eh?"

"Hell, no. They must be doing some hot trade up here."

"Sure. With the ecosystem and the economy recovering, the Kitasoo are a wealthy people. This is one of the choicest, least damaged areas of the coast and they steward the land and water for a hundred kilometers in all directions."

They found David and Simon breakfasting in a vaulted great-room with gleaming red-brown walls and tall windows that looked out over mountains and water. It smelled of cedar. David leaped up from the table and ran into his father's arms. Simon stood warily. Rigo put his hands on Simon's shoulders and gave him a gentle embrace, avoiding his injured rib cage, then Mary did the same, but Toni found herself feeling unexpectedly awkward and uncertain, so she held her hand out. Simon took it, giving her an intense, unreadable look from shadowed eyes. He looked pale and weary, heightening the impression of weird menace given by his altered face. And something else seemed worryingly different about him, but she couldn't quite put her finger on it.

Ron McCaskill stepped past her and offered his hand.

"Hello, Simon."

Toni saw a flicker of alarm in Simon's eyes, but he shook Ron's hand.

"Hello sir."

"Do you remember me?" asked Ron gently.

Simon wouldn't meet his eyes.

"From... from before? No. Sir."

"Well, I remember you from when you were a small child. You were a nice boy."

Simon had no idea what to do with that and Toni was ready to warn Ron off, but the old gentleman didn't say any more. He turned around and Toni noticed Colm Starr waving them to chairs that had been set in a large circle. In the middle of the circle a holo showed a fire burning on a low stone platform... or was it at holo? Toni stared, then caught a glint of reflection and realized that a transparent funnel rose over the stone fire pit. It was a live fire sculpture.

Mugs of tea were passed out, and Toni took one, eager for something warm even if it wasn't coffee. The taste surprised her. Unlike the watery stuff popular with the Guilds, this brew was strong, with a sharp taste of tannin and an almost nutty flavor. She noticed the locals dumping spoonfuls of sugar into their cups and copied them. The results weren't bad.

Colm Starr spoke first, introducing everyone present. He was a Kitasoo elder, and three other elders sat beside him: Kaytee Starr, Stone Robinson, and Big Bob Brown. Then Colm handed his talking stick to Simon. Toni tensed as Simon stood, his height dwarfed by the soaring rafters of the greatroom.

"My name is Simon Lau. I am charged with murder in the District of Vancouver and am on a medical, pre-sentencing parole. At this time I am in violation of the terms of my parole. Last night I surrendered myself to the custody of the Kitasoo Nation and asked for a hearing."

As he sat, Toni felt sweat breaking out. Surrendered? Mary must have briefed him. And she hadn't told Toni, probably because Toni vehemently distrusted legalities. Simon handed the talking stick to Colm who passed it to Kaytee Starr, a tiny wizened woman with a face wreathed in wrinkles. She did not stand and she spoke slowly.

"Simon Lau, the Kitasoo Nation can't change your parole but we can hear you speak and decide if you should be held in custody here or released. And we can make recommendations. Also, the Empress of Vancouver ran aground within our lands. We would like to hear all you know about this."

Even looking directly at Simon's scarred deathmask face, the old woman seemed calm. Mary at work again, guessed Toni. Mary held out her hand and the stick passed to her.

"I have just one request first. I'd like to ask David and Simon not to name the place Simon has been living. It would be safer for our families."

She waited until all the Elders nodded, then asked David to tell everyone what happened and passed the stick to him.

David started hesitantly. At first Toni thought he found the crowd of adults intimidating, then as he described how he'd been used to betray Simon, she realized he was ashamed. He flushed as he described the worst parts, but stood straight, kept his voice level and made no excuses. For the first time she could see the emerging adult in David, and she was impressed. He was also trying to protect Simon, she decided after a while. His account had plenty of detail about camping in the wilderness yet seemed vague about his interactions with Simon.

David finished and looked around uncertainly. Colm Starr spoke from his seat.

"Does anybody have questions?"

"Yes." It was Bahi, from the parole committee. "David, did you feel at any time that you were in danger from Mr. Lau?"

David looked uncomfortable. He shot a glance at Simon and then his father before answering.

"Well... I was scared for a while, especially on the ship when he wouldn't talk to me. But he didn't hurt me and when he started talking again, things were fine. Besides, if anybody's in trouble here it should be me. I got him into this mess, and then he saved my life."

Starr looked around the room, then nodded at David. The boy sat down, and the stick passed to Simon.

Toni had heard Simon give factual reports before, but it must have been an eerie experience for the others. He used his enhanced memory to recount conversations verbatim and described his actions in accurate, emotionless detail. For a while Toni got caught up in his story, trying to figure out what he might be omitting, then she pulled back. She was recording this on her phone and could listen to the content later. It was more urgent now to pay attention to Simon's behavior, which was nagging at her again. Something seemed different.... Then it struck her that he had not looked at her once for permission or direction. She felt a chill. He was reporting in Blade's habitual style, but those alert eyes, staring directly at his audience, were characteristic of Choi, and yet he wasn't mimicking Choi's voice or mannerisms.

He was integrating!

As that realization hit her, she became conscious of engine noise in the distance. A copter. She remembered them all too well from her childhood in the Zone, spewing riot glue and teargas into the streets. Major Kim had arrived.

Simon kept talking. The engine throbbed louder, then cut off. Simon finished. He remained standing while the elders whispered among themselves, then old Kaytee spoke.

"Simon." She waited for eye contact. "When you went to meet David at night were you disobeying Toni's orders?"

"Yes."

"Why?"

Simon shifted uncomfortably, his movements suddenly childish. When he spoke his voice was soft and anguished. "I was angry.

251

I didn't want to follow Toni's orders, didn't want to be her slave."

"You broke your parole also. Why did you do that?"

"I... I didn't think about it."

"But later, you told us you thought about your promise to David's father. And that you wanted to keep the promise."

"Yes."

"Was that promise different?"

"It... Yes. It was different. We shook hands."

This woman was good, decided Toni. She was persistent, yet gentle and very patient. She let a long silence hang before her next question.

"Did you shake hands at your parole hearing?"

"I wasn't there," said Simon. He shot a sudden glance at Rigo. "My father and Dr. Almiramez represented me."

"Ah."

Another elder spoke, the man called Big.

"If you aren't a slave, what are you?"

Simon looked at him, eyes wide with startlement. "A person," he said, then with sudden defiance: "I'm a person!"

The man nodded and Kaytee spoke again.

"A person must make his own promises and keep them for his honor and the honor of his family. Are you ready to do that?"

Simon didn't hesitate.

"Yes."

Toni barely heard what followed, she was dizzy with the implications of Simon's integration. He had survived a crisis and also pulled off yet another almost impossible feat. She should feel jubilant, she thought distantly as the Kitasoo conferred among themselves, but instead she felt weary.

Heavy footsteps crunched outside, then double doors banged open, admitting two Natives in Watch hats and two uniformed Patrol officers. One was Major Kim. He strode into the room.

"I demand an explanation for this runaround...."

Colm Starr rose.

"Please sit down. The Kitasoo Judicial Council is in session." He gestured to a chair outside the circle.

Kim's face went rigid with fury, and Toni saw the dawning realization that he'd been outmaneuvered. He walked stiffly to a chair and sat, folding his arms. The other officer, a lanky woman, followed. The two Native Watchers stood near the door.

The rest of the proceedings were brief and the outcome did not surprise Toni. The Elders released Simon into the custody of his father and forwarded a copy of the hearing to his parole committee, with the recommendation that he meet the committee in person. When the Council adjourned, Mary and Rigo went over to speak to the Elders and Ethan crossed the room to shake hands with Simon. Toni stayed seated, waiting for Major Kim. Sure enough, he rose and walked straight to her chair.

"Dr. Almiramez."

"Major Kim."

"May I have a private word outside?"

"Certainly."

Toni gathered herself and stood up very straight, wishing she wasn't wearing the clothes she'd slept in. To her surprise, she found herself looking at Kim's shoulder. On screen his apparent round-faced youth made him seem small, but in person he stood a head taller than her, square and muscular like a wrestler. He wasn't wearing the antique glasses either—perhaps they were just a prop programmed into his interface. They stepped outside into brisk morning air, fragrant with pine. Kim started talking the instant the door shut behind them.

"You may think you did a clever end run, doctor, but this construct is not a pet or a friend or a research project, this is a bioaltered assassin!"

Toni met his glare coolly.

"Your point?"

"I'm not letting this go. I have Cascadia-wide authority to apprehend persons suspected of complicity in unsanctioned or nonconsensual alterations."

"Simon isn't a suspect."

"But you are."

Toni felt a brief chill but shrugged indifferently at his furious eyes.

"Fine. You probably think I was a trainer Downtown, but I wasn't. Of course, I can't prove it and I'm sure you could find circumstantial evidence. You might be able to detain me, in which case

Simon will have to get a new therapist. Maybe a better one." She had let bitterness slide into those last few words.

Kim frowned, searching her face for signs of fear, but Toni felt none. She didn't give a damn.

"I'll be watching!" he snapped finally. "If there is any further irregularity, anything at all, I will file an intervention and get that thing slammed in a cell where it belongs. Do you understand?"

"Yes," she said, then sighed as he turned his back and marched back inside. Another thing she should have handled better—tried to plant seeds of cooperation that Simon would need in the future.

Toni leaned against a cedar house post and let her milling thoughts settle into a steady ache. She'd succeeded. She'd found Simon, and yet she had lost him as well. An integrated Simon would not be emotionally dependent on her. He was a new person, probably angry at her, perhaps not even a friend. That thought made her feel miserably alone. She couldn't help remembering that she had no future—no place to go when she left Cortes.

After a time Mary came out to see where she'd gone, so Toni put on her social face and went through the motions of interacting. Major Kim stomped off to his helicopter. Their Kitasoo hosts fed them breakfast, then escorted the group back to the yellow contraption. Throughout all of it, Simon never looked at Toni.

She walked at the back of the group as they headed down the wharf. David walked hand in hand with his father. Simon watched, then reached out for his own father's hand.

# 23

At dawn on the second day after the wreck Yasmin realized Tor had become an encumbrance. He lay across a bench seat in the cabin of the steam launch, moaning and feverish from the knife wound. Despite Yasmin's first aid, the perforated colon was leaking infection into his abdominal cavity. Cin-Cin sprawled in a stupor in a reclining seat, but her problem at least was straightforward—until Yasmin could reach a reasonably well equipped med lab, she would have to keep the babydoll drugged or unconscious to circumvent the implanted suicide directives that had kicked in when she left the Empress. But with a relatively small investment of effort, Cin-Cin would become useful again. Alone and desperate, already looking to Yasmin as her savior, the girl would require only minor tweaking.

Tor had been useful at first. He'd steered the launch out of the storm into sheltered waterways, and then located an automated ecosalvage barge lying dormant in a small inlet awaiting a satellite signal to send it back to work in the shipping channel. He tied up the steam launch in the scan shadow of the much larger log picker, where they were out of sight and would not attract sonar or satellite notice. And the barge contained a Refuge—a small room with cots, a toilet and emergency supplies. This proved more useful than Yasmin had anticipated since it turned out that most of the launch's emergency supplies were missing—more of Tommy Yip's incompetence.

Exhausted as she was from her long ordeal on the Empress, Yasmin still didn't like to take chances, so she alternated sleep shifts with Tor, spending her waking time reading medical texts on her phone and checking navsat. In the aftermath of the storm, marine traffic was light and no one approached the log picker. By nightfall Tor's wound had worsened and he was feverish. He thrashed and grunted so much that Yasmin sent him back to the launch so he didn't disturb her reading. She dosed herself with sleep suppressants and kept watch all night. When she checked him the next morning, his abdomen was distended and the skin around the wound showed ugly streaks of red. She replaced the dressing, but there was little else she could do. The supplies in the barge's first aid kit were rudimentary—designed on the assumption that anyone in distress would pull the prominent red emergency beacon handle and call for medevac.

When she returned to the refuge from checking on Tor she heard a high pitched wail and realized that Cin-Cin had woken her kiwi bear. The animal looked thin and glassy-eyed and the girl was trying to feed it crumbled pieces of oat bar. Yasmin looked at her in annoyance.

"There's no point giving the animal that, it'll just get sick."

The girl blinked stupidly up at her.

"What? Why?"

"Kiwis are bioconstructs. They're genetically engineered to require an enzyme that doesn't occur in nature. That way they can't escape and start feral populations."

"Huh?"

Yasmin sighed impatiently. Cin-Cin had undoubtedly been told this, but who knows how many memory wipes she'd had in the meantime.

"You had special kiwi food on the Empress, didn't you?"

"Yes. But I ran out last week and I didn't have any money and Uncle Tommy wouldn't buy any more for me. He said it was too expensive."

"Well, that's all she can eat. She's starving to death."

Cin-Cin pouted.

"But I used to give her food off my plate sometimes!"

"They can't digest it."

The kiwi clutched at the girl's hand and mewled hoarsely. Probably dehydrated, too, thought Yasmin. Cin-Cin had been keeping it asleep too much. They'd have to get rid of it. Apart from its nuisance value, the animal was conspicuous and its exotic food could easily be traced.

The girl looked down, mouth trembling, and Yasmin dug in her pocket. She held out an Eros patch, but for once Cin-Cin didn't grab eagerly for chemical bliss. Instead she looked up with tearful eyes.

"What do I do?"

"Nothing."

"I can't let Cocoa starve!"

"Then break her neck or drown her."

"No!"

"Oh for Christ's sake!" muttered Yasmin. She reached in her pocket for a medspray, but the girl sprang up and ran outside, clutching her pet. Yasmin went after her, seething with annoyance.

Cin-Cin bolted for the launch and tried clumsily to cast it off, but she hadn't managed to untie even one line before Yasmin grabbed her arm and shouted for Tor. He staggered up from where he'd been lying and took the girl's other arm. The kiwi fell between them. Yasmin got a firm grip on the squirming girl, then nodded to Tor.

"Tor, drown the animal."

"No!" screamed Cin-Cin.

"Now," said Yasmin firmly.

Tor frowned at the girl's hysterics, but followed orders. He grabbed the little pet by its collar, leaned over the side, and held it underwater until it stopped struggling. Afterward he pinned Cin-Cin's arms while Yasmin gave her a dose of sedative and then helped the sobbing girl to a reclining seat. He stood next to her, leaning his weight against the boat cabin, unable to sit, and looked up at Yasmin with distress.

"Yasmin...."

"I'll get you some pain meds."

But that wasn't his concern.

"Cocoa..."

"The kiwi was starving, Tor. It couldn't live, so we had to put it out of its misery."

"Oh." His face cleared. "It felt very thin," he said sadly.

With that melodrama out of the way, Yasmin turned her attention to their situation. Her first impulse was to continue south towards Port Hardy, but marine weather bulletins received on the launch's rudimentary netset reported continuing severe conditions in the open waters they'd have to cross. She scowled at the set, then pulled out her phone and tried raising the micro-beacons she'd implanted in Simon and David.

The biochips were tiny and crude, with a range of no more than one hundred kilometers, but they worked perfectly. She matched distance and direction readings to the map in the launch's netset and discovered, to her surprise, that Simon and the boy were no longer on the Empress. They might have been rescued, but more likely they'd fled on a life raft. And that left her with a dilemma—should she try to recapture them?

Her first instinct was to go after them immediately, and she nearly set off in the launch, but another look at Tor dissuaded her. He was in no condition to help her capture and restrain a bioenhanced enforcer—a job which would certainly be more difficult a second time. And she didn't have many meds left—certainly not enough to keep Simon sedated for the couple of days it might take her to find suitable facilities. With enormous reluctance she abandoned that plan and decided to wait for the storm to pass. By tomorrow she should be able to head south. There were lots of towns along the sheltered eastern shore of Vancouver Island where she could lose the launch and find other transportation. And with a little clever cosmetic work, she could pass Cin-Cin off as her sulky teenaged daughter.

That left a full day with nothing to do but read, and Yasmin chaffed at forced inaction. She examined the launch from bow to stern, explored the entire barge, and made periodic checks on Simon and David's micro-beacons, which did not move.

At first light on Monday she started the launch's boiler. It required a half hour to warm up, but she had other things to do in the meantime. A quick examination of Tor showed that he'd grown worse. He needed hospital treatment within twenty-four hours, she judged, or he would die. Port Hardy had a hospital, of course—only a few hours south. But the tongs and perhaps the Patrol would be alert for Yasmin and Tor. As a pair they were far too conspicuous, and on his own, Tor's complete ineptness at pretense made him a dangerous liability.

Back on the barge she filled a box with food, then hunted around and found a rope and a chunk of ancient, rusting machinery that the barge had collected. That would have to do.

Wrestling the derelict machine part down a ladder onto a rocking launch wasn't easy, but she managed, then she went back for the box of supplies before setting out. She revved the engine up to full speed, enjoying the exhilaration of slicing through waves. The controls were easy to master and she didn't bother with autonav. The clouds had lifted and as she headed south sunshine broke through, turning the seascape deep blue and foamy white. Wind still gusted, but it seemed gentle now compared to the storm.

Cin-Cin roused herself long enough to scowl at her surroundings and eat a corn cake, then she wrapped herself in a blanket and curled into a ball on the padded bench. Fine, thought Yasmin. She wanted the girl out of the way.

The launch's limited navsat display showed a few boats in the vicinity but most were traveling out in the main shipping lane. Yasmin hugged the coast. She continued south for an hour before finding the ideal spot—a stretch of deep water with no habitation for dozens of kilometers and no boats in sight. She throttled the engine back to idle, locked the wheel, and went back to Tor.

The painkillers she'd given him were wearing off and he lay awake, staring up at the cabin roof with frightened eyes. When she approached his face lit up.

"Yasmin!"

"Good, Tor," she told him and saw his pupils dilate. He smiled, then lapsed into the anxious tearful look she'd grown to loathe.

"I'm sorry I'm sick. I didn't mean to. I'm going to get better!"

"No you aren't, sweetie," she told him, reaching down and stroking his hair. "So I need you to do something for me. Will you do it?"

"Of course I will!"

"Can you get up?"

He grabbed the back of the seat and pulled himself up, blanching and grunting with the effort. She helped him stumble to the stern, where a small bench seat ran along the lowest section. He couldn't lift anything, so she had to heave the rusty machine part up off the seat onto the rear corner of the boat. As he sat down, she gave him a big reward that left him smiling even while he panted with pain. She got out the rope and ran it through the machinery, then tied it to Tor's ankle, wrapping it around a couple of times, and lashing it securely back to the machine. Tor watched with a dawning frown.

"Yasmin? What are you doing?"

"It's OK, sweetheart." She stroked his cheek, and then kissed him on the mouth, taking her time and enjoying it fully. She thought about fucking him one last time, but he hadn't been able to do it last night. When she drew away she smiled into his eyes. "Tell me how you feel about me."

"I love you, Yasmin!" His eyes shone.

"Good! Now, just sit up on the side here, like this, and then when I say 'now', push backward with your feet."

He pulled himself up onto the side of the boat, balancing on the edge in the sunshine as the launch rocked among glittering waves. Again she saw a spurt of fear in his eyes.

"Yasmin...?"

"Now!"

He responded instantly to her command, hurling himself back into the water with a splash that flung water into the boat. The rope pulled taut for a second, then the rusty machine plopped after him. He surfaced once, thrashing and gasping, but the anchor dragged him down. He didn't resurface.

Looking at the bubbles, Yasmin felt a wave of sudden fury. What a waste! She'd spent years training him, fixing his face, and now he was just fish food.

Damn Choi Shung Wai! It was all the old blackmailer's fault. Well, she'd get even. This time she would finance her new start using Choi's assets—funds from his horde, his camouflaged datashark, and his valuable, experienced trainer.

The key to it all was Almiramez, and Yasmin knew where to find her.

# 24

## September 23

Nothing had changed and yet everything about Cortes Island seemed different. Simon found himself looking at familiar people as if he'd only seen their shadows before. At the same time, his surroundings seemed less real. The big fir trees were only trees now and he knew with grievous certainty he could no longer find safety dancing in the sky among their branches.

The first day back they let him sleep in very late and he lay in bed listening to the sounds of the house and watching the pattern of light on the ceiling and feeling sick with fear. He wasn't invisible Simon any more. Could he still dance?

Finally he went down to the platform in the yard and, with his heart pounding in his throat, started slowly with his oldest dance. To his immense relief, music still brought joy. He ignored the stiffness in his arms and shoulders and pushed past the pain in his ribs to reach melting release, then he lay for a long time letting the music wash through him. Afterward he had to face his new world.

Being Simon all the time felt like balancing on slippery rocks at low tide. Sometimes he'd lose focus and slide one way or another, but Mary seemed to know when to put a hand on his shoulder and steady him. She seemed perfectly comfortable around him, but the others didn't. Klale gave him puzzled glances, his father looked worried and uncertain, and Toni kept almost entirely silent. That should have been convenient—Simon still felt angry and did not want to talk to her—but he found her distance made him miserable.

And when he looked at her closely, Toni's thin, listless condition alarmed him. For the first time it struck him that she was a tiny, unstable fifty year old woman in poor health. When she'd been his master he'd always thought of her as enormously powerful, but now he understood that she was frail and mortal. Like Choi.

That parallel frightened him profoundly.

Things had even changed between him and David. Tuesday evening after Klale and Blue finished laying the kitchen floor, they joined the Andersons for a belated Equinox dinner cooked by Ethan and Rigo. Simon tried a bit of duck with cranberry dressing—he'd never eaten bird before—and ate large helpings of roast potatoes, red chard from the garden and then trifle—fresh fruit and sponge cake, drenched in Ethan's plum wine. David, sitting next to him, seemed quiet and thoughtful. Simon wondered at first if David was still scared of him, but when they sat later in a corner of the living room, David wrapped his arms around his knees like he always did and began talking.

"Kinda too bad we didn't get to stay longer at Boat Bluff," he said ruefully. "I want to go back. Miz Starr said if I come to visit they'll give me a tour of the whole biostation, and show me all their marine monitoring sites."

He looked at Simon and grinned, just like old times and Simon felt a tightness in his heart ease. He smiled back.

"Granddad got a call from Dr. Srivastava at UBC. He's interested in the preliminary results from my microstudy. Of course it means my alias is blown and I won't be able to use granddad's account any more, but it's worth it. The professor is coming here to Cortes to look at my ADAT station and add some real equipment. He even said I can use him as a scholarship reference!"

David's eyes shone and Simon felt delighted for him.

"Does this mean you'll be going to university early?"

"Nah." David shook his head. "I didn't even ask. I've been thinking maybe it doesn't matter so much if I have to wait. I'll have this UBC project to work on so I can earn advance credits. Which reminds me, I wanted to ask if you'd check all the sites for me for a while. I've got to stay at school late to do make-up work and there's a big community marathon all weekend."

"Sure."

"We can get together next weekend and crunch all the September data. That prof asked about meeting my collaborator, too. He figures you're another kid." David grinned. "He'd sure get a surprise, huh? But I bet you can't," he added regretfully.

"No," said Simon. "And next weekend I'm meeting with my parole committee."

David looked up, startled.

"They aren't going to uh, throw you in jail or anything, are they?" he asked anxiously.

"I don't think so. Mr. McCaskill says they want my handshake."

David frowned at him, puzzled.

"Don't you want to?"

Abruptly Simon realized that his voice had been bitterly unhappy.

"I don't know."

"Oh."

An awkward silence fell before David spoke again.

"I've been thinking about Cin-Cin. You know, the girl who let me out of my cabin. She's posted as missing and since she didn't have a phone or any kind of emergency transmitter, there's no way to find her." He flushed and spoke with sudden intensity: "The Coast Patrol says she was just one of the hookers, like that makes her matter less than other people, but she saved our lives, didn't she? Mom and Dad say there's nothing we can do but I thought maybe you might know something....?"

Simon considered the problem doubtfully.

"I don't know anything about search and rescue."

"One of the launches is still missing. What if she got to a town? Or what if she was on the copter?"

"If she was airlifted out by the tongs they'll put her in a smut-shop or sell her."

"That's what I was afraid of," said David.

"Does the Patrol have her genescan?"

"Yeah, they got it off the Empress."

"Then I'll launch some seekers."

"Would you?" David dropped his voice. "Or you can show me how and I'll do it."

Simon had been teaching David some simple techniques for acquiring data through back doors on the net without leaving a trail. Now, for the first time, it occurred to him that David had maneuvered those lessons out of earshot of the adults—even Klale. His mind whirled as a whole new quagmire opened up in front of him. He had never considered Guild rules before, but the Andersons were Citizens. If they found Simon teaching David how to circumvent data fees they might be very angry. On the other hand, David wanted to learn. Would he get angry if Simon stopped teaching him? The thought of losing David's friendship alarmed him. It felt like losing his last handhold in this precarious new landscape.

"Simon. Are you OK?"

He looked into the boy's concerned eyes and nodded.

"I'm OK. David... You said once we were friends."

"Sure."

"But... things are changing."

"Yeah, things change all the time. And I'm still me and you're still you, right? Besides, you forgave me for a very big mistake, so I guess I owe you a gargantous screw up one day."

He grinned. Simon looked at him seriously.

"You don't owe me anything. You're the first person who ever talked to me like... like I was normal."

"Yeah and you're the first person who ever really liked me for who I am, instead of wanting me to be normal," said David with sudden vehemence. "Guess we better stay friends, huh?"

Simon felt a smile breaking through.

"Yes."

The good feeling lasted all evening, but that night he woke up with nightmares and in the morning he found his mind roiling with dark thoughts and unanswered questions. What were Toni's motives for working on him? And what exactly had she been doing? He'd never managed to see her closely guarded case notes, so it could be anything. She had been molding his emotions and behaviors; she could also have erased memories and created new ones. His neural interface chips coupled with virtual tech made this especially easy. How could he know that anything he saw or felt or knew was real? How could he even know that David was his friend and not someone hired to act the part, or even a completely simulated persona in virtual reality?

The more he looked at the problem the uglier it became, and the more sick and terrified he felt. Some moments he longed to go back to being a slave, to the certainty he'd felt when he knew that all he had to do was please Toni and she would protect him forever. Then he remembered her hot desperate kisses and the disgust on her face afterward and black rage surged inside him, bringing Blade perilously close to the surface.

On Wednesday he danced for hours, ignoring the pain in his rib cage. His father watched him from the kitchen window and finally came out and asked him to please ease off or else the cracked bones would not heal. So they went down to the beach to check David's ADAT monitors.

When he came home Toni and Mary were talking in the kitchen. Simon hovered in the dining area, eavesdropping.

"... have to get back to Vancouver so you can't put this off any longer," Mary was saying.

Toni sounded distraught.

"I hate being on the other end!"

"I know, love." Pause. "We'll need Rigo there. Do you want me to ask Klale to take Simon down to the beach during the morning?"

"Yes. No." He heard Toni sigh. "It doesn't matter a goddamn to me, Mary. You decide...."

Later Mary came out and told Simon and Klale she'd be doing therapy with Toni the next day. "Since you're the closest thing she has to family, she feels you're entitled to share this with her, if you choose to."

This struck Simon as curiously different from the conversation he'd overheard and he wondered for the first time if Mary's reputation for honesty was accurate. Certainly she was proficient in getting people to do what she wanted, and Choi, among others, had underestimated her capabilities.

In the morning Mary arranged the living room. She turned off all the phones and sets and pulled chairs around to form a circle that reminded Simon of Klemtu. The day was dull and gray outside and she closed the curtains, turning on a soft amber light that fluctuated subtly, like candlelight. Mary sat on the couch next to Toni, with Dr. Lau on her other side in a chair. Klale and Simon sat across from them, further away. Lau set up his medical monitor on the coffee table and taped a medpak to Toni's arm. Toni held her arm out, but sat with her legs drawn up to her chest, eyes squeezed shut, like she expected him to hit her.

When Lau finished, Mary took her hand and squeezed it.

"Dear, I want you to remember two things. First, I love you. Nothing you can say today will change that. Second, the past is past. It's gone. You have given old ghosts power to hurt you but when you look at them, bring them out in the light, they will fade."

Toni, gave a jerky nod, eyes fixed on the carpet. Mary glanced at Simon's father. He nodded. Then she looked at Simon and Klale.

"You may listen, but don't say anything. If you feel uncomfortable, just get up and leave quietly. OK?"

They nodded. She turned to Toni.

"We need to find the starting place, love. Rigo told me about the rats, but I think we should begin with something less frightening. I remember a long time ago you told me about your mother writing your name on the wall. Perhaps that's a good beginning. I can ask you to look at the wall and then look at your surroundings, OK?"

Again, the nod, but fractionally less jerky. Lau must have started the meds, perhaps dosing her with a tranq as well as a hypnotic agent.

Mary used a standard induction, asking Toni to visualize row upon row of trees on mountain after mountain. As she talked softly, Simon realized he had never seen another person undergo hypnosis. It felt very strange to be on the outside.

"All right, Toni. You told me once that you know your birth date because your mother wrote it on the wall of the apartment and she taught you to read it out loud. Can you picture that wall? Can you read it out loud for me?"

There was a silence, then Toni whispered:

"Toni, born of Teresa, April 19, 2058."

"Good. Your mother read it out, too, didn't she? Can you remember her voice?

"She said 'that's right!', then she said 'that's your birth notice, just like the Gentries got on the net.'"

Toni's voice had become higher, childlike. Mary nodded at Lau. He made adjustments to his set, triggering a higher dose of mnemonic.

"What does the writing look like, Toni? Dark or light? Big or small?"

266

"She wrote me in dark red pen with round letters, and she made a heart for the 'i' dot and a special curly 't.' She wrote Jamal bigger underneath after me but mine was prettier. But when the baby come...."

Toni stopped and clutched Mary's hand hard.

"What happened when the baby came?"

"Nothing!" Toni yelled. "There's no baby! I don't got no baby!"

Mary spent a moment stroking Toni's shoulder and hair, calming her down, then started again in a very soft voice.

"It's OK. It's safe. You can tell me about the baby. Did your mom write the baby's name on the wall?"

Toni spoke with obvious reluctance.

"I asked her, but she don't do it, so I wrote him there below Jamal. 'Raffayal, born of Teresa, March 4, 2068.' I spelled Rafael wrong but she said he was my baby and I could spell him any way I want and it would be special just for him, not like some stupid dictionary crap that don't do nobody no good anyhow."

Toni's American accent had grown thicker. Mary watched her face.

"She said Raffayal was your baby?"

"He born in the kitchen and they put him in my arms and mommy told me I was a big girl now and he would be my baby to take care of and love me. He was so beautiful, big brown eyes and dark skin, browner than mine and smooth like chocolate."

She paused, smiling in a way Simon had never seen her smile before, then her face crumpled.

"But he cry! He cry all the time! I hold him and rock him and do for him but he only stop a little bit and then he cry again and momma say keep him quiet girl, can't nobody sleep and the neighbors get mad. Some time she go and get some medpatch, put on his skin and he quiet down, and when her own milk stop she get some synth and give me the paper from the clinic with the directions what to do. I can read real good."

"But then she don't come home hardly at all and when she do she just sleep and sleep and I go through her pockets for money and lotsa time she don't got nothin so I got to steal food for me and Jamal. Baby can't eat real food, he spit it out when I bring some in my pocket from school, so I got to fill the bottle. This big girl down-stairs she show me how to mix sugar and water when there nothin else but it ain't enough and he wail all the time and be so thin that when I hold him in my arms I feel all his little bones and his heart thumpin and I wonder if it gonna stop...."

Simon found it hard to look at her naked misery, hard to listen to that anguished child voice. He looked at the floor.

"Did you ask a grown up for help?" asked Mary.

"Help a cholo trash brat? Alla people live in the Zone got trouble nuf of they own. And we gotta hide! Can't trust nobody, cause they wanna get the reward for turning in ills. We all illegal kids, and he be a third baby, too, so las pacas gonna kill him for sure mamma says, just break his neck right there and take Jamal and me off to the cylum where they put us in a shower with poison gas so we spit out our lungs and die. That what they do with ills, everybody know that."

The force of Toni's raw pain made Simon want to run. He looked around to see Klale watching wide-eyed, her hand across her mouth. His father's face was grave and sad as his gaze flicked between Toni and the monitor. Mary's eyes seemed heavy with knowledge, like she'd heard this before. She gave Toni a tissue and signed at Lau, who made an adjustment on the medset.

"Where do you go to school, Toni?"

Toni wiped her face with the tissue and sniffed.

"UN school. They take any kids, even chiggers and kooks, and don't tell the uniforms, and they give us breakfast and lunch. We all go."

"Who takes care of the baby when you go to school?"

"Momma take Raffayal with her mostly but he get bigger and she don't do it so much, he too heavy and messy and too much cryin' and she don't come home most nights. We got a big box we put him in like a crib but it don't got no bars cause rats they run between bars. But they chew at the box anyhow. They smell the bottle I put with him. I make the bottle in the morning, put in juice or milk if I got it or sugarwater and crush up some downer caps to mix in, make him quiet, then I close the blinds and lock the door so nobody find him.

"Since he be quiet all day, he don't want to sleep at night, but I got to sleep and I got to do homework and I hungry and tired and I get so mad! I hit Jamal and he run out to the street and I hit the baby and shake him and then I feel so bad and I hug him cause I know he don't mean to cry and I know he gonna hate me." Simon looked over to see tears streaming down Toni's face. "Baby hates me!

"It's OK, Toni," said Mary softly. "He doesn't hate you. It's a long time ago." She waited a long while before asking: "What happened next?"

"Momma don't come home no more. I go lookin, go in all the bars, all the joyhouses. One place this man tell me she dead. I go home and I scared. Can't tell nobody or las pacas come for us. I steal from the teacher, get caught, can't get no more from school. Baby puke up food and he can't stand on his feet no more. I carry him alla way to the free clinic—it so far and my arms hurt so much—and I wait and wait and wait, but when it be my turn the big white nurse be staring and asking questions. When she try to trap us in a little room I run away."

"Jamal mad and he won't help me none, he stay out on the street alla time. One day I come home...."

Abruptly she stopped, eyes wide.

"It's OK, Toni. Tell me what happened when you came home."

"No!" She stood up on the couch, arms wrapped around her torso, yelling down at Mary. "No! No! Don't got no baby! Didn't do nothin, don't know the bad thing!"

"Yes you do know the bad thing," said Mary, suddenly firm. She took Toni's arm gently, but firmly, and pulled her down onto the couch. Beside Mary's comfortable bulk, Toni, shaking with anguish, looked like a child. "Now, tell me what happened to the baby."

"I come home... I come home. Jamal he be sitting in the hall outside the door and I see by his face there be somethin wrong. He don't say nothin. I open the door and walk in.... Rats got into the box. They be chewing my baby's face. I scream and I chase them away but the baby dead. He dead and cold!"

She curled rocking on the couch, arms crossed over her head.

"I killed him! I killed my baby!"

Simon couldn't stand any more. He fled to the kitchen and stood quivering. Klale followed and put an arm around him but he wanted to put his arms around Toni and hug her like Mary was doing, wanted to pick her up and stroke her hair and love her. And he desperately, so desperately, wanted her to love him back.

Longing burned inside him, then sick misery as he remembered Yasmin's fingers against his cheek. Toni had made him feel this way! She had burned this emotion into his mind, shackled him to her with love instead of fear! He ran outside, picked up a chunk of lumber from the kitchen scrap heap and then pounded it against a tree, bashing again and again until it splintered and broke in his hands. He wanted to kill Toni! He wanted to love her!

He stood panting in front of the scarred trunk, thoughts screaming in his head. He couldn't live like this! And he didn't have to. He could kill himself. He could destroy this valuable asset of Toni's, make it worthless, make sure he could never be manipulated or enslaved again.

That idea brought calm. He tossed the wood aside and went over to sit on the dance platform, gradually ordering his thoughts. He saw Klale and Rigo watching him from the porch, looking worried, but they let him alone.

Did he want to die? He thought it over very carefully—thought about David and sweet trifle with plum wine and harbor seals poking their heads up from a glistening morning sea. No, he would prefer to live. But if he stayed with his father and Toni he must be certain they weren't using him.

Before he could live, he must know what they had done to him.

# 25

## September 27

On Friday, while the Salish Sea lay like poured steel under a high overcast, Simon made his preparations. An hour after they put him to bed, he stopped feigning sleep and got up, removing the Davidson cups adhering to his scalp. Fortunately the whole household had retired early, including Toni, who was still recuperating. They had reinstalled Simon's sleepware, but he'd glued a dot of foil on the inside of the suction cup surface, blocking infrared signals to his neural chips. He shut off the cabin's perimeter security on the housecomp, and went out through a window in case the doors were monitored. He retrieved the bag of clothes and food he'd stashed under the porch, put on night goggles and jogged along the upper trail beneath ghostly, motionless trees to the Anderson's woodwork shop.

Last night he'd overridden the door locks on the workshop and searched it for the handgun he suspected David's grandfather had hidden there. It was a recent model eleven millimeter Glock—almost ideal for his purposes. Like many amateurs, the old man hadn't understood how to fully secure the weapon, and Simon had been able to reprogram the gun's safety chip. Now it took him only a few seconds to get inside the workshop, take the gun from its hiding place and shove it into a capacious inner pocket.

With a hood up to hide his bald head and burn scars, goggles on his eyes and a scarf tied across the rest of his face, Simon was almost unrecognizable. Only his immense height could not be disguised. He ran along the winding rural road to Cortes Bay, twice diving into prickly clumps of salal bushes to hide from traffic. He had already identified several suitable boats in the marina and took the first one he found with a fully charged fuel cell. Three hours later he motored into Vancouver's inner harbor, dumped the boat at a maintenance dock near Pier B-C, and stole an automated garbage picker. The picker was only four meters long and had no cabin, but he could crouch in the empty refuse bin and override its navigation panel—a trick he'd seen local flot kids use. The picker wallowed under his weight, but chugged slowly through the harbor to the American refugee floats in False Creek channel.

The boat he was looking for lay moored in its usual spot. From the outside it looked like an ancient, decrepit fiberglass cabin cruiser, unremarkable among the ramshackle noahs tied up four deep along slimy floats. In reality it was a ghost boat—a radar-transparent surface glider with retractable wings. It could skim the top of calm water without a sonar ripple. As Blade, Simon had used it several times.

Simon felt a surge of relief when infrared revealed the familiar profile of the pilot, an Afroid man in his forties, waiting in the wheelhouse. Now that the Vancouver Council of Guilds had regained jurisdiction over Downtown, Simon hadn't been sure that flots would risk their lives on illicit errands, but evidently they still needed money. He checked the boat carefully for other heat signatures or traps, then jumped aboard.

The pilot did not need to see Simon's ghoulish face to recognize an enforcer and he looked terrified. He had been expecting a passenger, but not this one. For an instant he looked as if he might try to bolt, but the sight of the gun barrel froze him in place.

Simon signed "Seattle" and settled into Blade's old seat at the back of the wheelhouse. The pilot gave him a white-eyed glance and obeyed.

They left the harbor in a series of abrupt zigzags, interspersed with long, silent waits in the briny night. Simon sat motionless and mute, outwardly a menacing statue, but inwardly feeling peculiar and frightened. He'd never tried doing anything like this as Simon and he kept finding himself sliding into Blade. After a while he took out his phone and studied maps of his destination to help him focus and pass the time.

Getting clear of the marine traffic lanes around Vancouver took more time than usual, and by six a.m. the first hints of light began graying the sky. They would have to hide for the day. He gave another signed order and the flot changed course, pulling them in among the half submerged ruins of an old factory near Everett. They tied up to a large "Hazard" sign, then the pilot filled a starboard ballast tank, making the boat list like a derelict. Simon allowed the man to drink and eliminate, then motioned him to his smelly bunk and hit him with a sedative spray. The man recoiled in terror as he collapsed, but soon lay sprawled on his back snoring.

Simon ate, but he did not dare sleep. He spent the long day sitting motionless, so as not to rock the boat, and working on his phone. Its limited interface and slow speed frustrated him, although he eventually accessed the data he needed. Water slapped the boat's sides, sea gulls screamed and he heard distant sounds of human traffic. When dusk fell he stretched, ate again, then woke his pilot. The man looked relieved to be alive, but when Simon spelled out "Ballard Sea Gates" in Slang, his eyes widened and he began babbling about security and payoffs. Simon had anticipated the problem—getting through the gates to Lake Union was the riskiest part of trip—and he messaged a five hundred dollar untraceable credit to the pilot's gray market phone. That calmed the man.

Still, Simon found his shoulders aching with tension as he crouched in the cabin, unable to see any of the slow trip through the locks to Lake Union. Even with his gun trained on the pilot, he feared the man would betray him. The flot did a great deal of fast talking in a heavy American dialect, evidently passing as a local, because three successive officials accepted a phone zap and passed them through.

Simon's target lived on Capitol Hill over a kilometer from the water, but a former golf course covered much of the intervening distance. It wasn't yet ten o'clock when the ghost boat drifted beneath old concrete bridge pillars and let Simon off on a swampy stretch of land. That had gone as planned, but the subsequent journey proved agonizingly slow as Simon crept through scrub in the park then along residential streets, hiding for long stretches of time in bushes and shadows. At eleven all the street lights dimmed, traffic died, and Simon cursed his poor planning. He could have saved much effort and risk by checking the neighborhood utility schedule.

Dr. Dougherty occupied a spacious end unit in a recently-built upscale rez. His windows were dark so he might be asleep, but Simon's research had shown that the doctor usually spent his

Saturday nights attending concerts and theater, rarely returning before midnight. Simon didn't bother with the main door or ground floor windows—he watched the treed street until scans showed it to be deserted, then crossed to a shadowy corner of the building and climbed. The roof held a patio, shrubs in containers, and a poorly secured access door. He hacked the security and opened it in less than a minute.

The rez was empty—no food odors and no residual heat signatures. Simon made a brief, silent search of the upstairs bedrooms and office, then descended the stairs to an entrance hall across from the kitchen. Dougherty had left a light on. Simon reached up and unclipped the ceiling element, plunging the hall into darkness. Then he crossed to the kitchen and settled in to wait, aware of growing fatigue, a persistent ache in his partly healed ribs, and hunger. Not wanting to risk hypoglycemia, he ate the last of his sandwiches, drank water from the potable tap, and dosed himself with sleep suppressants. After the silence of Cortes Island he noticed the faint growl of city noise, but locally he heard only the occasional hiss of tires on the street or a banging door.

Footsteps. A single person only. Good. Simon checked the time as he flattened himself against the wall just inside the kitchen doorway. Twelve twenty. The door opened, revealing a smudge in the darkness, then a figure stepped inside with a fumble and a mutter, closed the door, and opened the closet. Simon stepped out and grabbed the man from behind, slapping one hand over his mouth and holding the Glock to his throat with the other. The man tensed rigidly and his coat fell.

Simon whispered: "Make no noise. Don't struggle."

In the darkness he smelled perfume in the soft hair below him; felt the warmth of a human body pressed against his chest and the cool smooth steel of the gun barrel. Heartbeats thudded urgently—Simon's and the other man's both—and suddenly it felt much too real and terrifying to do this as Simon instead of Blade. He desperately wanted to flee back into that safe numbness, but forced himself to continue.

"Follow my instructions and I will not hurt you. Nod if you understand."

The head nodded. Simon removed his hand from Dougherty's

mouth and frisked him thoroughly for weapons. He found none. He emptied the man's possessions on the floor, including a phone and an antique wristwatch with a luminous analog face.

"Now, walk over and sit on the chair next to the dining table. Put your hands on the table."

As Dougherty crossed the room, Simon flicked on a lamp. When the man reached the chair and turned, he saw Simon's death-mask face and looked terrified. Of course Dr. Dougherty would know all about enforcers and he must expect to die.

Dougherty matched his professional photos very accurately—a dapper Caucasian man, medium height, with bronze hair gleaming with metallic highlights, and a closely trimmed beard. His handsome features showed natural irregularity—either he hadn't had a facial sculpt, or he'd paid for subtle and costly custom work. He wore a white silk shirt and embroidered purple velvet jacket, stylish leather boots, and diamonds at his ears and throat. He looked about thirty-five but Simon knew him to be fifty-eight. Though he appeared almost chubby, Simon had felt muscles in his arms. He sat on the chair, staring at Simon with sick dread.

Simon seated himself across the room, holding the gun ready. He spoke calmly.

"Good evening Dr. Dougherty. I am here for a professional consultation."

Dougherty's eyes widened and Simon saw sudden surprise beneath the man's fear. A speech like that was far out of character for a tool of Simon's appearance.

"Consultation?" he said shakily. "At gunpoint?"

"I do not want you to call the Watch—or anyone else."

"I see.... And when you have consulted me, do you plan to kill me?"

"No."

"Then you don't need the gun."

That was true. Besides, Simon could easily kill an unarmed man in seconds and Dougherty must know it. Simon lowered the Glock, activated the safety, and slid it into his pocket.

Dougherty let out a breath and Simon saw a flicker of calculation before his face twisted in sudden fury.

"You son of a bitch! You break into my home and threaten

my life and then expect me to help you?!" He seemed to struggle for control, then continued in a shaky voice. "Now making extraordinary allowances for extraordinary circumstances, I'm willing to offer you a second chance. Your chance goes like this. Both of us walk back to that doorway, you give me back the items you took from my pockets, and then we start again."

He stood stiffly and strode toward the entrance hall, velvet clad shoulders tensed as though expecting a gunshot.

Simon sat paralyzed for several seconds, well aware that Dougherty was trying to assume the role of master, and unsure what to do about it. But Simon had never intended to kill Dougherty and his bluff had been called. He had little choice. He got up and followed. As he retrieved objects from the floor, he felt a flush of shame and then admiration for the man's courage. Dougherty took his belongings with unsteady hands, shoved them in a pocket and glanced up at the ceiling light. Simon reached up and snapped the fixture back into place. It glowed to life.

"Good." Dougherty's voice was a deep, cultured baritone which wavered with fear and fury. "Now you begin by apologizing."

Simon bowed his head and spoke quietly.

"Good evening Dr. Dougherty. I apologize for breaking into your house and threatening you. My name is Simon and I wish to consult you. I will pay you for your services."

"Good evening, Simon. I prefer that people knock on my door, but since you're already here, come in. I was just about to pour myself a night cap. If you'll be seated, I'll join you in a minute."

He strode stiffly towards the dining room. Simon frowned after him, then spoke sharply. Choi's high-pitched voice came out of his mouth.

"You did not offer me a drink, Doctor."

Dougherty turned, startled. Simon met his eyes, then remembering the peril that implied from an enforcer, let his gaze fall.

Dougherty spoke. "I beg your pardon, I forgot my manners. May I offer you a drink?"

"Thank you, yes."

Simon knew what Dougherty had assumed. Tools were taught never to eat or drink anything but their master's food. So Simon would prove that he was free. He followed at a cautious distance and stopped near a gleaming dining table as Dougherty opened tall glass doors to a wooden cabinet which contained shelves and shelves of glasses, all different shapes and sizes. There were enough for dozens of people, although Simon knew he lived alone.

"I can offer you cognac or armignac, and I also have a very acceptable '98 port."

"... port...?"

"It's a wine," said Dougherty coldly. "Cognac is a distilled liquor."

"Wine, please."

"Perhaps you should taste it first."

Dougherty pulled out a wine glass and poured a splash of ruby liquid from a tall bottle on the sideboard. He held the glass across the table to Simon. Simon reached forward cautiously, took it, sniffed, sipped. It burst on his tongue rich and sweet, a little like Ethan Anderson's black currant wine. He felt Dougherty's eyes watching so he swallowed the rest and passed the glass back.

"It tastes very good,"

"It ought to."

Dougherty poured more for Simon, then took a smaller bottle and poured amber liquid into a squat, bulbous glass, filling it only halfway. He gestured to the living room. Simon took his glass and turned his back, listening for footsteps, listening for Dougherty to pull out his phone and hit the emergency pad. If he hadn't done that already. Most likely he had triggered it in his pocket and the Patrol would arrive in minutes.

Dougherty turned on lights, then sat in a leather chair by the curtained window. He plucked the knees of his trousers before crossing his legs, just like Dr. Lau often did, then he leaned back and drank from his glass. Arriving in the dark and concerned only with an ambush, Simon hadn't noticed any details of the room. Now he saw the elegant gleam of a polished hardwood floor, partially covered with thick wool rugs. A couch and chairs circled an unlit fire sculpture, and paintings hung on the walls. Small tables held more artwork in wood, stone and metal. Something about the room seemed strange, then Simon realized there were no screens, sets or other devices visible.

"Excuse me." Dougherty fixed him with an assessing stare. "I don't usually gulp good cognac, but this was an emergency. Now... do you have a surname, Simon?"

"I will not give it."

"Then perhaps you would do me the honor of telling me why you wish to consult me."

"I'm a weapon," said Simon flatly and saw Dougherty's startled recognition of the meatmarket term. "I am thirty one years old. I have a thalamic plug and five custom neural chips, each with nine filament arrays, designed for sensory interface."

He paused, picking his words cautiously.

"Last year I was... rescued. Two doctors have been working on me, rehabilitating me. They say...." He swallowed, unable to keep the sick fear entirely out of his voice. "They say that they're making me better so I can be free. But I don't know that. They could be repatterning me, using me for their own purposes. So I came to you to find out if what I think I know is real."

For several seconds Dougherty stared, then he seemed to collect himself. "I... I hope you realize that's a very tall order."

"I need to be certain."

"I see. And what if you can't be certain?"

Simon had considered this and he spoke without hesitation.

"Then I prefer to die. I will not be a slave again. I won't be twisted and burned in and stroked like a pet!" His burst of vehemence startled both of them.

"I see." Dougherty's eyes were calculating and Simon felt a new wash of fear. He knew his own potential value to the institute. They had never been able to get their hands on a live weapon. He'd be a coup for any researcher.

"Since you know my name, may I assume that this wasn't a random assault?"

Simon nodded.

"Then I must ask: why me? As Clinical Convenor at the Institute I spend most of my time on administration and teaching these days. I'm certainly not the best qualified person to diagnose you."

"You are nonetheless qualified," said Simon. He would not betray Toni by using her old name or mentioning her background—

her former colleagues assumed her dead. But it had been Toni's reminiscences that had caught Simon's interest. She had talked to Dr. Lau one evening about the institute and her grudging respect for Dougherty, despite their frequent and profound professional disagreements. She said: "One thing I can say for him: Graeme never chose political expediency over patients."

Dougherty pressed. "What other reasons did you have? Can you give me an example?"

His caustic tone sparked Simon's annoyance.

"For example, Doctor, the original neurosurgery done on me was performed by an expert. I know the approximate date, and I have identified all the surgeons with the necessary skills inside an appropriate radius. There were fewer than a dozen candidates and you are one. However, eighteen years ago you were on sabbatical in South America."

"We have a very good surgeon on staff who was still in school eighteen years ago."

"That does not mean Dr. Yee isn't bent."

"Surely you can't know for certain about me either," countered Dougherty.

"No," admitted Simon. "I am taking a risk."

There was a silence. Dougherty stroked his beard.

"Tell me some more about yourself."

Simon started to describe what Choi had done to him, but Dougherty waved his hand to interrupt.

"No, no, no. If you can't trust your memory, you certainly can't trust what you've been told, and I never listen to apocryphal evidence. I'm asking about your personality. What kind of a person are you?"

Simon felt his irritation growing.

"I don't know how to answer. Is this relevant?"

"This is a standard interview question for patients who hold a gun to my head. What's your favorite food?"

"I don't have a favorite."

"Then name some foods you like."

Simon summoned patience and thought back on the last few days. "Orange peel tofu with pea pods. Butterscotch ice cream. Pizza with tomatoes and Parmesan. Honey wine. Congee with four kinds of mushroom. Pommes pommes. Salal jam on oat toast...."

"Enough. Have you read any good books lately?"

Simon stared, then said: "Yes."

"Examples....?"

"The Audubon Field Guide to North American Birds, Western Region, revised 2101 edition with Improved Interactive Targeting for Personal Phones. A History of Modern Dance, Cube II. Microclimate Gardening with Native Plants on the Pacific Northwest Coast. The Holiday Humor Omnibus, Print Companion. Is that enough?"

Dougherty's lips twitched.

"I see you have catholic tastes."

"You're wasting my time! You're just keeping me occupied while you wait for help!"

Dougherty leaned forward, glowering.

"What I'm doing is giving you a hearing that is probably pointless because you're asking too much of me, and too much of yourself. You realize that to make a diagnosis I will have to hook you up and run scans of your cerebral function?"

Simon swallowed and nodded, abruptly frightened. He knew that, he just hadn't wanted to think about it.

"Let me guess: when you panic or lose your temper, do you become uncontrollably violent?"

"...sometimes."

"Sometimes," echoed Dougherty. He leaned back in his chair. "Still, you present a fascinating challenge. Therefore, I'm willing to take you as a patient at the Institute."

"No!"

Dougherty frowned. "I'll admit you under my personal authority, no other doctors on your case."

"You would never release me. And once there I'd make an easy target—the tongs would kill me."

Dougherty waved his hand dismissively.

"We have security. We can hide you."

"Security?" All of Choi's icy disdain surfaced. "Do you know how easily I accessed the institute's secured records, Dr. Dougherty? Patient files, case notes, personnel files. Your personal stipend is four hundred and fifty-two dollars a month, of which you donate ten percent to the Guildless Medical Fund. Two days ago you convened an in-camera disciplinary meeting at which it was decided to censure attendant Gannet Philip Mathers and fine him fifty dollars for inappropriate use of chemical restraint on a patient and failure to obtain approval from a supervising physician. And your perimeter surveillance is riddled with holes. Your own office window is an easy sniper target."

"Don't threaten me!" Dougherty sounded furious, but the glass in his hand shook. He put it down.

Simon closed his eyes and rubbed his forehead, fighting back terror and exhaustion. He desperately regretted choosing this man now, but he had no other options left except to win his cooperation.

"I apologize," he said finally.

Dougherty let silence hang before he spoke again in a calmer tone.

"You must realize that I need the equipment in the medlab at the institute."

"But you have a portable medkit with diagnostic capability."

"How did you...? Ah. You checked the internal logs and saw I signed it out of inventory, didn't you?"

"Yes."

"First, you must know that your neural configuration is very rare. That portable isn't adequate to deal with it. And second, Simon, I make it a personal rule not to bring work home. The unit's in my office at the institute."

Simon felt a rush of despair. Dougherty might be lying, but his words sounded all too plausible. Had he come all this way for nothing? He felt weariness behind his eyes and hunched in the chair, squeezing his arms tight around aching ribs, trying desperately to think of anything else he could do.

Dougherty sat watching, then spoke in a gentler tone.

"Let me be very honest, Simon. It isn't possible for me to tell you what's real. Quite apart from issues that have troubled philosophers for millennia, you are an intelligent man with cerebral intrusions so extensive that it would be very difficult to determine which of your reactions are natural and which have been induced."

"And there's a much greater problem. You cannot possibly know beyond all doubt that your memories and thoughts are your own. Nobody living in the twenty-second century can. I may sit here and tell you that I despise the criminal use of neurotechnology, but I could have been tampered with and I wouldn't know it. I could even have done something in the past so horrible that I erased my own memory. The possibilities are endless, and contemplating them would only drive me mad, so I must live with a degree of doubt."

"But you check!" burst out Simon. "It's in your personnel file—you take regular screenings for evidence of physical or mental tampering!"

Dougherty raised his eyebrows.

"Touché," he muttered. "The price of freedom is eternal vigilance." He grimaced and twisted his glass between his hands. Amber liquid swirled. "Have you considered what you would do if I found something? For example, I might find that your rescuers have made clinically sound adjustments in order to override cemented paths from your earlier training. Then what?"

"I don't know!" said Simon desperately. "But... they should have told me!"

"These people who are helping you—have they said why they're doing it?"

"She... They say it's because they love me."

"And if that's true, and you decide to kill yourself, you'll hurt them."

"Stop!!! STOP IT!" Simon found himself on his feet, yelling, all thoughts of stealth and neighbors long forgotten. "Stop playing games! You're trying to confuse me! But what would you choose? What would you do if you were me, Doctor?"

Dougherty sat without expression for long seconds.

"I might ask somebody to diagnose me," he admitted finally. "But I sure as hell wouldn't hold a gun to their head and then expect an honest answer!"

"I made a mistake. I apologize."

"Apologizing doesn't mitigate the risk."

Simon said nothing. Dougherty sighed, then looked at him.

"May I touch you?"

"Yes."

Simon sat back down. Dougherty got up and walked slowly

over. He stopped in front of the chair, reached out and lightly touched Simon's shoulder, then his forehead. Simon didn't flinch. Dougherty moved around beside the chair and ran cool fingers over the crown of Simon's head, searching for the tiny betraying bumps of subdermal chips while Simon held himself very still. Fingers swept across, then down toward the thalamic plug at the back of Simon's neck....

Simon hurled himself out of the chair and fetched up by the curtained window. For long seconds all he could do was pant and struggle for control.

"I take it you've been tortured?" Dougherty asked quietly.

Simon nodded mutely.

"That was all I needed. Please take your seat again."

Simon didn't want to sit, he wanted to run or dance or hit something or curl up and cry, but he reluctantly forced himself to return to his seat as Dougherty settled back into the leather arm-chair.

"At the hospital we don't go near a patient like you without physical restraints and an emergency team standing by. And you want me to take this risk by myself in the middle of the night. Tell me, Simon. Why should I do that?"

Simon couldn't think of a reason. Not of his own. But Toni's words came back to him.

"I came to you because one of your colleagues said this: 'Dougherty is an arrogant, supercilious prick and he would fight to the death defending his worst enemy if he believed it was the right thing to do.'"

There was a very long silence, then Dougherty spoke very dryly.

"I suppose I can only hope you didn't find that in my person-nel record."

# 26

Giddy. That was the word, Toni decided. She'd heard patients describe it before—the sensation of having an enormous weight lifted from their shoulders, but she'd never felt it. After a torrent of tears she'd fallen into an exhausted sleep and she'd woken fourteen hours later feeling a century younger and lighter than she could ever remember. She'd even caught herself smiling at eight in the morning for no reason at all.

Across the breakfast table, Rigo smiled back. Klale slid closer on the bench seat and put an arm around Toni's shoulders. Mary had gone for her habitual morning walk, taking Simon with her.

"You look so much better," said Klale.

"I feel good," admitted Toni.

"When..." Klale hesitated, then continued. "When it's a good time, I wanted to ask you something."

"Now's good," said Toni serenely. Damn if it wasn't true, too. She took a second helping of oat toast and spread it with jam, ignoring the greasy cow butter Klale liked to eat—it made her shudder.

"Toni, what you said about the Zone... They didn't really kill children in gas chambers, did they?"

"No." Toni thought back, feeling sad, but no longer distressed. "No, they didn't, Klale. But we all believed they did. It wasn't until I was a med student working in a UN emergency clinic that I found out it wasn't true. We'd treated a small child with burns who didn't seem to have any family, and when a special constable arrived to take her, the kid became hysterical with terror and I got so upset I almost blew my pose as a townie. That's when I discovered the UN had a special facility in Detroit for unregistered orphans. I didn't believe it even then, I took the train on my day off to look at it myself and it wasn't until I walked down a hallway and saw well fed kids playing hakysak in dorms that I realized that what I'd believed all my life was just an ugly, evil myth."

Rigo was listening. She gave him a twisted smile.

"There's a terrible irony, too. It turns out the gas chamber stories were deliberately spread in the Zone by local activists who wanted to stir up rebellion. And for that cause they terrified their own people. I've always hoped they burned when the Zone burned."

"It burned?"

Toni looked at Klale, startled, suddenly realizing how young the girl was. The Burning of the Zone had made global headlines in '83—twenty six years ago. And Klale had just turned twenty-six.

"Yeah. Thousands of people died in the fire, trapped behind barbed wire fences. When the townies realized what was happening some of them came and pulled down the fences where they could, but it was an inferno. Almost the whole place went up. I was long gone, of course. I watched it on the net."

Almost true. She'd turned on coverage, then turned it off, not able to look. The world of her childhood had burned that day, and maybe Jamal had died with it. She would never know.

Klale looked somber. "I can't believe that your own mother.... Well, what she did to you was terrible."

"She wasn't much more than a child herself," said Toni very quietly. "She was fourteen when she got pregnant with me. I try to remember that."

When Mary returned from her walk she suggested tea and a therapy wrap-up. Remembering the tea from Klemtu, Toni asked Mary about it and Mary laughed, saying it was cheap black tea steeped much too long but she liked it, too. So they drank strong tea with sugar and Toni talked with an ease she could rarely remember feeling.

"It's like finding the key to a puzzle. My self-destructive behavior suddenly falls into place. I always believed..." Even now it was hard to say. She forced the words: "...that I was a terrible person. That I didn't deserve to live."

And she hadn't planned to live, she realized now. She hadn't looked past this job with Simon, hadn't made plans, hadn't considered anything in her future.

"And now that you remember, do you feel terrible?" asked Mary softly.

"I feel sad. Looking back as an adult at that poor ignorant, terrified child I feel sorry for her. She did everything wrong, but she tried so goddamned hard...." Her voice caught.

"No anger?"

"Yes. Of course. At my mother. And the people who built the Zone. No child should ever have to live like that," she said vehemently. Then she took a breath and looked into Mary's brown eyes. "But that's in the past. The Zone is gone."

Mary smiled, that wonderful glowing smile of hers that scrunched up all the brown seams of her face.

"Good. I'm so happy for you." They sat in silence for a moment, then: "Toni.... I've been wanting to tell you something."

Mary curled her fingers into Toni's palm and Toni felt an old surge of wariness. Eight years ago she and Mary had broken up after a vacation in this cabin—a wretched week during which Mary had tried to get closer to Toni and Toni had driven her off with increasing ferocity. The memory made her wince.

"I've met somebody," said Mary, her voice abruptly shy and girlish. Toni felt an unreasoning stab of jealousy, mingled with relief.

"Who is it?" she asked, and then listened while Mary told her. It felt good to be the listener again, and she truly wished Mary happiness. Mary's first wife, her childhood sweetheart, had been killed in a traffic accident, then her second wife, Jay, had contracted Lutwyche's Sarcoma. Jay had been born on Cortes. When she fell ill, she and Mary had moved back to the island and bought the cabin from Jay's cousin. Before she died, Jay had convinced the Island Council to allow a nonresidential ownership exception so she could will it to Mary.

So she listened and then hugged Mary, feeling their friendship stronger than it had been for a long time.

Mary left the next morning and at Rigo's urging, Toni spent the day resting and eating many small meals. She didn't do therapy with Simon, but she watched him. He seemed quiet, solemn and preoccupied—not an unreasonable response to the sudden changes in his life. Toni suspected he was worrying about his upcoming meeting with the Parole Committee—the first formal decision of his adult life. She had a great deal to discuss with him, but it could wait.

Klale seemed confused by the changes in Simon. She had become enamored of a charming child-man and suddenly he was gone, replaced by a wary adult. She made overtures which he rebuffed with distant politeness—too distant, decided Toni after a while. She'd assumed Simon was only angry at her, but perhaps he'd generalized his anger to all of them. Or perhaps something had happened on the Empress that he hadn't told them about. He had even retreated from his new progress with his father.

Increasingly worried, she called a team meeting with the others on for the next morning. But on Saturday, Toni woke to find her plans shattered. It was Rigo, this time, who found Simon missing and a note flashing on the netset by his bed.

"I have left Cortes Island. I will contact you within forty-eight hours. If you have not heard from me by then, this set will release my itinerary and a GPS tracking code. Do not phone. Major Kim is monitoring island calls. I do not intend to harm anyone. I apologize for breaking parole, but I must do this. Simon."

Toni stared at it a long time before looking at Rigo and Klale crouched on the futon beside her. Their faces mirrored her dismay and anger. Damn!

"Well," she said finally. "We have a choice. Either we call the parole committee and Major Kim, or we wait forty-eight hours and hope we can retrieve the situation then."

"Goddamn!" said Rigo explosively. He stood and kicked the nearest object, which happened to be the door. It slammed shut, narrowly missing his face, and he screamed at it in Chinese, then wrenched it open and stomped out, leaving Klale and Toni staring after him.

"Wow. I've never seen him blow before," said Klale.

"Last straw," said Toni. Despite her own upset, she was suddenly aware of a new underlying calm in herself. She deserved to live. And that felt good. She looked at Klale and found herself grinning. "Guess we should make tea."

Klale stared at her, then got up, shaking her head.

"The whole world is going tilt."

When Rigo returned half an hour later the two women were sitting at the kitchen table sipping tea. He pulled up a chair and ran his hand through his hair.

"Can we trust him?" he asked bluntly.

He looked at Toni. So did Klale. Toni took her time before answering.

"We can probably trust his intentions," she said at last. "I'm not so sure about his judgment. But I trust Major Kim even less."

"I don't like hiding this from Mary," said Klale unhappily.

"We can't tell her," said Toni. "It would put her in an impossible position."

"I know."

There was a long silence, eventually broken by Klale.

"We're going to do it, aren't we?"

"Yes," said Rigo bitterly. "But this is the last time. I will not do this again, ever. Even for my son."

"Agreed," said Toni.

And so another wait began, and this time they had no floor to work on. Klale finished up the last few touches, then pointed out that the beautiful new floor made the old walls look dingy. How about painting them? But Toni declined, noting that Rigo had had enough of cooking in the dining room. Instead she went for a walk to burn off some of her frustration. It was the longest walk she'd taken on the island and she looked up to find herself outside of Manson's Landing General Store. After a long hesitation she marched in and bought a few items, giving a big smile to the geezy rurro behind the counter. The woman nearly dropped Toni's bag.

Hiding Simon's absence from the Andersons was their biggest concern, but Ethan was away on a job, and the rest of the family were helping with the annual potato harvest at Linnea Farm all weekend. However, on Sunday afternoon, an unexpected visitor showed up—old David Anderson. Klale and Rigo had gone to the farm as well, so it was Toni who looked apprehensively out the kitchen window and saw him standing there. Simon had turned off the cabin's security net and she'd forgotten to switch it back on, she realized. Well, too late now. With great reluctance, she opened the door.

"Hello."

"Afternoon."

They stood looking warily at each other. After several long seconds Toni realized she couldn't avoid inviting him in, so she stepped back. Anderson removed his hat, scraped his boots on the mat, and stepped inside, then stood there uncomfortably.

"Went down to the store today," he said gruffly. "Found a message from a Major Kim."

Toni felt her blood pressure soar but kept her face expressionless. Damn. Did Kim know?

"He wanted to know about the Island Council, were we fully aware of hazards of having Simon here."

"Oh," said Toni, simultaneously relieved and annoyed. Kim hadn't taken long to track them down.

"I told him he was wasting his time," said Anderson unexpectedly. He paused, then held out his hand. "I owe you an apology."

Toni found herself gaping up at the old bastard. He had the look of a man braced to perform some dreadful duty.

"Please don't bother," she told him. "Let's stay enemies. It's easier."

"I'd love to." Anderson's voice was heartfelt. "But it's no good for the families." He shoved his hand at her. "Friends?"

She looked down at the proffered hand and wrinkled her nose. "That's a big step for a recovering therapist. How about we try for a truce?"

That won a smile and Toni abruptly realized she hadn't seen Anderson smile before. It gave her a sudden glimpse of a young man with craggy good looks and a gentle side buried under fearful responsibilities.

"I think I can just about manage that."

Toni shook. Damn. Now she couldn't avoid asking him to stay. On cue, Anderson produced a bottle from under his coat.

"Blackberry wine? It's one of Ethan's better attempts."

"No, thanks," said Toni hastily. Too hastily. Anderson stiffened. "But... you wouldn't tell Rigo if I had coffee, would you? He cut me off after breakfast."

"Course not."

Anderson hung up his coat and sat while Toni got a glass for him and made herself coffee. Then she excused herself, saying she had to check on Simon. She hurried to his room and called up a noisy vidshow on the netset, hoping it would cover the suspicious silence in the cabin. When she returned, Anderson was already half way through his first glass of wine.

She sat. He sipped. She sipped.

"So," she said finally. "Was this Blue's idea?"

"Blue still won't say a word to me beyond 'pass the potatoes'. But young Rory, she's another story, doesn't shut up that girl. Got all her mother's steel will and a mouth on her like a band saw."

"Uh huh."

Toni sat impatiently, waiting for the old man to get to the point. He finished the first glass of wine and poured himself another. She sighed inwardly, steeling herself for a long story. Or a confession. Yes, that felt like it.

"I know I been hard on you. So I wanted to explain a bit about... well, about what it was like around here years ago."

He lost momentum, fortified himself with more wine and started in again.

"See, the younger people don't know what it's like to starve. What it does to you. And I can't tell them."

"Been there," said Toni shortly.

"Yeah, I heard."

"Small neighborhood," she grumbled, unsurprised. Klale had been talking to Blue, she guessed. Or Rigo to Ethan. Or Simon to David. Shit. No hope of keeping her life private.

"Well, I guess that's why I thought you might understand."

He took a deep breath and visibly plunged in.

"When I was fifteen my Dad died of Bloom. We never figured out where he picked it up, and by the time we knew what was happening it was too late. Sunday he was fine. Tuesday he was dead. So then I was alone in the house with mom and my little sister. Mom worked when she could, sold what she could, but the winter I was sixteen we were starving.

"That was a bad year. The climate was going apeshit and a blight hit the island—killed most of the vegetables, even the potatoes. We ate anything we could think of that winter—seaweed, mussels, seagulls, tree bark—and people died anyway. Making it worse, there were refugees streaming north from all the big cities— Vancouver, Seattle, Portland. They seemed to think they could come up here to the 'wilderness,' camp in any spot they wanted and live off the land. Like hell!" He snorted.

"I heard stories all the time. Refugees landing, stealing food, shooting families, taking their houses. We were terrified."

He shot a glance at Toni.

"It was a racist thing, too. We'd see the news vids—gangs of blacks in the big American cities killing each other, looting. And these islands were white—Caucasian, Asian, Native Indian. Growing up here I'd hardly even met an Afroid."

"Anyway...."

He paused so long Toni almost decided to prod, then he poured more wine and started again.

"Winter of '42. February. I'm looking out the kitchen window and I see this tall black guy coming up through the garden. He's wearing an army jacket, has a big semi-automatic and he's moving slow, like he's sneaking up on the house to kill us. I'm scared shitless but I grab Dad's rifle and run to the front door and I throw it open and yell: "Stop!" He looks like he's raising his weapon, so I aim and shoot. Twice. Drop him dead."

"Then I walk out and see all the blood spilling out of him and wonder what in hell I've done, was he really meaning to shoot? He's a young man, not a lot older than me, and so thin, just bones...."

Anderson took a long unsteady breath.

"He'd come from the direction of the dock so after I threw up I went down there and saw this stupid fiberglass speedboat pulled in. It had oars rigged, and those boats didn't row worth a shit. And there was a woman lying in the bottom of the boat, shivering. She didn't look like she could move, so I put my gun down and went to lift her up and I found she had a baby in her arms...."

A baby. Toni felt her own ghosts rising as his words continued.

"Its face was terrible, like a tiny old man. I got my mother and we carried them up to the house and tried to warm them up and feed them, but they were too far gone. The baby died that night, and the woman died the next day."

Anderson wiped the back of his hand across his eyes. Toni spoke quietly.

"And you couldn't tell anybody, right?"

"Hell, no! I dug a hole. Bitch of a job, too. Had to go at it with a pick axe to shift all the rocks and still couldn't get it deep enough.

So in the spring I planted a couple apple trees on top."

"Ah." The puzzle fell into place. Toni found her hands clenched together on the table and put them in her lap. "Does Ethan know?"

"Never told him. Times were different by then, and he was always such a gentle kid. Somehow... well, I just couldn't." Anderson stared into his glass, not meeting Toni's eyes. "That gun the guy had.... It was nothing but rust. No bullets."

Toni kept quiet. He took a long unsteady breath, then cleared his throat.

"Every spring when I walk around the island I look in people's yards and wonder what's underneath 'em. There was a hell of a lot of rectangular gardening going on those years, even in winter. Some strange lookin' crab pots, too."

"I see," managed Toni, suddenly aware of her own anger. She'd grown up hating the people who walked on the other side of the barbed wire fence while she starved and bled inside it. They hadn't all been white, any more than all the people in the Zone had been Afroid or Hispanic, but it had felt that way. It had felt like genocide.

Put it away, she told herself. That time is over. And there were victims on all sides.

"Why did you tell me this?"

"Had to start with someone."

She studied him.

"If you're looking for absolution, that's Mary's department."

"Nope. Nobody can do that for me. I got to do it myself."

The steady determination in his voice took her by surprise.

"You got a program in mind?"

"Uh huh. First... well, I've got to talk to Ethan. Then I thought I'll take those damned apple trees down, dig the grave up, move whatever's left over to the cemetery where it should be. And hold a memorial service down at the hall. That should stir up one hornet's nest around here." There was a hint of relish in his voice. He'd enjoy raising a ruckus, thought Toni.

"Are you going to post the DNA to missing persons?"

He hesitated, uncertain.

"You think I should? It's a hell of a long time ago."

"Other families need to put the past to rest, too."

Anderson nodded, then pushed his chair back.

"Thanks for listening. And I'm sorry for what I did over at the Empress."

"You know..." Toni stood up with him and followed him to the door. "The person you really should be apologizing to is Simon."

Then she could have kicked herself. Damn! What if he took her up on it?

But the old man stopped by the door, a flash of humor in his eyes.

"Doctor... you owe me a bottle of vodka."

He strode out, leaving Toni smiling in spite of herself.

When a rap sounded at the same door barely half an hour later, she opened it without hesitation and found herself looking at a red-haired woman supporting a young girl on one arm.

"I'm Yasmin Paroo," said the woman. "You must be Dr. Almiramez."

# 27

"Sneaking in to my own laboratory in the middle of the night. Preposterous!" muttered Dougherty as he pressed his finger against the old pad on the door panel. Strangely, his voice held an undertone of relish.

In contrast, Simon felt terrified. It had been appallingly easy for Dougherty to smuggle an enforcer into the Institute, albeit an unarmed one. At Dougherty's insistence, he'd left the gun back at the rez. The doctor had phoned ahead with a story about an anonymous VIP patient, and the guards at the gate had allowed him to drive a luxury sharecar through the main entrance, barely glancing at the slouched figure of Simon in the passenger seat, his face muffled. Either security here was appallingly lax, or Dougherty had set a trap.

They'd driven between tall, slablike buildings to a blocky old wing with deeply inset windows. Everything about it seemed ominous. No patients in this building, Dougherty told him, just offices, labs and surgeries. They entered through a side door secured by an ancient metal key and a fingerprint reader, climbed a stairwell, and now Dougherty stood at a security door repeating the key and fingerprint routine.

This door let onto a long, high ceilinged hallway, lit only by dim emergency lights and so silent that their footsteps echoed. Simon felt his breathing start to race. Something about the sound of the hard floor, the stir of vented air against his face and the faint chemical smells seemed too horribly familiar, like Choi's bunker. He knew with sudden certainty that something terrible was about to happen. Panic flooded him. He spun and bolted out the door.

Dougherty found him crouched in the bottom of the concrete stairwell, shaking. Simon heard his footsteps come down the stairs, then slow and stop half a flight up.

"You can't do this, can you?"

"I can! I just...." He swallowed, tried to breathe slower, tried to deepen his voice so he didn't sound like a frightened child. "Something about that hall.... I think it's the smell." He forced himself to stand, arms still clutched tightly around his chest.

"We have to get to the lab immediately," said Dougherty. "I asked them to blank the hall and stairwell security vids for ten minutes, and that's almost up."

"I'm coming," said Simon grimly.

He started for the stairs. Dougherty shot him a doubtful look but turned and led the way again. He'd exchanged his wine-colored velvet jacket for a suede coat, but still wore the diamonds at his ears.

Fifty meters down the hallway Dougherty stopped in front of a door labeled "Cognitive Imaging Laboratory - Authorized Admittance Only." Simon watched over his shoulder, appalled again. This panel required a retinal scan from Dougherty, but permitted him to admit another, unscreened individual simply by holding the door open. Then Dougherty waved the lights on and he stared in surprise.

He'd expected a cold, functional room, but this looked like a staff lounge and the air smelled of cinnamon. Comfortable chairs nestled in groups between potted plants. To Simon's left, tall bar stools stood by a counter with built-in cupboards and a mini kitchenette. The room had no windows but the lights were fully programmable across the spectrum. A wall to Simon's right featured original flat art, the rear wall held a floor-to-ceiling screen, and an angled corner contained a fish tank, in which neon fish swum lazily through fronds of seaweed. Simon had almost touched the glass before he realized he was looking at a top quality screen, framed in steel to mimic a tank.

"Compromise decision," Dougherty said, throwing his coat on a chair. "Therapists wanted fish, but facility staff didn't want to clean a tank. So we installed twenty-four hour holofeed from the Biology lab's exotic breeding project. Soothing and cheap—an inspired solution if I do say so myself."

Simon nodded. His panic had eased the moment he stepped into this room, but he felt tension building again as he spotted a reclining chair whose blue patterned upholstery didn't quite disguise the restraint anchors.

"Help me with this, would you?" said Dougherty. He opened a cupboard, brought out carbonweave restraint straps, and handed them to Simon. Strangely, it made Simon better to attach the straps to the anchors himself. He perched on the recliner, hands and feet clammy with nerves. But at least this room didn't smell like a lab— scents were cycling through and now he caught whiffs of sesame and pine.

Dougherty opened a closet and rolled out a trolley that held an interface array. He set it up beside a chair, angling the chair so that he had a direct view both of Simon and the wallscreen. He waved his set on, and displays blossomed to life on the wall.

"Do you want me to fasten the restraints?" asked Simon, unable to keep an edge out of his voice.

"Please," said Dougherty, then looked at him. "I'll be running through all your filaments to gauge your reactions, and I'd much prefer it if you didn't jump up and kill me."

Simon nodded. He understood that. He also understood that he'd chosen to put himself in Dougherty's hands and must trust him. But it had only been a week since he'd woken up as Yasmin's prisoner, and it took everything he had to sit and fasten leg straps, then a waistband, a chestband and finally straps on his left arm and wrist. Dougherty fastened his right arm with swift efficiency, checked all the restraints and the headrest, and adjusted angles so Simon could comfortably watch the wallscreen and also see Dougherty. Then he produced a wide, padded forehead strap.

"To prevent neck strain."

"No! Please." Simon clenched his eyes shut. Seconds crawled past. He looked again, to find that Dougherty had put the strap down and returned to his own chair, taking a lapset from the trolley.

"May I assume that you usually use Davidson cups?"

"Yes." Optical cables delivered maximal bandwidth and prevented eavesdropping or signal jamming.

"Well, you don't need them here. This lab is shielded and has extremely sensitive high load data transference. All I need is a signal address and your passcode."

Simon told him, feeling stark terror in his stomach, even though he'd prepared for this eventuality by setting up a once-only gateway with a three hour time limit. Still, three hours could destroy him.

"We don't use headsets in this room," said Dougherty in conversational tones. Simon focused desperately, trying to distract himself from fear by watching Dougherty work. "Using the big screen allows us to observe our patient directly and lets the patient watch us. Good, I'm in, and.... Oh my. I've never seen an array like this...."

Multiple readouts opened on the wallscreen. They looked similar to the displays in Simon's sleepware, though more numerous and complex. Then a holographic image of Simon's skull flashed up, showing the implanted chips and filaments radiating into his brain tissue. Dougherty stared avidly at the screen, then began manipulating his lapset.

"Diagnostics coming up... I see your chips are standard Sensei, four-one-twos. Very reliable."

A chip flashed red.

"The thalamic chip is damaged. Were you aware of that?"

"Yes."

"Has it been damaged long?"

"A year," said Simon.

Dougherty frowned and threw him a sharp glance.

"It should be removed as soon as possible. Now, I'm running a scan for scarring and other neural damage. You'll see that in orange."

Orange bloomed around the implant sites, with heavy concentrations near the damaged chip. Dougherty studied the screen without expression.

"Mmm hmm. All right, now I'm going to test a random location on each filament for response and signal degradation. When I say the word 'now', tell me what you experience." The screen zoomed in on a single filament and the surrounding brain tissue. "Now."

"I smell salt water."

Text appeared near the filament: "89% spec function."

"Now."

"I itch." Reflexively Simon reached to scratch, but restraints pinned him in place. "Left shoulder."

"Now."

Simon stood on the end of Pier B-C in the rain, water beading and dripping off him. A cargo picker rolled past, heading for a passenger foil tied up alongside.

"What is it?"

"A memory," said Simon shortly. The pier vanished and he lay in the lab again. He stared at the wallscreen, trying to ignore hunger and exhaustion and the sensation of being trapped. Dougherty continued through all the filaments, checking the ones on the damaged chip twice and frowning.

"Fine," he said finally. "That's an intriguing design, similar to wizard modifications, but I don't see much evidence of chemical burn in. Who trained you?"

"My owner."

"Amateur?"

"Yes."

"I thought so. Burning neural pathways is finicky work and it's unforgiving. Amateurs who try it often fail. It's fortunate your owner didn't make that mistake."

"Yes, he did," said Simon, as comments from Choi's training logs suddenly fell into place. "He had other tools before me. And he... experimented." Simon studied his new awareness with an odd sense of vertigo. He'd always felt utterly alone at Choi's hands, but others had suffered before him. Simon had been unique only in being the last.

"You will almost certainly have a few burned in commands, such as a restraint—usually a voice-keyed word or phrase synonymous with 'stop' but less commonly used. 'Halt' is popular."

"I don't remember any commands like that."

"You wouldn't. I'd like to locate one, but I'd need your owner's voiceprint."

"I can imitate his voice," said Simon.

"You can?" Dougherty sounded dubious.

"Very accurately. You must have a list of common commands. He preferred to speak Mandarin, so I'll translate and read them off, then you can play them back."

"It's a long shot."

"I want to know."

Dougherty looked at him, eyes unreadable.

"All right."

A list of words flashed up on the screen. Simon read them in English, then gave a Mandarin equivalent, leaving a pause between each word. When he finished, Dougherty played them back. As always the sound of that Chinese accented voice made Simon flinch. His own voice sounded high pitched when he heard himself speak, but in playback it precisely echoed the old sadist.

Abruptly he felt Dougherty's hand on his shoulder, shaking him. He blinked. An instant before Dougherty had been sitting in his chair.

"What happened?"

"Control word. The one that means 'cease.' Watch, I'll show you a playback."

Dougherty regained his seat and opened a new window onscreen. Simon saw himself strapped into the reclining couch. Abruptly his eyes rolled up and his jaw slacked. He looked at the image, feeling queasy, then something struck him.

"Why didn't he use it?"

"What?" Dougherty looked up sharply. Simon hesitated, realizing his mistake, but Dougherty prodded. "When didn't he use it?"

"When I killed him," said Simon, hearing savage satisfaction in his own voice. He did not regret that murder, would not pretend to regret it.

"I see. Well... I must assume either you surprised him or he couldn't speak. Certainly the command works." Dougherty's voice was calm, but the tension in his shoulders betrayed him and Simon realized he shouldn't have made himself seem more dangerous. Worse, he'd just recorded the command for Dougherty. That thought brought a new flood of fear.

Dougherty called up more diagnostics.

"Trained young, I see. Eidetic memory enhancements?"

"Yes."

"Typical concentration of scarring and highly developed pathways in the thalamic regions, but also in areas of the frontal lobe usually associated with creativity. Intriguing.... Did you have an obedience ritual?"

"Yes."

"And it was...?"

Simon spoke very reluctantly, the words bitter in his mouth.

"I kneeled, leaned forward to touch my forehead to the floor, and recited words."

"All right. I want you to close your eyes and pretend you're performing the ritual and then say the words. Can you do that?"

Simon never wanted to do it again. Never. He steeled himself.

"Yes."

"Now."

He pictured the mahogany desk in Choi's office and prostrated himself before it on the polished floor. He spoke in Mandarin.

"Master, I am grateful for your patience with such a miserable servant. I am grateful for the pain of correction so that I may learn from my errors. I...."

Dougherty interrupted him.

"Enough. Good. Now I'll play back your neural activity at one third realtime."

Simon opened his eyes and saw blue pathways flickering through his brain tissue like forks of lightning. To the left of that image, graphs writhed. He wished he'd studied up on medical software so he'd know what they meant.

"I'll play it again and pull up a library profile for comparison. Now, see the similarity? This sequence is a typical trauma-etched behavior. Note the unusually high activity level here and here. At the same time, there's activity in other areas, designated green by this imaging software. We call this 'peripheral static.' To put it in subjective terms, you are performing this behavior, and you may even believe the words you say, but in some small corner of your mind you know that you are doing this under duress. Correct?"

"Yes," said Simon vehemently.

"By contrast, a chemically etched behavior—here's a sample profile—is characterized by strong pathways that show no natural variation on repetition, and a complete lack of peripheral static. In other words, a person performing an etched behavior believes utterly and never deviates. There is no doubt, can be no doubt. Prolonged torture produces effects that seem outwardly identical, but scans show the difference. Now, do you have a reward ritual?"

"No!" said Simon before he could stop himself.

Dougherty gazed at him calmly.

"For the diagnosis you requested, I need data. I'm asking you for an absolute minimum."

Simon took several long, uneven breaths. "I need access to a music library."

For an instant Dougherty looked surprised. Then he smoothed his expression and called up a menu.

"This is the university music library."

Simon didn't want to use any of his favorite dance music, so he picked an old waltz he both loved and loathed because Choi had often given it to him. He thought of asking for headphones, but as the first strains of the Blue Danube sounded, he realized the lab had superb acoustics. So he lay back and closed his eyes, letting calm gradually blanket his fear, and imagined a wide dance floor....

When he came back to himself he found tears rolling down his face. His body hummed with pleasure, but he yearned desperately to escape and he realized he'd been thrashing against the restraints. He felt ashamed, horribly vulnerable and furious.

"I'm sorry, but it was necessary," said Dougherty quietly. "Tell me when you feel able to continue." He did not meet Simon's eyes.

Simon blinked and cleared his throat, unable to quench these emotions without Blade, unable even to wipe the tears from his face, and aware that Dougherty was watching every nuance of his mood.

"Continue," he said roughly.

"Very well. I intended to ask you some questions about your owner, but we're short of time and I think I can surmise your feelings about him. So I'll to move on to your therapist. What's her name?"

"Toni."

Simon braced for further questions about her identity, but to his surprise, Dougherty didn't ask. Instead he quizzed Simon about her professional techniques and then about Simon's responses. What did Simon feel when she touched his face? How did he feel when Toni gave him orders? Haltingly Simon forced himself to describe the night Toni got drunk, what had happened, and how he'd felt afterward. Dougherty's voice remained cool and clinical, but Simon sensed intense interest. Finally he closed most of the vid-panes and looked at Simon.

"That's sufficient for the time being. I need to discuss my find-ings with you, and I'd like to calm your emotions. May I do that?"

Simon didn't want to be manipulated, but he knew he needed it.

"Yes."

Almost instantly his fear faded, his muscles relaxed and he felt a warm sense of well-being. Dougherty blanked the wallscreen and leaned back in his chair, swiveling to face Simon.

"Very well, here's my preliminary opinion. You understand that I'm basing it on one very brief exam. However, I see no evi-dence of recent tampering with your memories or emotions, and no recent traumatic etching. You have strong, conflicted feelings about your therapist, but I'd judge those feelings to be entirely appropri-ate to the circumstances you describe."

"Isn't it possible to program responses that mimic natural emotions?" asked Simon.

"Certainly. But even with your neural array it would require a great deal of expertise and sophisticated wetware."

"There might not be a cabin on an island and I might never have lived there. It might all be virtual."

"Well I won't use the word 'impossible,' but I think it's very unlikely. A simulated scenario that complex is far more difficult to build than most people appreciate, and a man of your intelligence would notice even subtle flaws—bits of artifice, lack of sensory detail, time distortions or repeating patterns. And fictional realities usually promote stability, whereas your experience seems chaotic. Why, for example, write a scenario where your therapist gets drunk? Finally, if you were under the control of such sophisticated experts, it seems to me improbable that you'd be able to escape and come here."

"I see."

Simon tried to focus, to decide what he should do with this information. Now that his fear and anger were damped, he felt fatigue descending like heavy fog. With his raised tolerances meds like sleep suppressants were only mildly effective and wore off quickly.

"What do you plan to do next?"

"Uh...." Simon wanted to rub his forehead. "Please release the restraints."

"I need to know your intentions, first," said Dougherty.

Simon knew that should frighten him, but it didn't. He felt calm and content.

"I'm not sure," he admitted. "I didn't plan this far."

"You expected to kill yourself, didn't you?"

Simon examined that idea.

"The odds of obtaining your diagnosis were not good. And... Well, death would be the safest option."

"Of course. Death is very safe," Dougherty said gravely. "Whereas life as a free human being is complex and bewildering and often painful."

"My death would release others from difficult responsibilities and great risk," pointed out Simon.

"And you'd be doing nothing to pay them back for all the responsibility and risk they've taken for you. You'd be committing the ultimate selfish act."

Simon looked at him in puzzlement.

"I've given them money."

"Please don't insult my intelligence. Or your own. If you think about it, I believe you'll discover that you could choose to give a great deal back. For example, the research we do here at this institute is used to develop medical therapies and to treat victims of torture. You could help us."

Simon studied Dougherty's face.

"You're not planning to release me, are you?"

Dougherty sighed and for the first time Simon realized that the dapper man was weary, too.

"Frankly, I'm trying to decide. I must tell you that everything we've said since you assaulted me has been monitored by my security staff."

Simon stared, then realization hit him. "Your earrings." He should have noticed earlier. Fear must have been clouding his thought process.

Dougherty hesitated an instant, then nodded.

"That's right, they're transmitters. Ever since some threats were made.... Well, that's not pertinent. Initially I signaled Security to hold off because I couldn't see any point getting my staff killed in the faint hope of rescuing me from an enforcer. Then I realized you were a potential patient of very great value."

"So you led me into your trap."

"I risked my life to help you, damn it!"

"You risked your life to achieve a professional coup," said Simon.

"Is that what you believe?!" Dougherty glowered. "Of course. You were molded by an egocentric sadist, I should hardly expect anything else."

"I don't want to be your lab rat."

"Even if it helps other people? Even if it helps other tools like yourself?"

An emotion tugged at Simon, slipped away before he could identify it. He closed his eyes, trying to pull it back from beneath the shroud of pleasant blandness. Hurt. Why hurt?

"It's not right. What you're doing isn't right."

"Isn't it, now. Then tell me, Simon: what is right?"

He thought about it for a long time while Dougherty waited in silence.

"Getting them out," said Simon finally. "Toni said that. She said you help the smuts and love birds and tools after they've been burned in and used and discarded, but nobody will take on the machine that builds them. Nobody will fight the bent surgeons who make them and the rich johns who fuck them and the tonglords who buy everyone with the profits. And nobody will make the Guilds do something to stop it instead of pretending it doesn't happen."

He thought back, remembering all the other victims he'd seen on Vancouver's streets. He'd never seen their commonalty before. The reflection of Blade's deathmask face stared at him from the wallscreen. He moved his eyes to Dougherty.

"I was a child sold to a sadist to be tortured and mutilated and twisted into a monster. I had no hope. No one tried to help me. But I would try to help the people who are sold. I would get them out."

These words should evoke strong emotion, Simon knew, but serenity lay across him like wet concrete. Dougherty studied the fish tank with a troubled expression, then sighed.

"Touché. Again. It appears that I keep underestimating you,

Simon. So here is the course of action I propose. As much as I may wish to keep you here, I won't do it at the expense of your freedom and my own conscience. Come home with me and avail yourself of my guest bedroom. Then, when we've both had some sleep and a decent meal, we'll discuss what to do next."

Simon hesitated.

"What about security?"

"I'll arrange it."

"And this session? Did you save it to the university node?"

Dougherty gave him a sour look, then reached over to the lapset and popped out a data cube.

"For some unaccountable reason, I have resolved to keep my confidential records on cube from now on."

"Thank you," said Simon. "Yes, I would like to stay in your guest room."


The trip back was, if anything, worse than the trip to the institute. Released from restraints and tranquilizing routines, Simon found himself distraught and shivering uncontrollably. He panicked in the hallway again and had to throw up in a shrub outside the exit, then the ten minute drive back to Dougherty's rez seemed endless.

Though it was growing light, none of Dougherty's neighbors were in sight. Dougherty let Simon run in the door while he dismissed the car, then he went to the kitchen and put several meal paks on to heat. Simon knew he was desperately hungry, but he couldn't think about food, couldn't even stand still. He found himself pacing and swaying with distress, unable to cope with a tumult of memories and feelings. Dougherty shot him increasingly alarmed glances as he set cutlery out on the dining table.

"Can I get you juice or tea? Or wine?"

Simon flinched at his voice, then burst out, "I need to dance!"

Dougherty froze.

"To.... Did you say dance?"

"There's enough space here if I move your furniture. May I? I'll move it back again!" Simon heard himself pleading, his voice a shrill child's.

Warring expressions crossed Dougherty's face—fear, annoyance, curiosity.

"Fine. Move it."

He stood behind the table, arms crossed, while Simon stacked furniture and sculptures against the wall by the kitchen and rolled up the rugs. It left him with a cleared space about eight by ten meters. He stripped off his sweater, shirt, shoes and socks with shaking hands, and took out a headset. Then he called up his personal music library on his phone. Seconds later he gasped as the first deep chords of music shook him to his bones.

On Cortes Island he'd often woven light, joyous dances, but tonight he called back all the old black dervishes—the angry, crying, howling, bleeding dances—the ones he'd thrown himself into when he found blood painted on his hands and face, and heard screams echoing in some locked corner of his mind. With no throwing knives he couldn't do the dance of knives, but he danced all the others in a nonstop blur of throbbing sound and motion until the last notes died and left him gasping in the stillness of an empty room.

He ached all over, sweat ran down his head and chest, and he thrummed with joy—once again a child washed clean of Blade's filth. For long seconds he savored the rapture with closed eyes as his breathing slowed, then he reluctantly opened his eyes to an adult world.

Dougherty sat at the dining table, Simon's phone by his hand. He'd been listening to the music, Simon realized. The doctor stood up and Simon saw tears on his face.

"Thank you," Dougherty voice was husky. "That was an extraordinary privilege."

Simon found himself blinking, not sure what Dougherty meant and having no idea what to say. He started toward the furniture, but the doctor waved at him.

"Leave it. Have a shower while I put food out. There's a spare bathrobe in the closet in the tub room."

Before showering, Simon took a moment to send a forged courier notice via several blind bounces to Toni's ID: "Parcel delivered, return shipment pending." Then he sat down in a thick, soft robe to a meal of linguini and salad. The food smelled and tasted wonderful, but as soon as Simon's hunger eased he began to droop.

After eating, he followed Dougherty to the guest room, yawning.

"Do you usually use sleepware?" Dougherty asked at the door.

Simon nodded.

"I'll get my medset."

Simon blinked at Dougherty's retreating back through a haze of exhaustion.

"But... you said it was in your office at the institute."

"I lied."

Simon blinked after him, then looked around the beautifully furnished guest bedroom. He found himself drawn to an oil painting—a surrealistic seascape, all wet reflections from moonlight and sand.

"You like it?" asked Dougherty from the doorway.

"Yes."

"It's by the painter Frans Klerkk."

"Your lover."

Simon heard a sharp intake of breath.

"How the hell did you know that?!"

"I researched you. Klerkk was one of your first patients when you were apprenticing in Vienna thirty years ago. You became lovers. When he died, you initiated an inquest because you felt that the hospital had erred in his treatment. The ruling did not support your view and the hospital censured you for inappropriate conduct."

"Those records were supposed to be purged after ten years!"

Simon shrugged, and turned to meet the doctor's angry eyes.

"Confidentiality systems are unreliable. It's almost impossible to purge records once they've been written to a node. And data mining is my expertise."

He knew he should feel afraid. He'd angered Dougherty and now he was about to lie down and plug into Dougherty's set. But physical and emotional exhaustion left no room for fear. Simon simply removed his borrowed bath robe, slid between the smooth sheets of the too-short bed, and attached optic cables. Dougherty watched him, then sat on the edge of the bed frowning down at the set.

"Simon... I know you're tired, but I have one more question.

Why were you so very sure that Toni manipulated your emotions?"

"Because...." Simon's voice dropped to a shamed whisper. "Because the way I feel about her is so... strong. Just like the feelings burned in me. Like dancing. Normal people don't feel that way. They don't feel that much."

"Ah. But there you're wrong." Dougherty's brown eyes met his with deep sadness. "Normal people feel towering passion and terrible grief, Simon. We just learn to hide it. Or hide from it." He touched Simon's shoulder very gently, then stood. "Sweet dreams."

# 28

Lost in the sheer delight of floating in the sky, Simon leaned eagerly forward, staring out the window of the air ambulance. To his left, the late afternoon sun shot rays through scattered clouds, smearing the rippled Salish Sea with bronze and silver. To his right, mountains reached up from green roots to blue ridges. And beneath him islands lay scattered in the strait, emerald oases encircled by white flecks of surf.

Simon glanced to his right and found Dougherty watching him intently. Unexpectedly the doctor smiled. Simon grinned back and saw his surprise.

"Having fun, are you?" asked Dougherty.

"Yes. Flying is wonderful. Are you having fun?"

"Ah. Well, strictly between you and me, I confess it, yes. You know, ever since the pandemics, senior medical personnel have had enormously broad powers—rather like a ship's captain at sea—but we rarely have occasion to use them these days. Ordering top priority secured air transport on my personal say-so is the most fun I've had in years. All this cloak and dagger brings back fond memories of illicit hours uplinked to CyberChase when my parents thought I was asleep in bed."

Dougherty was smiling, but abruptly his face turned serious and he looked in Simon's eyes. "It's time to talk."

Simon nodded, feeling anxiety rush back at him. He'd woken at two p.m., and immediately accessed the net. Coastal Justice showed no record of his parole committee being notified of his absence, but when Simon checked uploads from the taps in the cabin he discovered that they had all been disabled. It couldn't be a coincidence. Someone knew he was missing, and the most likely candidate was Major Kim. If Kim caught Simon in violation of parole, he'd have grounds to arrest him, so it seemed likely that Kim was laying in wait at the cabin.

As Simon hadn't planned his return trip and had no idea how

to handle this new problem, he'd had little choice but to reveal his situation to Dougherty, who surprised him by proving immensely competent. By four in the afternoon Dougherty had conjured up legal formware naming him Simon's physician of record, had arranged for air transport to any destination in five hundred kilometers, and had produced a large meal—delivered direct to his table from an Indian restaurant. He'd also laundered Simon's clothes while he slept and rescheduled all his administrative appointments and meetings for the next few days. Simon, devouring a third helping of eggplant subji, felt very impressed. It had never before occurred to him that legitimate transactions could be efficient.

Now he sat in the cabin of a STOL jumpjet watching downtown Vancouver—the entire world he'd known for the first thirty years of his life—pass beneath him like a gray stain on pavement. Despite his worries, he felt a burst of elation. Perhaps he truly was free. And perhaps he really could do what he'd told Dougherty—rescue other victims and lift them out of their tiny hells into this vast, bright world.

"Simon?"

Reluctantly, Simon dragged his eyes from the dazzling view. He looked at Dougherty, then gestured at the pilot who sat no more than five meters ahead of them. They sat in medics' jumpseats, with empty cargo space stretching between them and the cockpit—for stretchers, Dougherty had told him. The jet's cabin was almost silent except for a muffled roar of wind outside, and the pilot's headset dangled around his neck. He was flying manually, gazing ahead at the view and occasionally flicking curious glances back at Simon.

"Speak softly," advised Dougherty.

Simon pulled out his phone and set a jammer. It was far from foolproof, and it wouldn't defeat a hard-wired spy device, but it made Simon feel better. Dougherty watched, amused.

"Ready?"

"Yes."

"Very well, we land in Powell River, and then what?"

"I rented a boat using your net account," explained Simon. "We pick it up at the transfer pad in Powell River."

"My account? You might have asked," said Dougherty with annoyance.

Simon gave him a puzzled look.

"You said: 'make the necessary arrangements.'"

"An error I won't repeat. Why not fly all the way to this island of yours?"

"There's no airstrip, and floatplane hires are conspicuous."

There was a short pause.

"It's time," said Dougherty sharply. "I've trusted you a long way, but I need to know the details now. Names, dates, locations, everything."

Simon lowered his eyes, troubled. Revealing the cabin meant putting everyone in danger—including David. And Dougherty was still wearing his diamond earrings.

Dougherty spoke.

"There's an old saying—in for a penny, in for a pound. And I've already guessed a great deal. For example, I can only think of one therapist with the sheer bloody-mindedness you've described. It's Ann Almiramez, isn't it?"

Simon swallowed and nodded.

"Did you tell her you were consulting me?"

"No." Simon gave Dougherty a worried look, then finally blurted out: "What will you do to her?"

"Do?" Dougherty sounded surprised.

"She said she left Seattle 'one jump ahead of prosecution' for stealing meds and falsifying personal records."

"Ah. That. Well, that was a decade ago, Simon, and in the interim...." He sat back, stroking his beard thoughtfully.

"I think you need some background here. Ann's departure caused a very large shake-up at the Institute. Inevitably information about her past surfaced, and we faced the acute embarrassment of admitting that one of our own senior staff was an untreated plug victim who'd been fooling her 'expert' colleagues for years. I'm grateful I wasn't convenor at the time—my predecessor lost her post over the scandal though it was hardly her fault.

"It also sent incendiaries up posteriors far outside our walls. Ann was a rising star in her field, but if she hadn't lied about her past and forged her psych profiles, she'd never have been admitted to medical school. In the subsequent furor, she and her theories became something of a cause célèbre. So now, while I'm sure it will prove most inconvenient to have her show up large as life and twice as belligerent, I doubt that anyone will care to persecute an icon who has a fellowship and a prestigious award named after her."

Dougherty sounded amused, but Simon frowned.

"You didn't answer my question."

"Lord, you're persistent! Very well, the short answer is, I will not pursue charges against her at this remove, nor is it likely anyone else would do so, but I expect she'll have a good deal of trouble with the medical association if she tries to re-register."

"I see," said Simon. In fact, he didn't. Listening to Dougherty made him realize how little he knew about the Guild world.

"Details!" prodded Dougherty.

"You're very persistent," said Simon. But, having run out of delays, he sent a prepared datafile from his phone to Dougherty's. While the doctor read it over, he stretched his legs, longing to work out. Vancouver had passed behind and now the pilot was following the crinkled shoreline of the Sunshine Coast.

I could fight the tongs, thought Simon. The prospect filled him fierce exhilaration. Mary might not approve, but he didn't care. He'd found a purpose worth spending his life on.

"Doctor? How long will I live?"

"Ah...." Dougherty looked up, startled, then wary. "That's not my area of expertise."

"I know that tools are usually euthanized around forty, because of instability and cumulative physiological damage, but I don't know how long I might live with medical treatment."

"I'd only be speculating."

"Please speculate. Forty-five?"

Dougherty looked very troubled. He sighed.

"Long term damage to your immune system is the real culprit. I wouldn't count on seeing fifty if I were you. But please get a proper diagnosis."

Simon nodded. "Thank you."

Dougherty's sharp eyes were fixed on Simon. He seemed to expect a reaction, but Simon didn't have one. If he could anticipate ten functional years, that was a long time. It was half the time he'd spent with Choi, and that had been an eternity. Simon could do a very great deal in a decade.

The STOL craft landed at the air/marine transfer station in Westview, just south of the Powell River townsite. Simon raised his hood and wrapped the scarf around his face, but Dougherty's use of a contagion warning had been effective. When they stepped out there wasn't a person in sight, and they walked across the pad and down onto the dock unmolested. Rays of setting sun lit up a rental boat lying motionless in the arranged berth. The strait was still calm, with only small ripples on the water's surface. Dougherty climbed into the driver's seat and called up the interface, then glowered.

"Something's wrong. I can't get the traffic grid."

"There isn't one here," said Simon, squeezing beside him into the cramped seat.

"Good lord, we've fallen off the edge of the Earth. I'm supposed to drive this contraption manually?"

"There's a tutorial," pointed out Simon. Dougherty fixed him with a sour look.

"Have you done this before?"

"Yes. I stole a boat to leave the island."

"Saints have mercy. Very well, I have a doctorate, I can master this."

In fact, the controls were simple, and once Dougherty managed to detach the boat from the berth's security system, the trip went without incident. After some discussion, they decided to land at the Anderson's float. If Major Kim was waiting, subterfuge was pointless. And as Dougherty pointed out, the best weapon against an official was a bureaucrat. He seemed to relish the prospect.

They were less than fifteen minutes from dock when Simon's phone rang. Simon checked the ID and felt a stab of worry. Toni. So Major Kim must know about Simon's absence, otherwise she'd never risk the call. He took a couple of seconds to confirm that her phone was located at the cabin and connected the call.

"I need you back now," said Toni's voice, cold and very slightly slurred, as if she was very tired. "Abort your attempt to get to Choi's stash; we can try again later."

Somebody was forcing her to make the call, or listening in, thought Simon, but 'stash'?

"Acknowledged," he said flatly.

"How long will it take you to get back?"

Choi's imaginary stash would probably be in Vancouver.

"Three hours," he said.

Toni disconnected. Simon was left staring at his phone, alarmed and baffled.

"I don't understand," he told Graeme. "She wanted me to lie about my location, but why? Kim could trace this phone in seconds; I left its locator beacon intact so Toni could find me if I was unable to contact her. And why invent this 'stash'?"

Graeme's voice sounded grim.

"What if the tongs have found her?"

Simon stared at him, feeling like he'd been kicked in the stomach. The tongs. Since the Empress's sinking he'd discounted them, and he had left for Seattle without even considering Toni's safety. That had been a critical mistake. Major Kim would not harm Simon's family or David's. The tongs, on the other hand, would capture Toni and kill any witnesses. Toni's phone call had probably alerted Kim, but it would take Kim at least two hours to respond.

Toni! Simon fought back a wave of panic. He still felt a turmoil of confusing, painful emotions when he thought of her, but it had never occurred to him that he might lose her. The very idea of having to live without her made the world shake underneath him.

Abruptly he realized that Graeme was slowing the boat. Simon looked at him desperately.

"Hurry! They may take Toni now and not wait for my return. She's worth more than I am."

"Or you could be walking into a trap," said Graeme sharply. "If they already have Ann it's foolish to risk you as well. Let's wait for the cavalry."

"I have to help Toni!" Simon felt dismayed and furious to hear a quaver in his voice.

"And what if they know that—know that you'll risk anything to save her?" As the boat lost headway, Graeme turned in the pilot's seat to face him. "Simon, heroics are not in my repertoire. We need help. Is there somebody nearby we can call? A local Watch?"

"They're amateurs, not even armed," said Simon. "Tong soldiers would slaughter them." Abruptly he noticed a sparkle from Graeme's earrings and felt a flare of hope.

"What about your security team?"

"Ah." Graeme grimaced and scratched his ear awkwardly. "Hmm. Well, I'm afraid that sometimes an earring is just an earring."

It took Simon a second to realize what Graeme was saying.

"You lied."

"Yes."

Simon took a breath and fought for calm. He needed Blade's detachment and Choi's tactical reasoning, but he didn't dare slide too far either way into those personas. If he was going to get Toni back he had to focus and keep Simon in control. He closed his eyes for a long second, then looked at Graeme and spoke with utterly certainty.

"I'm going to the cabin. Now. If you will not assist me, I will remove you from that seat."

A wave slapped against the boat, rocking them. The wind was rising. For the first time Graeme looked indecisive, even afraid.

"Surely you're not going to launch a frontal assault!"

"That would risk Toni," said Simon. "I'll reconnoiter. I know the surroundings well, and I upgraded the perimeter security myself. I can get past it."

"And then you'll consult me before you do anything!"

"Very well."

Graeme grimaced and studied Simon's face unhappily. "And if you're lying, there's not a damned thing I can do, is there?" He swivelled back to the instrument panel. "I hope like hell you know what you're doing."

As waves slapped past and the island grew closer in the fading light, Simon felt exposed and unprepared. He searched the shoreline repeatedly with his goggles and saw no sign of ambush. There was very little activity at nearby houses and docks, but that wasn't unexpected—most islanders would be attending the Harvest Dinner. He debated pulling into another cove and cutting through the woods, but he was acutely aware of minutes ticking away. The heart of the trap was Toni, and her phone signal had come from the cabin.

As they pulled into the Anderson's dock and tied up, Simon saw movement inside the Anderson's house, then David's grandfather emerged, carrying his rifle loosely under one arm. Simon considered evading him, but a noisy altercation would attract attention, and the old man might have information.

They met at the garden end of the dock.

"Mr. Anderson, this is Dr. Graeme Dougherty, from the Seattle Neurological Institute. Doctor, this is David Anderson Senior, my neighbor."

Anderson glowered suspiciously for a second before stepping forward and taking Graeme's proferred hand in his work-roughened one. "Doctor, huh? He turned to glare at Simon from under bushy white eyebrows. "Aren't you supposed to be with an authorized keeper at all times?"

"I'm authorized," said Graeme smoothly.

"News to me," snapped Anderson, not taking his eyes off Simon. "You planning to return that item of mine you took?"

"Ah...." Simon felt the weight of the Glock in his jacket pocket. "Yes. I didn't... use it."

"Damn well better not of."

"Have you seen Toni today?" he asked urgently.

Anderson's eyebrows rose.

"Yeah. Matter of fact. This afternoon."

"What time?"

"Left around four."

"Was she alone?"

"Well, she told me you were upstairs, but that was obviously a crock ..."

"And Rigo and Klale?"

"Went over to the farm this morning with Blue and the kids. Where have you been?"

Simon looked at Graeme.

"Stay here."

He turned and jogged along the beach, moving as fast as he could over the slippery, uneven shoreline in the fading light. He heard Anderson shout behind him:

"Where do you think you're going?!"

Then Graeme's voice—sharp with urgency.

"Simon! Talk to me before you take action! Do you hear?!"

Simon ignored them both.

Nearing the foot of the cabin trail, he almost collided with

David, emerging from the path at a run. The boy tripped and stumbled, so Simon grabbed his shoulder and steadied him, taking in his appearance. The boy wore mud-spattered work clothes and appeared annoyed, but not injured or frightened. He looked up at Simon reproachfully.

"Simon! I've been looking all over for you! You didn't check the ADAT stations for me yesterday and you didn't answer your phone. I had to deke out of the harvest dinner and bike home to catch the tide."

"I'm sorry." Simon ignored a distant pang of remorse. "Were you just at the cabin? Have you seen Toni?"

David shook his head, frowning. "No. I came straight down from the road to get here before all the light's gone. Is something wrong?"

"Yes," said Simon bluntly. "I think the tongs have found us. Please go straight back to your house. Your grandfather can defend it."

David's eyes widened and he looked scared. A few weeks ago, he wouldn't have understood the urgency of the situation, but he did now. He didn't even argue.

Simon turned away, then a thought struck him and he looked back at the boy, who was already starting for home.

"David, wait! You told me you used to get into the cabin, even though Mary kept it locked."

"Yeah, sure."

"How?"

"From the old chestnut tree. You can climb along a branch onto the roof, then down the ivy on the chimney to Tony's window. But I think she fixed the broken window latch and..." he looked dubiously up at Simon, "I don't think the branch would take your weight."

It wouldn't thought Simon. Unfortunate.

He put on his night goggles and started up the trail, picking his footing carefully, grateful that he still wore the dark clothes he'd chosen for his trip to Seattle, but aware of growing fear. He could avoid the perimeter security system and he thought he could refine his infrared scans sufficiently to tell him how many people the cabin held, but he had no taps inside, and no way of finding out what was happening without crossing ten meters of open yard. Going in blind was a huge risk, yet he could think of no other plan.

He was not afraid of dying; as Graeme had pointed out, dying was easy. He was afraid for Toni. And he would risk anything to save her.

# 29

There had been a time, only a few hours earlier, when Toni had thought that handling a violent, delusional seven foot bioenhanced enforcer was a challenge. But she now knew that was nothing compared to entertaining a brilliant, predatory psychopath. Yasmin was growing restive and Toni could barely conceal her own terror as she considered what a bored, sadistic trainer might do for fun—or for revenge.

Yasmin had started by trying to dupe Toni. She'd arrived at the kitchen door with the girl, Cin-Cin, leaning semi-conscious against her shoulder. She'd claimed tearfully that the tongs were after them and Cin-Cin urgently needed medical help. She made such a convincing show of desperation and concern for the girl that Toni had even felt a sliver of doubt. She'd let them into the kitchen, keeping a cautious distance.

Just inside the door, Yasmin stumbled, letting Cin-Cin slip from her grasp, but Toni had grown up watching her mother roll drunks in bars and she knew that move. Instead of stepping instinctively forward to catch the girl, she'd stepped back and let the girl fall heavily to the floor.

Yasmin eyed her speculatively and smiled.

"No fool, are you?"

Then she pulled a gun.

"Where's Simon."

"Not here," Toni told her, keeping her face expressionless.

"I guessed that. I've been watching this place all day and there's been no sign of him. Where did you send him? And," she smiled again, "please don't bother lying, Dr. Almiramez. You know I can get the information out of you."

"Vancouver."

"And he'll be back....?"

"Some time tonight."

"And the others, where are they?"

No point lying; Yasmin could easily have checked the island newsnet.

"At a community dinner. They should be home around ten."

"Fine. Now, turn around, remove your clothes and put both hands against that wall."

Toni did as she was told. Behind her, Yasmin chatted like a sparkling social hostess as she made preparations, then pressed the gun against Toni's head and proceeded to glue an explosive packet to her hostage's stomach.

"This little toy is a Viet Ching specialty. It has a range of ten meters from my phone. If you stray further you'll hear a chime, then if you don't move back into range within five seconds, it will detonate. It's a small charge, but the blast is directed straight inward. It will rip your intestine to shreds."

Or in my case, more shreds, corrected Toni silently, feeling a sick wave of fear. Strange, she'd been able to face many threats stoically, but this bomb on her stomach kicked up unreasoning panic. She could smell the stink of her own fear and had to fight to maintain a semblance of calm.

"And of course I can detonate it at any time if you cause trouble," chirruped Yasmin. "You can dress."

She bound Toni's hands behind her, then led her into the dining room and lashed her to a chair with flexible strapping cord. After dumping the semi-conscious girl on the couch, she proceeded to bolt all the doors and windows securely and reactivated the security system before searching the cabin. Cin-Cin roused herself enough to put on a headset and then sat watching vids on her phone with a vacant, incurious expression, her eyes periodically drifting closed. Tanked on opiates, decided Toni. Her incapacity was clearly a nuisance, so Yasmin must have a reason for keeping her that way.

When Yasmin returned, she decided to risk a question.

"What's wrong with the girl?"

"Implanted suicide directives," said Yasmin, placing her knapsack on the dining room table. "Treatable, of course, but..."

"You need time and equipment," supplied Toni.

"Precisely. Whereas all I have right now is a supply of meds. Sufficient for symptomatic treatment... or, as it happens, for interrogation." She flashed Toni a bright and all too sincere smile, and

Toni felt a fresh surge of fear.

When she was twenty, a john from the Gentries had beaten Toni and left her for dead. Yasmin had the same eyes he'd had. And Toni felt precisely the same sensation she'd felt around violent tricks—that horrible prickly sense of dancing on the edge of a precipice, waiting for a random gust.

She swallowed and kept her voice level with effort.

"Please check the dosage. I'm underweight, and I've been seriously ill. You won't get answers if I'm unconscious or dead."

Yasmin raised a skeptical eyebrow, but brought out a medical scanner and did a cursory exam.

"My, you have been a sick girl, haven't you?. Well you're about to feel much much better."

A medspray hissed against Toni's upper arm. A second later she felt a dizzy rush of pleasure, much stronger than she'd expected. The relief from tension was intense; she felt herself sagging against her bonds, relaxing into a stupid grin. Some kind of amphetamine derivative, she guessed, and a muscle relaxant. Damn, she hadn't felt this good in years... Don't relax! she told herself. Concentrate!

"Truth" drugs relied on convincing patients that they were compelled to tell the truth. That wouldn't work on Toni, of course, but the meds would cloud her thought processes and make it difficult to lie consistently. While Yasmin was searching the cabin, Toni had concocted a story; now she had to concentrate on keeping it straight. Yasmin would be an expert interrogator, but she still knew little about Simon. Nor did she know just how much experience Toni had at lying convincingly while frightened and tripped—lying to an angry pimp, angry johns, teachers, colleagues, friends, her ex-husband; hell, to everybody. Toni found herself giggling. She had a doctorate in lying—five doctorates!

Yasmin checked Toni's blood work on the monitor.

"Good. You're ready. Now, how do you control Simon?"

"Affection," said Toni. She started to describe how severely touch deprived he'd been when she first met him, but Yasmin cut effectively through her babble.

"Does he have burned in commands?"

Toni smirked.

"It's not like Choi was going to hand me the keys, sweetie. You

321

know I got Simon to kill him?"

Again Yasmin ignored the red herring.

"Where is Simon?"

"Sent him to Vancouver."

"What did you send him for?"

"Choi's stash. Stuff we couldn't get out of the bunker last fall."

As she expected, this interested Yasmin. She questioned Toni closely, checking and rechecking for inconsistencies in the story, but Toni managed to hold her pastiche of truth and lies together. She hadn't sent Simon to Vancouver sooner because he wasn't stable enough and she'd been sick, but she couldn't delay any longer since the site of Choi's bunker was slated to be redeveloped for the Maglev railroad terminal. Choi had kept a special horde of rare metals; platinum, indium, tantalum; and it was down there somewhere in the ruins of the bunker. She had told Simon not to contact her because she was worried about Major Kim. She'd barely been able to get Simon away from the Empress without Kim taking him, and she feared Kim was getting close. She didn't think she dared stay at the cabin much longer.

"Why didn't you get treatment for the colitis?"

"I'm officially dead. If I go to a hospital, they'll run a gene scan and I'll be back on record."

"What's your long term plan?"

"Retire."

"And you expect me to believe that?" said Yasmin disdainfully. She paced the dining room, occasionally perching on a chair for a few seconds, then rising again and moving, circling behind Toni's chair with the grace of a large predator. It was a distracting routine, intended to further confuse a fogged interviewee, but Toni sensed that Yasmin's restlessness wasn't feigned. The red-haired woman seemed hyper.

She kept probing, managing to reveal Toni's passion for her work and her utter inability to picture a life of leisure. Toni put up an effort to derail and distract her; distantly aware that she must keep the interrogation away from the subject of Simon. It had clearly never occurred to Yasmin that Toni might really emancipate Choi's slave, or that he was capable of independence.

"When's he due back?" asked Yasmin for the fourth or fifth time.

"I'm not sure. Soon."

"Call him."

The demand took Toni by surprise, and she blurted: "Can't."

"Why not?"

"Dangerous," she managed, then risked a near truth. "Someone might tap the call."

"But he's due back soon." Yasmin scowled, and circled the table impatiently. She grabbed up Toni's phone. "Call him now. Find out where he is and order him back here!"

Toni did it. Yasmin put the call through and Toni spoke, knowing Simon would suspect a trap, but unable through her thick brain to think of some way to warn him about Yasmin. How far away was he really? She had no idea where he'd gone; only that he'd reached his destination. She wasn't even sure he could return by his original deadline of ten pm. Damn!

Yasmin's interrogation was losing momentum, so Toni tried questioning her again, hoping to engage the woman's ego. A little to her surprise, it worked. Yasmin wanted to talk; wanted to boast, in fact, to an expert audience. Toni readily took on the role; asking technical questions, and pretending to be impressed. Actually, she didn't have to pretend. Bent she might be, but this woman had a brilliant, subtle grasp of behavior modification. Toni worked at being a subtly flattering audience, while a distant concern nagged at her. This seemed too easy. What was wrong?

When Yasmin paused to shoot herself up, the shoe finally dropped. Yasmin was manic, and once she knew that, Toni recognized the formula—sleep suppressants, stimulants and cognition enhancers. Several versions of the illicit cocktail, known as "boost," were popular with students, and Toni had used it almost continuously through her first years of medical school. She vividly remembered the seductive feeling of boundless energy and capability. If Yasmin had been continuously on the run for the last week, she might easily have stayed awake all that time. In her muzzy state Toni couldn't add up how many hours it had been since the Empress ran aground, but it was a lot. Most individuals started displaying impaired judgment after a hundred hours on boost and borderline psychotic behavior at about a hundred and fifty. Or in Yasmin's case, presumably, more psychotic behavior.

Under the impetus of a fresh dose, Yasmin expounded on her theories of building better humans. Toni didn't bother to feign agreement. Instead, she put forth ethical counter-arguments, guessing Yasmin would enjoy the chance to demolish them. She did. Her green eyes gleamed with anticipation as she promised that Toni would soon see her point of view. Toni's high was wearing off and she could feel the first edges of terror at the prospect of being "persuaded" by Yasmin.

Abruptly Yasmin leaned over and kissed Toni full on the mouth. Toni flinched back so hard she knocked the chair over and landed hard on her back on the floor. Her relaxed muscles absorbed the shock, but air burst out of her lungs and she gasped, feeling tears in her eyes. Yasmin stood laughing down at her. Yasmin knew about cascades—she had to. She'd just been toying with Toni, checking out her tolerance for trips. Now she'd start the real work. Cascades and old addictions made Toni a dismayingly easy target, and as the trip crashed, Toni was dismayed to find herself starting to cry.

The cabin's proximity alarm wheeped loudly. Yasmin whipped around, startled, then strode over to the security console on the wall by the stairway.

"Well doctor, let's see which of our pigeons have come home to roost."

Toni said nothing but felt her own heart thud. Surely Simon wouldn't walk into such an obvious trap. But the thought of Rigo and Klale was almost as appalling.

A loud bang echoed from the woods. Toni blinked. Yasmin scowled.

"What the.... "

Distant bellowing echoed through the trees, growing louder.

"...final straw. I want you and that goddamned ghoul the hell off my island. NOW!"

What in hell?" wondered Toni, recognizing old David Anderson's voice. Yasmin frowned at her suspiciously.

"Who is that?"

"Neighbor."

Recognition dawned on Yasmin's face. "Anderson?" She stepped cautiously to the window and peeked through the curtain.

And Toni's cloudy brain finally caught up. It must be a diversion—with Anderson playing the role of an enraged rurro bigot. He sounded so convincing that if she hadn't spoken to him just hours ago she might have believed every word.

"Do you hear me Almiramez? My family's away, so it's just us. Don't you skulk around inside, I know you're there. Come out on the porch and bring it with you!"

"Feisty old bastard," Yasmin said half admiringly. "But very bad timing."

Another rifle blast shook the house.

And from her vantage point on the floor, Toni felt the rug heave underneath her, saw the dining room table shudder and tilt. The trap door! Someone was trying to come up through the crawl space. But the trap door lay under the dining room table, the rug, and Toni's own inert weight strapped to the chair. She tried throwing herself forward and sideways, hoping to hop the chair out of the way, but her muscles seemed to have turned to water, and she only managed an awkward rocking motion.

"...plenty of ammo, can keep this up all night! You don't come out, the neighbors gonna phone the Coast Patrol—they'll get rid of you if I don't."

At the window, Yasmin scowled. On the couch, Cin-Cin stared into her phone, oblivious.

Anderson bellowed again, his voice moving around the cabin to the back door, and Yasmin turned abruptly. Toni caught her breath, but the carpet stopped moving. Whoever was below must be listening to Yasmin's footsteps.

Anderson's voice: "Almiramez! Get out here NOW!"

Yasmin strode over and grabbed Toni's chair.

"We have to get him inside and shut him up. Come on."

She released the cords binding Toni to the chair and pulled her up roughly. Toni swayed and leaned on the table. Her hands were still bound behind her, her knees felt like water and her head swam. Yasmin grabbed her roughly by the upper arm and herded her toward the kitchen. She had the gun in her pocket and held the phone in her hand. Toni staggered along, barely able to keep her feet underneath her; wishing she was faking her weakness. She knew how to fight, but Yasmin was taller, stronger, fitter, and tanked on boost. It would be no contest.

At the back door, Yasmin loosed Toni's wrists and shoved her forward.

"Get him in here!" she hissed.

Toni flicked her hands for a second to get the blood flowing, then awkwardly unbolted the door and opened it a cautious crack. She found herself looking straight at old Anderson. He glared at her, red-faced, his white hair standing up in tufts.

And she found her mind completely blank.

"Uh... hi," she finally managed.

He stared at her incredulously. Small wonder.

Then he began yelling—a torrent of every insult and complaint he'd made since they arrived, leaving no chance for Toni to get a word in edgewise. She stood, leaning her weight on the door handle, feeling her sweat turn clammy in the draft from the door, feeling the itchy cling of the explosive pak against her stomach, and doing nothing at all while she hoped desperately for something to happen behind her. Had she heard a scrape of furniture?

Nonetheless, the crash startled her. She turned just in time to see Yasmin whirl, pulling her gun. Simon skidded into the doorway, crouched low, and threw a scrap of lumber. Yasmin's shot rang out an instant before the wood hit her hand, knocking the gun to the floor.

Anderson shoved through the back door, rifle pointed at Yasmin, but Yasmin was faster. She grabbed Toni by the scruff of the neck, hauled her backward, and held up the phone.

"STOP or she dies!"

Silence. Toni looked anxiously at Simon, but Yasmin's shot had evidently gone wide. He crouched unmoving in the doorway. His face, backlit from the living room, looked particularly skull-like and she could not read his expression.

"Call him off," Yasmin told her roughly.

"Simon, don't move," ordered Toni.

Anderson still had his rifle trained, but he looked uncertain.

"I've taped an explosive pak to Dr. Almiramez and I will activate it if you don't lower that weapon," said Yasmin in an even, cold voice. Toni could feel the woman's warm breath tickling the back of her neck.

"It's unfortunately true," Toni told him.

Anderson lowered his gun with visible reluctance.

Toni staggered a little, then let herself fall heavily sideways against Yasmin's rough grasp. Yasmin compensated, but she didn't expect Toni to writhe suddenly in her arms, spinning around and grabbing her in a bear hug. Toni pressed her stomach tight against Yasmin's.

"OK, set it off!" she gasped. "Let's see how directed that charge is."

Yasmin instinctively tried to push Toni away, and the distraction gave Simon the opening he needed. He grabbed Yasmin. Toni was wrenched out of the other woman's grasp, then she heard a crack as Yasmin's phone hit the floor and skittered across it. She closed her eyes, braced for an explosion that didn't come. Hands grabbed her from behind; old Anderson taking her shoulder and leading her to the kitchen counter, which she leaned against for support, struggling to keep her feet under her. It was several seconds before she could focus on the scene in the kitchen.

Simon sat on the kitchen floor, Yasmin pinioned in front of him, her arms twisted behind her back. With his free hand he reached down and stroked her face. Toni could hear his harsh breathing, and see the rage blossoming in his eyes.

"Call him off!" yelled Yasmin, her voice shrill.

Simon spoke in a harsh whisper.

"I'm not her dog. Or your dog."

He ran his fingers along her jawline, found a nerve cluster near her ear and pressed.

Yasmin screamed. Simon's face twisted into a macabre smile that Toni had never seen before and he spoke in Choi's voice.

"It's my turn now, trainer. I shall teach you the ways of pain and obedience...."

"Simon, stop!" said Toni with all the force she could muster. Her voice came out thin and reedy. Simon ignored her. And she realized he wasn't going to stop.

Beside her Anderson stared at the tableau in wide-eyed horror and clutched at his rifle.

I'm too sick, I can't take control, I can't handle this, thought Toni desperately. She felt her knees buckling, fought it, then let go and started sliding to the floor. Use what you have, she thought grimly. If weakness is all I have, I'll use that.

When Anderson reached out to grab her, she waved him urgently back. He stepped away, confused. Toni's backside hit the floor.

"Simon!" she said, letting her voice crack. "Please help me! I need your help!" She squeezed out a few tears, seeing the madness in his eyes as he met her gaze.

"Simon!" she tried again. "Please!"

For several long seconds the tableau held; all of them motionless. Then she heard Simon take a deeper breath and he blinked.

"Toni?" It was his small boy voice.

Thank gods.

"Please take Yasmin to the other room and have Mr. Anderson tie her up. Then come and help me," said Toni.

Had she overplayed it?

Simon stood up, hauling Yasmin to her feet. He turned her around and stared down at her, and for a moment Toni thought she'd lost him again. Then he struck her across the face with a crack that echoed through the house. She slumped. He dragged her into the living room.

"Follow them," hissed Toni at Anderson. "Make sure she isn't hurt but for chrissakes don't believe anything she says. And if you need help with Simon, yell."

"I'll gag her," snarled Anderson, and stomped off.

Toni leaned her head back against the kitchen cupboard. She didn't need to do anything more—and a good thing, too, because she couldn't do anything more. She closed her eyes.

The back porch creaked. Footsteps approached, walked in through the door. Friend or enemy? wondered Toni vaguely. She was too tired to care. With great reluctance she opened her eyes, wondering if this hellish night would ever end.

What she saw was an impeccably coiffed man in a tailored jacket advancing into the room, holding an axe nervously in front of him. She blinked, thinking he looked familiar, then felt her mouth slide open in incredulous recognition.

"Graeme?! Graeme Dougherty?"

He looked down.

"What's happening?"

"It's OK. Everything's OK," she managed, still staring stupidly at him.

He lowered the axe with an expression of profound relief. "Thank all the gods. Bravado is not my forté. Hello, Ann."

"Graeme!?... Simon went to see you?"

"On the basis of your very eloquent recommendation. And I must say you look suitably appalled." He frowned down at her and held out a hand. "Ah... may I be of assistance?"

Toni nodded, and fought back a wave of dizziness, aware that she was barely coherent.

"Just give me a second. Goddamn trips. The bitch shot me up and I haven't quite come down..." She took several long breaths. "OK, would you look around the floor for a phone. It's around here someplace. Pick it up very carefully—I mean very VERY carefully. It has a proximity trigger on it keyed to an explosive pak glued to my stomach. I lived through this much, I'd hate to bleed out all over the floor now...."

She stopped abruptly, aware that she was hovering on the edge of hysteria.

Graeme wiggled his fingers at her.

"Hands of a surgeon, remember?"

This couldn't be real—it must be a drug-induced nightmare, she decided, watching the surreal vision of Graeme Dougherty on his hands and knees searching the kitchen floor, and finally fishing Yasmin's phone out from under the cooker with a broom handle. He carried it to the kitchen table, and put it down with exaggerated caution.

Then Simon came and kneeled down beside her, and Toni grabbed his hand. We're going to make it, she thought. We're going to be all right.

The next hour was a blur. The men searched Yasmin's knapsack for riot glue solvent and couldn't find any, so Anderson went over to his workshop to hunt down an alternative. Graeme checked Toni over, made her drink a large glass of juice, and had Simon carry her up to her bedroom and lay her on top of the covers. She tried very hard not to remember the last time he'd carried her. Graeme followed them with the phone, which he put on the dresser. Simon left, not looking at Toni.

"I've examined the girl. Opiates, all right, but I think it's best to leave her that way until we can get her to a hospital."

Toni nodded, though she couldn't think of much except the damned thing on her stomach. And she couldn't stop shivering. Graeme spread a blanket over her and sat on the edge of her bed. She tried to focus.

"So what did Simon want from you?"

"A second opinion."

"And your opinion is?"

Dougherty looked thoughtful.

"He's extraordinary. Have you considered his potential in the dance world?"

Toni let out an explosive snort.

"For christssakes Graeme, I've been struggling to get through another hour or another day. I haven't considered next frigging week, never mind the long term!"

"Ah yes, now I remember your clinical strategy."

She rolled her eyes.

"Look, quit trying to provoke me and bring me some coffee! Hot, strong coffee! Please!"

He had just gone downstairs when Toni heard Klale and Rigo arrive. A din of explanations ensued and seemed to stretch on for hours. Toni had begun wondering if she could crawl down the stairs and make coffee herself, when Rigo came upstairs with a tray. He insisted she swallow a cup of soup and half a sandwich, before allowing her a much-too-small mug of tepid coffee.

Finally the solvent arrived. Rigo dabbed it on cautiously, peeling away the edges of the pak for what seemed like an eternity before the horrid clinging weight sucked away from her skin. When Rigo left to dispose of it, Toni got shakily to her feet, pulled her trousers up over sticky skin and put on her heaviest sweater.

When she turned, Simon was leaning against the door frame, his posture rigid, staring at her bed. His gaze moved to her.

"Did you train me to love you?"

"No," she said, holding very still. He walked into the room, loomed over her, so close she could feel his breath when he shouted.

"All those years you touched me—held my hand! You were training me!"

"No! I was building an emotional bond. That's not slavery. Real bonds stretch both ways. You grew to love me. And I grew to love you."

"You only said you loved me when you were drunk. Then you said you made a mistake!"

His voice had started sliding into child Simon. Toni felt relief. She could deal with that.

"I did a very wrong thing, Simon. I'm supposed to help you with your problems, not to use you for my own gratification. I didn't invite you to have sex with me, did I? I ordered you to give me sex. I used you because you couldn't refuse me. That was terribly wrong." And hard to admit. She could feel her cheeks burning.

Simon paced.

"You did order me," he said finally.

"Yes. And I apologize."

He whirled.

"I won't take orders from you any more!"

"Good," she said, meeting his eyes. "You never really belonged to me, Simon. I was just taking care of you until you could stand on your own. You are a free person. You make your own decisions."

She watched him carefully, decided to risk a little more.

"You know, you made a mistake, too," she said quietly. "That night... you knew I was crazy drunk, out of control, and you knew about cascades. You could have called for help. But you let me give you orders that were dangerous...."

Simon evaded her gaze, uncomfortable. So, some part of him had been aware he could refuse; he just didn't want the responsibility.

"I did what you said," he told her petulantly.

"And from now on that's not an excuse; you're responsible for yourself and all your decisions."

Toni was distantly aware of activity downstairs—knocking at the door, voices. But she had more to say. She kept her concentration pinned on Simon.

"And what you did to Yasmin was wrong. Vengeance is not an answer. You can't erase the pain Choi inflicted on you by hurting others."

"She deserved it!"

"Nobody deserves torture. You did it because it felt good, didn't you?"

He hesitated a long moment, then nodded.

"It felt SO good," he whispered.

"It's the release of rage," said Toni quietly. "Like dancing. But dancing doesn't create more victims, doesn't perpetuate pain. Somebody once hurt Choi, and he turned his rage on other people, leaving a trail of horror behind him. You can make a better choice."

"Dr. Almiramez!"

Rigo's voice from below. She gave Simon an startled glance, then they both hurried for the stairs. She started down ahead of Simon and saw Major Kim stride into view and look up at her.

Toni's heart lurched and she jolted to a stop, then forced herself to keep going. Simon's heavy footsteps creaked behind her. When she reached the bottom of the stairs, Kim held out his phone. He wore combat gear, she noticed—heavy boots, a navy beret with an insignia pin, and a smart-weave cloak that mimicked his surroundings so his body seemed to vanish into a mirage of the sitting room. Two other soldiers, identically camouflaged, stood by the front door, their heads seeming to float above invisible bodies.

"Doctor, I am serving you with this Cascadia-wide warrant for the apprehension of Simon Lau."

"I'll take that," came Dougherty's voice. He strode across the living room, holding his own phone out.

"Who are you?"

"I might ask you the same."

Kim stiffened. "Major Sage Boden Kim, CFPR, Major Crimes Unit."

"Dr. Graeme Oliver Dougherty, Clinical Staff Convenor and Chief of Neurosurgery, Seattle Neurological Institute. I am Mr. Lau's physician of record."

Toni kept her face expressionless as Kim shot her a startled glance.

"But..."

"I will, of course, relay this warrant immediately to my legal staff for advice. In the meantime, perhaps you and I could have a private discussion outside?"

Silence hung in the room. Toni held still, hoping Simon would do the same. She had no doubt Kim would take any motion on his part as an excuse to use force. Dougherty stood waiting, then gestured at the door. With obvious reluctance, Kim turned and left, Dougherty following.

Toni waited until the front door shut, then looked at Simon.

"Your physician of record?"

"He advised it."

Rigo stepped forward, giving Toni a worried look.

"Do you think Dougherty can really call Kim off?"

"I have confidence in him," said Simon.

"What?" said Toni.

"You do?" Even Rigo looked surprised.

"He's a superb liar," said Simon.

Graeme's negotiations with Kim took the better part of an hour during which they could only wait. Kim's soldiers watched Yasmin, while the others congregated in the kitchen around the inevitable pot of tea. Rigo had given his son a bear hug, and now Klale sat in Simon's lap with one arm wrapped around him. He hugged her back, and Toni realized with a pang that she hadn't done any of those things—hadn't welcomed him or hugged him or told him how relieved she was to see him back. And now just didn't seem to be the time. So she sat at the table with a mug of tea and made weary attempts at conversation.

When Dougherty finally returned with Major Kim, they all fell silent. Kim caught sight of Klale in Simon's lap and Toni saw startlement in his eyes, before he turned to her.

"Dr. Dougherty has proposed an agreement," he announced stiffly. "I will release Mr. Lau into the custody of his father on the condition that he cooperate with us by providing information on tongs in Vancouver and specifically the activities of Choi Shung Wai. He must also agreed to 24 hour surveillance of his domicile by CFPR. Do you agree, Mr. Lau?"

Toni tensed, but Simon answered without hesitation.

"Yes."

"What about them?" asked Rigo, nodding toward the living room.

"The girl will be transferred to Vancouver Hospital for emergency treatment. I am taking Dr. Smith back to headquarters for questioning."

Toni frowned, worried.

"Major, she's extremely dangerous and very persuasive."

"I'm aware of her profile, doctor. In fact, I have an extensive dossier on her. I think you can rest assured that she will never leave custody again."

Toni nodded, thinking: good move, Graeme. Major Kim wasn't going home empty handed—he had a prestigious catch.

Major Kim thrust his phone toward Simon.

"I require your voice signature and fingerprint on the undertaking displayed onscreen."

Simon took it with a glance at Dougherty, who nodded. Nonetheless, Simon read through the entire text before signing. Dr. Lau signed after him, then Dougherty. Toni felt a surge of indignation not to be included, then remembered she was legally dead. She couldn't sign anything.

She followed them into the living room and watched Kim's soldiers untie Yasmin, then handcuff her and lead her outside. With her red hair artistically tousled around her youthful face and a bruise blooming on her cheek, Yasmin put on a stellar performance as a bewildered innocent, grateful to be rescued from the brutal enforcer. Toni felt a fresh surge of fury. Kim regarded Yasmin stonefaced, but Toni could already see the young soldiers reacting with sympathy. For a bitter moment she wished they had killed the woman when they had the chance and damn the consequences. She saw that same thought in Simon's eyes, and had to drop her gaze from his, annoyed at her own hypocrisy.

If only Mary was here. Mary could look up at him with shining eyes and tell him convincingly why killing was wrong, whereas Toni could only try to play the role while secretly longing to put an end to Yasmin herself. Shit!

After the soldiers left, Rigo and Graeme went upstairs to put Simon to bed and Klale started cleaning the kitchen with unnecessary vigor. Toni looked around the living room, seeking a place to settle, but she kept seeing the dining room table, remembering the bite of cord tying her to that chair and the warmth of Yasmin's lips on hers. On impulse she grabbed her mug and a coat and went out to the back porch. She couldn't sleep yet; didn't dare. Simon had always found sitting on the porch soothing, maybe she should try it. When Pauline Johnson jumped up in her lap she glowered into the cat's yellow eyes, but let it dig its claws into her thigh and lie down.

The door banged. Graeme strolled over and gestured at the wicker chair next to her.

"May I?"

"Sit," said Toni.

He settled in with a creak and a sigh.

"It's good to see you again, you know," he said quietly. I didn't expect I ever would."

She relaxed a little at his gentle tone. She was too tired for sparring.

"I... I didn't expect this either. Have you told anyone at the institute?"

"About you? Or Simon?"

"Either."

"No. Not yet."

"Simon's very impressed with you," said Toni. "He says you're a 'superb liar.'"

Graeme smiled.

"I'll have to tell him that's it's called an aptitude for administration." He let silence hang, then: "You've done an astonishing job with him."

"Simon's the astonishing one. He found me, not the other way around. Then he found David. And now you."

"Found isn't quite the word," said Graeme dryly. "It's more like being sucked into a vortex."

Toni found herself smiling. "True," she admitted. "What happened?"

While Graeme gave a brief summary she studied his profile. He looked precisely the same, she thought bleakly. Bronze and mauve highlights in his hair rather than copper and crimson, but he didn't seem a day older than he had when she'd left eleven years ago. She, on the other hand, had lines and scars in her face and gray in her hair. She'd looked less than thirty then; now she looked every day of fifty-one.

"Thank you for all your help," she said when Dougherty finished. "Especially after the way Simon treated you."

"You're not upset at him?"

"For checking up on me? No, it was a smart thing to do, though the way he chose to do it put us through hell...." She broke off and looked down at her cooling mug with distaste. "You know, tea's not going to cut it tonight."

"Your friends opened a bottle of bucolic plonk," suggested Graeme politely. "Honey wine, I think."

"I believe Rigo has some single malt stashed in the sideboard."

"Thank God!" Graeme jumped up. "Be right back."

"Plonk for me," called Toni.

Graeme returned with a tumbler half full of whiskey for himself and a generous glass of Ethan's honey wine for her. She sipped it, discovered she liked it, drank some more.

"May I still call you Ann? Or do you prefer Toni?" Graeme asked.

"Either is fine."

"Why Toni?"

"It's my real name. My mother never told me my surname. Almiramez was my pimp's name. He gave it to me when he forged my ID, and I added 'Antonia.' I thought it sounded very upper crust." She sipped some more, then lobbed back. "Why didn't you call for help when Simon showed up at your rez?"

"Perhaps because I'm an 'supercilious prick'?"

Toni ignored the jibe.

"I don't recall you being suicidal."

"No." Dougherty sat for a long time, staring out into the darkness, then he looked at her and for the first time, Toni noticed the age in his eyes.

"I didn't call for help, Ann, because I've been afraid for a long time that the institute's security is compromised. No, it's worse than that—I suspect we're rotten with corruption. And last night... Last night I took a bioenhanced assassin in and out of SNI right through the main security gate, and I got away with it! If I can do that, what the hell else is going on?"

Graeme's voice shook with frustration and Toni listened in surprise. She'd never heard him speak like this; rarely glimpsed the man behind the polished armor.

"Have you tried to do anything?"

"Oh, yes, of course," he said bitterly. "But I began to realize that the only real solution would involve drastic measures. And the chancellor and governors are not willing to take drastic measures. I hope it's because they're complacent fools who think they have an alarmist on their hands. But I fear that some of them are corrupt, and occasionally—very late at night—I wake up wondering if I would be wiser of me to stop poking at these ugly shadows lest I be seen to be a nuisance and be struck down. Literally."

A very real danger, thought Toni. But she was surprised that he knew it.

"Apropos of which, I must ask you," he continued, looking out into the yard. "Were you moonlighting on the dark side?"

Toni swallowed, tried to breathe. Admitting this hurt, even after so many years.

"Yes. I got into debt. And the Yakuza came calling. It started as small mom and pop jobs—adjust the kids to study harder at school, or give invalid grandma a plug to keep her smiling instead of complaining. Then, of course, the work got uglier. When I hit my limit I ran. I had no other choice. I couldn't tell SNI. They would have prosecuted, dug up my past, destroyed my career at the very least. I couldn't stay in Seattle. The Yakuza were planning to give me an attitude readjustment so I'd love their work. And..." She gave a humorless snort... "I couldn't manage to commit suicide either. So I ran."

"Were you first approached through the Institute?"

"No. Outside. But they knew about me, Graeme—knew too much about my finances and far too much about my clinical work. I'm quite sure I was lined up by somebody inside. I can't prove it, though."

Dougherty took that in grim silence.

"For what it's worth, I've been clean since. I stayed in hiding and worked as a bartender. Truly." She felt tears burning in her eyes and realized that it mattered to her that he believe. Damn!

"I may believe you, Ann, but you can rest assured that I'll check your story every way I can think of."

She nodded, knowing he was right.

"And there is one other thing."

"Only one?" she said dryly, fighting to regain detachment.

"Simon..." Graeme shot her a wary look. "Simon told me about the night you got drunk."

"Shit!" Shame and embarrassment flared in her face, then she felt a rush of anger as Dougherty continued.

"He should get another therapist."

"STOP!" She held up her hand, keeping her voice steady with effort, aware of the liquor and fatigue eroding her shaky self control. "Look, this is not something I want to talk about but I understand your concerns, so I will say this exactly once."

"I'm a woman who's been abandoned, terrorized, tortured, and prostituted. I've been beaten almost to death twice. I've never felt safe. Anywhere. I know that I have an ocean of neediness that I keep locked down with steel bars. Then along comes Simon—strong, fierce, willing at any instant to die protecting me, and also so gifted, so sweet, so desperately eager to pour out unconditional love, and finally, castrated so he doesn't need a cock hole. If that's not temptation, I don't know what in hell is."

"Yes, I'm exactly the wrong person to be his therapist. But, you know something Graeme, I'm also the only one who could have been. Not one of your responsible, well behaved, safe, smug doctors would have thrown themselves out on a limb for a no-hope ghoul from Downtown. Sometimes..." she found her voice trembling, had to clear her throat to continue, "sometimes the only person who will do a crazy, dangerous job is a crazy, dangerous person."

For once, Graeme didn't have a glib retort. They sat in silence, listening to odd night rustles in the yard. Finally Toni pulled herself together again and managed a calm tone.

"You have a hell of a problem at the institute. And if the whole thing spills, your career will go with it. I'm surprised you haven't left."

"I've thought about it." His chair creaked as he recrossed his legs. "And I've justified staying by telling myself that destroying the institute would hurt the many patients we manage to help. Now I'm not so sure. Simon left me with a great deal to think about. I may even have to cultivate the acquaintance of Major Kim."

Toni found herself bristling.

"We have to keep Simon hidden!"

"Too many people have seen him, Ann. He can't possibly hide much longer. And you must know that he needs surgery on that chip. Urgently. You're damned lucky he hasn't had seizures."

"I know, I know! I'm just trying to keep this house of cards together for a few more months, give him a chance to stabilize, find his feet, grow up."

"He's done that already," said Graeme quietly. "It's time to let go."

Oh hell, thought Toni, as a flood of emotion engulfed her. She put her hands across her face, feeling as fragile as eggshell. This was where she'd always fallen down as a therapist—especially with the hopeless cases. She'd never been able to quit, and she'd taken out her fury on colleagues and students. Well, that was eleven years ago, before she'd looked into the black recesses of her own psyche. She could do better now. She took a deep breath.

"I know it's time to let go. And I can do it."

I have to.

# 30

Dr. Dougherty slept two nights on the couch and spent the intervening day talking with all of them and reviewing Toni's case notes. The morning he departed, he shook Simon's hand and said casually that he would see him in Seattle when Simon "left the island." Simon, stunned by sudden revelation, stood in his wake unable to focus on anything but the thought: "I'm leaving."

He had never considered it before, never consciously understood what it meant that this was Mary's cabin and she'd loaned it to them. But of course they would go, and Simon must abandon his entire new world—his bedroom with the pictures he'd posted on the slanting cedar ceiling, the dance platform they'd built in the long grass under soaring evergreens, a sky dizzy with stars, and life teeming underneath that sky in everything Simon touched and tasted and smelled.

He loved this place so fiercely it burned inside him, and yet the others seemed utterly casual. He'd heard all of them talk about living in one place and another place as if all the places were just simsettings to paint into their personal scapes. Were they blind to the miracle around them? Didn't they care? Or were they like Dougherty—hiding their feelings in some jail behind their faces.

Simon couldn't even find a dance for this new anguish. His dances seemed to have become part of the island, but this island wasn't his place, couldn't ever be his place. Worse, when he tried to think of where he might go next, he couldn't imagine it. Where in this world could Simon live?

He knew he had a few weeks remaining, so he tried not to think about leaving, but somehow the more he tried to focus on present joy, the more it charred with future pain. Only a few months ago the future had been a new concept; now he couldn't seem to live anywhere else and he walked through the days in a daze, barely able to focus even on his upcoming parole hearing.

On Friday afternoon Simon had arranged to go to the beach

with David. The weather was perfect. Arbutus leaves gleamed green and alders glowed gold in the autumn sunshine. Eagles circled overhead, giving weird whinnying cries. But when Simon and Rigo went to meet David at the Andersons' woodwork shop, David was busy with his father at the back bench, and his grandfather stood near the door, polishing a small table. Simon paused outside, but Rigo strode in and greeted Ethan, then David looked up and waved. With a wary glance at old Anderson, Simon stepped inside among the motes of sawdust and the resiny smell of wood oils.

"Hi, Simon! Sorry this is taking longer than I thought. Can you wait?"

"Sure," said Simon, then stood awkwardly, feeling very much out of place. The old man straightened up with a grunt and looked at him.

"You can give me a hand. I want to move this over to that corner."

Simon stepped up and took one side of the table. Its top was fashioned from a horizontal slice of tree trunk a meter in diameter, with growth rings radiating outward to an asymmetrical, cleverly beveled edge. Dark and light squares of contrasting wood had been inlaid seamlessly in the polished surface. This was the board for old Anderson's chess set, he realized suddenly. The tabletop was mounted on a base containing two drawers. When he picked up the table, even the underside of the drawers felt satiny.

"What happened to your hand anyway?" asked Anderson suddenly.

Simon looked down at his stiff left hand, and felt a faint shadow of old self loathing.

"I punched it into a concrete wall."

"Mmph." The old man maneuvered, then set his side down. "You play chess?"

"Yes sir."

"Huh. Suppose you play that net rubbish. Ever played a real game with real players and pieces?"

"No."

"Time you learned."

Simon didn't like chess—it had been part of Choi's education—but he needed to talk to Anderson and he'd been wondering

341

how to arrange it. Anderson led him upstairs to the loft where he dug out a pair of beautiful, straight backed chairs with seats made from wood that matched the table. Simon carried them down and helped dust them off, then Anderson passed him a shammy cloth and showed him how to rub each carved chess piece with fragrant oil before placing it on the board.

On the other side of the shop David helped his father feed boards through a table saw, while Rigo looked on. The roar of an old electric motor and whine of microfilament biting into wood masked conversation. Simon oiled the black queen—a native woman with a long braid—and looked at Anderson.

"My parole hearing is on Sunday. I presume you were notified."

"Yup."

Simon hesitated, then continued.

"That item of yours I borrowed—it was a violation of my parole conditions."

"No shit."

"I believe that possession of such an item is also a very serious offense for a Guild member."

Anderson glanced up at him, blue eyes suddenly hard.

"So?"

"So, if you don't mention it, I won't mention it either," said Simon calmly.

"Are you telling me you plan to lie to your parole committee?" asked Anderson with a dangerous gleam in his eyes.

"Not lie. Omit," said Simon.

Anderson held Simon's gaze a second longer, then returned to polishing the white king's face with his agile, long-fingered hands. He put the king down and started on a rook before speaking again.

"I'm gonna tell you something for free, kid. When I brought AnderCraft back from dry-dock last week, I lost an item overboard off Cape Mudge. And since no one ever saw it, no one could ever prove I had it."

Simon knew that ploy.

"Perhaps not," he said coolly. "But that proof isn't necessary. It would only be necessary for a similar item to be found hidden in your workshop."

The table saw stopped. So did Anderson's hands. In the sudden silence he leaned forward, glaring, and said softly. "That sounds a lot like blackmail."

"Blackmail would also be a parole violation," pointed out Simon. "I was merely trying to arrange an equitable exchange."

"Uh huh." The saw revved up to speed. "That what you're going to do when you leave here?"

"Sir...?"

"Go into equitable exchanges?"

It was a reasonable supposition, thought Simon. But he would not become Choi.

"No. I have other plans."

"You want to tell me about them?"

"No."

"Think of it as an equitable exchange."

"Oh." Simon dipped his shammy in oil, smoothed it carefully across carved eyebrows. "I intend to set up an organization dedicated to rescuing bioaltered slaves. For example," he gave Anderson a challenging look, "if David had been snatched, your chances of finding him again would have been poor, even with the resources of the Guilds behind you. The Guildless have no hope of escape."

Anderson grunted.

"Sounds very noble. You finished? OK," he picked up two pawns, and thrust his hands behind his back. "Pick a hand." Simon looked at him blankly. Anderson gave an impatient grunt. "Left or right?!"

"Left?"

Anderson brought his hand forward. It held a black pawn. He replaced the pawns on the board.

"OK, my first move." He slid a pawn forward. Simon followed and they made three more quick moves before Anderson stopped to study the board. Simon looked at it, too, fascinated again by the lifelike faces.

"David said you're selling the chess set."

"Yup. Going to list it for auction. Got an appraiser coming here next week to look at it."

"An appraiser?" asked Simon, puzzled. "All you need is a hologram for the auction site."

343

Anderson glared.

"Hologram! You take a holo of your toilet when you sell it, not a piece of art! A holo doesn't tell you that the finish on this is softer than silk sheets or that you can close your eyes and feel the different kinds of wood by how they warm up in your hand." His voice caught. He slid a piece and snarled. "Your move!"

Simon reached forward and found himself picking up the Afroid woman. He turned her over in his hands, drawn by the desperation in her eyes. He'd seen women much like her aboard the American noahs, and this portrait was so good he felt sure he could have picked her out of a crowd.

"Is this an accurate likeness?"

Anderson shot him a sharp glance.

"Almiramez told you, eh?"

"No." Simon hesitated, then continued. "I read the article you sent to the local paper."

"It isn't published yet."

"It will be in the next issue."

"Huh." Anderson glowered, then looked down. "For most of these I had photos to go by. Those three I carved from memory, but I've got a good memory for faces. Especially those ones." He looked down for a long moment, then shrugged. "Hell, the set's no big loss. Isn't another serious chess player in the family. Rory's not bad, but she's at the age for hormones. Won't practice." He gave Simon a sudden look. "When are you leaving?"

Simon felt a jolt of anguish and fought for self control, managed to speak matter-of-factly.

"After Solstice."

"Well, sooner would be better."

Simon stared at the chess board, unseeing, thinking about the taste of sea salt on his lips and the whoosh of raven's wings, loud in the stillness of the forest.

"I don't want to leave," he whispered.

"Yeah," said Anderson gruffly. "That's the whole history of this island in a nutshell. People come here, fall in love with it, give up everything to move here, and then find out you can't eat scenery." He shook his head.

"Thing about living on an island is you start thinking you're safe. We don't bother much with the rest of the world and we start to think it won't bother us. But we're all part of the world and it catches up with us sooner or later. You'd think I would've learned that growing up when I did, but almost losing David was a reminder. I owe you for that, by the way."

"In that case, perhaps you could forget about the item," suggested Simon.

Anderson gave a sour snort.

"OK, let's get this straight. I owe you for David, but that's personal. I owe a lot of other people, too. I have a duty to my neighbors and my Guild. And the fact is, you're dangerous. I still think Mary should have put you in some kind of custody instead of bringing you here, and I'm not going to sleep well at night until you're gone. Maybe you don't mean to be dangerous, but you are."

"I need to be dangerous," said Simon bitterly. "The tongs will never leave me alone, and if I oppose the training business, they will declare war."

"Yeah, well, you're liable to have parole problems over that one, but for what it's worth, I approve."

"You do?" said Simon, startled.

Anderson nodded.

"Sure. This Guild malarkey, it's all right as far as it goes, but there are times that talking doesn't do jack shit. You got to fight."

"Oh." Simon couldn't think how to respond. He waited for Anderson to move again, then played. Anderson glowered.

"You always move this fast?"

"I'm used to timed games."

"Well, in a real chess game you set a deliberate pace. Think. Look in your opponent's eyes. It's not just a sim, it's real. It's personal."

"Like the chess set," said Simon, understanding suddenly. "Like death."

Anderson's bushy white brows rose and he gave Simon a startled look. Simon barely noticed as he studied the set, realizing how many layers of meaning and beauty it encompassed. Like a concerto. And it was a part of this place—part of Cortes Island and part of the Anderson family.

"I would like to buy the set."

"Huh." Anderson looked doubtful. "I'll think about it."

345

Simon studied him.

"Fifteen thousand."

Anderson said nothing.

"And I'll write a will leaving it to David."

"Not too optimistic about that war of yours, eh?"

"I'll win the war," said Simon, "but I'll die of the side effects of the tailored immunities I was given. David will likely have the set by the time he's thirty."

"Huh." Anderson pointed at one of the white knights, a young man with shaggy hair and a rueful smile. "Back in the forties when they first brought out those immune retroviruses, Blake here volunteered for accelerated trials. I remember all the hoopla. They were sure this was going to be the great solution to the pandemics, so they speeded up the schedule, got volunteers for clinical trials. Worked like stink for a while, too, but then they ran up against the ugly long term.... Well, I'm sorry to hear it."

He sat in silence. Simon watched him and listened to the sounds of the shop—the saw rising and falling, Ethan calling directions to David, Rigo asking questions.

"OK," said Anderson finally, "here's my offer. Between you and me only, right? Nobody else to know. I forget about the gun. And," he shot Simon a sharp look, "the blackmail. And a few other things. You buy the chess set from me at the appraised price, plus cost of appraisal. And then you agree that once you leave here you will never come back to Cortes Island and you will break off all contact with David."

Simon stared at him, stunned then furious.

"David's not part of the deal!"

Old Anderson leaned back in his chair and crossed his arms.

"Maybe nobody else wants to say it, but I will. Tongs wouldn't of taken him if they hadn't been looking for you in the first place. And now you're going to war. Fine with me, but I'm not going to let you drag my grandson into it. He's got a future, and you're not wrecking it."

The table saw stopped again. Simon leaned forward and hissed.

"If you tell the parole committee about the gun, you also give them evidence against yourself. You could lose your Guild membership! And without your pension you could lose this home."

Anderson didn't flinch.

"I'd rather lose all of that than my grandson."

Simon glared, longing to knock the chess table aside and throw himself at the old bastard. But an assault would only play into Anderson's hands. And if he let himself think about the man's words even a little, he faced their implacable truth.

"Simon, I'm ready!" called David. He walked over, pulling off his work apron. "Who's winning?"

Simon swallowed, tried to sound normal, but his voice came out harsh in his own ears.

"Your grandfather wins. I concede."

He didn't want to touch Anderson's outstretched hand but he couldn't avoid it. He shook callused old fingers, then strode outside, misery burning in his chest.

He wasn't just losing this place, he realized, he was about to lose all the people, too. They weren't his either, not the way David and his house and land and family belonged together for generations. Rigo was his only family here. Toni was his therapist, and Klale was a friend. He had only a few more mornings to spend etching tai chi characters in the dew with Rigo while Klale sang in the shower and Toni stomped downstairs to make coffee and grumble about the plumbing. Then it would all be gone.

He barely heard David's chatter as they walked down the springy, needle-matted path to the beach; barely even noticed when David stopped to examine a cluster of delicate mushrooms and a striated orange shelf fungus on an old log. He was trying to create a new dance: the leaving dance.

"Simon?"

Simon started, realized they'd emerged from the trees onto the beach, and looked down into David's worried face.

"What's wrong?" the boy asked.

"I...." He couldn't say all of it. "I don't want to leave," he finally managed.

"You're not leaving right away are you?"

"No."

"Oh good." David gave him a smile, then looked back over his shoulder—a gesture that Simon had come to translate as 'are the adults out of earshot?' Rigo stood with his hands in his pockets looking out at the water. David led Simon down to one of their markers on a boulder about half way down the beach. A blue heron wading at the tideline watched them approach, then leaned forward, unfurled its wide wings and flapped ponderously into the air. They watched as it flew further along the beach and soared to a new landing spot.

They crouched in the briny shadow of the boulder and David stared into a tide pool, frowning. He seemed distracted, also.

"Cin-Cin said some things.... I talked to her the other night, you know. She told me that Tor drowned her kiwi. And then Dr. Paroo told Tor to drown himself. And he did. He just stepped off the boat. Cin-Cin said she pretended to be asleep because she was scared Yasmin would drown her, too. But she was pretty tripped when she talked to me.... You think she made that up?

"No."

David looked troubled.

"I can't believe anybody would do that!"

"That's what tools are for," said Simon bitterly. "We're disposable. We cannot refuse anything."

David turned frightened eyes on him.

"Nobody could do that to you, could they? Not now?"

"No. Not now."

Simon made his voice sound certain, though he wasn't sure. He'd never be sure.

"Good." David looked relieved. "What... Well, what about Cin-Cin? People used her, too, and now what happens to her? She doesn't have any family, they checked. I wanted to call her at the hospital today but mom wouldn't let me. She says Cin-Cin's being taken care of, and I may need more social interaction but I'm not going to get it from a hooker twice my age thanks very much. But it's not fair! I mean," his face had turned red, "that's not why I wanted to call her. I don't think she has any family or friends—nobody. All she had was the kiwi and it's dead."

Simon opened his mouth to offer to contact her, then realized that he wouldn't be here much longer. And contact with Simon would merely endanger the girl.

"You could call Dr. Dougherty. He said he would admit her for therapy at the Seattle Institute."

"You think he'd talk to me?"

"I'll make sure he does," promised Simon.

"Great!" David brightened, then looked down at his bio-marker and made a face.

"I wish it was spring again and we could start a whole new set of studies."

"Me, too," whispered Simon.

Toni came down to the beach to spell Rigo, then it was time for David to go home for dinner and Simon stood looking after him, wishing with sudden desperation that he could change everything—change into a normal person who could live on a lush green island in the sparkling blue inland sea and be David's friend all his life.

He wanted to curl up and cry, and go back to being the dancing boy who didn't hurt like this and didn't have to make horrible choices.

"You OK?"

He looked down into Toni's perceptive eyes.

"No."

She studied him, then sat down and patted the log beside her. He sat, then slid off the log onto the shingle so he wouldn't loom above her. The rocks felt cool, and the air was losing heat quickly as the sun sank low. Toni kept silent, waiting for him. Finally, he found a place to start.

"Have you ever loved a place?"

"Oh yeah." Toni sighed. "I loved my apartment."

"It was beautiful," said Simon, remembering the plants and pictures and the smell of honey. It had been Toni's home, he realized, and it had been demolished.

"I built it over ten years," continued Toni, unexpectedly. "I started when I got through withdrawal, I hid up on that floor and barricaded myself in and then worked on it every spare moment, with every spare dollar. I did it all—plumbing, cabling, floors, walls, cupboards, tilework, woodwork, mosaic windows. Some things I had to tear out and do over three or four times. I built it up, and it built me up so I could live again."

"And it's gone," said Simon.

"Yeah. Well that's what happens when you nest in a condemned building."

"Will you build another apartment?"

The question seemed to surprise her. She frowned at Simon, then at the water before answering.

"I don't know. I put so much of my heart into it. Right now I don't feel like I could do that again." Then she added softly. "How's your heart?"

"It hurts!" Simon found tears in his eyes. "I don't want to leave."

Toni nodded. She waited while he cried, letting the time stretch out easily. She didn't seem as tense these days. He looked at her, sudden fear welling.

"Are you going to leave me?!"

"Not yet," she said calmly. "But eventually, yes. That's how therapy works. You get better, I move on."

"I'm not better!" he protested. "I'll never be completely better, will I?"

"No."

"So I need you!"

She met his desperation with soft brown eyes.

"You'll need a therapist, but it won't be me. We're too close, Simon. And I have too many problems of my own. But we'll still be friends."

All his hurt and neediness rose in a storm.

"You don't even touch me any more!"

Toni winced, lowered her eyes.

"Sorry. I'm overcompensating. Made such a fucking mess of it in one direction...."

Simon reached up and grabbed her hand. Toni took his hand between both of hers, squeezed his fingers, stroked his wrist. He closed his eyes to savor that sensation and clung to the anchor of his world, the touch that had brought him through hell, not wanting ever to let go,

"I love you, Simon," she said quietly.

That same voice hot and urgent against his chest in the dark had pleaded "never leave me!" and he knew with sudden certainly that she hadn't lied that night, she'd lied all the days afterward.

# 31

October 6, 2109

The parole committee met Sunday afternoon in the Building Trades Guild Hall in Campbell River. Toni, arriving with Klale and the Andersons in a wheezy old sharecar, looked around at the parking stalls and bike racks and felt relieved to see most of them empty. The building was surrounded by tall chestnuts and maples which glowed yellow and scarlet against a gray autumn sky. They formed a harmonious backdrop for the cedar shake siding of the big hall and the low wing of administrative offices behind it. Klale sent the sharecar back for Rigo and Simon—Campbell River's traffic grid ran short of cars on weekends—and then walked toward tall double doors. Toni stared up at the massive cedar door posts and the crest over top of the lintel.

The inside of the hall was much like community halls Toni had seen before—a large high ceilinged room with a raisable floor section at one end and a kitchen and bathrooms at the other. But the quality of construction was stunning.

Tall opaquing windows let in columns of dappled forest light, and a series of clever skylights allowed autumn sun to pour down on the polished floor, inlaid with a Guild crest that stretched from wall to wall. Each corner of the room was dominated by a wooden pillar that reminded her of a stylized totem pole. Toni couldn't read the writing in the scrollwork at the top of the columns, but she didn't need to. These were the four pillars of the Guilds: Community, Cooperation, Integrity, and Harmony. The end wall near the door was covered with framed holopix of Guild execs and members. Along another wall children's drawings had been tacked up, depicting Citizenship duties.

Toni felt terribly out of place. David led Klale to a closet near the kitchen and began taking out battered folding chairs. Toni started to follow, then caught sight of Mary's sea-green salwar kameez in a group of people standing near the end of the room. She walked up and saw another familiar face.

"Alberta!"

The KlonDyke's muscular blonde chief of security turned and flashed a brief, uncomfortable smile. The ex-military woman looked as dressy as Toni had ever seen her in black pants, a pearl gray shirt, and a cobalt blue flash jacket.

"Hi, Toni. Good to see you." She gripped Toni's hand tightly and frowned down at her. "You've lost weight."

"I'm fine. How's Rill?" Alberta's wife had been one of the victims on Pier B-C a year ago. Simon had thrown her across the concrete wharf, breaking her spine. Even with modern nerve regeneration techniques, an injury that severe could not be entirely repaired and Toni braced for anger or distress from Alberta, but to her surprise, the tall woman's face lightened.

"She's doing a lot better. Everyone at Sisters' Rez has been great, and she's finally back at work."

"Glad to hear it," said Toni sincerely. She looked around, spotting elderly Ron McCaskill leaning on his cane beside a middle-aged Chinese woman who must be Esme Fung, mother of Harbour Patrol Officer Adam Fung, and a bearded, turbaned man who would be Devinder Singh Dhillon, brother of Captain Baljeet Dhillon. They were the only two members of the parole committee she hadn't met in person.

She also hadn't met the jurist—a lean, sandy-haired Citizen named Baz Bell-Irving who wore conservative clothes and a boxy Guild-issue phone. He looked as four Pillars as they came, thought Toni, but apparently he was another pal of Mary's. Toni could never get over how many people Mary swapped favors with.

They had arrived early. As Toni chatted with Alberta, other people drifted in. Among them Toni recognized Miz Guthrie, with her off-the-rack face sculpt and appalling pink hair. She glowered at young David, who kept his head down and clattered chairs with renewed energy. Even though notice hadn't been posted about the parole hearing, Toni knew the news would be all over Cortes and the committee would not refuse to let Citizens attend. In her view, the Guilds took open process to an extreme. She would have much preferred a closed session.

Rigo and Simon were among the last arrivals and the committee members—seated in a semi circle at the front of the room—looked up at their entrance. Simon came through the door in step with his father, striding with confident grace. Rigo wore his Byronic suit, and Simon, towering a head above his tall father, wore his best ensilk clothes and the scarlet headscarf Klale had given him. A gleaming ear cuff dangled from his undamaged right ear—too flashy for a hearing, Toni felt, but it was a gift from Simon's mother. Just like the bitch to send baubles and beg off.

Since this special meeting had been called for a handshake, Toni had held out the faint hope it might be a mere formality, but it soon became evident that the committee was taking it very seriously indeed. The jurist went through all the correct process—reading out the charges against Simon, describing the people he had killed or injured, and then introducing each parole committee member. As he spoke, Toni watched the solemn, worried group, and suddenly realized that she was looking at people who had never expected to be here, never expected Simon to recover, and didn't know what to do about it. Her heart sank. If she'd realized that, she would have put this off longer.

After introductions, the jurist called witnesses. Toni went first. She gave a general description of Simon's recovery and her assessment of his current condition. Several committee members asked her questions—all pertinent. They'd done their homework.

The next witness up was Graeme Dougherty, linking in from Seattle. He used every pompous trick—even addressing the committee from behind his desk, with ornate certificates visible on the wall behind him. His report, while clinically accurate, included some masterpieces of misdirection and omission about how he'd been called into the case, and Toni kept her face expressionless only with effort.

Witness statements and questioning went on for over three hours, with a coffee break after two hours. Major Kim's curt, harsh testimony, also delivered via phone, worried Toni the most. Kim stated that he had no direct evidence of intentional parole violations or crimes since last November, but he did not believe that such a physically bioenhanced, psychologically damaged individual should ever have been granted parole. He strongly urged that Simon be kept in indefinite custody in a secure facility.

In the chill atmosphere following his words, young David Anderson proved a savior as he solemnly described how he had first met Simon on the beach. His account drew reluctant smiles from the committee and Toni saw them relax. David didn't talk about Simon as a criminal or a monster or even a medical case, just a wonderful friend who was patient enough to sit all afternoon watching heron nests, and who had risked his life to save David. Even Alberta and Dhillon—the two committee members Toni had identified as most hostile to Simon—visibly thawed.

The last witness was Simon himself. David gave him a grinning thumbs up as he left the witness chair, and the spectacle of Simon smiling back riveted everyone's attention. So did his soft, confident tenor voice, issuing from that deathmask face. He gave a rehearsed statement, expressing remorse for his crimes and asking for the forbearance of his victims' relatives.

The committee members took turns asking questions, and Alberta went first. She didn't mince words.

"When you were Choi's enforcer you killed other people, didn't you?"

"Yes."

"What about them? Do you feel remorse for them?"

Simon hesitated, frowning, though Toni doubted most people would notice the subtle facial movements that told her that. To them he would seem impassive.

"I feel revulsion. And sadness," he said slowly. "But remorse implies responsibility. I do not take responsibility for my actions when I was Choi's slave. I was not able to refuse his orders."

Mr. Dhillon leaned forward. "You made your own choice on the pier in last year. No one ordered you to attack my sister. Could that happen again?"

"I was psychotic at that time. I did not understand the consequences of my actions."

"And now that you understand, you could chose to kill, couldn't you?"

"I chose not to kill," said Simon quietly. "I have given my word to my father and will give it to this parole committee that I will not kill again."

Mary was holding back, Toni noticed, letting Simon speak for himself. At the original hearing she had been his passionate advocate. Old Ron McCaskill spoke next.

"Major Kim believes you are dangerous. What do you say about that, Simon?"

Simon took his time to answer, though Toni had warned him to prepare for that questions.

"I was a prisoner for twenty years, Mr. McCaskill. I do not wish to be imprisoned again. But I know that I require supervision and assistance. Living by myself is not feasible."

The jurist intervened, frowning.

"I believe you have evaded Mr. McCaskill's question. You were trained to kill, Mr. Lau. If I came up behind you by surprise and slapped your shoulder, what would happen?"

Simon's eyes dropped and his shoulders hunched slightly.

"I might hit out from reflex," he admitted.

"You might kill me."

"It's possible."

"May I speak to this?" asked Rigo.

"We're here to listen to your son today," said the jurist firmly. "I want to hear his answers. Mr. Lau, how do you propose to keep society safe from you?"

Simon didn't hesitate this time.

"I will take the advice of Dr. Almiramez and Miz Smarch and my father. They set up conditions to keep me safe and keep the people around me safe and they succeeded. I will trust them to help determine conditions for my future life."

Alberta was watching with sharp eyes.

"And if those conditions include a permanently installed neural restraint?..."

"If we could come to no other satisfactory arrangement, I would agree."

Mary spoke up in her soft voice.

"Simon, I know you've been busy with therapy, but have you thought about what you'd like to do in the future?"

"Yes," he said. "I'd like to help others—other people who've been enslaved."

Oh, oh, thought Toni. On the surface it sounded fine—she could see Ron smiling, no doubt thinking about the group he worked with that rescued children from the tongs—but she suspected that Simon had far more direct action in mind. If his parole committee got wind of it, they might well panic. Time to forestall more questioning along those lines. She stood and spoke out of turn.

"Excuse me for interrupting. I just want to point out that the extent of Simon's recovery has caught all of us by surprise and there's still a lot of assessment required, including treatment in hospital. I don't believe it's appropriate to make any long term plans yet."

The jurist frowned at her outburst, but as Toni had hoped, the committee was quietly relieved—she'd given them a good reason to postpone tough decisions. Ron moved to extend Simon's medical parole for another six months and the motion, with some refinement of detail, attained consensus. Simon stood and gave a verbal oath, shook hands with each committee member, and then signed a paper contract—unnecessarily melodramatic, thought Toni, but the Guilds loved old fashioned ceremony. Then the jurist wrapped up with a short speech in which he congratulated everyone for everything—another typical Guild exercise.

Afterward there was much hand-shaking and the inevitable pots of tea, served with home made cookies. Toni drank her tea and smiled until her face hurt. Simon stayed by his father's side, with Klale on his other side, talking to one committee member after another. All of them wanted to stare up at him from close range. However she noted with amusement that the space directly behind him cleared whenever he turned around.

After another awful but mercifully short boat ride, they arrived at dusk at the feast-ready cabin. Rigo and Klale had been cooking for three days in anticipation of a celebration. And a box had been delivered that afternoon—a case of champagne sent with Graeme's compliments.

Rigo popped a cork immediately and even poured a glass for Toni without a word about her stomach. Toni took it and retired with Mary to the couch. Ron had been invited, too, but he'd decided to go back to Vancouver with the rest of the committee. They clinked glasses.

"Cheers!" said Mary, beaming.

Toni made a face at her.

"Don't tell me, let me guess: you didn't warn me how serious this was going to be because I would only have worried."

"That's right, dear. I knew Simon could handle it."

"Thanks for your confidence."

"Miracles do happen. Look at Davy Anderson. I expected complaints from him and not a word."

Toni snorted.

"Rigo says he and Simon had an intense conversation the other day. I suspect they struck a deal and I would dearly love to know who paid what."

Mary winced. "Toni, you really must work on Simon's ethics!"

Toni couldn't help it. She laughed.

"You're talking to the woman who cheated her way into medical school with a forged ID, stole meds to get tripped on the job, and moonlighted as a trainer. I think ethics are your department."

The Andersons came in carrying a big sheet of wood which they placed on top of the dining table, making it large enough for ten people to crowd around. Toni found herself wedged in between Klale and Rory, facing David and his parents across the table. Ethan gave David a small glass of champagne, so he could toast Simon's future with the rest. David tasted the bubbly wine and put it down with a shrug.

"I like yours better, Dad."

Ethan smiled. "You know what I wanted to be when I was your age?"

David's boggled expression made it clear he had never considered such a thing. "Uh... a carpenter?"

"No, a vintner."

"Oh. Um... why didn't you?"

"Well, there were a lot of reasons." From beneath his unruly beard and hair, Ethan's eyes flicked across the table to his father, then away again. "It was hard to get into any of the wineries in those days—you practically had to be born in or marry in. And I was needed here."

David digested that, then asked cautiously: "Are you sorry?"

"A little," he admitted. "But I have a good life and a great family.

Besides," Toni caught a wicked glint in his eye, "I haven't given up on it yet. I may still apply for transfer to the Husbandry Guild."

Toni caught Blue grinning, then turned back to see David frown anxiously down at his plate.

"Dad, I'm sorry I'm such a thumb-bound retro in the shop, but I don't do it on purpose. It's just that I can't get interested in wood. I mean...." he looked up, eyes intense, "Wood is dead, and everything out there is alive!"

Ethan squeezed his shoulder.

"I have managed to notice your lack of aptitude for carpentry. We're looking into that early university program. But to get into university at all, you're going to have to bring up your grades and study all those 'Other Stupid Subjects'."

David gave an abashed grin and Toni caught Simon watching from the foot of the table, his eyes alight.

After dinner Mary called them outside for a ceremony. They put on coats and went into the crisp autumn darkness to find lanterns hanging from trees, and torches burning around Simon's dance platform. A low, carved table had been placed at one end of the stage with dozens of unlit candles beside it; at the other end were cushions. Toni looked around and caught a glimpse of Simon in one of his abrupt persona shifts—he stepped out the door as a grave adult, then caught sight of the flames and stared with the wide-eyed awe of a child. Toni picked a cushion and sat down cross-legged, feeling a bit like Simon as she looked up at flickering shadows of tree limbs and a sky full of stars. The air was still and she could hear a distant murmur of surf.

Mary stood by the makeshift altar. Beads and abalone shells shone on her Tlingit dance shirt, reflecting firelight just as they had been designed to do centuries ago by her ancestors. The cloak lent her a solemn presence as she looked around at everyone.

"We've all been through fear and distress lately, so it's time to take an hour to dismiss old hurts and anger and guilt, and to remember and forgive our dead. It's very simple. We light candles, and we say who we are lighting them for and why. I'll start."

She turned, picked up a candle, and lit it from a fire wand in her hand.

"Jay, love, it's always been so hard for me to come back to

your cabin that I've stayed away and let it fall apart. I'm so sorry. But now it's become a haven and a place of healing for others, and I know it would give you joy to know that."

She put the candle in a holder and set it on the table, then came and sat on a cushion. There was an uneasy pause, then Rigo stood. He lit a candle and spoke in Chinese, then in English:

"For my father. Father, I should have been a better son to you. I should have been kinder and more patient. You made terrible mistakes, but I know that some of the fault was mine and I forgive you. Rest in peace."

He took his seat, tears shining on his face.

What the hell, thought Toni. She stood and lit two candles.

"Jamal and Raffayal, my brothers," she said, then found she couldn't say more. She sat.

When she blinked the scene back into focus, she saw old Mr. Anderson placing three candles on the table "for the people buried in the garden."

Klale went next, lighting candles for her parents, and Blue followed, also lighting candles for her parents who died in the plagues. She returned and gave an inquiring look to her husband who shook his head quietly and said "Not tonight."

"I want to," said David unexpectedly. He got up and lit a lone candle, then spoke with nervous intensity. "This is for Tor. I think he tried to be kind to us and it wasn't his fault what Dr. Paroo did. It was terrible to die like that."

Simon went last. To Toni's surprise he picked up a hand full of candles, set them up, and lit them in succession—she counted eleven. He stood haloed by torch light, eyes shadowed.

"Deepank, James, Ali, Chung Hon, Kwenu and the others whose names are lost. You are my brothers. Choi tortured and killed you before me. You are not forgotten and I will avenge you."

"Simon." Mary spoke in a soft, troubled voice. "This ceremony isn't for revenge, it's for remembrance and forgiveness."

"There are some things I cannot forgive."

"I understand that you aren't ready yet," said Mary calmly.

Simon's eyes glittered and he loomed tall in the darkness.

"I will never be ready to forgive Choi."

As a therapist she should disapprove, thought Toni, but as a victim she understood entirely. There was a lot she had no intention of forgiving either. She spoke up.

"Mary, some of us find redemption in different ways. I revenge myself for all the brutality of my childhood by healing other people."

Simon nodded.

"Yes. Exactly. I will not be Choi. My vengeance will not make victims. My vengeance will save victims."

Toni knew Mary felt uncomfortable with that ending, but she led them in an old hymn—another typical Guildism. Still, it felt quite wonderful to be part of a chorus singing to the starry sky. Then Simon announced that he wanted to thank all of them by giving them a dance. While he got ready, Klale moved the table and cushions, set up two netsets to broadcast, and directed the others to stand circling the stage. When Simon waved at her, she started the music.

Simon danced naked, his body gleaming in torch light as he leaped and spun. Even Toni, accustomed to his enhanced strength and his eerie gracefulness, found it like watching some wondrous, supernatural demon. Old David Anderson actually gaped and young David stared wide-eyed, seeing an entirely unexpected aspect of his friend. Toni watched the audience, then turned her attention back to the dance, impressed despite her familiarity with Simon. "Graeme was right," she thought. "He's astounding.

Then it struck her. Simon's really going to make it. This man will grow well enough to have a life, to make friends, to find work. My gods, we did it!

No, I did it. I was right. All those years defending my methods, fighting to give my patients more time to recover, all that rhetoric I spouted about building real community, real connections, real hope and healing instead of paid staff overseeing a medical prison, all those failures I blamed on institute not giving me free rein. Well, fuck it, I was right!

And, she thought with a burst of savage delight, I'm going back to tell them so.

# 32

After dancing, Simon showered, and when came out of the bathroom he found Klale sitting on the stairs with two champagne glasses on the step beside her. A din of conversation drifted up from the living room. Mary, Rigo and Toni were saying good night to the Andersons. Simon considered going down to say good-bye again, but Klale smiled up at him and held out a glass.

"You were wonderful."

"Thank you." He took the champagne and drank some because it was Graeme's gift and they all seemed to value it. He preferred Ethan's wines, though.

He sat next to Klale, a step lower so their heads were almost level. He could relax around Klale almost the same way he could with David because she wasn't complicated and moody and full of hidden shadows. She danced with abandon and, best of all, she often put her arms around him. He loved to be touched, stroked, held, but there seemed to be endless rules about "appropriateness" that always left him wanting more.

Still, it caught him by surprise when she leaned over and kissed his cheek. He pulled away and looked at her, an obvious question occurring to him for the very first time.

"Why are you here? Living with us? Instead of going to university?"

Klale looked taken aback.

"Because I'm your friend."

Simon frowned, unsatisfied. Beside him Klale sighed and pushed unruly auburn hair out of her face.

"OK, that's not the whole story. It's because you saved my life, Simon. But you don't remember that, do you?"

She sounded sad. Simon shook his head.

"No. I only remember fragments. Toni says it's because of the accident that damaged my chip."

"I know." Klale sat in silence for a moment, then spoke again, her voice uncharacteristically somber.

"There's another reason, too. You see, I'm partly responsible for those people you killed. It wasn't your idea to go to Pier B-C. I ordered you. Toni and Alberta both warned me that you were unstable and violent, but I didn't listen. If I hadn't sent you there, maybe nobody would have died. Everyone's been ignoring that, being very kind like I'm some cretting Zit kid who didn't know any better, but you know something? It's my responsibility, too, and I came here to work it out."

"Oh." Simon hadn't understood that. For the first time, he voluntarily thought back on that ugly memory. "I thought I killed you," he said in a low voice.

"Yeah, well for the ten thousandth time, you didn't. I'm just fine, and I forgive you, OK?"

Simon echoed her smile though he didn't quite understand why she found it funny.

"And of course I wanted to help Toni because she's my friend," Klale added.

"I remember you lived with her at the KlonDyke," said Simon, voicing something that had been puzzling him. "But you're not sharing a room here."

"Toni said she needed her privacy and I understand. It's a big step to go from living as a hermit on the twenty-first floor of a mostly empty building to sharing a tiny bedroom in a crowded cabin. And anyway it wasn't... well, there wasn't a lot between us. I was never serious about Toni or her about me, it was just friendly sex."

"So, you aren't having sex with her?" asked Simon cautiously.

"No."

"Are you having sex with my father?"

"What?!" Klale's eyes went wide and she sputtered indignantly. "No! Simon...! Why did you think that?"

"You touch each other frequently," he observed.

"Well, yeah, but not like that."

"Why not?"

"He's..." Klale trailed off and then rolled her eyes. "Look, just trust me, it's not appropriate."

"Oh." Simon thought it over, then risked another question. "As it was also inappropriate to have sex with me?"

"Well... Toni thought so. I didn't."

"Oh." Simon felt like sighing. It seemed like the more he longed for a simple answer, the vaguer and more complicated the explanations got.

"Your father and I had a talk," Klale continued. "He was OK on my having a pash for you but he agreed with Toni that I should wait until you were able to make your own decisions."

"That's now," said Simon.

Klale looked at him, startled, then with blooming mischief in her eyes.

"So it is."

She sat, looking him straight in the eyes, saying nothing. Simon looked back at her, then suddenly got it. He leaned over very cautiously and kissed her lightly on the mouth. She kissed back, warm and soft and slippery. After a while she pulled away and grinned at him.

"Your room or mine?"

"Mine," said Simon. "But I have to do something first."

"Okay. That gives me time to primp."

Primp? He thought they would take off their clothes so why primp? But he didn't ask. It seemed unlikely he'd get a simple answer to that question, either.

It was quieter downstairs now. Mary, Rigo and Toni were in the kitchen, cleaning up. Simon started to ask Toni's permission to use the netset, then thought it over and instead stated politely that he needed to use it for half an hour. She looked surprised, but nodded.

He took it outside and set it up beside the stage. Instead of mating his optic cables directly to the set, he put them on and connected them to a small transmitter he hung from his neck. Then he opened a remote link on the set, closed his eyes, and fell into Choi's office.

The severe, echoing room with its big mahogany desk looked just the same. But this time he rose from the desk, walked around it, and then looked back, facing the frozen figure of Choi Shung Wai.

He'd never dared do this before, and he struggled with instinctive terror. It had been burned into him never to raise his eyes, never to look in Choi's face and he hadn't—not even when he killed the man. But he did it now, circling the desk and studying that expressionless parchment face. Somehow he'd felt certain that face must be stained with appalling cruelty, but the figure in the sim seemed ordinary now, just a frail old Chinese man. He sat unmoving, eyes frozen, hands immobile on the desk. Those hand had never touched Simon except carefully swathed in surgical gloves when Simon lay unconscious.

"I hate you!" he whispered. "I hate everything you were, everything you did! And I killed you. I stabbed you dozens of times and then I killed you again! I dumped your hoards of blackmail data onto the net—gave it away. And now I'm killing you again. I'm ripping you out of me, out of Simon!"

He reached out, feeling the air of Cortes Island against his skin and the platform under his bare feet and the tears running down his face, and he danced on the floor of Choi's office—danced and twirled and leaped between the walls of his old hell. When the music faded, he deleted the sim for good.

Then he went to share another kind of dance with Klale lying warm and alive and beautiful in his bed.

introducing...

# OLD ENEMIES

In 22ⁿᵈ century Cascadia no one dares take on the brutal tong lords who use neural programming to enslave people, and who buy silence with the profits. Until now. Simon Lau is a slave who escaped. He wants revenge.

But before he can act, Simon is felled by seizures triggered by damaged neural filaments in his brain. Disoriented and unable to speak, he is wheeled into emergency surgery, only to realize that the man who is about to operate on him is the same surgeon who did the first cruel and highly illegal alterations twenty years before.

Returning to Seattle Neurological Institute with Simon also brings unwelcome flashbacks for Dr. Antonia Almiramez, who fled SNI eleven years ago in a cascading crisis of lies, rage, and addiction. Her former colleagues still don't know her most shameful secret—that she was moonlighting criminally as a "trainer". But the Yakuza have not forgotten.

**Drowned City Press**

www.drownedcitypress.ca

LaVergne, TN USA
20 March 2010
176609LV00001B/3/P